Nouvellettes
Of
The Musicians

by

Mrs. E. F. Ellet

Double 9
BOOKS

Nouvellettes Of The Musicians
by Mrs. E. F. Ellet

ISBN: 978-93-64288-92-7

Published by

DOUBLE 9 BOOKS

2/13-B, Ansari Road
Daryaganj, New Delhi – 110002
info@double9books.com
www.double9books.com
Tel. 011-40042856

ABOUT THE AUTHOR

Mrs. E. F. Ellet, a distinguished author of the 19th century, captivated readers with her masterpiece "Nouvellettes of the Musicians." Renowned for her meticulous research and vivid storytelling, Ellet's work delves into the lives and experiences of prominent musicians, offering a rich tapestry of their struggles, triumphs, and contributions to the world of music. Through her eloquent prose, she transports readers into the vibrant world of classical music, painting portraits of composers and performers with depth and nuance. Ellet's keen insight and passion for her subject shine through in each narrative, as she explores the creative process, the societal influences, and the personal anecdotes that shaped these musical geniuses. "Nouvellettes of the Musicians" stands as a testament to Ellet's literary prowess and her dedication to preserving the legacies of these iconic figures. With meticulous attention to detail and a deep reverence for her subject matter, Mrs. E. F. Ellet's work continues to inspire and educate readers, ensuring that the stories of these musical luminaries endure for generations to come.

CONTENTS

PREFACE

In the following series of Nouvellettes, something higher has been attempted than merely the production of amusing fictions. Each is founded on incidents that really occurred in the artist's life, and presents an illustration of his character and the style of his works. The conversations introduced embody critical remarks on the musical compositions of great masters; the object being to convey valuable information on this subject—so little studied or known except among the few devoted to the art—in an attractive form. The view given of the scope and tendency of the works of different artists, and their relation to personal character, may also enforce a striking moral; showing the elevating influence of virtue, and the power of vice to distort even the loveliest gift of Heaven into a curse and reproach. Of the tales—"Tartini," "Two Periods in the Life of Haydn," "Mozart's First Visit to Paris," "The Artist's Lesson," "The Mission of Genius," "The Young Tragedian," and "Tamburini," only are original; the others are adapted from the "*Kunstnovellen*" of Lyser and Rellstab. The sketch of the great pianist, Liszt, is translated from a memoir by Christern, a distinguished professor of music in Hamburg.

HANDEL

In the parlor of the famous London tavern, "The Good Woman," Fleet street, No. 77, sat Master John Farren, the host, in his arm-chair, his arms folded over his ample breast, ready to welcome his guests.

It was seven in the evening; the hour at which the members of the club were used to assemble, according to the good old custom in London, in 1741. Directly before John Farren, stood Mistress Bett, his wife, her withered arms akimbo, and an angry flush on her usually pale and sallow cheeks.

"Is it true, Master John," she asked, in a shrill tone; "is it possible! do you really mean to throw our Ellen, our only child, into the arms of that vagabond German beggar?"

"Not exactly to throw her into his arms, Mistress Bett," replied John, quietly; "but Ellen loves the lad, and he is a brave fellow—handsome, honest, gifted, industrious——"

"And poor as a church mouse!" interrupted Bett; "and nobody knows who or what he may be!"

"Yes! his countryman, Master Händel, says there is something great in him."

"Pah! get away with your Master Händel! he is always your authority! What is he to us, now that it is all over with him in the favor of His Majesty! While he could go in and out of Carlton House daily, I would have cared for his good word; but now that he is banished thence for his highflown insolent conduct, what is he, but an ordinary vagabond musician?"

"Hold your tongue!" cried John Farren, now really moved; "and hold Master Händel in honor! If he gives Joseph his good word, by my troth I have ground whereon I can build. Do you understand, Mistress Bett?"

The "good woman" seemed as though she would have replied at length; but before she could speak, the door opened, and two men of respectable appearance entered. Tom, the waiter, snatched up a porter-mug, filled and placed it on the round table in the middle of the room, and stood ready for further service; while Mistress Bett, flinging a scowl at both the visitors, silently left the apartment.

"Well," cried the eldest of the two—a colossal figure, with a handsome and expressive countenance, and large flashing eyes—"well, Master John, how goes it?"

"So, so, Master Händel," was the reply, "the better that you are just come in time to silence my good woman."

Händel gave his hat and stick to the boy, and turned to his companion, a man about the middle height, simple and plain in his exterior; only in the corner of his laughing eye could the observer detect a world of shrewdness and waggery. His name was William Hogarth; and he was well esteemed as a portrait painter.

"You think, then," asked Händel, keenly regarding his companion— "you think, then, Bedford would do something for my Messiah, if I got the right side of him?"

"You shall not trouble yourself to get the right side of him," exclaimed Hogarth eagerly; "that I ask not of you; no honorable man would ask it. Speak to the point at once with him; and be sure, he will use all his influence to have your work suitably represented."

"But is it not too bad," cried Händel, "that I must flatter such a shallow-pate as his Grace the Duke of Bedford, to get my best (Heaven knows, William, my *best*) work brought before the public? If his Grace but comprehended a note of it! but he knows no more of music than that lout of a linen-weaver in Yorkshire, who spoiled my Saul in such a manner, that I corrected him with my fist."

Hogarth replied with vivacity—"You have been eight-and-twenty years in England; have you not yet found out that the patronage of a stupid great man does no *harm* to a work of art? You know me, Händel; and know that I abhor nothing so much as servility, be it to whom it may. Yet, I assure you, should I deal only with those who understand my labors, and have no good word from others, I should be glad if I obtained employment enough to keep wife and child from starving. As to luxuries, and my punch clubs, that have pleased you so well, I could not even think of them. You know as well as I, that talent, a true taste for art, and wealth to support both, are seldom or never found together. Let us thank God, if the unendowed are good-natured enough not to grudge us our glorious inheritance, while they deny us not a portion of the crumbs from their luxurious tables."

Händel was leaning with both arms on the table, his head buried in his hands. Without looking up or changing his position, he murmured, "Must it ever be so; must the time never come, when the artist may taste the pure joy he prepares through his works for others! Hogarth," he continued, with sudden energy, while he withdrew his hands from his face, and looked earnestly at his friend, "Hogarth, would you consent to leave your country, and exercise your art in other lands?"

"What a question! Not for the world," replied the painter.

"There it is!" cried Händel, hastily: "you have held out, and begin now to reap the reward of your constancy; but I left my dear fatherland, just as new life in art began to be stirring. Oh, how nobly, how magnificently, is it now developed there! What could I not have done with the gifts bestowed upon me? Have my countrymen achieved any thing great—they have done it *without me*, while I was here, tormenting myself in vain with your asses of singers and musicians, to drive a notion of what music is, into their heads. I have scarce yet numbered fifty years. I will return to my own country; better a cowherd there, than here again Director of the Haymarket Theatre, or Chapel-master to His Majesty, who, with all his court rabble, takes such delight in the sweet warblings of that Italian! Hogarth, you should paint the lambling, as the London women worship him as their idol, and bring him offerings?"

"I have already," answered Hogarth, laughing; "but hush, our friends!"

Here the door opened, and there entered Master Tyers, then lessee of Vauxhall, the Abbe Dubos, and Doctor Benjamin Hualdy; they were followed by Joseph Wach, a young German, who had devoted himself to the study of music under Händel's instruction, and Miss Ellen Farren, the young lady of the house. Master John arose; and Tom filled the empty porter mugs, and produced fresh ones.

Händel gave his pupil a friendly nod, and asked: "How come you on with your part? Can I hear you soon?"

"I am very industrious, Master Händel," replied Joseph, "and will do my best, I assure you, to be perfect. You must only have a little patience with me."

"Hem," muttered Händel; "I have had it so long with the stupid asses in this country, it shall not so soon fail with you. Enough till to-morrow; to your prating with your little girl yonder."

"Ah! Master Händel," cried Ellen, pouting prettily, "you think, then, Joseph should only be my sweet-heart when he has nothing better to do?"

"That were, indeed, most prudent, little witch," said Händel, laughing: "but 'tis ill preaching to lovers; that knows your father by experience, eh! old John?"

"Master Händel," said the Abbe, taking the word, "do you know I was not able to sleep last night, because your chorus—'*For the glory of the Lord shall be revealed,*'—ran continually in my head, and sounded in my ears? I think, good Master Händel, *your* glory shall be revealed through your Messiah, when you can once get it brought out suitably. But the Lord Archbishop, it seems, is against it."

Händel reddened violently, as he always did when anger stirred him: "A just Christian is the Lord Archbishop! He asked me if he should compose me a text for the Messiah; and when I asked him quietly if he thought me a heathen who knew nothing of the Bible, or if he thought to make it better than it stood in the Holy Scriptures, he turned his back on me, and represented me to the court as a rude, thankless boor."

"It is not good to eat cherries with the great," observed wise John Farren.

"I thought," muttered Händel, "this proverb was only current on the continent; but I see, alas! that it is equally applicable in the land of freedom!"

"Good and bad are mingled all over the earth," said Benjamin Hualdy, smiling: "and their proportion is everywhere the same. We must take the world, dear Händel, as it is, if we would not renounce all pleasure. Confess then: never felt you more joy—never were you more conscious of your own merit—never thanked you God more devoutly for his gifts to you, than when at last, after long struggle with ignorance and intrigue, you produced a work before the world, that charmed even enmity and envy to admiration!"

"And what care I for the admiration of fools and knaves?" interrupted Händel. Benjamin continued, in a conciliating tone—"Friend, he who *can* admire the beautiful and the good, is not so wholly depraved, as oft appears. There lives a something in the breast of every man, which, so long as it is not quite crushed and extinguished, lets not the worst fall utterly. I cannot name, nor describe it; but art, and music before all arts, is the surest test whereby you may know if that something yet exists."

"Most surely," cried Master Tyers. "I myself love music from my heart, and think with your great countryman, Doctor Luther, 'He must be a brute who feels not pleasure in so lovely and wondrous an art.' But, Master Händel, judge not my dear countrymen too harshly, if they have not accomplished so much as yours in that glorious art. Gifts are diverse; we have many that you have not."

"You have been long in England," observed the Abbe, "and have experienced many vexations and difficulties, particularly among those necessary to you in the production of your works. But tell me, Master Händel, supposing it true, that the court and nobles often do you injustice;

that our musicians and singers are inferior to those in your own country; that we cannot grasp *all* the high spirit that dwells in your works; are you not, nevertheless, the darling of the people of Britain? Lives not the name of Händel in the mouth of honest John Bull, honored as the names of his most renowned statesmen? Well, sir, if *that* is true, give honest John Bull (he means well and truly, at least) a little indulgence. Let us hear your Messiah soon; your honor suffers nought, and you remain, after all, the free German you were before."

"Aye!" cried Hogarth, "that is just what I have told him." "And I," — "And I," exclaimed Tyers and Hualdy; while John added, coaxingly, "Only think, Master Händel, how often I have to give up to my good wife, without detriment to my authority as master of the house."

Händel sat a few moments in silence, looking gloomily from one to another, around the circle. Suddenly he burst into a loud laugh, and cried in cheerful tone—"By my halidome, old fellow, you are right. Give us your hand; to-morrow early I go to the Duke of Bedford; and you *shall* hear the Messiah, were all the rascals in the three kingdoms and the continent against it. Tom, another mug!"

Loud and long applause followed his words: John Farren essayed a leap in his joy, which, 'spite of his corpulence, succeeded beyond expectation, and moved the guests to renewed peals of laughter. Joseph whispered to the maiden at his side—"Oh, Ellen! if it prospers with him, our fortune is made; I have his word for it."

The next morning Händel went, as he had promised his friends, to the Duke of Bedford. His Grace had given a grand breakfast, and half the court was assembled in his saloon. As soon as the servants saw Händel ascending the steps, they hastened to announce his arrival to their lord.

The Duke was not much of a connoisseur, but he loved the reputation of a patron of the arts, and took great pleasure in exhibiting himself in that light to the court and the king. It was his dearest wish to win the illustrious master to himself; particularly as he knew well that the absence of Händel from Carlton House was in no way owing to want of favor with the sovereign. The king, on the contrary, appreciated and highly valued his genius. But Händel's energetic nature could not bend to the observance of the forms and ceremonies held indispensable, not only at Carlton House, but among all the London aristocracy; and it was natural that this peculiarity should gradually remove him from the circles of the nobility. His fame on this account, however, only rose the higher. His Oratorio of Saul, which the preceding year had been produced, first in London, then in the other large cities of England, had stamped him a composer whom none hitherto had surpassed. The king was delighted; the court and nobles professed, at least, to be no less so. Among the people, his name stood, as his friend had truly observed, with the proudest names of the age! When informed of his arrival, the Duke hastened out, shook the master cordially by the hand, and was about leading him, without ceremony, into the hall. But Händel, thanking him for the honor, informed him he was come to ask a favor of his Grace.

"Well, Master Händel," said the Duke, smiling—"then come with me into my cabinet." The master followed his noble host, and unfolded his petition in few words, to wit: that his Grace would be pleased to set right the heads of the Lord Mayor and the Archbishop of London, so that they should cease laying hindrances in the way of the representation of his Messiah.

The Duke heard him out, and promised to use all his means and all his influence to prevent any further obstacle being interposed, and to remove those already in the way. Händel was pleased, more, perhaps, with the manner in which the polite but haughty Duke gave the promise, than with the promise itself.

"Now come in with me, Master Händel," said the Duke; "you will see many faces that are not strangers to you; and moreover, a brave countryman of yours, whom I have taken into my service. His name is Kellermann, and he is an excellent flute player, as the connoisseurs say."

"*Alle tausend!*" cried Händel, with joyful surprise; "is the brave fellow in London, and indeed in your Grace's service? That is news indeed! I will go with you, were your hall filled besides with baboons."

"Oh! no lack of them," laughed the Duke, while he led his guest into the saloon; "and you will find a fat capon into the bargain."

Great was the sensation among the assembled guests, when Bedford entered, introducing the celebrated composer. When he had presented Händel to the company, the Duke beckoned Kellermann to him; and Händel, without regarding the rest, greeted his old friend with all the warmth of his nature, and with childlike expressions of joy. Bedford seemed to enjoy his satisfaction, and let the two friends remain undisturbed; though the idol of the London world of fashion, Signor Farinelli, hemmed and cleared his throat many times over the piano, in token that he was about to sing, and wanted Kellermann to come back and accompany him. At length, Kellermann noticed his uneasiness; he pressed his friend's hand with a smile, returned to his place, took up his flute, and Signor Farinelli, having once more cleared his throat, began a melting air with his sweet, clear voice.

Händel, a powerful man, austere in his life, vigorous in his works, abhorred nothing so much as the singing of these effeminate creatures;

and all the luxurious cultivation of Signor Farinelli seemed to him only a miserable mockery of nature, as of heaven-born art. But, however much displeased at the soft trilling of the Italian, — whom Kellermann dexterously accompanied and imitated on his flute, — he could not refrain from laughing inwardly at the effect produced on the whole company. The men rolled up their eyes, and sighed and moaned with delight; the ladies seemed to float in rapture, like Farinelli's tones. "Sweet, sweet!" sighed one to another. "Yes, indeed!" lisped the fair in reply, drooping her eyelids, and inclining her head. Signor Farinelli ceased, and eager applause rewarded his exertions.

The Duke now introduced Händel to the Italian.

Farinelli, after some complimentary phrases, addressed the master in broken English.

"I have inteso," he said, with a complacent smile, "that il Signor Aendel has composed una opera — il Messia. Is there in that opera a part to sing for il famous musico Farinelli — I mean, for *me*?"

Händel looked at the ornamented little figure from head to foot, and answered in his deepest bass tone, "No, Signora."

The company burst out a laughing; the ladies covered their faces. Soon after, the German composer, with his friend Hogarth, took his leave. In the vestibule the artist showed Händel a sketch he had made of Farinelli singing, and his admirers lost in ecstasy. "By the Duke's order," whispered he.

"That is *false* of him!" exclaimed Händel, indignantly.

The satirical painter shrugged his shoulders.

Händel sat in his chamber, deep in composition. Once more he tried every note; now he would smile over a passage that pleased him; now pause earnestly upon something that did not satisfy him so well; pondering, striking out and altering to suit his judgment. At length his eyes rested on the last "Amen:" long — long — till a tear fell on the leaf.

"*This* note," said he, solemnly, and looking upwards — "*this* note is perhaps my best! Receive, Oh benevolent Father, my best thanks for this work! Thou, Lord! hast given it me; and what comes forth from Thee — *that* endureth, though all things earthly perish: — Amen."

He laid aside the notes, and walked a few times up and down the room. Then seating himself in his easy chair, and folding his arms, he indulged in happy dreams of his youth and his home. Thus he was found by Kellermann, who came at dusk to accompany him to the tavern. They discoursed long of their native land, of their art, and the excellent masters then living in

Germany. At length they broke off from the theme, fearful of keeping their assembled friends waiting too long.

"Well, friend," cried Hogarth gaily to the master as he entered; "was not my advice good? Has not Bedford helped you? and is your self-respect a whit injured?"

Händel nodded good-humoredly, and smiling, seated himself in his wonted place. "You remember, some time ago," the painter continued, "when the Leda of the Italian painter Correggio was sold here at auction for ten thousand guineas, I said—'If anybody will give me ten thousand guineas, I will paint something quite as good.' Lord Grosvenor took me at my word; I went to work, and laid aside everything else. At last my picture is ready; I take it to his lordship; he calls his friends together, and, as I said, they all laugh at me; I have to take back my picture, and go home to quarrel with my wife!"

All laughed except Händel, who, after a few moments' silence, said; "Hogarth, you are an honest fellow, but often wondrous dull! You cannot judge of the Italian painters. In the first place, their manner is entirely different from yours, and then you know nothing of their best works. Had you been, as I have, in Italy, and particularly in Rome, where live the glorious creations of Raphael and Michael Angelo, you would have respect for the old Italian painters; you would love and honor them, as I do the old Italian church composers. As to the modern painters, they are like, more or less, in their way, to Signor Farinelli."

"Well!" cried Hogarth; "we will not dispute thereupon. Tell us rather how you are pleased with your singers and performers, and if you think they will acquit themselves well to-morrow."

"They cannot do very badly," answered Händel; "I have drilled them diligently, and Joseph has helped me with assiduous study. Only the first soprano singer is dreadfully mediocre; I am sorry for it—for the sake of a few good notes—"

Here Joseph put his head in at the door, and said, "Master Händel, a word if you please."

"Well, what do you want?" asked Händel: and rising, he came out of the room; his companions looked smiling at one another; and John Farren sent forth from his leathern chair a prolonged "ha! ha! ha!" Joseph took his master's hand, and led him hastily across the passage and upstairs into his chamber, where Händel, to his no small astonishment, found the pretty Ellen.

"Ha! what may all this mean?" he asked, while his brow darkened; "what do you here, Miss Ellen, in the chamber of this young man—and so late too?"

"He may tell you that himself, Master Händel," answered the damsel pettishly, and blushing while she turned away her face. But Joseph replied quickly and earnestly: "Think not ill of me and the good Ellen, my dear master; for what we do here, I am ready to answer before you."

"Open your mouth, then, and speak," said Händel.

Joseph went on: "For what I am, and what I can do, I thank you, my dear master. You befriended me when I came hither a stranger, without means of earning a support. To make me a good singer, you spent many an hour, in which you could have done something great."

"Ho! ho! the fool!" cried Händel; "and do you think to make a good singer was not doing something great—eh?"

"You see, master, it has often grieved me to see you forced to vex yourself beyond reason with indifferent singers, because their education is far behind your works."

"That is a pity, indeed," sighed Händel.

"And I have tried," continued Joseph, "to instruct a singer for *you*: I think I have so far succeeded, that she may venture before you. There she is!" and he pointed to Ellen.

Händel opened his eyes wide, looked astonished on the damsel, and asked, incredulously, "Ellen! what, Ellen there?"

"Yes, I!" cried Ellen, coming to him, and looking innocently in his face with her clear hazel eyes. "I, myself," she repeated, smiling; "and now you know, Master Händel, what Joseph and I were about together."

"Shall she sing before you, Master Händel?" asked Joseph.

"I am curious to see how your teaching has succeeded," said Händel, while he seated himself: "Come, then, let her sing." Joseph sprang joyfully to the harpsichord; Ellen went and stood beside him, and began.

How it was with the composer,—how he listened, when he heard the most splendid part in his forthcoming Messiah—the noble air, "*I know that my Redeemer liveth;*"—and how Ellen sang it, the reader may conjecture, when, after she had ceased, Händel still sat motionless, a happy smile on his lips, his large flashing eyes full of the tears of deep religious emotion. At length he drew a deep breath, arose, kissed the forehead of the maiden, kissed her eyes—in which likewise pure drops were glancing,—and asked in his mildest tone: "Ellen, my good—good child, you will sing this part tomorrow, at the representation, will you not?"

"Master Händel—*Father* Händel!" cried the maiden; and overcome with emotion, she threw herself sobbing on his neck. But Joseph sang—

"Erwach'—erwach'—zu Liedern der Wonne;
Frohlocke!—frohlocke du!"

"Amen!" resounded through the vast arches of the church, and died away in whispered melody in its remotest aisles. "Amen!" responded Händel, while he let fall slowly the staff with which he kept time. Successful beyond expectation was the first performance of his immortal master-piece. Immense was the impression it produced, as well on the performers as upon the audience. The fame of Händel stood now immovable.

When the composer left the church, he found a royal equipage in waiting for him, which, by the King's command, conveyed him to Carlton House.

George the Second, surrounded by his whole household and many nobles of the court, received the illustrious German. "Well, Master Händel," he cried, after a gracious welcome, "it must be owned, you have made us a noble present in your Messiah; it is a brave piece of work."

"*Is it?*" asked Händel, and looked the monarch in the face, well pleased.

"It is, indeed," replied George. "And now tell me what I can do, to express my thanks to you for it?"

"If your Majesty," answered Händel, "will give a place to the young man who sang the tenor solo part so well, I shall be ever grateful to your Majesty. He is my pupil, Joseph Wach, and he would fain marry his pupil, the fair Ellen, daughter to old John Farren; the old man gives consent, but his dame is opposed, because Joseph has no place as yet. And your Majesty knows full well, that it is hard to carry a cause against the women."

"You are mistaken, Master Händel," said the King, with a forced smile; "I know nothing to that effect; but Joseph has from this day a place in our chapel as first tenor."

"Indeed!" cried Händel, rubbing his hands with joy, "I thank your Majesty from the bottom of my heart!"

George was silent a few moments, expecting the master to ask some other favor. "But, Master Händel," he said at length, "have you nothing to ask for yourself? I would willingly show my gratitude to you in your own person, for the fair entertainment you have provided us all in your Messiah."

The flush of anger suddenly mantled on Händel's cheek, and he answered, in a disappointed tone—"Sire, I have endeavored not to *entertain* you—but to make you *better.*"

The whole court was astonished. King George stepped back a pace or two, and looked on the bold master with surprise. Then bursting into a hearty fit of laughter, and walking up to him—"Händel!" he cried—"you are, and will ever be, a rough old fellow, but"—and he slapped him good-naturedly on the shoulder—"a good fellow withal. Go—do what you will, we remain ever the best friends in the world." He signed in token of dismission; Händel retired respectfully, and thanked Heaven as he turned his back on Carlton House, to hasten to his favorite haunt, the tavern.

We shall not attempt to describe the joy his news brought to the lovers, Joseph and Ellen, nor their unnumbered caresses and protestations of gratitude. John Farren took his good wife in his arms and hugged her, 'spite of her resistance and scolding, crying, "Nonsense, Bett! we must be friends to-day, though all the bells in old England ring a peal for it."

For ten years more Händel travelled throughout England, and composed new and admirable works. When his sight failed him in the last years of his life, it was Ellen who nursed him as if she had been his child, while her husband Joseph wrote down his last compositions, as he dictated them.

Proud and magnificent is the marble monument erected in Westminster to the memory of Händel. Time may destroy it; but the monument he himself, in his high and holy inspiration, has left us—his Messiah—will last forever.

TARTINI

It was late one evening in the summer of 171-, that a party of wild young students at law in the University of Padua were at supper in the saloon of a restaurateur of that city. The revelry had been prolonged even beyond the usual time; much wine had been drunk; and the harmony and good feeling that generally prevailed during their convivial meetings had been interrupted by furious altercation between two of their number. As is almost always the case, the rest took sides with one or other of the disputants; all rose from table; high words were exchanged, and a scene of confusion and tumult was likely to ensue, when the offenders were imperiously called to order by one of their number. He was evidently young; but his slender limbs were firmly knit, and his form, though slight, so well proportioned as to give promise both of activity and strength beyond his years.

"For shame!" he cried, angrily, after producing a momentary silence by a vigorous thump on the table; "are you but a set of bullies, that you stand here pitching hard words at each other, and calling all the neighborhood to see how valiant we can be with our tongues? Fetch me him that can swear loudest, and give us space for our swords!"

Here the clamor was redoubled by all at once explaining, and contradicting each other.

The first speaker struck the table again till all the glasses rang.

"Have done," he cried, "with this disgraceful uproar, or San Marco! I will fight you all myself—one by one!"

This threat was received with cries of "Not me—Giuseppe!" and after a few moments, the two disputants stood forth, separated from their companions. A space was speedily cleared for the combat.

The combatants needed no urging; but scarcely was the clashing of their swords heard, when Pedrillo, the restaurateur, ran in, followed by his servants, and with a face pale with terror protested against his house being made the scene of riot and bloodshed. It would be his ruin, he averred; he should be indicted by the civil authorities; he should be banished the country; he could never again show his face in Padua! If young gentlemen would kill one another there were places enough for such a purpose besides a reputable establishment like his; and with ludicrous rapidity enumerating the localities resorted to by duellists of the city, he besought them with piteous entreaties to transfer themselves elsewhere, offering even to remain minus the expenses of their supper. But Pedrillo's solicitations had little effect on the wilful young men, till backed by threats that he would call the guard. Most of them had known what it was to fall into the hands of the police for midnight disturbances, and duels were favorite pastimes among the students of the University; so that immediately on the disappearance of Pedrillo's servant, the whole party precipitately left the house. First, however, Giuseppe, the one who had recommended a resort to the duel, laid the amount of the reckoning on the table.

As the party turned the corner of a narrow street, they came close upon a carriage, attended by several servants. At this sudden encounter with so many half intoxicated and noisy students, recognised by their dress and well known to be always ready for any deed of mischief, the attendants fled in every direction. The horses caught the alarm, and, wild with fright, plunged, reared, and set off at full speed down the street. A shout of laughter from the revellers, who thought it capital sport to see the dismay created at sight of them, greeted the ears of the terrified inmates of the carriage. But Giuseppe sprang forward, and at the peril of his life, threw himself upon the horses' necks, pulling the bits with such violence as to check them at once. The animals, quivering with fear, stood still; the coachman recovered his control over them; and Giuseppe, opening the door, assisted an elderly gentleman, very richly dressed, to alight, and inquired kindly if he had suffered injury.

"I have only been alarmed;" replied the gentleman, carefully adjusting his dress, and drawing his cloak about him. "But my daughter" —

Giuseppe had already lifted from the carriage the nearly lifeless form of a young girl. As the lamp-light fell upon her face, he could see it was one of matchless beauty.

"My Leonora!" exclaimed the father, in a tone of anxious apprehension. The young girl opened languidly a pair of beautiful dark eyes, started up, gazed with an expression of surprise upon the young student who had been supporting her, then threw herself into her father's arms. With an expression of joy that she had recovered from her fright, the gentleman ordered his servants, who had returned when the danger was over, to procure another conveyance. This was immediately done; and turning to Giuseppe, he thanked him with lofty courtesy for the service he had rendered, and invited him to call next day at the house of the Count di Cornaro, in the Prado della Valle.

All night wild thoughts were busy in the brain of the young student. Never had such a vision of loveliness dawned upon him. And who was she? One elevated by fortune and rank so far above him that she would regard him but as the dust beneath her feet. As he had seen her in her delicate white drapery, like floating silver, her hair bound with pearls, she had moved, in some princely palace, among the nobles of the land. Many had worshipped; many had doubtless poured forth vows at her feet. How would she look upon one so poor and lowly? Giuseppe heaved a bitter sigh, but he resolved nevertheless to love her, and only her, for the rest of his life. A new sensation was born within him. He had hitherto cared only for frolic and revel and fighting; had been known only as Giuseppe, the mad student; the mover and leader in all mischief; a perfect master of his weapon, and the most skilful fencer in Padua. So great was his passion for fencing, and so astonishing the skill he had acquired in the art, that the most finished adepts in that noble science were frequently known to resort to him for lessons. So fond was he, moreover, of exhibiting this accomplishment, that he shunned no opportunity of exercising it at the expense of his acquaintances. Many were the duels in which he had been engaged; whether on his own account or for the sake of his friends, it mattered little. His love of fighting was as well known as the fact that few could hope to come off victorious in a strife with him; and this may account for the ascendancy he evidently had over his companions, their unwillingness to chafe his humor, and submission to the imperious tone in which he was wont to address them.

Of late, disgusted with the study of law, to which he had been consigned by his parents as a last resort—their first wish having been that he should embrace a monastic life—he had adopted the resolution of leaving Padua, of taking up his abode in one of the great capitals, and pursuing the profession of a fencing-master. Thus he would have opportunity for the cultivation of his favorite science, and at the same time would be unfettered by the control of others, a yoke galling beyond measure to his impatient spirit. Already he had announced this determination to his fellow students, and waited only a favorable opportunity to effect his escape from the University.

How often are the plans of a human mind changed by the slightest accident! How many fortunes have been made or marred by occurrences so trivial that they would have passed unnoticed by ordinary observation! How many events of importance have depended on causes at the first view scarce worth the estimation of a hair! In the present instance, the Count di Cornaro's horses taken fright cost a capital fencing-master, and gave the world—a Tartini!

In due time next day, Giuseppe appeared in the Prado della Valle. As he was about to ascend the steps of the noble mansion belonging to the Count di Cornaro, a window above was hastily thrown open, and a rose fell at his feet. Glancing upward, he caught a glimpse of the bright face of Leonora; she smiled, and vanished from the window. The youth raised the flower, pressed it to his lips, and hid it in his bosom.

At the door, the porter received him as one who had been expected, and ushered him into a splendidly furnished apartment. The marble tables were covered with flowers; a lute lay on one of them; the visitor took it up, not doubting that it belonged to the beautiful Leonora, and while waiting for the Count, played several airs with exquisite skill.

"By my faith! you have some taste in music!" cried Cornaro, who had entered unperceived, as he finished one of the airs. The young man laid down the instrument, embarrassed, and blushing deeply, stammered an apology for the liberty he had taken.

"Nay, I excuse you readily, my young friend," said the Count, cordially—extending his hand. Then motioning him to a seat, he asked his name.

"Giuseppe Tartini."

"A native of Padua?"

"No; I was born at Pisano, in Istria."

"Your business here?"

"I am a student at law, in the University."

The speaker colored again; for he had suddenly become anxious to obtain the Count's good opinion.

"And where," asked Cornaro, after a pause, "did you acquire your knowledge in music?"

"You are pleased, Signor," replied the youth, modestly, and bending his eyes to the ground, "to commend what is indeed not worthy—"

"Allow me judgment, if you please," interrupted the Count, sharply. "I am myself skilled in the art. I ask, where did you receive instruction?"

"I took some lessons at Capo d' Istria," answered Giuseppe, "when very young; my parents had placed me there to be educated for the church; and I found music a great solace in my seclusion."

"The church! and why have you changed your pursuits?"

"I could not, Signor, conscientiously devote myself to a religious life— when I knew myself in no way fitted for it."

"I understand; you wished to act a part in the world; you were right. Your parents were wrong to decide for you prematurely. I like your frankness and simplicity, Giuseppe. You may look upon me as a friend."

This was said in the lofty tone of a patron. The young man bowed in apparent humility and gratitude.

"You rendered me a service last night, at great risk to yourself—ay, and some injury, too!" Here he noticed, for the first time, a slight wound on the cheek of his young visitor.

"Oh, it is nothing, Signor!" cried Giuseppe, really embarrassed that so slight a hurt should be alluded to.

"You may esteem it such, but I do not forget that I owe you thanks for your timely aid; nor do I fail to observe that you are modest as brave. I perceive, also, that you have talents, and lack, perhaps, the means of cultivating them. In such a case, you will not find me an ungenerous patron. In what way can I assist you now?"

Tartini made no reply, for his head was full of confused ideas. His former purposes and plans were wholly forgotten. The Count remarked his embarrassment, and graciously gave him permission to go home for the present and consider what he had said.

The young man lingered a moment before the door, and stole a glance upward, hoping to see once more the angelic face that had smiled upon him; but the window was closed and all was silent. He departed with a feeling of sadness and disappointment at his heart. He knew not how powerful an advocate he had in the bosom of the maiden herself. Under the sun of Italy love is a plant that springs up spontaneously; and the handsome face and form of the youth who had perilled his life to save her from harm had already impressed deeply the fancy of the susceptible girl. Unseen herself, she watched his departure from her father's house; and, impelled by something more than mere feminine curiosity, immediately descended to know the particulars of his visit. It was to be supposed that her woman's wit could point out some way in which the haughty Count could discharge his obligation to the humble student. And she failed not to suggest such a way.

Two days after, Giuseppe was surprised by a message from the Count di Cornaro, proposing that he should become his daughter's tutor in music, and offering a liberal salary. With what eagerness, with what trembling delight he accepted the offer! How did his heart beat, as he strove in the Count's presence to conceal the wild rapture he felt, under a semblance of respect and downcast humility! How resolutely did he turn his eyes from the face of his beautiful pupil, lest he should become quite frantic with his new joy, and lest the passion that filled his breast should betray itself in his looks! As if it were possible long to conceal it from the bewitching object!

It was a day in spring. The soft air, laden with the fragrance of flowers, stole in at the draperied windows of Cornaro's princely mansion, and rustled in the leaves of the choice plants ranged within. In the apartment to which we before introduced the reader, sat a fair girl, holding a book in her hand, but evidently too much absorbed in melancholy thought to notice its contents. She was reclining upon a couch in an attitude of the deepest dejection. Her face was very pale, and bore the traces of recent tears. As the bell rang, and the door was opened by the domestic, she started up and clasped her hands with an expression of the most lively alarm. But when a young man, apparently about twenty years of age, entered the room, she ran towards him, and throwing herself into his arms, wept and sobbed on his bosom.

"Leonora! my beloved!" cried the youth; "For heaven's sake, tell me what has happened!"

"Oh, Giuseppe!" she answered, as soon as she could speak for weeping, "We are lost! My father has discovered all!"

"Alas! and his anger has not spared thee!"

"No—Giuseppe! He has pardoned me; thou art the destined victim! Stay—let me tell thee all—and quickly; for the moments are precious! The Marchese di Rossi, thou knowest, has sought my hand. He saw thee descend last night from my window."

"He knows, then, of our secret marriage?"

"No—he knows nothing; but seeing thee leave my chamber at night, he gave information this morning to my uncle, the Bishop."

"The villain! he shall rue this!" muttered Tartini, grasping the hilt of his weapon.

"Oh, think not of punishing him! it will but ruin all! Fly—fly—before my uncle——"

"Tell me all that has happened."

"This only—the Bishop revealed what he knew to my father; I was summoned to his presence scarce an hour since. He reproached me with what he called the infamy I had brought upon his house. I could not bear his agony—Giuseppe! I confessed myself thy wedded wife!"

"Thou wast right—my Leonora! and then?"

"He refused to believe me! I called Beatrice, who witnessed our marriage, with her husband. My father softened; I knelt at his feet, and implored forgiveness."

"And he?" asked Tartini, breathlessly.

"He pardoned me—he embraced me as his daughter; but required me to renounce thee forever."

The young man dropped the hand he had held clasped in his.

"Wilt thou—Leonora?" he asked.

"Never—Giuseppe!"

"Beloved! let us go forth; I will claim thee in the face of the world."

"Nay, my husband—listen to me! I have seen our friend, the good Father Antonio—and appealed to him in my distress. He counsels wisely. Thou must leave Padua, and that instantly! My father's anger is not to be dreaded so much as that of my haughty uncle, who would urge him to all that is fearful. They would sacrifice thee—Giuseppe! Oh, thou knowest not the pride of our house! They would shrink from no deed—"

Here the speaker shuddered—and her fair cheek grew pale as death.

"I have no fears for myself—Leonora. They cannot sever the bonds of the church that united us; my own life I can defend."

"Ah, thou knowest them not! the dungeon—the rack—the assassin's knife—all will be prepared for thee. As thou lovest me, fly!" And gliding from his embrace, she sank down at his feet.

"Forsake thee—my wife! Abandon thee to the Cardinal's vengeance—"

"I have naught to fear from him. Oh, hear Antonio's advice! When thou art gone, the Bishop's anger will abate. A few months may restore thee to me. Go—Giuseppe: there is safety in flight—to stay is certain death! Must Leonora entreat in vain?"

Their interview was interrupted by Beatrice, the nurse, who came in haste to warn Tartini that her master, with his brother the Bishop of Padua, was approaching the house, and that they were accompanied by several armed servants. There could now be no doubt of their intentions towards the offender. He comprehended at once, that even the forbearance the Count had shown his daughter had been dictated by a wish to secure his person. To stay would be utter madness; and yielding to the passionate entreaties of his young wife, he clasped her for the last time to his heart, pressed a farewell kiss on her forehead, and was gone before his pursuers entered the house.

That night, while the emissaries of the Bishop of Padua were searching the city, with orders to arrest the fugitive, and to cut him down without mercy should he resist, Tartini, disguised in a pilgrim's dress, was many miles on the way towards Rome.

More than two years after the occurrence of this scene, one evening in the winter of 1713, the Guardian of the Minors' Convent at Assisi was conversing with the organist, Father Boëmo, on the subject of one of the inmates, whom Boëmo had taken under his peculiar care.

"The youth is a relative of mine," continued the Guardian; "but considerations of humanity alone moved me to grant him an asylum, when, poor, persecuted and homeless, he threw himself on my compassion. Since then his conduct has been such as to secure my favor, and the respect of all the brethren."

"In truth it has," said Boëmo, warmly. "And believe me, brother, you will have as good reason to be proud of him as a kinsman, as I of my pupil. It is my knowledge of his worth that causes me such pain at his loss of health."

"The wearing of grief, think you?"

"Not wholly. His anxiety for the safety of his wife was set at rest long ago by intelligence of her welfare. He knows well that the only daughter of so proud a house must be dear to her kinsmen—even by their unwearied efforts to discover his retreat. And I have taught him to solace the pains of absence."

"Fears he still the Bishop's resentment?"

"Oh, no; these convent walls are secure, and his secret well guarded, since only in your keeping and mine. His enemies may ransack Italy; they will never dream of finding him here."

"What is the source, then, of his depression?"

"It is a mystery to me. I have marked it growing for weeks. And sure I am, it is not weariness of the solitude of this abode. Since his spirits rose from the sadness of his first misfortunes—since he breathed the air of comparative freedom, and joined in the exercises of our pious brethren, Giuseppe has been a changed man. Sorely hath he been tried in the furnace of affliction, and he hath come forth pure gold. The religious calm of this retreat has taught him reflection and moderation. His past sorrow has chastened his spirit; the holy example of the brethren has nourished in his breast humility and resignation and piety. The ardent aspirations of his nature are now directed to the accomplishment of those great things for which Heaven has destined him. Never have I known so unwearied, so devoted a student."

"With your training and good counsel, brother, he might well love study," said the Guardian, with a smile.

"Nay, brother," replied Boëmo, modestly, "I have but directed him in the cultivation of his surprising genius for music. And you know he excels on the violin. It is for that he seems to have a passion—a passion that I fear is consuming his very life."

They were interrupted by one of the brethren, who had some business with the Guardian; and Father Boëmo proceeded to the cell of his pupil, whom he was to accompany to vespers.

He found the object of his care seated by his table, on which he leaned in a melancholy reverie. His form was emaciated; his face so pale that the good monk, who had seen him but a few hours before, was even startled at the increased evidence of indisposition. His violin was thrown aside neglected—strongest possible proof of the malady of one who had worshipped music with an idolatry bordering on madness.

Boëmo laid his hand kindly on his pupil's shoulder, and said, in a tone of mild reproof—"Giuseppe!"

The young man made no reply.

"This is not well, my brother!" continued the worthy organist. "The gifts of God are not to be thus slighted; we offend Him by our despondency, which, save abuse of power, is the worst ingratitude."

"It is your fault!" said the youth, bitterly, and looking up.

"Mine—and how?"

Giuseppe hesitated.

"How am I to blame for this sinful melancholy you indulge?"

"Your lessons have given me knowledge."

"And does knowledge bring sorrow?"

"Saith not your creed thus? Since Adam tasted the fruit—"

"Of a knowledge forbidden."

"So is all knowledge—of things higher than we can attain to. To aspire—and never reach—that is the misery of humanity." And the speaker again buried his face in his hands.

"I understand you, my brother;" said Boëmo, after a pause. "I have been to blame in suffering you to pursue your studies in solitude. Knowing nothing of the outer world, you have wrought but in view of that ideal which, to every true artist, becomes more glorious and inaccessible as he gazes—as he advances. You despond, because you have labored in vain after perfection. Is it not so?"

"I have mistaken myself;" answered Tartini; "you have mistaken me. It was cruel in you to persuade me I was an artist."

"And who tells you you are not?"

"My own judgment—my own heart."

"It deceives you, then."

"It does not," cried Tartini, with sudden energy, and starting up with such violence that the worthy monk was alarmed. "It is you who have deceived me. You have taught me to flatter myself; to imagine I could accomplish something; to thirst for what was never to be mine. You have pointed me to a goal toward which I have toiled and panted—in vain—while it receded in mockery. You have given me wishes which are to prove my everlasting curse. Yes,"—he continued, striking his forehead, "my curse. What doom can be more horrible than mine?"

"You have but passed," answered Boëmo, mildly, "though the trial of every soul gifted by Heaven with a true perception of the great and the beautiful."

"It is not so," exclaimed his pupil, passionately. "I have striven to soar—and fallen to the earth, never more to rise. I have dreamed myself the favorite of art—and awaked to find myself outcast and scorned. My soul is dead within me. You must have foreseen this. Why prepare such anguish for one already the victim of misfortune?"

"Young man," said the organist, impressively, "this feeling is morbid. I will not reason with you now; come with me, and let us see what change of subject——"

"Ay," muttered Tartini, his face distorted, "to show the brethren what you have done; that they, too, may mock at me! I see them now—"

"Holy Mother! what ails you, my son?" cried Boëmo, much alarmed at the wild looks of his pupil.

"You will deem me mad, good father;" said Giuseppe in an altered voice, and grasping the monk's arm; "but I swear to you—'tis the truth. I see them every night!"

"See whom?"

"The spirits—the demons, who come to mock at me! They range themselves around my cell—and grin and hiss at me in devilish scorn. As soon as it is dark they throng hither. See—they are coming now! stealing through the window——"

"My brother! my brother! is it come to this?" cried Boëmo in a tone of anguish.

"Sometimes," said his pupil, "I have thought it but an evil dream. I strove against it till I knew too well it was no delusion of fancy."

"Why—why did I not know of this before?"

"It was needless. I would not grieve you, father. Besides—I would not have the demons think I sought aid against them. That would have been cowardly! No—they do not even know how much their malice has made me suffer."

"This must be looked to!" muttered the monk to himself; and drawing Giuseppe's arm within his, he led him out of the cell and down to the chapel, intending after the evening service to confer with the Guardian respecting this new malady of his unfortunate friend.

They decided that it was best to leave Giuseppe no more alone at night. The melancholy he had suffered to prey so long on his mind had impaired his reason; repose and cheerful conversation would restore him. Father Boëmo resolved to pass the first part of the night in his cell; but as he had to go before the hour of matins to pray with a poor invalid, he engaged a brother of the convent to take his place at midnight.

When the organist the next day saw his pupil, he was surprised at the change in his whole demeanor. Giuseppe received him in his cell with a face beaming with joy, but at the same time with an air of mystery, as if he almost feared to communicate some gratifying piece of intelligence.

"You passed a better night, my son," said the benevolent monk. "I am truly rejoiced. I have prayed for you."

"Listen, father!" said Giuseppe, eagerly. "I have conquered them. I have put them all to flight."

"The evil one fleeth from those who resist him," said Father Boëmo, solemnly.

"But I have done better; I have made a compact with him."

"Giuseppe!" The monk crossed himself, in holy fear.

"Nay, father Boëmo! I have yielded nothing. The devil is my servant— the slave of my will. Last night the demons came again so soon as you were gone, and while brother Piero slept, to torment me. They mocked me more fiercely than ever. I was in despair. I cried to the saints for succor."

"You did right."

"The evil spirits vanished; but the mightiest of all, Satan himself, stood before me. I made a league with him. Do not grow pale, father! Satan has promised to serve me. All will go now according to my will." [1]

Boëmo shook his head, mournfully.

"As a test of his obedience, I gave him my violin and commanded him to play something. What was my astonishment when he executed a sonata, so exquisite, so wonderful, that I had never in my life imagined anything approaching it! I was bewildered—enchanted. I could hardly breathe from excess of rapture. Then the devil handed the violin back to me. "Take it, master," said he, "you can do the same." I took it, and succeeded. Never had I heard such music. You were right, father! I have done wrong to despair."

The monk sighed, for he saw that his poor friend still labored under the excitement of a diseased imagination. He made, however, no effort to reason with him, but sought to divert his mind by speaking of other matters.

"You shall hear for yourself," cried Tartini; and seizing his violin, he walked several times across the room, humming a tune, and at last began to play. The music was broken and irregular, though in the wild tones he drew from the instrument, the ear of an artist caught notes that were strangely beautiful. It seemed, in truth, the music of a half-remembered dream.

Again and again did Giuseppe strive to catch the melody; at length throwing down the instrument, he struck his forehead and wrung his hands in bitterness of disappointment.

"It is gone from me!" he cried, in a voice of agony. Father Boëmo sought in vain to lead his mind from this harrowing thought. Now he would snatch up the violin and play as if determined to conquer the difficulty; then fling it aside in despair, vowing that he would break it in pieces and renounce music forever.

After a consultation with the Guardian, Father Boëmo summoned medical assistance, and that night himself administered a composing draught to his young friend. He had the satisfaction of seeing him soon in a profound slumber; and having given him in charge once more to Piero, withdrew to spend an hour or two in prayer for his relief.

Just before matins the organist was aroused by a cry without. Being already dressed, he hastily descended to the court where the brother who had given the alarm stood gazing upward in speechless terror. Well might he shake with fear! Upon the edge of the roof stood a figure, clearly visible in the moonlight, and easily recognized as that of the unhappy Giuseppe.

"Hush! not a word—or you are his murderer!" whispered Boëmo, grasping the arm of the affrighted monk. Both gazed on the strange figure; the one in superstitious fear—the other in breathless anxiety. Boëmo now perceived that Giuseppe held his violin. After a short prelude he played a sonata so admirable, so magnificent, that both listeners forgot their apprehensions and stood entranced, as if the melody floating on the night wind had indeed been wafted downward from the celestial spheres. [2]

A dead silence—a silence of awful suspense, followed this strange interruption. Neither dared to speak; for Boëmo well knew that a single false step would cost his friend's life. And he was well aware that the sleep-walker often passes in safety over places where no waking man could tread. The great danger was that his slumber might be suddenly broken.

The sonata was not repeated. The figure turned and slowly retraced his steps along the roof, taking the way to Tartini's cell. Father Boëmo breathed not till his pupil was in safety; then with a faint murmur of thanksgiving he sank on his knees, while the liberated monk hastened to communicate to the superior what he had seen. The worthy organist watched by the bed of his friend, after blaming severely the negligence of the brother who had been left to guard him. Giuseppe awoke feverish and disturbed—the workings of an unquiet imagination had worn out his strength and an illness of many weeks followed. During all this his faithful friend scarcely left him, but sought to minister to the diseased mind as well as the feeble frame. His care was rewarded. With returning health, reason and cheerfulness returned.

It was a holiday in Assisi. The inhabitants came in crowds to the church to join in the services; in fact so goodly an assemblage had never been seen in that old place of worship. The fame of the admirable music to be heard there formed a powerful attraction. It is almost needless to say that the execution was that of the brothers of the Minors' Convent.

Much curiosity had been excited among the people by the circumstance that a curtain was drawn across a part of the choir occupied by the musicians, during all parts of the service. As usual, general attention was fixed by the least appearance of mystery. The precaution had, in fact, been adopted for the sake of Tartini, who played the violin. He still stood in fear of the vengeance of the Cornaro family, who had spared no pains to discover his abode.

The service was nearly ended. While the music still sounded, the wind suddenly lifted the curtain and blew it aside for a moment. A suppressed cry was heard in the choir, and the violin-player ceased. He had recognized in the assembly a Paduan who knew him well.

The Guardian and Father Boëmo, when informed of this discovery, opposed Giuseppe's resolution of quitting the convent. Both pledged themselves to protect him against the anger of the Bishop of Padua; besides, who knew that the same accident had discovered him? Even among the brethren he passed by an assumed name; it was probable that all was yet safe.

"Come, Giuseppe, you must play to-day in the chapel; the Guardian has guests, who have heard of our music, and we must do our best."

The grateful pupil and the pleased instructor did their best. When the service was over, Father Boëmo took his young friend by the arm and led him into the parlor of the convent.

A lady of stately and graceful form, her face concealed by a veil, stood between two distinguished looking men, one in the robes of a cardinal. Tartini gave but one glance; the next instant—"Leonora!—my wife!" burst from his lips, and he clasped her, fainting, in his arms.

"Receive our blessing, children," said the cardinal Cornaro. "Years of religious seclusion, Giuseppe, have rendered thee more worthy of the happiness thou art now to possess. Not to the wild disobedient youth, but to the *man* of tried worth, do I give my niece. Give him thy hand, Leonora."

The young couple joined hands, and the cardinal pronounced over them a solemn benediction.

"In one thing, my son, thou art to blame," he resumed—"in hiding thyself from us, instead of trusting our clemency. We have sought thee, not for the purpose of vengeance, but to restore thee to thy wife and country. But for a happy chance, we should still have been ignorant of the place of thy retreat. Yet Heaven orders all for the best. Sorrow has done a noble work with thee."

"And it has made thee only more beautiful—my beloved!" whispered the happy artist, "my own Leonora—mine—mine forever!"

We do not question the sincerity of Tartini's joy at his reunion with his lovely wife. But we must have our own opinion of his constancy, when, not long after, we find him leaving her side and flying from Venice for fear of the rivalship of Veracini, a celebrated violin-player from Florence. Perhaps this want of confidence was necessary to the development of his qualities as an artist. But we leave his after life with his biographer. One thing, however, is certain; of all his compositions, the most admirable and the most celebrated is "The Devil's Sonata."

FOOTNOTES

[1] Lalande, to whom Tartini himself communicated this curious anecdote, relates it in his Travels in Italy.

[2] It may be seen by a reference to any detailed biography of Tartini, that nearly all the incidents recorded in this little tale are real facts.

HAYDN

THE APPRENTICESHIP

I

In a small and insignificant dwelling in the village of Rohrau, on the borders of Hungary and Austria, lived, at the beginning of the last century, a young pair, faithful and industrious, plain and simple in their manners, yet esteemed by all their neighbors. The man, an honest wheelwright, was commonly called "merry Jobst," on account of the jokes and gay stories with which he was always ready to entertain his friends and visitors, who, he well knew, relished such things. His wife was named Elizabeth, but no one in the village, and indeed many miles round it, ever called her any thing but "pretty Elschen." Jobst and Elschen were indeed, to say truth, the handsomest couple in the country.

Mc Rae, sc.

HAYDN.

The Hungarians, like the Austrians and Bohemians, have great love for music. "Three fiddles and a dulcimer for two houses," says the proverb; and it is a true one. It is not unusual, therefore, for some out of the poorer classes, when their regular business fails to bring them in sufficient for their wants, to take to the fiddle, the dulcimer, or the harp; playing on holidays on the highway or in the taverns. This employment is generally lucrative enough, if they are not spendthrifts, to enable them, not only to live, but to lay by something for future necessities.

"Merry Jobst" was already revolving in his own mind some means to be adopted for the bettering of his very humble fortunes, when Elschen one day said to him, "Jobst! it is time to think of making something more for our increasing family!" Jobst gave a leap of joy, embraced pretty Elschen, and answered, "Come then! I will string anew my fiddle and your harp; every holiday we will take our place on the road side before the tavern, and play and sing merrily: we will give good wishes to those that listen to and reward us, and let the surly traveller, who stops not to hear us, go on his way!"

The next Sunday afternoon merry Jobst and pretty Elschen sat by the highway before the village inn; Jobst fiddled, and Elschen played the harp and sang to it with her sweet clear voice. Not one passed by without noticing them; every traveller stopped to listen, well pleased, and on resuming his journey threw at least a silver twopence into the lap of the pretty young woman. Jobst and his wife, on returning home in the evening, found their day's work a good one.—They practised it regularly with the like success.

After the lapse of a few years, as the old cantor of the neighboring town of Haimburg passed along the road one afternoon, he could not help stopping, admiring and amused at what he saw. In the same arbor, opposite the tavern, sat merry Jobst fiddling as before, and beside him pretty Elschen, playing the harp and singing; and between them, on the ground, sat a little chubby-faced boy about three years old, who had a small board, shaped like a violin, hung about his neck, on which he played with a willow twig as with a genuine fiddle-bow. The most comical and surprising thing of all was, that the little man kept perfect time, pausing when his father paused and his mother had solo, then falling in with him again, and demeaning himself exactly like his father. Often too, he would lift up his clear voice, and join distinctly in the refrain of the song. The song pretty Elschen sang, ran somewhat in this way:

"The Spring it is come—and the blithe earth is green,
Birds and flowers are abroad, and how glistening the sheen!
O'er the broken stones sparkling, the stream murmurs nigh,
And how fresh from the mountains the breezes sweep by.

"The bees hum around us, the lambs frolic too,

And golden clouds sport in the heavens' deep blue!

The young mountain shepherd, his shawm he hath wound,

And the maiden steps softly, and follows the sound.

"The bell in yon valley breaks faint on the air,

Stranger! haste not away! pause and breathe first a prayer,

And give thanks to our Maker, on whom good men call—

Who created in love, and sustaineth us all."

"Is that your boy—fiddler?" asked the teacher, when the song was at an end. Jobst answered,

"Yes, sir, that is my little Seperl." [3]

"The little fellow seems to have a taste for music."

"Why not? if it depends on me, I will take him, as soon as I can do so, to one who understands it well, and can teach him. But it will be some time yet, as with all his taste and love for it, he is very little and awkward."

"We will speak further of it," said the teacher, and went his way. Jobst and Elschen began their song anew, and the little Joseph imitated his father on his fiddle, and joined his infant voice with theirs when they sounded the 'Hallelujah!'

The cantor came from this time twice a week to the house of merry Jobst to talk with him about his little son, and the youngster himself was soon the best of friends with the good-natured old man. So matters went on for two years, at the end of which, the cantor said to Jobst, "It is now the right time, and if you will trust your boy with me, I will take him, and teach him what he must learn, to become a brave lad and a skilful musician."

Jobst did not hesitate long, for he saw clearly how great an advantage the instruction of Master Wolferl would be to his son. And though it went harder with pretty Elschen to part with Seperl, who was her favorite and only child, yet she gave up at last, when her husband observed—"The boy is still our own, and if he is our only child, we are—Heaven be praised!—both young, and love each other!"

So he said to Wolferl, the next time he came—"Agreed! here is the boy! treat him well—and remember that he is the apple of our eye."

"I will treat him as my own!" replied the teacher. Elschen accordingly packed up the boy's scanty wardrobe in a bundle, gave him a slice of bread and salt, and a cup of milk—embraced and blessed him, and accompanied him to the door of the cottage, where she signed him with the cross three times, and then returned to her chamber. Jobst went with them half the way to Haimburg, and then also returned, while Wolferl and Joseph pursued their way till they reached Wolferl's house, the end of their journey.

Wolferl was an old bachelor, but one of the good sort, whose heart, despite his grey hairs, was still youthful and warm. He loved all good men, and was patient and forbearing even with those who had faults, for he knew how weak and fickle too often is the heart of man. But the wholly depraved and wicked he hated, as he esteemed the good, and shunned all companionship with them; for it was his opinion "that he who is thoroughly corrupt, remains so in this world at least; and his conversation with the good tends not to his improvement, but on the contrary, to the destruction of both."

Such lessons he repeated daily to the little Joseph, and taught him good principles, as well as how to sing, and play on the horn and kettledrum; and Joseph profited thereby, as well as by the instruction he received in music, and cherished and cultivated them as long as he lived.

In the following year, 1737, a second son was bestowed on the happy parents, whom they christened Michael.

Years passed, and Joseph was a well instructed boy; he had a voice as clear and fine as his mother's, and played the violin as well as his father; besides that, he blew the horn, and beat the kettledrum, in the sacred music prepared by Wolferl for church festivals. Better than all, Joseph had a true and honest heart, had the fear of God continually before his eyes, and was ever contented, and wished well to all; for which everybody loved him in return, and Wolferl often said with tears of joy—"Mark what I tell you, God will show the world, by this boy Joseph, that not only the kingdom of heaven, but the kingdom of the science of music shall be given to those who are pure in heart!" The more Wolferl perceived the lad's wonderful talent for art, the more earnestly he sought to find a patron, who might better forward the youthful aspirant towards the desired goal; for he felt that his own strength could reach little further, when he saw the zeal and ability with which his pupil devoted himself to his studies. Providence ordered it at length that Master von Reuter, chapel-master and music director in St. Stephen's Church, Vienna, came to visit the Deacon at Haimburg. The Deacon told Master von Reuter of the extraordinary boy, the son of the wheelwright Jobst Haydn, the pupil of old Wolferl, and created in the chapel-master much desire to become acquainted with him.—The Deacon would have sent for him and his protector, but von Reuter prevented him with "No—no—most reverend Sir! I will not have the lad brought to me;

I will seek him myself, and if possible, hear him when he is not conscious of my presence or my intentions; for if I find the boy what your reverence thinks him, I will do something, of course, to advance his interests." The next morning, accordingly, von Reuter went to Wolferl's house, which he entered quietly and unannounced. Joseph was sitting alone at the organ, playing a simple but sublime piece of sacred music from an old German master. Reuter, visibly moved, stood at the door and listened attentively. The boy was so deep in his music that he did not perceive the intruder till the piece was concluded, when accidentally turning round, he fixed upon the stranger his large dark eyes, expressive of astonishment indeed, but sparkling a friendly welcome.

"Very well, my son!" said von Reuter at last; "where is your foster-father?"

"In the garden," said the boy; "shall I call him?"

"Call him, and say to him that the chapel-master, von Reuter, wishes to speak with him. Stop a moment! you are Joseph Haydn; are you not?"

"Yes, I am Seperl."

"Well then, go."

Joseph went and brought his old master, Wolferl, who with uncovered head and low obeisance welcomed the chapel-master and music director at Saint Stephen's, to his humble abode. Von Reuter, on his part, praised the musical skill of his protegé, enquired particularly into the lad's attainments, and examined him formally himself. Joseph passed the examination in such a manner that Reuter's satisfaction increased with every answer. After this he spent some time in close conference with old Wolferl; and it was near noon before he took his departure. Joseph was invited to accompany him and spend the rest of the day at the Deacon's.

Eight days after, old Wolferl, Jobst and pretty Elschen, the little Michael on her lap, sat very dejectedly together, and talked of the good Joseph, who had gone that morning with Master von Reuter to Vienna, to take his place as chorister in St. Stephen's church.

II

The clock struck eight, and all were awake in the Leopoldstadt. A busy multitude crowded the bridge—market women and mechanics' boys, hucksters, pedlars, hackney coachmen and genteel horsemen, passing in and out of the city; and through the thickest of the throng might be seen winding his way quietly and inoffensively, the noted Wenzel Puderlein, hairdresser, burgher and house-proprietor in Leopoldstadt. Soon he passed over the space that divides Leopoldstadt from the city, and with rapid steps approached through streets and alleys, the place where resided his most distinguished customers, whom he came every morning to serve.

He stopped before one of the best looking houses; ascended the steps, rang the bell, and when the house-maid opened the door, stepped boldly, and with apparent consciousness of dignity through the hall to a side door. Here he paused, placed his feet in due position, took off his hat modestly, and knocked gently three times.

"Come in!" said a powerful voice. Wenzel, however, started, and hung back a moment, then taking courage, he lifted the latch, opened the door and entered the apartment. An elderly man, of stately figure, wrapped in a flowered dressing-gown, sat at a writing table; he arose as the door opened, and said,

"'Tis well you are come, Puderlein! Do what you have to do, but quickly, I counsel you! for the Empress has sent for me, and I must be with her in half an hour." He then seated himself, and Wenzel began his hairdressing without uttering a word, (how contrary to his nature!) well knowing that a strict silence was enjoined on him in the presence of the first physician to Her Imperial Majesty.

Yet he was not doomed long to suffer this greatest of all torments to him, the necessity of silence. The door of the chamber opened, and a youth of about sixteen or seventeen years of age came in, approached the elderly man, kissed his hand reverently, and bade him good morning.

The old gentleman thanked him briefly, and said, "What was it you were going to ask me yesterday evening, when it struck eleven and I sent you off to bed?"

The youth, with a modest smile, replied, "I was going to beg leave, my father, if your time permitted, to present to you the young man I would like to have for my teacher on the piano."

"Very well; after noon I shall be at liberty; but who has recommended him to *you*?"

"An admirable piece which I was yesterday so fortunate as to hear him play at the house of Mlle. de Martinez."

"Ah! your honor means young Haydn," cried Puderlein, unwittingly, and then became suddenly silent, expecting nothing less than that his temerity would draw down a thunderbolt on his head. But contrary to his expectation, the old gentleman merely looked at him a moment, as if in surprise, from head to foot, then said mildly, "You are acquainted with the young man then: what do you know of him?"

"I know him!" answered Puderlein; "Oh, very well, your honor; I know him well. What I know of him? Oh, much; for observe, your honor, I have had the honor to be hairdresser for many years to the chapel-master, von Reuter, in whose house Haydn has long been an inmate—it must now be ten or eleven years. I have known him, so to speak, from childhood. Besides I have heard him sing a hundred times at St. Stephen's, where he was chorister, though it is now a couple of years since he was turned off."

"Turned off? and wherefore?"

"Aye; observe, your honor, he had a fine clear voice, such as no female singer in the Opera; but getting a fright, and being seized with a fever—when he recovered, his fine soprano was gone! And because they had no more use for him at St. Stephen's, they turned him off."

"And what does young Haydn now?" asked the Baron.

"Ah, your honor, the poor fellow must find it hard to live by giving lessons, playing about, and picking up what he can; he also composes sometimes, or what do they call it? Well, what helps it him, that he torments himself? he lives in the house with Metastasio, not in the first story, like the court poet, but in the fifth; and when it is winter, he has to lie in bed and work, to keep himself from freezing; for, observe, he has indeed a fire-place in his chamber, but no money to buy wood to burn therein."

"This must not be! this shall not be!" cried the Baron von Swieten, as he rose from his seat. "Am I ready?"

"A moment, your honor,—only the string around the hair-bag."

"It is very good so; now begone about your business!" Puderlein vanished. "And you, help me on with my coat; give me my stick and hat, and bring me your young teacher this afternoon." Therewith he departed, and young von Swieten, full of joy, went to the writing-table to indite an invitation to Haydn to come to his father's house.

Meanwhile, Joseph Haydn sat, sorrowful, and almost despairing, in his chamber. He had passed the morning, contrary to his usual custom, in idle brooding over his condition; now it appeared quite hopeless, and his cheerfulness seemed about to take leave of him forever, like his only friend and protectress, Mlle. de Martinez. That amiable young lady had left the city a few hours before. Haydn had instructed her in singing, and in playing the harpsichord, and by way of recompense, he enjoyed the privilege of board and lodging in the fifth story, in the house of Metastasio. Both now ceased with the lady's departure; and Joseph was poorer than before, for all that he had earned besides, he had sent conscientiously to his parents, only keeping so much as sufficed to furnish him with decent, though plain clothing.

Other patrons and friends he had none! Metastasio, who was nearest him, knew him only by his unassuming exterior, and was too indolent to enquire particularly into his circumstances, or to interest himself in his behalf. He had briefly observed to the poor youth, that since the Lady Martinez had left Vienna and his lessons were over, he could look about till the end of the month for other lodgings; and Joseph was too retiring, if not too proud, to answer anything else than that "he thanked the Signor for the privilege hitherto enjoyed, and would look out for another home." But where? thought he now, and asked himself, sobbing aloud. "Where— without money?" Just then, without any previous knocking, the door of his chamber was opened, and with bold carriage, and sparkling eyes, entered Master Wenzel Puderlein.

"With *me!*" cried the friseur, while he stretched his curling irons like a sceptre towards Joseph, and pressed his powder-bag with an air of feeling to his heart, "With me, young orphan! I will be your father,—I will foster and protect you! for *I* have feeling for the grand and the sublime, and have discerned your genius—and what you can, with assistance, accomplish; I know, too, your inability to cope yet with the world,—for you have not my experience of men. I will lead you to Art—I myself; and if before long you be not in full chase, and have not captured her, why you must be a fool, and I will give you up!"

"Ah, worthy Master von Puderlein!" cried Haydn surprised; "You would receive me now, when I know not where to go, or what to do? Oh! I acknowledge your goodness! but how have I, poor knave! deserved it? and how shall I thank you?"

"That is nothing to you!" said Puderlein shortly; "all that will appear in due time! Now sit you down on the stool, and do not stir till I give you leave. I will show the world what a man of genius can make of an indifferent head!"

"Are you determined, then, to do me the honor of dressing my hair, Master von Puderlein?"

"Ask no questions, but sit still."

Joseph obediently seated himself, and Wenzel began to dress his hair according to the latest mode. When he had done, he said with much self-congratulation, "Really, Haydn, when I look at you, and think what you were, before I set your head right, and what you are *now*, I may, without presumption, call you a being of my own creation. But I am not so conceited; and only remark to you, that so long as you have walked like a man on two legs, you have first been enabled through me to present the *visage* of a man! Now pay attention; you are to dress yourself as quickly as possible, or to express myself in better German, you are to put yourself prestissimo into your best trim—and collect your moveables together, that I can send to fetch them this evening. Then betake yourself to the Leopoldstadt, to my house on the Danube, No. 7; go up the steps, knock at the door, make my compliments to the young lady my daughter, and tell her you are so and so, and that Master von Puderlein sent you, and if you are hungry and thirsty call for something to eat and a glass of Ofener or Klosterneuburger; after which you may remain quiet till I come home, and tell you further what I design for you. Adieu!"

Therewith Master Wenzel Puderlein rolled himself out of the door, and Joseph stood awhile with his hair admirably well dressed, but a little disconcerted, in the middle of his chamber. When he collected his thoughts at length, he gave thanks with tears to God, who had inclined the heart of his generous protector towards him, and put an end to his bitter necessity; then he gathered, as Puderlein had told him, his few clothes and many notes together, dressed himself carefully in his best, shut up his chamber, and after he had taken leave, not without emotion, of the rich Metastasio, walked away cheerfully and confidently, his heart full of joy, and his head full of new melodies, towards the Leopoldstadt and the house of his patron.

III

When young von Swieten came half an hour later to ask for the young composer, Signor Metastasio could not inform him where "Giuseppo" might have gone. How many hours of despondency did this forgetfulness of the wise man and renowned poet prepare for the poor, unknown, yet incomparably greater artist,—Haydn!

When Joseph after a long walk stood at length before Puderlein's house, he experienced some novel sensations, which may have been naturally consequent upon the thought that he was to introduce himself to a young lady, and converse with her; an idea which, from his constitutional bashfulness, and his ignorance of the world, was rather formidable to him. But the step must nevertheless be taken. He summoned all his courage, and went and knocked at the door. It was opened, and a handsome damsel of eighteen or nineteen presented herself before the trembling Joseph.

The youth, in great embarrassment, faltered forth his compliments and his message from Master Wenzel. The pretty Nanny listened to him with an expression both of pleasure and sympathy—the last for the forlorn condition of her visitor. When he had ended, she took him, to his no small terror, by the hand, without the least embarrassment, and leading him into the parlor, said in insinuating tones, "Come in, then, Master Haydn, it is all right; I am sure my papa means well with you, for he concerns himself for every dunce he meets, and would take a poor wretch in, for having only good hair on his head! He has often spoken to me of you, and you may rely upon it, he will assist you; for he has very distinguished acquaintances. But you must give in to his humors a little, for he is sometimes a trifle peculiar."

Joseph promised he would do his best, and Nanny went on, "you must also accommodate yourself to my whims, for, look you, I lead the regiment alone here in the house, and even papa must do as *I* will. Now, tell me, what will you have? Do not be bashful; it is a good while since noon, and you must be hungry from your long walk."

Joseph could not deny that such was the case, and modestly asked for a piece of bread and a glass of water.

Pshaw! cried Nanny, laughing; and tripped out of the room. Ere long she returned, followed by an apprentice boy, whom she had loaded with cold meats, a flask of wine, and a pair of tumblers, till his arms were ready to sink under the burden, while yet he dared not make a face,—for he had been in the family long enough to be sufficiently convinced of Mademoiselle Nanny's absolute dominion. Nanny busily arranged the table, filled Joseph's glass, and invited him to help himself to the cold pastry or whatever else stood awaiting his choice. The youth fell to, at first timidly, then with more courage; till, after he had at Nanny's persuasion emptied a couple of glasses, he took heart to attack the cold meats more vigorously than he had done in a long time before; making at the same time the observation mentally, that if Mademoiselle Nanny Puderlein was not quite so distingué and accomplished as his departed patroness, the honored Mlle. de Martinez, still, as far as youth, beauty, and polite manners were concerned, she would not suffer by a comparison with the most distinguished dames in Vienna.— In short, when Master Wenzel Puderlein came home an hour or so after, he found Joseph in high spirits, with sparkling eyes, and cheeks like the rose— already more than half in love with the pretty Nanny.

Joseph Haydn lived thus many months in the house of Wenzel Puderlein, burgher, house proprietor, and renowned friseur in the Leopoldstadt of Vienna, and not a man in the Imperial city knew where the poor, but talented and well educated artist and composer was gone. In vain he was sought for by his few friends; in vain by young von Swieten; in vain at last, by Metastasio himself; Joseph had disappeared from Vienna without leaving a trace. Wenzel Puderlein kept his abode carefully concealed, and wondered and lamented like the rest over his loss, when his aristocratic customers asked him, whom they believed to know everything, if he could give them no information as to what had become of Joseph. He thought he had good reasons, and undoubted right, to exercise now the hitherto unpractised virtue of silence; because, as he said to himself, he only aimed at making Joseph the happiest man in the world! But in this he would labor alone; he wanted none to help him; and even his protegé was not fully to know his designs, till he was actually in possession of his good fortune.

Joseph cheerfully resigned himself to the purposes of his friend, and was only too happy to be able undisturbed to study Sebastian Bach's works, to try his skill in quartettos—to eat as much as he wished, and day after day to see and chat with the fair Nanny. It never occurred to him, under such circumstances, to notice that he lived in a manner as a prisoner in Puderlein's house; that all day he was banished to the garden behind the house, or to his snug chamber, and only permitted to go out in the evening with Wenzel and his daughter. It never occurred to him to wish for other acquaintance than the domestics and their nearest neighbors, among whom he was known only as "Master Joseph;" and he cheerfully delivered every Saturday to Master Wenzel the stipulated number of minuets, waltzes, &c., which he was ordered to compose. Puderlein carried the pieces regularly to a dealer in such things in Leopoldstadt, who paid him two convention guilders for every full toned minuet—and for the others in proportion. This money the hairdresser conscientiously locked up in a chest, to use it, when the time should come, for Joseph's advantage. With this view, he enquired earnestly about Joseph's greater works, and whether he would not soon be prepared to produce something which would do him credit in the eyes of the more distinguished part of the public.

"Ah—yes—indeed!" replied Joseph; "this quartetto, when I shall have finished it, might be ventured before the public; for I hope to make something good of it! Yet what shall I do? No publisher will take it; it is returned on my hands, because I am no great lord, and because I have no patron to whom I could dedicate it!"

"That will all come in time," said Puderlein, smiling; "do you get the thing ready, yet without neglecting the dances; I tell you a prudent man begins with little, and ends with great; so to work!"

And Joseph went to work; but he was every day deeper and deeper in love with the fair Nanny; and the damsel herself looked with very evident favor on the dark, though handsome youth.—Wenzel saw the progress of things with satisfaction; the lovers behaved with great propriety, and he suffered matters to go on in their own way, only interfering with a little assumed surliness, if Joseph at any time forgot his tasks in idle talk, or Nanny her housekeeping.

But not with such eyes saw Mosjo Ignatz, Puderlein's journeyman and factotum hitherto; for he thought himself possessed of a prior claim to the love of Nanny. No one knows how much or how little reason he had to think so, for it might be reckoned among impossibilities for a young girl of Vienna, who has reached the age of fourteen, to determine the number of her lovers. The Viennese damsels are remarkable for their prudence in what concerns a love affair. However that may have been, it is certain that it was gall and wormwood to Ignatz to see Joseph and the fair Nanny together. He would often fain have interposed his powder-bag and curling irons between them, when he heard them singing tender duets; for it must be owned that Nanny had a charming voice, was very fond of music, and was Joseph's zealous pupil in singing.

At length he could endure no longer the torments of jealousy; and one morning he sought out the master of the house, to discover to him the secret of the lovers. How great was his astonishment, when Master Wenzel, instead of falling into a violent passion, and turning Joseph out of doors without further ado, replied with a smile,

"What you tell me, Mosjo 'Natz, look you, I have long known, and am well pleased that it is so."

"Nein!" cried Ignatz, after a long pause of speechless astonishment; "Nein, Master von Puderlein! you should not be pleased. You seem as if you knew not that I—I, for several years have been the suitor of your daughter."

It was Wenzel's turn to be astonished, and he angrily replied, "I knew no such thing; I know not, nor will I know any such thing. What—Natz! is he mad? the suitor of my daughter! What has come into the man? Go to! Mind your powder-bag and your curling irons, and serve your customers, and set aside thoughts too high for you; for neither my daughter nor myself will wink at such folly."

"Oho, and have you not both promised? There was a time, Master von Puderlein, when you and mademoiselle your daughter—"

"Hold your tongue and pack yourself off."

"Master von Puderlein, you are a man of honor; are you doing me justice for my long years of faithful service? I have always taken your part. When people said 'von Puderlein is an old miser and a blockhead,' I have always said, 'that is not true;' even if it has been often the truth that people said."

"Have done, sir, will you?"

"Master von Puderlein, be generous; I humbly entreat you, give me your daughter to wife."

"I will give you a box on the ear presently, if you do not come to reason."

"What!" cried Ignatz, starting up in boiling indignation, "a box on the ear, to me—to me, a free spoken member of the society of periwig makers?"

"And if you were a king, and if you were an emperor, with a golden crown on your head, and a sceptre in your hand, here in my own house I am lord and sovereign, and I will give you a box most certainly, if you provoke me much further."

"Good," answered Ignatz, haughtily; "very good, Master von Puderlein; we are two, henceforth; this hour I quit this treacherous roof—and you and your periwig stock. But I will be revenged; of that you may be sure; and when the punishment comes upon you and your faithless daughter, and your callow bird of a harpsicord player, then you may think upon Natz Schuppenpelz."

The journeyman then hastened to pack up his goods, demanded and received his wages, and left the house vowing revenge against its inmates. Von Puderlein was very much incensed; Nanny laughed, and Joseph sat in the garden, troubling himself about nothing but his quartetto, at which he was working.

Wenzel Puderlein saw the hour approaching, when the attention of the Imperial city, and of the world, should be directed to him, as the protector and benefactor of a great musical genius. The dances Joseph had composed for the music seller in the Leopoldstadt, were played again and again in the halls of the nobility; all praised the lightness, the sprightliness and grace that distinguished them; but all enquiries were vain at the music dealer's, respecting the name of the composer. None knew him; and Joseph himself had no idea what a sensation the pieces he had thrown off so easily, created in the world. But Master Wenzel was well aware of it, and waited with impatience the completion of the first quartetto. At length the manuscript was ready; Puderlein took it, carried it to a music publisher, and had it sent to press immediately, which the sums he had from time to time laid by for Joseph, enabled him to do. Haydn, who was confident his protector would do everything for his advantage, committed all to his hands; he commenced a new quartetto, and the old one was soon nearly forgotten.

They were not forgotten, however, by Mosjo Ignatz Schuppenpelz, who was continually on the watch to play Master Puderlein some ill trick. The opportunity soon offered; his new principal sent him one morning to dress the hair of the Baron von Fürnberg. Young von Swieten chanced to be at the Baron's house, and in the course of conversation mentioned the balls recently given by Prince Easterhazy, and the delightful new dances by the unknown composer. In the warmth of his description, the youth stepped up to the piano and began a piece, which caused Ignatz to prick up his ears, for he recognized it too well; it was Nanny's favorite waltz, which Joseph had executed expressly for her.

"I would give fifty ducats," cried the Baron, when von Swieten had ended, "to know the name of that composer."

"Fifty ducats," repeated Ignatz, "your honor, hold a moment; your honor—but I believe *I* can tell your honor the name of the musician."

"If you can, and with certainty, the fifty ducats are yours;" answered Fürnberg and von Swieten.

"I can, your honor. It is Pepi Haydn."

"How? Joseph Haydn? How do you know? Speak!" cried both gentlemen to the friseur, who proceeded to inform them of Haydn's abode and seclusion in the house of Wenzel Puderlein; nor did the exjourneyman lose the opportunity of bepowdering his ancient master plentifully with abuse, as an old miser, a surly fool, and an arch tyrant.

"Horrible!" cried his auditors, when Ignatz had concluded his story. "Horrible! This old friseur makes the poor young man, hidden from all the world, labor to gratify his avarice, and keeps him prisoner! We must set him at liberty."

Ignatz assured the gentlemen they would do a good deed by doing so: and informed them when it was likely Puderlein would be from home; so that they could find opportunity of speaking alone with young Haydn. Young von Swieten resolved to go that very morning, during the absence of Puderlein, to seek his favorite; and took Ignatz along with him. The hairdresser was not a little elated, to be sitting opposite the Baron, in a handsome coach, which drove rapidly towards Leopoldstadt. When they stopped before Puderlein's house, Ignatz remained in the coach, while the Baron alighted, entered the house, and ran up stairs to the chamber before pointed out to him, where Joseph Haydn sat deep in the composition of a new quartetto.

Great was the youth's astonishment, when he perceived his distinguished visitor. He did not utter a word, but kept bowing to the ground; von Swieten, however, hesitated not to accost him with all the ardor of youth, and described the affliction of his friends (who they were Joseph knew not) at his mysterious disappearance. Then he spoke of the applause his compositions had received, and of the public curiosity to know who the admirable composer was, and where he lived. "Your fortune is now made," concluded he. "The Baron von Fürnberg, a connoisseur, my father, I myself—we all will receive you; we will present you to Prince Esterhazy; so make ready to quit this house, and to escape, the sooner the better, from the illegal and unworthy tyranny of an avaricious periwig maker."

Joseph knew not what to reply, for with every word of von Swieten his astonishment increased. At length he faltered, blushing, "Your honor is much mistaken, if you think I am tyrannized over in this house; on the contrary, Master von Puderlein treats me as his own son, and his daughter loves me as a brother. *He* took me in when I was helpless and destitute, without the means of earning my bread."

"Be that as it may," interrupted young von Swieten, impatiently, "enough, this house is no longer your home; you must go into the great world, under very different auspices, worthy of your talents. Speak well or ill of your host, as you please, and as is most fitting; to-morrow the Baron and I come to fetch you away."—Therewith he embraced young Haydn with cordiality, quitted the house and drove back to the city, while Joseph stood and rubbed his forehead, and hardly knew whether all was a dream or reality.

But the pretty Nanny, who listening in the kitchen had heard all, ran in grief and affright to meet her father when he came home, and told him everything. Puderlein was dismayed; but he soon collected himself, and commanded his daughter to follow him, and to put her handkerchief to her eyes.

Thus prepared, he went up to Haydn's chamber; Joseph, as soon as he heard him coming, opened the door, and went to meet him, to inform him of the strange visit he had received.

But Puderlein pushed him back into the chamber, entered himself, followed by the weeping Nanny, and cried in a pathetic tone, "Hold, barbarian, whither are you going?"

"To you," answered Joseph. "I was going to tell you—"

"It is not necessary," interrupted Puderlein; "I know all; you have betrayed me, and are now going to leave me like a vagabond."

"Ha, surely not, Master von Puderlein. But listen to me."

"I will not listen; your treachery is clear; your falsehood to me and to my daughter. Oh, ingratitude, see here thine own image! I loved this boy as my own son; I received him when he was destitute, under my hospitable roof, clothed and fed him. I have dressed his hair with my own hands, and labored for his renown, and for my thanks, he has betrayed me and my innocent daughter. There, sir, does not your conscience reproach you for the tears you cause that girl to shed?"

"For Heaven's sake, Master von Puderlein, listen to me. I will not leave you; I will not be ungrateful; on the contrary, I will thank you all the days of my life for what you have done for me, so far as it is in my power."

"And marry that girl?"

"Marry her?" repeated Joseph, astonished, "marry her? I—your daughter?"

"Who else? have you not told her she was handsome? that you liked her? have you not behaved as though you wished her well, whenever you have spoken with her?"

"I have indeed, but—"

"No buts; you must *marry* her, or you are a shameless traitor! Think you, a virtuous damsel of Vienna lets every callowbird tell her she is handsome and agreeable? No! the golden age yet flourishes among our girls! Innocence and virtue are paramount with them! they glance not from one to another, throwing their net over this one and that one; they wait quiet and collected, till the one comes who suits them, who will marry them, and him they love faithfully to the end of their days; and therefore are the Viennese maidens famed throughout the world.—You told my innocent Nanny that she was handsome, and that you liked her; she thought you wished to marry her, and made up her mind honestly to have you. She loves you, and now will you desert and leave her to shame?"

Joseph stood in dejected silence. Puderlein continued, "And I, have I deserved such black ingratitude from you, eh? have I?" With these words, Master Wenzel drew forth a roll of paper, unfolded and held it up before the disconcerted Joseph, who uttered an exclamation of surprise as he read these words engraved on it, "Quartetto for two violins, bass viol, and violoncello, composed by Master Joseph Haydn, performer and composer in Vienna.—Vienna, 1751." "Yes!" cried Puderlein, triumphantly, when he saw Haydn's joyful surprise; "Yes! cry out and make your eyes as large as bullets; *I* did that; with the money I received in payment for your dances, I paid for paper and press work, that you might present the public with a great work. Still more! I have labored to such purpose among my customers of rank, that you have the appointment of organist to the Carmelites. Here is your appointment! and now, go, ingrate, and bring my daughter and me with sorrow to the grave."

Joseph went not; with tears in his eyes he threw himself into Puderlein's arms, who struggled and resisted vigorously, as if he would have repelled him. But Joseph held him fast, crying, "Master von Puderlein! listen to me! there is no treachery in me! Let me call you father; give me Nanny for my wife! I will marry her; the sooner the better. I will honor and love her all my days. Ah! I am indeed not base nor ungrateful."

Master Wenzel was at last quiet; he sank exhausted on an arm chair, and cried to the young couple, "Come hither, my children, kneel before me, that I may give you my blessing. This evening shall be the betrothal, and a month hence we will have the wedding."

Joseph and Nanny knelt down, and received the paternal benediction. All wept and exhibited much emotion. But all was festivity in No. 7, on the Danube, that evening, when the organist, Joseph Haydn, was solemnly betrothed to the fair Nanny, the daughter of Wenzel Puderlein, burgher and proprietor in the Leopoldstadt in Vienna.

The Baron of Fürnberg and young von Swieten were not a little astonished when they came the next morning to take Haydn from Puderlein's house, to find him affianced to the pretty Nanny. They remonstrated with him earnestly in private, but Joseph remained immoveable, and kept his word pledged to Puderlein and his bride, like an honorable young man.

At a later period he had reason to acknowledge that the step he had taken was somewhat precipitate; but he never repented it; and consoled himself, when his *earthly* muse mingled a little discord with his tones, with the companionship of the immortal partner, ever lovely, ever young, who attends the skilful artist through life, and who proved herself so true to *him*, that the name of Joseph Haydn shall, after the lapse of centuries, be pronounced with joyful and sacred emotion, by our latest posterity.

FOOTNOTES

[3] The diminutive for "Joseph" in the dialect of the country.

TWO PERIODS IN AFTER LIFE

I

It was about noon of a day in the spring of 175-, that a man of low stature and pale and sallow complexion might have been seen entering a meanlooking house in one of the narrow streets of Vienna. Before he closed the door, the sound of a sharp female voice, speaking in shrill accents, was quite audible to the passers-by. As the person who entered ascended the stairs to his lodgings, he was greeted by a continuance of the same melody from the lips of a pretty but slovenly dressed young woman, who stood at the door of the only apartment that seemed furnished.

"A pretty mess is all this!" she exclaimed. "Here the printers have been running after you all the morning for the piece you promised to have ready for them, and I nothing to do but hear their complaints and send them away one after the other!"

"My good Nanny——"

"But, my good Joseph, is not my time as precious as yours, pray? What have you from this morning's work?"

"Seventeen kreutzers," sighed he.

"Ay, it is always so—and you spend all your time in such profitless doings. At eight, the singing desk of the brothers de la Merci; at ten, the Count de Haugwitz's chapel; grand mass at eleven—and all this toil for a few kreutzers."

"What can I do?"

"Do? What would I do in your place? Give up this foolish business of music, and take to something that will enable you to live as well as a peasant, at least. There is my father, a hairdresser, did not he give you shelter when you had nothing but your garret and skylight?—when you had to lie in bed and write for want of coals to warm you? Yes, in spite of your boasted genius and the praises you received, you were forced to come to him for bread!"

"He gave me more, Nanny," said her husband, meaningly.

"Yes—his daughter, who had refused half the gallants in Vienna—for whom half-a-dozen peruke-maker's apprentices went mad. Yes—and had he not a right to expect you would dress her as well as she had been used at home, and that she should have servants to wait upon her as in her father's house? A fine realizing of his hopes and schemes for his favorite child—this miserable lodging, with but a few sous a day to keep us from starving!"

"You should not reproach me, Nanny. Have I not worked incessantly till my health has given way? And if fortune is still inexorable——"

"Ah, there it is, fortune!—as if fortune did not always wait, like a handmaid, upon industry in a proper calling! Your patrons may admire and applaud, but they will not pay; and yet you will drudge away your life in this ungrateful occupation. I tell you, Joseph, music is not the thing."

"Alas!" sighed Haydn, "I once dreamed of fame."

"Fame—pshaw! And what were that worth if you had it? Would fame clothe you or change these wretched walls to a palace? Believe me for once, and give up these idle fancies."

Here a knock was heard at the door, and the wife, with exclamations of impatience, flounced away. The unfortunate artist threw himself on a seat, and leaned his head on a table covered with notes of music—works of his own, begun at various times, which want of health, energy or spirits, had prevented him from completing. So entirely had he yielded himself to despondency, that he did not move, even when the door opened, till the sound of a well known voice close at his side startled him from his melancholy reverie.

"How now, Haydn, what is the matter, my boy?"

The speaker was an old man, shabbily dressed, but with something striking and even commanding in his noble features. His large, dark, flashing eyes, his olive complexion and the contour of his face, bespoke him a native of a sunnier clime than that of Germany.

Haydn sprang up and welcomed him with a cordial embrace. "And when, my dear Porpora, did you return to Vienna?" he asked.

"This morning only; and my first care was to find you out. But how is this? I find you thin and pale, and gloomy. Where are your spirits?"

"Gone," murmured the composer, and dropped his eyes on the floor. His visitor regarded him with a look of affectionate interest.

"There is something more in this than there ought to be," said he, at length. "You are not rich, as I see; but that you were not when we last parted, nor when I first found—in the youthful, disinterested friend, the kind companion of a feeble old man—a genius such as Germany might be well proud of. Then you were buoyant, full of enthusiasm for art, and of hope for the future."

"Alas!" replied Haydn, "I was too sanguine. I judged more favorably of myself— —"

"Did I not say you were destined to something great?"

"Your friendship might deceive you."

"And think you I had lost my judgment because I am old?—or am a fool, to be blinded by partiality?"

"Nay, dear Porpora— —"

"Or that, because you were fain to serve me like a lacquey from pure love, I rewarded you with flattering lies, eh?"

"Caro, you mistake me. I know you clearsighted and candid—yet I feel that I shall never justify your kind encouragement. I have toiled till youth is passing away in vain. I have no heart to bear up against the crushing hand of poverty—I succumb."

"You have lost, then, your love of our art?"

"Not so. What your valuable lessons, dear master, have opened to me, forms the only bright spot in my life. Oh that I could pursue—could grasp it!"

"Why can you not?"

"I am chained!" cried Haydn, bitterly—and giving way to the anguish of his heart, he burst into tears.

Porpora shook his head, and was silent for a few moments. At length he resumed—"I must, I see, give you a little of my experience; and you shall see what has been the life of a prosperous artist. I was, you know, the pupil of Scarlatti; and from the time I felt myself capable of profiting by the lessons of that great master, devoted myself to travel. I was more fortunate than you, for my works procured me, almost at once, a wide-spread fame. I was called for not only in Venice, but in Vienna and London."

"Ah, yours was a brilliant lot!" cried the young composer, looking up with kindling eyes.

"The Saxon court," continued Porpora, "which has always granted the most liberal protection to musical art, offered me the direction of the chapel and of the theatre at Dresden. Even the princesses received my lessons— in short, my success was so great, that I awakened the jealousy of Hasse himself."

"That was a greater triumph still," observed Haydn, smiling.

"So I thought; and still greater when I caused a pupil of mine, the young Italian Mengotti, to dispute the palm of song with the enchantress Faustina [4] —aye, to bear it away upon more than one occasion. All this you know, and how I returned to London upon the invitation of amateurs in Italian music."

"Where you rivaled Händel!" said Haydn, enthusiastically.

"Ah, that was the turning point in my destiny. Farinelli, the famous singer, gloried in being my scholar. He turned all his splendid powers to the effort of assuring the triumph of my compositions. I could have borne that these should fail in commanding popularity; I could have borne the defeat by which Händel was elevated at my expense to an idol shrine among the English—but it grieved me to see that Farinelli's style, so really perfect in its way, was unappreciated by the most distinguished connoisseurs. I did justice to the strength and grandeur of my rival; should he not have acknowledged the grace, finish and sweetness of Italian song? But he despised Farinelli, and his friends made caricatures of him."

"Händel, with all his greatness, had no versatility," observed Haydn.

"I wished to attempt another style, for this repulse had somewhat cooled my zeal for the theatre. I set myself to cultivate what was new—what was not born with me. I published my sonatas for the violin—the connoisseurs applauded, and I was encouraged to hope I could face my rival on his own ground. I composed sacred music——"

"And that," interrupted his auditor, "will live—pardon me for saying so—when your theatrical compositions have ceased to enjoy unrivaled popularity."

"When they are forgotten, say rather—for such, I feel, will be their fate. My sacred compositions may survive and carry my name to posterity—for taste in such things is less mutable than in the opera. After all, the monks may claim me," and he smiled pensively. [5] "You see now, dear Haydn," he resumed, after a pause, "for what I have lived and labored. I was once renowned and wealthy—what did prosperity bring me? Envy, discontent, rivalship, disappointment! And did art flourish more luxuriantly on such a soil? With me the heavenly plant languished, and would have died but that I had some energy within me to save it. I repine when I look back on those years."

"You?" repeated Haydn, surprised.

"Would you know to what period I *can* look back with self-approbation, with thankfulness? To the toil of my early years; to the struggle after an ideal of greatness, goodness and beauty; to the self-forgetfulness that saw only the glorious goal far, far before me; to the undismayed resolve that sought only its attainment. Or to a time still later, when the visions of manhood's impure and selfish ambition had faded away; when the soul had shaken off some of her fetters, and roused herself to a perception of the eternal, the perfect, the divine; when I became conscious of the delusive vanity of earthly hopes and earthly excellence, but at the same time awakened to the revelation of that which cannot die!

"You see me now, seventy-three years old, and too poor to command even a shelter for the few days that yet remain to me in this world. I have lost the splendid fame I once possessed; I have lost the riches that were mine; I have lost the power to win even a competence by my own labors—but I have *not* lost my passion for our glorious music, nor enjoyment of the reward, more precious than gold, she bestows on her votaries; nor my confidence in Heaven. And you, at twenty-seven, you—more greatly endowed—to whom the world is open—*you* despair! Are you worthy to succeed, O man of little faith?"

"My friend—my benefactor!" cried the young artist, clasping his hand with deep emotion.

"Cast away your bonds; cut and rend, if your very flesh is torn in the effort; and the ground once spurned, you are free. Come, I am pledged for your success—for if you do not rise, I am no prophet! What have you been doing?" and he turned over rapidly the musical notes that lay on the table. "Here, what is this—a symphony? Play for me, if you please."

So saying, with a gentle force he led his young friend to the piano, and Haydn played from the piece he had nearly completed.

"So, this is excellent, admirable!" cried Porpora, when he rose from the instrument. "This suits me exactly. And you could despair while such power remained to you! When can you finish this? for I must have it at once."

"To-morrow, if you like," answered the composer, more cheerfully.

"To-morrow then—and you must work to-night. I see you are nervous and feverish; but seize the happy thought while it flies—once gone, you have no cord to draw it back. I will go and order you a physician;—not a word of remonstrance;—he will come to-morrow morning;—how madly your pulse throbs—and when your work is done, you may rest. Adieu for the present." And pressing his young friend's hands, the eccentric but benevolent old man departed—leaving Haydn full of new thoughts, his bosom fired with zeal to struggle against adverse fortune. In such moods does the spiritual champion wrestle with the powers of the abyss and mightily prevail.

When Haydn, late that night, threw himself on his bed, weary, ill and exhausted, his frame racked with the pains of fever, after having worked for hours in the midst of reproaches from her who ought to have lightened his task by her sympathy, he had accomplished the first of an order of works destined to endear his name to all succeeding time. Who that listened to its clear and beautiful melody, could have divined that such a production had been wrought out in the gloom of despondency, poverty and disease?

While the artist lay on a sick bed, attended only by the few friends whom compassion more than admiration of his genius called to his side, and forgotten by the great and gay to whose amusement so many years of his life had been devoted, a brilliant fête was given by Count Mortzin, an Austrian nobleman of immense wealth and influence, at which the most distinguished individuals in Vienna were present. The musical entertainments given by these luxurious patrons of the arts were, at that time and for some years after, the most splendid in Europe, for the most exalted genius was enlisted in their service—and talent, as in all ages, was often fain to do homage to riches and power.

When the concert was over, Prince Antoine Esterhazy expressed the pleasure he had received, and his obligations to the noble host. "Chief among your magnificent novelties," said he, "is the new symphony, St. Maria. One does not hear every day such music. Who is the composer?"

The Count referred to one of his friends. The answer was—"Joseph Haydn."

"I have heard his quartettos—he is no common artist. Is he in your service, count?"

"He has been employed by me."

"With your good leave, he shall be transferred to ours; and I shall take care he has no reason to regret the change. Let him be presented to us."

There was a murmur among the audience, and a movement, but the composer did not appear; and presently word was brought to his highness that the young man on whom he intended to confer so great an honor was detained at home by indisposition.

"So, let him be brought to me as soon as he recovers; he shall enter my service—I like his symphony vastly. Your pardon, count, for we will rob you of your best man."

And the great prince, having decided the destiny of a greater than himself, turned to those who surrounded him to speak of other matters.

News of the change in his fortune was brought to Haydn by his friend Porpora; and so renovating was the effect of hope, that he was strong enough on the following day to pay his respects to his illustrious patron. Accompanied by a friend who offered to introduce him, Haydn drew near the dwelling of the prince, and was so fortunate as to find admittance. His highness was just preparing to ride, but would see the composer; and he was conducted through a splendid suite of rooms to the apartment where the proud head of the Esterhazys deigned to receive an almost nameless artist. What wonder that Haydn blushed and faltered as he approached this impersonation, as he felt it, of human grandeur?

The prince, in the splendid array suited to his rank, glanced somewhat carelessly at the low, slight figure that stood before him, and said, as he was presented—"Is this, then, the composer of the music I heard last night?"

"This is he—Joseph Haydn," was the reply.

"So—a Moor, I should judge by his dark complexion." [6]

The composer bowed in some embarrassment.

"And you write such music? You look not like it, by my faith! Haydn—I recollect the name; and I remember hearing, too, that you were not well paid for your labors, eh?"

"I have not been fortunate, your highness——"

"Why have you not applied to me before?"

"Your highness, I could not presume to think——"

"Eh? Well, you shall have no reason to complain in my service. My secretary shall fix your appointments; and name whatever else you desire. Understand me, for all of your profession find me liberal. Now then, sir Moor, you may go; and let it be your first care to provide yourself with a new coat, a wig and buckles, and heels to your shoes. I will have you respectable in appearance as well as in talents; so let me have no more of shabby professors. And do your best, my little duskey, to recruit in flesh—'twill add to the stature; and to relieve your olive with a shade of the ruddy. Such spindle masters would be a walking discredit to our larder, which is truly a spendthrift one."

So saying, with a laugh, the haughty nobleman dismissed his new dependent. The artist chafed not at the imperious tone of patronage, for he felt not yet the superiority of his own vocation. It was the bondage-time of genius; the wings were not yet grown which were to bear his spirit up, when it brooded over a new world.

The life which Haydn led in the service of Prince Esterhazy, to which service he was permanently attached by Nicolas, the successor of Antoine, in the quality of chapel-master, was one so easy, that, says his biographer, it might have proved fatal to an artist more inclined to luxury and pleasure, or less devoted to his art and the love of glory. Now, for the first time relieved from care for the future, he was enabled to yield to the impulse of his genius, and create works worthy of the name—works not only pleasing to himself and his patron, but which gradually extended his fame over all the countries of Europe.

II

On the evening of a day in the beginning of April, 1809, all the lovers of art in Vienna were assembled in the theatre to witness the performance of the oratorio of the "Creation." The entertainment had been given in honor of the composer of that noble work, the illustrious Haydn, by his numerous friends and admirers. He had been drawn from Gumpendorf—his retreat in the suburbs, the cottage surrounded by a little garden, which he had purchased after his retirement from the Esterhazy service, and where he had spent the last years of his life—to be present at this species of triumph. Three hundred musicians assisted at the performance. The audience rose en masse, and greeted with rapturous applause the white-haired man, who, led forward by the most distinguished nobles in the city, was conducted to the place of honor. There seated, with princesses at his right hand, beauty smiling upon him, the centre of a circle of nobility, the observed and admired of all, the object of the acclamations of thousands, who would not have said that Haydn had reached the summit of human greatness—had more than realized the proudest visions of his youth? His serene countenance, his clear eye, his air of dignified self-possession, showed that prosperity had not overcome him, but that amid the smiles of fortune he had not forgotten the true excellence of man.

"I can never hear this oratorio," remarked one of his friends, whom we shall call Manuel, to another beside him, "without rejoicing for the author. None but a happy spirit could have conceived—only a pure, open, trustful, buoyant soul could have produced such a work. His, like the angels, is ever fresh and young."

"I agree," replied his friend, "in your judgment of the mind of Haydn. All the harmony and grace of nature, in her magnificent and beautiful forms, in her varied life, breathe in his music. But I like something deeper, even if it be gloomy. There is a hidden life, which the outward only represents; a deep voice, the echo of that which we hear. The poet, the musician, should interpret and reveal what the ordinary mind does not receive."

"Beethoven's symphonies, then, will please you better?"

"I acknowledge that I am more satisfied with them, or rather I am not satisfied, which is precisely what I want. The longings of a human soul are after the ineffable, the unfathomable; and to awaken those longings is the highest triumph of the artist. We are to be lifted above the joys of earth; out of this sunny atmosphere, where trees wave and birds fly, though we rise into a region of cloud and storm, chilly and dark and terrific."

"You are more of a philosopher than I am," returned Manuel, laughing. "You may find consolation for your clouds and storms in the thought that you are nearer heaven; but give me the genial warmth of a heart imbued with love of simple nature. I will relinquish your loftier ideal for the beauty and blessing of reality and the living present. For this reason is Haydn, with his free, bright, child-like, healthful spirit, bathing itself in enjoyment, so dear to me. I desire nothing when I hear his music; I feel no apprehension; I ask for no miracles. I drink in the bliss of actual life, and thank Heaven for its rich bestowments."

"I thought our great composer, on the verge of life, would have looked beyond in his last works," said the other, thoughtfully; "but I see plainly he will write no more."

"He has done enough, and now we are ready for the farewell of Haydn."

"The farewell?"

"Did you never hear the story? I have heard him tell it often myself. It concerns one of his most celebrated symphonies. The occasion was this:— Among the musicians attached to the service of Prince Esterhazy, were several who, during his sojourn upon his estates, were obliged to leave their wives at Vienna. At one time his highness prolonged his stay at the Esterhazy Castle considerably beyond the usual period. The disconsolate husbands entreated Haydn to become the interpreter of their wishes. Thus the idea came to him of composing a symphony in which each instrument ceased one after the other. He added, at the close of every part, the direction, 'here the light is extinguished.' Each musician, in his turn, rose, put out his candle, rolled up his notes, and went away. This pantomime had the desired effect; the next morning the prince gave orders for their return to the capital."

"An amiable thought; I have heard something of it before."

"As a match story, he used to tell us of the origin of his Turkish or military symphony. You know the high appreciation he met with in his visits to England?"

"Where, he maintains, he acquired his continental fame—as we Germans could not pronounce on his claims till they had been admitted by the Londoners."

"True; but notwithstanding the praise and homage he received, he could not prevent the enthusiastic audience from falling asleep during the performance of his compositions. It occurred to him to devise a kind of ingenious revenge. In this piece, while the current is gliding softly, and slumber beginning to steal over the senses of his auditors, a sudden and unexpected burst of martial music, tremendous as a thunder peal, startles the surprised sleepers into active attention. I should like to have seen the lethargic islanders, with their eyes and mouths thrown open by such an unlooked-for shock!"

Here a stop was suddenly put to the conversation by the commencement of the performance. "The Creation," the first of Haydn's oratorios, was regarded as his greatest work, and had often elicited the most heartfelt applause. Now that the aged and honored composer was present, probably for the last time to hear it, an emotion too deep for utterance seemed to pervade the vast audience. The feeling was too reverential to be expressed by the ordinary tokens of pleasure. It seemed as if every eye in the assembly was fixed on the calm, noble face of the venerated artist; as if every heart beat with love for him; as if all feared to break the spell of hushed and holy silence. Then came, like a succession of heavenly melodies, the music of the "Creation," and the listeners felt as if transported back to the infancy of the world.

At the words, *"Let there be light, and there was light,"* when all the instruments were united in one full burst of gorgeous harmony, emotion seemed to shake the whole frame of the aged artist. His pale face crimsoned; his bosom heaved convulsively; he raised his eyes, streaming with tears, towards Heaven, and lifting upwards his trembling hands, exclaimed—his voice audible in the pause of the music—"Not unto me—not unto me—but unto Thy name be all the glory, O Lord!"

From this moment Haydn lost the calmness and serenity that had marked the expression of his countenance. The very depths of his heart had been stirred, and ill could his wasted strength sustain the tide of feeling. When the superb chorus at the close of the second part announced the completion of the work of creation, he could bear the excitement no longer. Assisted by the prince's physician and several of his friends, he was carried from the theatre, pausing to give one last look of gratitude, expressed in his tearful eyes, to the orchestra who had so nobly executed his conception, and followed by the lengthened plaudits of the spectators, who felt that they were never to look upon his face again.

Some weeks after this occurrence, Manuel, who had sent to inquire after the health of his infirm old friend, received from him a card on which he had written, to notes of music, the words "*Meine kraft ist dahin*," (my strength is gone.) Haydn was in the habit of sending about these cards, but his increased feebleness was evident in the handwriting of this; and Manuel lost no time in hastening to him. There, in his quiet cottage, around which rolled the thunders of war, terrifying others but not him, sat the venerable composer. His desk stood on one side, on the other his piano, and he looked as if he would never approach either again. But he smiled, and held out his hand to greet his friend.

"Many a time," he murmured, "you have cheered my solitude, and now you come to see the old man die."

"Speak not thus, my dear friend," cried Manuel, grieved to the heart; "you will recover."

"But not here," answered Haydn, and pointed upwards.

He then made signs to one of his attendants to open the desk and reach him a roll of papers. From these he took one and gave it to his friend. It was inscribed in his own hand—"Catalogue of all my musical compositions, which I can remember, from my eighteenth year. Vienna, 4th December, 1805." Manuel, as he read it, understood the mute pressure of his friend's hand, and sighed deeply. That hand would never trace another note.

"Better thus," said Haydn, softly, "than a lingering old age of care, disease, perhaps of poverty! No—I am happy. I have lived not in vain; I have accomplished my destiny; I have done good. I am ready for thy call, O Master!"

A long silence followed, for the aged man was wrapt in devotion. At length he asked to be supported to his piano; it was opened, and as his trembling fingers touched the keys, an expression of rapture kindled in his eyes. The music that answered to his touch seemed the music of inspiration. But it gradually faded away; the flush gave place to a deadly pallor; and while his fingers still rested on the keys, he sank back into the arms of his friend, and gently breathed out his parting spirit. It passed as in a happy strain of melody!

Prince Esterhazy did honor to the memory of his departed friend by the pageant of funeral ceremonies. His remains were transported to Eisenstadt, in Hungary, and placed in the Franciscan vault. The prince also purchased, at a high price, all his books and manuscripts, and the numerous medals he had obtained. But his fame belongs to the world; and in all hearts sensible to the music of truth and nature, is consecrated the memory of Haydn.

FOOTNOTES

[4] "Faustina Bordoni, born at Venice in 1700, was one of the most admirable singers Italy ever produced. She was a pupil of Gasparini, but adopted the modern method of Bernacchi, which she aided greatly to bring into popular use. She appeared on the stage at the age of sixteen; her success was so great that, at Florence, a medal was struck in her honor; and it was said that even gouty invalids would leave their beds to hear her performance. She was called to Vienna in 1724; two years afterwards she came to the London theatre with a salary of 50,000 francs. Everywhere she charmed by the freshness, clearness and sweetness of her voice, by the grace and perfection of her execution, so that she was called the modern siren. It was at London she met the celebrated Cuzzoni, who enjoyed a brilliant reputation; and the lovers of song were divided in their homage to the two rivals. Händel took part in these disputes. Faustina quitted England in 1728, and returned to Dresden, where she became the wife of Hasse." — *Biog. Universelle.*

[5] It is related of Porpora, who was a man of much wit as well as one of the first pianists of his age, that, in reply to certain monks who boasted of the music as well as the piety of their organist, he observed — "Ah yes, I see that this man fulfils to the letter the precept of the evangelist — he does not let his left hand know what his right hand doeth!"

[6] This interview, but little varied in the circumstances, is related by several of Haydn's biographers.

FRIEDEMANN BACH

It was on Sylvester night of the year 1736, that a man closely wrapped in his mantle, his hat drawn over his brows, was leaning against the wall of the castle at Dresden, looking upward at the illuminated windows of a mansion opposite. Music sounded within, and the burst of trumpet and the clash of kettledrum accompanied, ever and anon, the announcement of some popular toast. A moment of silence at length intervened, as if one of the guests were speaking aloud; till, suddenly, in a jovial shout, the name "Natalie" was uttered, and every voice and instrument joined in tumultuous applause.

The listener in the street turned to depart, but the next instant felt himself seized by the hand, and looking up, saw the royal page M. Scherbitz.

"*Bon soir—mon ami!*" cried the page, pressing cordially the hand he had taken. "I am right glad to have met you; I have sought you the whole evening, but never dreamed of finding you here. What are you doing?"

"Philosophizing!" answered the other, with something between a laugh and a sigh.

"*Bon!*" cried the page—"and just here, opposite the lord premier's mansion, is the best occasion, I grant, but not exactly the best place for it. Besides it is terribly cold! You will have the goodness, *mon ami*, to come with me to Seconda's cellar? We shall not fail there of some capital hot punch, and excellent company." And taking his friend's arm, he walked with him to a then celebrated Italian house of refreshment, on the corner of Castle Street and the old market.

Signor Seconda received his guests with many compliments, and officiously begged to know with what he should have the happiness and honor to serve milord, the page, and milord, the court organist. The page ordered hot punch, and passed, with his friend, into an inner apartment, which, to the surprize of both, they found quite empty.

"They will be here presently," observed von Scherbitz. "Meantime, we will take our ease, and thaw ourselves a little. *Parbleu!* there is no place on earth so delicious; and I thank fortune, so far as I am concerned, that I can spend the night here! *Eh bien!* make yourself at home, friend."

The other threw off his hat and cloak, and stood revealed a handsome man, of about five and twenty, of a figure tall, symmetrical, and bold in carriage, and a countenance whose paleness rendered more striking the effect of his regular, noble, and somewhat haughty features. About his finely chiselled mouth lurked something satirical whenever he spoke; there was a fierce brightness in his large dark eyes, which sometimes, however, gave place to a wild and melancholy expression, particularly when he fixed them on the ground, suffering the long lashes to shade them.

"You are very dull to-night, *mon ami!*" said the page, while he pressed his friend to a seat next him. "Has any thing happened? *Non?* Well then, banish your ill humor, and be merry; for life, you know, is short at best."

"Never fear," replied his friend. "My resolution is taken, to live while I live, in this world. Yet have patience with me, that I cannot go all lengths with you at all times. You know I am but a two years' disciple."

"Pah! *one* year sufficed to spread your fame in *music* through Europe! Who knows not the name of Friedemann Bach? You have but one rival, the admirable Sebastian, your father!"

Friedemann colored deeply as he replied, "How durst I think of comparing myself with my father? If *my* name is celebrated, whom have I to thank but my father? Beside him, I feel, with pride as well as pain, his greatness and my own insignificance. Ah! my love for him elevates me; his love crushes me to the dust, for I know myself unworthy of it!"

"Nay, you are too conscientious," observed Scherbitz.

"Too conscientious!" repeated Friedemann, with a bitter smile.

"Yes!" returned Scherbitz, "I know not how otherwise to express it. What is the head and front of the matter? The old gentleman is, in certain respects, a little strict; *pourquoi?* because he is old! you are young, impetuous; have your adventures, and your liberal views, and conceal them from him; not, mark me, out of apprehension, but because things he has no power to change, might cause him chagrin. *Enfin!* where is the harm in all this?"

Friedemann was sitting with his head resting on his open palm. At the last question he sighed deeply, and seemed about to make a quick reply, but on a second thought, only said, passing his hand over his brow, "Let it alone, Scherbitz; it is as silly as useless to discuss certain matters. Enough, that I have strength, or if you will have it—perverseness, to enjoy life after my own heart. Let us be merry, for here comes the punch!"

Signor Seconda entered, followed by two attendants carrying the hot punch, with glasses; serving his guests at the round table in the midst of the apartment, and providing for the new comers, who entered one after another. These consisted of several officers, and some of the most distinguished musicians and painters then living in the capital.

"Said I not—*mon frère*?" whispered Scherbitz to his companion, "said I not, they would be here presently? See: Monsieur Hasse," he said aloud, as he rose to greet a distinguished looking man, who just then came in. Hasse returned his salutation, and after a rapid glance round the company, seated himself at a distant corner table, and motioned to an attendant to take away the light just placed on it. The man obeyed, and set before him a cup and a flask of burgundy.

"The poor fellow," observed Scherbitz, in a low tone to Friedemann, "dismisses the old year with an 'Alas!' and greets the new with an 'Ah, me!' *tout comme chez nous!* If *he* drink much to-night, 'tis all in honor of his fair Faustina. Well—" he lifted his glass, to drink with Friedemann.

"I am sorry for him," replied Bach; "but why not separate himself from the wife no longer worthy his esteem and love? they say it is out of gratitude for her having taken care of him when an unknown youth; but this gratitude is weakness, and will be the destruction not only of the man, but of the artist. All his works show too well what is wanting in him—namely: strength. In everything he writes there is a softness, the offspring of deep, hidden sorrow. But not the grief of a man; it is, if not thoroughly womanish, the sorrow of a stripling!"

"Is it not on this account that he is the favorite composer in our world of fashion?"

"Very possibly; but I am sure he would give much not to be so on *this* account!"

Their discourse was here interrupted; for many newly arrived guests took their places at the table. The glasses were rapidly emptied and replenished; the conversation became general, and assumed more and more of a jovial character.

An elegant groom of the chambers, whom a mischievous lieutenant of the guard had enticed thither, and introduced, before he was aware, into the midst of the company, occasioned infinite amusement among the guests, whose unbridled festivity he endeavored to awe by a mien of importance. His efforts, however, produced a contrary effect from that which he intended; and after he had joined the revellers in pledging a few toasts, he was himself the merriest of all. He laughed, he strode about—he clapped applause. Friedemann watched the scene with secret pleasure; it nourished the scorn which he, in common with others who stand ill with themselves, cherished for the whole human race. He could not refrain, now and then, from stealing a glance at the corner where Hasse sat, apparently indifferent to all that was passing about him.

"Apropos—sir groom!" cried Scherbitz, suddenly—"what was that admirable poem you had the pleasure of presenting to a famous *artiste*, a few days ago?"

The groom winked at him with a smile, pursed up his mouth, and said, "Monsieur Scherbitz, at your service—the poem runs in this way—

> "On earth's warm breast the pensile beams fall goldenly and bright— The mountain gales, the merry flowers—are swelling with delight; But nothing can such rapture yield unto this heart of mine, As—Oh, Faustina Hasse, that radiant neck of thine!"

"Ah! *c'est bien dit, sur mon honneur!*" cried Scherbitz.

"Is it not?" returned the groom, self-complacently; "it is composed by our best poet, and I paid for it five august d'ors, besides a tun of stadt beer."

"Here's to the 'radiant neck,'" cried one of the guests with a laugh. All joined in the toast, and the glasses clashed.

Hasse rose from his seat, and approaching the table, said, with a courtly bow—

"Messieurs! I commend myself to your remembrance, one and all! To-morrow early I leave Dresden, to return to Italy, perhaps for ever."

The company were astonished. An officer asked—"How, Monsieur Hasse—you leave us? And your lady—?"

"Remains here," interrupted Hasse, with a smile of bitterness. There was universal silence. Hasse, turning to Friedemann, and offering him his hand, said mildly, though earnestly—"Farewell, Bach! Present my adieus to your esteemed father, and tell him he may depend on hearing something good, one day, of the disciple of Scarlatti. May Heaven keep you from all evil!" He then, visibly affected, left the room.

Friedemann looked after him with much emotion, and murmured, "Poor wretch! and yet, would I not exchange with him? I might be the gainer!"

Peals of laughter interrupted him; they were occasioned by the comical groom, who, scarcely master of his wits, was going over the secret *chronique scandaleuse*, to the amusement of his auditors, relating the most surprising events, in all which he had been the hero, though few of them redounded to his honor. From these he went on to others; from the *chronique scandaleuse* to the disputes of the artists; in all matters of gossip proving himself thoroughly at home, and, finally, as the crown of all his merits, avowing himself a devoted adherent of Voltaire, whose epoch had then just commenced. The chamberlain received a full tribute of applause; the clapping of hands, cries of "bravo!" and fresh toasts, attested the approbation of the spectators at his speech, not the less, that the speech was in part unintelligible. At length he fell back in his seat quite overcome, and was asleep in a few moments. This was just what his mischievous friends desired. They stripped him of his gay court dress, and put on a plain one; some wild young men then carried him out of the house, and delivered him into the custody of the watch, as a drunken fellow whom no one knew, to be taken to the great guard-house. The company then amused themselves with imagining the terror and despair of the poor groom, when, awakening on New-year's morning, he should find himself in his new quarters.

The last hour of the old year struck, like a warning, amid the mirth and festivity of those guests; they heeded it not. Clamorous revelry filled up that awful interval between the departing and the coming time; revelry echoed the stroke of the first hour in the new year, mingled with the tumult of the storm that raged without; nor was the bacchanalian feast at an end till the morning broke, troubled and gloomy. The revellers then, one after another, reeled homewards; Friedemann Bach alone retained the steadiness of his gait, and his self-possession. The youthful vigor of his frame enabled him to withstand the effects of a night's festivity; but the bitter contempt with which he had early learned to look upon the ordinary efforts and impulses of men, found sufficient to nourish its growth.

On the morning of the New year, Friedemann, pale and disturbed, was pacing up and down his chamber, when Scherbitz came in.

"The compliments of the season to you!" cried the ever merry page. "Health, contentment, fortune, and all imaginable blessings!"

"The blessing is here!" sighed Friedemann, handing his friend an open letter.

Scherbitz read it through, and said, with some appearance of emotion — "*Mon ami!* your papa is a dear, charming old gentleman, whose whole heart is full of kindness for his Friedemann; every line of this letter expresses it. May he have a long and happy life! But I pray you, for the thousandth time, to recollect that it is quite impossible to satisfy, honestly, all the claims of such distinguished virtue of the olden time. Believe me, *mon ami*, the time will come when we, madcaps as we now are, shall be pointed out as wig-blocks that frown upon the disorderly behavior of our juniors. The wheel of time rolls on, and no mortal hand can check its course; it should suffice that we keep ourselves from falling, and being crushed in the dust beneath it."

"Can we do that?"

"*Mon ami!* Do I not stand, albeit I am a page forty years old? And look you, I know that I shall remain so, as long as I serve my lord faithfully. I might have opposed the all-powerful minister, and the country would have glorified me; yet I am a *page*, no captain, at forty years of age! I have been the talk of the capital, yet I stand firm!"

"And your consolation?"

"A knowledge that it has always gone thus in the world; that I am not the first whose life is a failure; that I shall not be the last; a perverse determination to live through a life which a thousand others would end in despair; in fine, curiosity to see what will be the end of the whole matter. Be reasonable, *mon ami!* I am really something of a hero! Were I an artist, as you are, I should have nobler consolations than perverseness and curiosity. Enough of my own insignificance; but let me ask you, have you forgotten the heroic Händel, whom, three years ago, you welcomed here in the name of your father?"

"How could I forget that noble being?"

"Ah, there I would have you, friend! You tell me yourself, Händel is not, as an artist, like your father; his fantasy is more powerful, his force more fully developed; he soars aloft, a mighty eagle, in the blaze of eternal light; while your father, a regal swan, sails majestically over the blue waters, and sings of the wonders of the deep. Well! we all know Monsieur Händel an honorable man—a man *comme il faut*; yet how different is he from your father! What the one, in limited circles, with calm and earnest thought, labors after, what he accomplishes in his silent activity—the other reaches amidst the tumult of a stormy life; amid a thousand strifes and victories. Yet your father honors and loves him, and blames him not for the path by which he travels towards the goal. It is also your path, and is not the worst that you might take. So—*en avant—mon ami!*"

"You forget," said Friedemann, gloomily, "you forget that Händel, in all his wild and agitated life, never lost himself; and that his belief was such as he might acknowledge even to my inflexible father."

"That I well remember, friend; and also that if Händel had been born in 1710, instead of 1687, he must have had more liberal views of certain things than he now has, if he thought it worth while to spend time upon matters of belief at all. He is a mighty musician; he lives and lets live; and credit me, did as others do, before he was your age; Faustina Hasse could tell you many pretty stories thereof, if she placed not so much stress upon outward demeanor."

"He never played the hypocrite to his father!"

"Because it was not worthwhile to lie to the old dupe. And now, *mon ami*, do not flatter yourself you can mislead a page forty years old! To speak fairly and honestly, your self-reproach and your—*pour ainsi dire*—profligacy, have a cause very different from that you have chosen to assign. I tell you, between ourselves, there is another secret, whose discovery you dread far more than the unmasking of your petty hypocrisy."

Friedemann reddened as he asked, "What do you mean, von Scherbitz?"

"Ha, ha!" laughed the page, "you need not look so gloomy because I have guessed the truth. *Non, non, cher ami.* If you really wish to keep your secret, you must govern your eyes better, when the name, 'Natalie' is uttered. Your last night's behavior opposite the minister's palace was not necessary to convince me that you have looked too deeply into the dark eyes of the little countess."

The flush on Friedemann's cheeks gave place to a deadly paleness; but mastering his emotions by a violent effort, he said, in a husky voice—

"You have discovered all; but you will be silent—will you not?"

"*O ma foi!* said I not, *mon enfant*, that I only warned you to be cautious before others? I will be silent, as a matter of course, and so, no more of it. Farewell! I am going to the guard-house, to see the happy waking of our noble chamberlain! You go to church, to edify the faithful with your organ-playing; come afterwards to Seconda's, where the groom shall give a splendid breakfast as his ransom. Courage! be not too philosophical! I hate the old Italian who made you so melancholy!"

The page departed, and Friedemann, having dressed himself, left his house to go to the church of Saint Sophia.

The service was at an end; the organ's last tones died tremulously along the vast arches, like the sighs of a suppliant angel. All was still again, and the worshippers departed from the sanctuary. Friedemann, too, arose, closed the instrument, and descended from the choir, more composed, if not more cheerful, than he had gone there. Just as he was going out, he felt himself clasped in a pair of vigorous arms; and looking up, with a joyful cry of—"Ah, my father!" flung himself on the bosom of Sebastian Bach.

"God's grace be with thee, on this New year's morn," cried Sebastian, clasping his son to his heart. "And my best blessing! Yea, a thousand,

Friedemann! You made my heart leap, ere yet I saw you, with pure joy! Truly, you have bravely—*greatly* acquitted yourself, in this morning's work! Ay, you know, to make others skilful in our sacred art, was ever my pride; Heaven will not reckon with me for presumption, nor must you take it for such, when I say—that as you were always my dearest pupil, you have become my best! Now conduct me to your lodgings, Master court-organist; Philip is already there, and unpacking; for eight days I propose to tarry with my Friedemann. We have been long separated, and though you wrote me charming letters, that, as you know, between father and son, is not like discoursing face to face, with hand in hand!" So saying, he took Friedemann's arm with affectionate pleasure, and walked with him towards his dwelling, talking all the while.

A new surprise awaited Friedemann there; for his younger brother, Philip Emanuel, in the three years that had flown since his departure from Leipzig, had grown a stately youth, and as his father testified, a ripe scholar in his art. He was a gay, light-hearted boy, "a little subtle upon the organ," as his father observed with a smile, "and certainly more at home on the piano; but a true and pious spirit, that scorned disguise."

Friedemann suppressed a sigh at the last remark of Sebastian, and gave his brother a heartfelt welcome. A servant in a rich livery interrupted the conversation. He presented a note to Friedemann, and said he was ordered to wait for an answer. Friedemann colored as he took the billet, opened it, glanced at the contents, and said briefly, "I will be there at the appointed hour." The servant bowed and disappeared.

"Ha!" observed Sebastian, with a smile, "it seems our court-organist has to do with very distinguished people."

"It was the livery of the Lord Premier," said Philip.

Sebastian started, and asked, "Eh, Friedemann, is it so? A domestic of His Excellency, the Count von Bruhl, comes to your house?"

"He was sent," replied Friedemann, with some embarrassment, "only by the niece of His Excellency, the Countess Natalie."

"Eh? you are acquainted with the young lady, then?"

"She is my pupil. This billet instructs me to come to her this afternoon, to arrange a concert she wishes to give on her aunt's birth-day."

"Eh? how come you to such an honor? I thought those matters were under the jurisdiction of M. Hasse."

"My dear father, as the young lady's music-master, I cannot well decline commissions of the sort, especially as they here promote one's reputation.

With regard to M. Hasse, he departed hence early this morning; we shall no more have the pleasure of hearing new songs from him."

"Hasse gone hence?" repeated Sebastian, with astonishment—"the excellent, amiable Hasse? Eh? where is he gone? Tell me, Friedemann!"

"It is a long story," replied his son, with a meaning glance at his young brother.

The father understood the hint. "You may go till meal-time, Philip," he said, "and amuse yourself by seeing the city." Philip bowed obediently, gave his hand to his brother, and quitted the room. "Now, my son," said Sebastian, "we are alone; what has happened to M. Hasse?"

Friedemann gave him an account of Hasse's departure—of his contemplated journey to Italy, and the well known cause of his disquiet and exile. Bach listened attentively. When his son had ended, he said, confidentially—"It was right that Philip should not hear such a tale—and that you suggested it to me to send him away. Hem! at court, indeed, all is not as it should be; there is much said in our Leipzig, as I could tell you, about it. Well, one must not listen to every thing; our most gracious Elector and sovereign means well with his subjects, and whoever is a faithful subject, will acknowledge that, and speak not of things which he who commits them has to answer for. We will say no more about it; you will go this afternoon to her gracious ladyship, and I warrant me, know how to demean yourself. I have cared enough, methinks, for your manners." Friedemann pressed his father's hand, and looked fondly on the good old man. "Tell me now, sir court-organist," continued the elder Bach, "what you have been doing of late. You have sent me but little for a long while; I hope you have not been idle."

"Surely not, my father! I have worked assiduously, but have done little that satisfied me; and what does not satisfy me, I would rather destroy, than venture before the world. In art, one should accomplish the best, or nothing at all."

"No, no!" cried Sebastian, interrupting his son; "that would be, indeed, a hard condition for many; for the greatest number among those who earnestly and honestly devote themselves to art; who find therein, often, the only consolation and happiness of their lives. The chosen are few—the called are many! And trust me, Friedemann, the called are not held in less esteem for the sake of the chosen, if they prove themselves true laborers! Art is like love. We all bear and cherish love in our hearts, and whether the bosom is covered by a regal mantle, or by a beggar's cloak, love, which dwells within, owns but *one* home—Heaven. Could the highest and the best alone avail in art, how should we and our equals stand? I can do little, but my will is honest, and vast is my reward! Yes! I am, as regards earthly good, like the poor man in the Evangelist; yet I would not exchange with a monarch! I rejoice in humility over my success, great or small as it may be; and for the rest, I submit me to the will of God!"

"Oh, that all had your apprehension of Art, my dear father; that all would strive to practise it as you do!"

"You will, my boy!" said Sebastian, tenderly. "I find much that is excellent in your *Fughetten*. Be not too severe with yourself; and remember that the fresh, free impulses of a young heart are ever accordant with the dictates of justice and truth."

"They are, indeed!" murmured Friedemann, gloomily.

His father continued—"Since we are permitted, my boy, to meet on this New-year's morning, allow me to ask how it stands with you in other respects? Eh, Friedemann, will you not soon seek out a wife among the daughters of the land? I warrant me, the court-organist need not seek long, to find a comely and willing damsel. Eh? speak, boy!"

"Dear father! there is time enough!"

"Pah! pah! I was not as old as you are, when I espoused your mother; and by my faith! I would have married sooner, if I had had my place. So make haste, Friedemann! 'Early wooed, has none rued!'"

"It is a serious step, father."

"That is very certain, and I am sure you would not take it precipitately; but I pray you, dear son, do it speedily. How merry a grandfather I shall be! and if the child is a boy, he must be named after me; and I will teach him his first notes. Ay, 'tis very true, marriage is no child's play. I can tell you, son, I have toiled unweariedly, oft oppressed with care, to furnish you, my boys and girls, with your daily bread. Yet, has not the Almighty blessed my labors? Have I not brought you all up happily, to be brave men, and skilful musicians? It is singular, Friedemann, that from my great grandfather down, all the sons of the Bach family have had taste and talent for music. Look you—as I wrote down my last fugue, I thought of my sons, and of you, particularly, and confessed myself happy! I used often to think I might write something, like the old masters, which, centuries hence, could edify and delight men—that they would love my memory. May I be forgiven if there was aught of worldly arrogance in the thought. Now, however, I have become less ambitious; but I have *one* vision, in which my fancy will revel as long as I live! It is this—how rapturous will it be—when all the Bachs meet together in the Kingdom of Heaven, and unite in singing to the glory of God—their 'hallelujahs' resounding forever and ever in the presence of the Uncreate—who was, and is, and shall be! Friedemann! child of my heart! let me not miss you there!"

"Father!" cried the young man, and sank overpowered at Sebastian's feet.

The elder Bach, unacquainted with the wo that struggled in his son's breast, saw only in his agitation a burst of filial feeling. He laid both hands on the head of the kneeling youth, and said, devoutly, "God's peace be with you, my Friedemann, now and ever, Amen!"

Friedemann arose, pale, but with a smile on his face. He kissed his father's hand, and slowly withdrew from the apartment; but scarcely was the door closed behind him, than he rushed impetuously through the hall, down the steps, and through the streets to the open space, where he threw himself on the frozen earth, hid his burning forehead, and cursed aloud his miserable being.

After the lapse of an hour, having collected and composed himself, he returned to his father, and conversed with apparent cheerfulness. The elder Bach chatted at table with Philip, who was required to give him an account of all the magnificence he had seen in the capital. The splendor of Dresden had reached its utmost under the administration of the luxurious and prodigal Count von Bruhl; and no court, not even that of Vienna, rivalled the Polish Saxon in this respect.

After dinner, the father reminded his favorite that it was time to dress, so as to be in season at the minister's palace; and Friedemann hastened to do so. With a beating heart, with feelings that partook both of pleasure and despair, he found himself at the palace. As he entered the hall, a side door was suddenly thrown open, and a small man, with striking features, and soft, clear blue eyes, richly dressed, with a blazing star on his breast, came forth: it was the minister himself. As Friedemann stopped and bowed to him, he advanced, speaking in the gentlest and blandest tone imaginable—

"Ah! bon jour, Monsieur Bach! Much happiness with the New year! My niece has sent for you? I am pleased to see you so punctual. I see, with satisfaction, you are attached to our house, and shall remember your zeal where it will do you good. I shall improve the first opportunity to convince you by deeds, of my good will. Now to the Countess!"

He nodded to the young man, smiled, and skipped out of the door and down the steps to his carriage, which soon drove away with him.

Young Bach looked after him, and murmured to himself, "Can he have guessed my secret? The smile of that man ever bodes disaster! Well, come what may, what can make me more wretched than I am? On, reprobate!"

He crossed the hall, and passed through one of the galleries towards the apartment of the Countess Natalie.

"This way," said the maid, who was waiting for him in the ante-room, and without further announcement, she opened the door of the cabinet, where Natalie, charmingly dressed, was reclining on a divan. Friedemann entered.

Natalie arose quickly, and stood a moment gazing earnestly on the visitor. She might have seen twenty summers; her figure was not tall, but perfectly symmetrical, and voluptuous in its rounded fulness; her head was beautiful, though not classical in its contour; a curved nose, and a pair of well defined, though delicately pencilled eyebrows, gave an expression of decision and pride to her countenance, while the exquisite, rosy mouth, and eyes shadowed by their long lashes, exhibited more the character of softness and tenderness. A profusion of dark hair floated unconfined over her neck, and relieved the outlines of her somewhat pale, but lovely face.

She stood still a moment before Friedemann, who cast down his eyes embarrassed; then approaching, she laid her small white hand lightly on his shoulder, and said, in a mild voice—"Tell me, Bach, what were you doing last night so late, opposite our house?"

Friedemann raised his dark, flashing eyes to hers, but dropped them the next instant. Natalie continued—"I saw you plainly, as I stepped a moment out on the balcony for a breath of fresh air—and I knew you at once. You were leaning against the castle wall; it seemed as if you were waiting for some one. Come—Bach, answer me!"

The young man struggled down his emotions, and after a pause, said coldly—"You sent for me, most gracious Countess, to honor me with your commands respecting the arrangement of a concert."

Natalie turned her back pettishly, and cried in an angry and disappointed tone—"Thus—haughty man! you thank me, too weak of heart! for my trust—for my concessions! Out on ungrateful man!"

Friedemann's pale face became crimson, and in a subdued voice, which had something in it absolutely terrific, from the deep sorrow and the wild passion it expressed, he replied—"What shall I—what can I say to you? Look at me, and enjoy your triumph! You have made me wretched—but I conjure you, let me have the only consolation that remains—the conviction that I alone am to bear the wrath and curse of offended heaven!"

"Friedemann!" cried the maiden, shocked, and she turned again to him, her eyes suffused with tears—"spare me; master this agitation, I entreat you!"

"I will *not!*" returned the young man, impetuously, "I will not spare you! you have yourself torn open, in cruel sport, the wounds of this heart! Look, how it bleeds! and yet, oh, fate, cannot cease to beat! I will not spare you! you are the only being on earth, to whom I dare unveil myself; I have purchased that right with my happiness here and hereafter; and this only, last right none shall tear from me! I gave you all! truth for falsehood—pure, undying love, for frivolous, heartless mockery!"

"I mocked you not!" protested Natalie, looking earnestly at him. "Believe me, I meant well."

"With *me?* Did you love me?"

"Ask me not."

"Natalie, answer! Did you love me?"

"How can it help, if I tell you I loved you? Are we not parted for ever?"

"No! by my soul! *no!* If you love me, nothing on earth shall part us! For the sake of your love, mark me—I would not spare even the heart of my father, though it should cost his life! But I must know—if you have loved—if you yet love me! If you have not, if you do not, I will ask—woman! wherefore did you tempt the free-hearted youth, who lived but for his art, with encouraging looks and flattering words? Wherefore did you give yourself—"

"Hold, unhappy man!"

"Wherefore?" repeated Friedemann, with a burst of passionate grief.

"I honored your mind—your genius—your heart."

"And you loved me not?"

"You will madden me with these questions!"

"And you loved me *not?*"

"I could not see you suffer—I wished to restore your peace—to have you acquiesce—"

"All that you gave without love, I *despise!* If you do love me, how can you bear to think of becoming the wife of another?"

"Ah! you know well, my station—the will of my uncle—"

"And *my* happiness, *my* peace is nothing to you?"

"Why can you not be calm—happy, when you know that my affection is still yours—that I can never love another!"

Friedemann's brow kindled, he stamped fiercely with his foot, and muttered—"Hypocrite, liar, coward! and all for the sake of a coquette!"

"Your passion makes you unjust and weak," said Natalie, with displeasure. "I am no coquette. Is not the story of my education familiar to you? My parents died early; they were poor, but descended from one of the oldest families in the land; my proud uncle, whose nobility was younger, surrounded me with all the state and splendor his power could command. I will not indulge in self-commendation, for that I early perceived the worthlessness of all this magnificence; but it is *something*, that I yielded not to temptation, which, in the midst of pomp and luxury, approached me in a thousand enticing shapes. It is much; I dare commend myself therefor, and be proud; for I had no loving, careful mother, to teach me the lessons of virtue. I grew thus to womanhood, flattered by puppets, by venal slaves, by smiling fools; for I had not yet seen a *man*. I saw you—I *loved* you. Must I excuse to you my too mighty love?"

"Ah! Natalie! what must I think? You love me, yet scorn to be my true and wedded wife! You love me, and will marry the creature of your uncle, whom you regard with indifference—with aversion? Must I never know what to make of you?"

"You must know that interest impels me not to this step, but a sense of duty."

"Sense of duty?"

"Yes! and towards you. I feel that as your wife I could never make you happy—could never be happy myself. You are a great artist, can accomplish much; but you cannot rise beyond a certain sphere—and I—think you it would be so easy for a princely maiden to fulfil the duties of a quiet citizen's wife? And were I willing to sacrifice all for you, where should we find a refuge from the pursuit of my incensed uncle? Nay—if we even found that, in some desert solitude, how long could the high-minded, ambitious artist endure this inglorious concealment?" Friedemann looked mournfully on the ground, and was silent; the lady continued,—"If I knew you discontented, could I be happy? Or you, if you saw my grief? I will do all for you that a woman in my circumstances can do for her beloved; my uncle's minion can never obtain any portion of my heart. I will live for you alone! And you— live for your art and me!"

"And must I enjoy your affection as a dishonorable thief?" asked Friedemann, angrily.

"Our regard cannot remain concealed—yet, for your sake, I will bear the condemnation of the world!"

"And the world's scorn? No—you shall *not*! The woman whom I love—for whom I am miserable—for whose sake I have deceived father, brother, friends—that woman shall none dare to scorn! Farewell, Natalie! we never meet again! Be what your future husband is not—be noble and true. And believe me, low as I am sunk, *all* virtuous resolution has not yet left my heart! I must be unhappy, but no longer utterly wretched, for you shall *esteem* me!"

"Friedemann!" cried the maiden, and threw herself weeping on his breast, "I honor, I admire you!"

Here the waiting maid entered hastily, and not without alarm, announced the minister's approach.

"Recollect yourself!" whispered Natalie, as she disengaged herself from the arms of her lover.

The minister cried in a cordial tone as he entered—"Ha! Monsieur Bach, here still? I am delighted to see you again. Well, *ma chére nièce!*" turning to the blushing girl, "how goes it? Is all arranged for the concert—and will it suit?"

"I hope so, most gracious uncle!"

"That is charming, my love; my wife will be enchanted with this kind attention. You, my dear Monsieur Bach, will certainly arrange all for the best, of that I am assured. Come very often to my house! understand—very often! I place the highest value upon you and your talents."

The young man thanked him, somewhat bewildered, and took his leave.

"A strong head, and great, great talent," observed the minister, looking after him, while he took a pinch from his jewelled snuff-box. He said more in his praise, then passed to indifferent subjects, and at length retired from the apartment, after having pressed his lips to the white forehead of his niece, who dutifully kissed his hand.

As Friedemann left the palace, the page rushed hastily from round a corner to him, and asked—"Whither?"

"Home!"

"Not there. Come with me instantly to Faustina's."

"Are you mad?"

"More reasonable than yourself, *mein engel*! Out on the blindness that cannot see the trap the wary bird-catcher has laid for the bird!"

"What mean you? What is the matter?"

"*Sacre-bleu!* Come to Faustina's with me, or you are to-night on the road to Konigstein! The lord Minister knows all!" And he led him away.

Twilight had come on; Philip had called for lights, and placed himself beside his father, who, sitting at the table, was diligently perusing Friedemann's last exercises and compositions, giving what he had read to his son, for the same purpose. At last, looking up, he asked—"Well, Philip, what think you of our Friedemann?"

"Ah, father," replied the lad, "do not make sport of me! But indeed, I know not how to express what I think and feel. I am moved, rapt—I admire my brother. It seems to me often as if I were reading something of yours; and then all is again so strange to me—so different from yours—I feel troubled—I know not why. In short, I cannot feel undisturbed joy in these compositions."

Sebastian looked grave and thoughtful for a moment, then turning with a smile to his son, he said—

"Yes, Philip, there is to me also something strange and paradoxical in Friedemann's works; and this is more the case in his exercises and sketches, than in his finished pieces; yet I am not disturbed; yea, I deeply rejoice therein."

"Rejoice?" repeated Philip, and looked doubtingly on his father; the latter continued—

"I know what you mean by this question; your own light, glad spirit accords not with the earnest, oft gloomy character displayed in Friedemann's works. Heaven knows, he inherits not the gloomy from me, though I have always dealt earnestly with art. But, observe, Friedemann's character is not yet fixed. All assures me there is something great in the man; but he is hardly yet determined how to develop it. He seeks the form, by which he shall represent what lives within him. I have examined closely and dispassionately; it is not a father's partiality that leads me to speak as I do. Friedemann seeks for himself a new path to the goal. Will he succeed? I hope so, when I reflect that every strong spirit has sought and discovered a new path, winning what his predecessor would have given up as impossible. I know not if I deserve so high a degree of praise as has been accorded to me; but this I know, Philip, and acknowledge, that from her origin, Art has ever advanced, and still advances, and her temple is not yet completed. Will it ever be? I think *not*; for the perfect dwells not on earth; yet therefore is Art on earth so divine and eternal, that we may ever long for her fairest rewards, and strive after them with our best strength."

"It is so," said Philip, struck with his father's remarks; "if one thinks he has accomplished something worthy, he soon finds there exists in his fantasy images far nobler and fairer, than with all his industry and taste he can produce."

The conversation was interrupted by a stout knock at the door. The elder Bach answered by a "Come in!" the door opened, and two tall men entered, and inquired for the court-organist.

"I expect my son every moment," answered Bach, and asked if the gentlemen had any message to leave. They replied that they were friends of the court-organist, and would wait for his coming. They seated themselves without farther ceremony; Sebastian also resumed his seat, and endeavored to introduce general conversation. But his politeness and his trouble were in vain; the two visitors only answered in monosyllables, and in a tone by no means encouraging, so that an awkward silence soon prevailed, and Sebastian, as well as Philip, wished, with all their hearts, for Friedemann's arrival. Still Friedemann came not; but after the lapse of a quarter of an hour, the door was opened without a previous knock, and the page, von Scherbitz, entered.

"*Bon soir!*" cried he, in an indifferent tone, while he fixed a keen look on the two strangers, who rose from their seats as they perceived him.

"Whom have I the honor—" asked Sebastian, somewhat surprised at the unceremonious intrusion.

"Von Scherbitz," replied he, "page in the service of His Highness, and a friend of your son Friedemann, if so be that you are the elder Bach."

"I am," returned Sebastian, smiling. "My son must be in soon; these gentlemen, also his friends, are waiting for him."

"Friends?" repeated von Scherbitz, "friends of Friedemann! So, so!" He placed himself directly before the two men, who were visibly embarrassed, and looked down. The page stood awhile in silence; at length he said in a cold, ironical tone, "Messieurs! you are come too late, in spite of the haste with which his Excellency thought proper to send you, and indeed you are here quite unnecessarily. Go, messieurs! Carry your lord the compliments of the page, M. Scherbitz, and tell him the court-organist, Bach, is with the Signora Hasse; I myself took him there, informed the sovereign of my doing, as in duty bound, and have already obtained my pardon!"

The two men started up and left the apartment without answering a word; the page threw himself on a seat, and burst into loud laughter.

The elder Bach, who knew not what to make of the whole scene, stood in blank surprise in the middle of the room, looking inquiringly at Philip, who, with equally astonished and anxious looks, was gazing at the page.

At length von Scherbitz ceased laughing, arose, approached the old man, and said with earnestness and respect, "Pardon, Master Cantor, for my strange behavior. I will explain it to you; I have much to communicate, but to you alone. It concerns your son, Friedemann—"

"My son?"—"My brother?" cried Sebastian and Philip in the same breath. "Where is he?"

"As I told those men," replied the page, "at the house of Signora Hasse."

"And what does he there?" asked Sebastian.

"I must tell you alone."

"Go, Philip, to your chamber," said the father mildly; and as the boy lingered, he repeated with more earnestness—"Go!" With a look of anxiety the youth retired.

Sebastian, full of serious misgiving, seated himself, and said, "Now, M. Scherbitz, we are alone; what have you to tell me of my Friedemann, whose friend you are pleased to call yourself?"

"I am his friend!" said the page, not without feeling; "and that I am, I have not first proved to-day!"

"And those two men, who marched off so quickly, when you told them my son was at Madame Hasse's?"

"Were in no way his friends—*tout au contraire, mon ami*! and on this account I wish to speak with you."

"Speak, then, M. Scherbitz!"

Scherbitz seemed at a loss in what manner to communicate to Bach the information he could no longer keep from him. For the first time in his life, in the presence of that worthy old man, his bold levity deserted him. Sebastian sat opposite with folded hands, his clear and searching eyes fixed steadily upon him. Recollecting himself, at last he began—

"Your son, Friedemann, my good sir, has told me how different, even when a child, he always was from his brothers and sisters, in that, with an earnestness far beyond his years, he apprehended and retained whatever moved his fancy."

"Yes, yes, it was so!" exclaimed Bach. "This peculiarity endeared the boy to me at first; but in later years it has made me anxious for him."

"You have brought him up strictly, sir."

"Very strictly, M. Scherbitz; in the fear of God, as is a parent's duty! yet I have constrained him to nothing—and only when he was convinced, have I led him strictly to follow his conviction. He who discerns the truth and the right, and obeys it not, is either a fool or a knave; not a man!"

"Ah! my dear sir, may not an excess of strength lead a well meaning man out of the way; yea, even to his ruin?"

"That is possible; but he should reserve his strength to struggle, not weakly yield. He should either rouse himself, and atone for his faults, or perish like a man."

"Heaven grant the first!" murmured the page.

"Do you fear the last?" asked Sebastian, quickly, and alarmed.

"No, M. Cantor; I trust Friedemann's strength to rise again."

"To rise again? Monsieur, tell me, in few words—what of my son?"

"Well, then! you have brought up your son as a man of honor; but you yourself, sir, are too little acquainted with the present ways of the world, to be able to shield him against the dangers that beset the path of youth, when, without a guide or counseller, he enters the great arena of life. Your son, till then, had known nothing of the world, beyond his paternal dwelling and your church of Saint Thomas. He was called to Dresden. He was received as the son—as the first disciple of the famous Sebastian Bach; and it was soon found that he was himself a master in his art. Esteem, admiration, were his; the great treated him with favor, his inferiors flattered him as the favorite of the great. Is it surprising that his head was somewhat turned, and that he forgot his place? Yet all would soon have been right again, when he learned to separate appearances from realities; but as ill luck would have it, the young Countess de Bruhl employed him as her music-master. In a word, your son loves her!"

"Is the boy mad?" cried Bach, angrily, and rising from his chair.

"Gently, papa!" interrupted the page; "if you knew the young Countess, you would confess, that for a young man like your son, it would be impossible not to love her; particularly as she was resolved to be loved; and in truth, she has excellently well managed it!"

Sebastian sank again on his seat, and his brow became clouded. The page continued—

"Friedemann struggled bravely against his passion, but the little Countess would not allow resistance—"

"Poor Friedemann!" sighed the father.

"When the first violence of his passion was over, he thought upon his father. He would have torn himself from his beloved—but could he? ought he? Everything was against their union. Was he to discover all to you, who had no misgiving? Disturb your peace, and that of your family? He resolved to bear all the anguish alone. The resolution was a noble one, but it made him so much the more wretched, since he, who so reverenced truth, had to dissemble with his father."

"Cease, M. Scherbitz!" said Sebastian, in a low, mournful voice.

"I have little more to say, M. Cantor. Friedemann's conscience gave him no peace day or night; and he suffered much from the fear of discovery. He fled to dissipation for relief. There were about him younger and older libertines. Thus I became acquainted with him; I, whose life has been an error! I would fain have aided him; but I saw then was not the time. His grief was too new; his passion reigned too fiercely in his breast; I looked to time for the cure, and sought only to keep him from too wild company. I was not always successful. Now, however, he has taken a wise step. He himself has broken off his connection with the Countess."

"Heaven be praised!" cried Sebastian with joy; the page continued—

"First hear me out, M. Cantor; the minister has discovered their intimacy. He swears your son's destruction—there I have baffled him; but I cannot prevent the necessity of Friedemann's quitting this place."

"It needs not!" said Sebastian, with quickness. "My poor son shall go hence; he needs comfort, and he can find it only with me!"

"He may come to you, then?" asked Scherbitz.

"What a question! Where is the father who can repel his unhappy child? And I know, sir, how unhappy my poor Friedemann must be; for I know, better than any other, his fiery soul! Bring him to me. I know he has ever loved his father; he must learn also to trust me with filial confidence!"

"My good sir!" cried Scherbitz with emotion, taking Sebastian's hand, and pressing it to his bosom, "had I had such a father, I should have been something more than a page, in my fortieth year. Your Friedemann is saved!"

He left the apartment. Sebastian looked sadly after him, and murmured to himself, "Ah! you know not what is in my heart, and that I dare not speak the whole truth, if I would save my boy! My fairest dream is melted away—the dream I indulged, of finding in my first-born a friend, pure and true—such as I have sought my life long in vain! Oh! now I acknowledge, the truest friend, the purest joy, is Art! Without her, where should I find comfort? All thanks and praise to Him who has given the children of earth such a companion through their pilgrimage of life!"

He passed from the room into an adjoining dark one, where a small but excellent work of Silbermann's was set up; he opened the piano, played a prelude, and began, with a full heart, the beautiful melody of an old song by Paul Gerhard, the first verse of which ran as follows:—

"Commit thy ways, Oh, pilgrim,
And yield thy sick heart's sighs
Unto the faithful caring
Of Him who rules the skies!"

More steady, more powerful rose the harmony; it filled the apartment, and was heard even in the streets, where it brought peace and consolation to more than one sick heart, as the passers-by stopped to listen.

In a luxuriously decorated room, lighted by a splendid astral lamp, reclined on a rich ottoman Faustina Hasse, the most beautiful woman, and the greatest dramatic singer, not only of her own, but perhaps of all times.

She wore a simple white robe, of the finest material; a costly necklace of pearls was rivalled by the snow of her lovely neck; her lofty brow was somewhat paler than usual, and a touch of melancholy about her mouth softened the pride that generally ruled the expression of those exquisite features.

"Let him come in!" said she, carelessly, to the waiting-maid, who had just announced a visitor. The maid withdrew, and the minister, Count von Brühl, entered, with a low and courtly bow. Faustina replied by a slight inclination of her head, and without changing her own easy position, motioned him to a seat. The minister sat down, and began smilingly—

"My late visit surprises you, does it not, Signora?"

"I am not yet aware of its object."

"Oh, that is plain! I am a good spouse, as is known; in fourteen days comes my consort's birth-day, and I intend giving a fête, as handsome as my poor means will allow. But how will it surpass in splendor all other fêtes in the world, if Faustina Hasse will honor it with her presence! Will the Signora let me sue in vain?"

"I do not sing, my lord minister."

"How have I deserved, Signora, that you should so misinterpret my well meant petition?"

"Will His Highness honor the feast with his presence?"

"He received graciously his most faithful servant's petition, and was pleased to promise me."

"Good—I will be there."

"Divine Faustina! My gratitude is unbounded!"

He kissed her hand, and was about to retire. Faustina started up hastily, and cried with flashing eyes—

"Hold—a word!" The minister stood still. "Where is Friedemann Bach?" asked she.

The Count could not suppress a start of surprise, but he answered blandly—"This question, most honored lady, from you—"

"Where is Friedemann Bach?" repeated Faustina, with vehemence. "I *will* know!"

"Well, then; he is probably on his way to Konigstein."

Faustina smiled scornfully, and asked—"For what?"

"To save him from yet severer punishment. The whole parish is disgusted at the scandalous life their court-organist leads, who, if he edifies the devotional with his organ-playing on Sunday morning, celebrates the wildest orgies with his fellow rioters, at Seconda's, on Sunday night!"

"And what is done with his fellow rioters?"

The Count von Brühl shrugged his shoulders, and replied dejectedly—"They are of the first families."

"And therefore pass unpunished? Very fair, my lord minister! But you are mistaken; Bach is not on the road to Konigstein; he is here, in my house, and has seen His Highness."

"How, Signora!" cried the Count, really shocked—"what have you done?"

"Silence—I command you!" said Faustina, haughtily. The minister was silent, and she continued—"His Highness knows all; knows why you pursue the unhappy youth, and would bring unspeakable misery on the whole family—and such a family! Heartless courtier! You cannot comprehend the worth of such a man. Friedemann must leave this city, but he goes freely, and must not be unprovided for. Give him another place, one worthy of his genius. That is His Highness's will!"

She left the apartment. The minister stepped in much embarrassment to a window, looked out into the darkness, and drummed with his fingers upon the pane. When he turned round, he saw Friedemann and the page, who had entered the room. There was a storm in his breast, but he suppressed all signs of agitation, and walking up to the young man, said in a gentle, though earnest tone, "Monsieur Bach, it grieves me much that you must leave us so suddenly; but since that cannot be helped, we must yield to what is unavoidable. You will go as soon as possible to Merseburg; the place of organist in that cathedral is vacant, and I have appointed you to it. Adieu!" And he retired.

"*Bravissimo, mon comte!*" cried the page, laughing as he looked after him—"where is there a better actor? Roscius is a poor bungler to him! But now, *mon ami*—he turned to Friedemann—"come with me to your father. Courage! he knows all."

"All!" repeated the youth, and with a look of despair he followed his friend. They passed out into the open air. It was a clear winter's night; the stars glittered in the deep blue firmament, recording in burning lines their hymn of praise to Infinite love; but in the heart of the young man dwelt hopeless anguish.

The pious melody Sebastian sang, was yet unfinished, when they arrived at the house. They entered. Philip, who saw them first, hastened to tell his father. Sebastian came into the room; as he approached his son, he said, "You come back to me—you are welcome!"

"Can you forgive me, father?" murmured Friedemann, fixing his looks gloomily on the ground.

"You have deeply sinned against your first, your truest friend; but I trust you will have ability to amend, and I *have* forgiven you!"

"And without a word of reproach?"

"Your own conscience has suggested more than I could say; it is now my part to console you. Come with me to Leipzig, and if I alone cannot comfort you, why, the others shall help me!"

"No, by my life!" cried Friedemann, looking up boldly. "I pass not again the sacred threshold of my home, till I am worthy of you—or quite resigned to despair!"

"Is that your firm resolve?" asked Sebastian.

"It is, my father! Henceforward I will be true to you. I know not if I shall overcome this anguish, but I will struggle against it, for I have yet power! If victorious, more is won than lost! But if I am overcome—"

"Then come to my heart, Friedemann!"

"I will!"

Sebastian held out his hand to his son. Friedemann flung himself into his father's arms.

The next morning they parted. Sebastian returned to Leipzig, and Friedemann prepared for his journey to Merseburg.

SEBASTIAN BACH

"If the lessons were only over!" cried impatiently Lina, the youngest daughter of Sebastian Bach.

"They will soon be over," said her mother; "it has already struck twelve."

"Ah! what with the beating and blowing above there, my father often does not hear the hour strike. He is too zealous with his pupils."

Madam Anna Bach smiled good humoredly at the impatience of her favorite, and replied—"Take care your father does not hear you talk so. He would interpret it ill. He regrets often enough, already, that his daughters have no gift for music, while his sons have been skilled on the piano and the organ from their earliest childhood."

Lina fixed her beautiful hazel eyes earnestly on her mother, and said with some petulance—"Yet my father, if he would be just, must acknowledge that we three girls give him more pleasure than all his sons, skilful musicians as they are!"

Mᶜ Rae, sc.

SEBASTIAN BACH.

"Silence!" said her mother, gravely. "It does not become you to boast of your father's regard, nor to accuse your brothers. Go to your sisters, and to work."

Lina obeyed; but when at the door she turned suddenly round, ran back to her mother, seized her hand, kissed it affectionately, and said—"Be friends with me, mamma! I meant no harm by what I said."

"That I well know," replied Madam Bach; "you are a good girl, but you have not the quiet manners of your other sisters. You are hasty and vehement, like the brother you resemble in outward features—whom you always blame, because he has grieved your father, and yet whom you love better than all the rest."

"Friedemann!" cried Lina, and threw herself sobbing into her mother's arms. Then recovering herself, with a "I will be good, mamma!" she left the apartment.

Madam Bach, after speaking a moment with her youngest son, Christian, was about to follow, when the door opened and her excellent husband, Johann Sebastian, entered. He was still a stately and handsome man, of steady carriage, and eyes that beamed with the brilliancy of youth; but thirteen years had considerably changed him; deep furrows were in the once open and smooth forehead; his cheeks were fallen in, and their color betrayed disease.

"Is your lesson over?" asked his wife.

Sebastian held out his hand affectionately, and answered—"Yes, for to-day." He placed himself in his arm-chair, and Madam Bach continued—

"You are glad of it, for you seem to-day very much exhausted."

"Ay; old age will have its claims satisfied, and rest does me good now and then; but glad—no! I am not glad that the hours are at an end, in which I must do my duty. I can impart instruction yet—I have strength to make good scholars, and so long as I can work, none shall find me remiss."

"You will do much good yet!"

"That is in God's hand, Anna! My will indeed is to do—you look so pleasant—what have you there?"

"A letter for you from Philip."

"Ho, ho!" cried Sebastian, while he joyfully rose; "has the scapegrace at last found time to write to his old father? By my faith, I have doubted whether he has ever learned letter-writing, since he has been concert-master

in the service of His Majesty of Prussia! Well—what says he?" and he opened
the letter, and read—

"My dear and honored father—

"You will pardon your most dutiful son, that he has not
written in so long a time to his beloved and honored parent,
and will impute this neglect of duty by no means to any lack
of filial affection, or of dutiful esteem, since it is solely and
entirely owing to the pressing business of my situation. This
magnificent capital is all life, as far as music is concerned.
At court there is a great concert two or three times a week,
without numbering the private entertainments, which His
Majesty has every evening in his cabinet, where I accompany
him on the pretty Silbermann's piano, on which my beloved
father played before His Majesty.

"His Majesty plays on the flute quite surprisingly; and I think
his tone fuller and better than Herr Quantz can produce. But,
as respects time, I am obliged to give good heed to keep with
him, for His Majesty is capricious, and troubles himself little
with the notes—going forward and backward and stopping
at his own will and pleasure. This is pleasant enough when
he plays alone, but in concerts occasions much confusion.

"His Majesty has always been very well pleased with my
accompaniment; and after every piece we have executed
together, His Majesty has been pleased to say—'You have
done this well.'

"His Majesty always inquires in a friendly manner after my
esteemed father, and often asks me—'Will not your papa
come once more to Berlin?' This I would propose, with
proper discretion; and I can promise beforehand, if my
dear and esteemed father will visit us, he will be received
with joy and honors by all. Be pleased to pardon my hasty
writing; convey my best love and duty to my most honored
mother, my beloved brothers and sisters, and make happy
with a speedy answer

"Your dutiful son,
"Philip Emanuel Bach.

"*Berlin, July 18th, 1750.*"

Sebastian folded the letter again, and said, with a good humored smile—"His *hasty* writing I must indeed pardon for this once; for he has never written to me otherwise."

"What think you of his proposition to visit Berlin once again?" asked Madam Bach. "The journey, I think, would do you good."

"It would indeed!" replied Sebastian, cheerfully. "I would gladly see Berlin and His Majesty once more! Ay! twice in my life have I been wrought to believe there was something good in me; the first time was in the year seventeen, when Monsieur Marchand took himself quietly off, the evening before our appointed contest, so that I held the field alone in Dresden— ha! ha! ha! The second time, was three years ago, when the great King of Prussia came into the ante-chamber to meet me and give me welcome; and when some rude chamberlains began to laugh at my expressions of duty and homage, His Majesty chid them with '*Messieurs! voyez vous, c'est le vieux Bach!*' That pleased me wonderfully, and Friedemann, too!"

"You will go, then?"

"Yes—if they will give me leave here—and there be a small overplus of money in the purse, I should be glad. It is strange that in my old days, I should be seized with a roving propensity, of which I had little or nothing when I was young. Enough for this time; let us go to dinner."

The day was near its close, and Sebastian sat before the door of his dwelling, by the side of his wife, and surrounded by his family; his two eldest sons only, Friedemann and Philip, were wanting. The mother and daughters were employed in sewing and knitting work, and whispered now and then to each other. The sons listened to what the elder Bach was telling them of his youthful studies, particularly under the century-old organist, Reinecken, in Hamburg.

The setting sun threw his last rays upon the quiet group under the green and stately linden which shaded the entrance to the old Thomas school. A picture was presented, which in its true keeping might have inspired the genius of the greatest painter of that day.

In the midst of Sebastian's story, Caroline, who had been looking towards the corner where Cloister street runs into Thomas' church-yard, sprang to her feet with a cry of surprise.

"What is the matter?" asked her mother, alarmed: while the others all rose, leaving the venerable father alone sitting on the bench. Before the maiden could answer, the tall figure of a man was seen hastily crossing the church-yard towards the house, and now Sebastian rose too, for he recognized his son Friedemann.

"*Salve!*" cried the old man. "Do you come to stay?"

"I have kept my word!" answered Friedemann, "and if you think right, I will stay!"

Sebastian, nodding a pleased assent, held out his hands to his son, and embraced him with transport. His mother and the rest crowded round him, all but Caroline, who stood in her place, looking inquiringly at her brother. After he had returned the greeting of his family, he turned and addressed her. Then her eyes sparkling, her lovely face suffused with the flush of joy, she cried—

"I also bid you welcome!"

After the first surprise was over, Sebastian led his son into his chamber, and with gentle earnestness repeated his question.

"Come as you will, you are welcome;" said he: "yet what brings you here so suddenly?"

"That it is not the old story, my father," replied Friedemann, "you will believe upon my assurance. Ah! thirteen years are enough to blunt one sorrow—the more certainly, the greater it is! But a thousand new ones are born to me, and one among them yields not in bitterness to the first!"

"And what is that, Friedemann?"

"I despair of ever doing anything truly great in my art! I have only pride, not power, to support me against daily vexations. I have purposed well—true! I have purposed well. I wished to strike out a new path, without neglecting the excellent old school. I might err—ay! I *have* erred! the result proves it; but the motive of my exertions was pure; what I strove after was great and noble. But I have been slandered—insulted! my aim ridiculed—my endeavors themselves maliciously criticised—decried!—"

"And by whom, Friedemann?"

Friedemann started at this question; at length he said—"I am wrong, I know, to permit the judgment, or rather the silly prating of a malignant fool to destroy the pleasure arising from my exertions; and yet it is so. There is a certain schoolmaster Kniff in Halle, who, though all he accomplishes himself is contemptible, yet passes for a luminary in the musical horizon; I think they call his works reviews."

"Ay," cried Sebastian, "I know them to be ridiculous. I think the schoolmaster must be the cause of some sport in Halle."

"You are mistaken, father," replied Friedemann. "He is not derided, but feared on account of his malice; and those who fear him not, are pleased at the base libels by which he strives to bring down others to his own level."

"And can that disturb you?" asked Sebastian, "notwithstanding your knowledge that only the base and the evil array themselves against the good? Methinks I have ever taught you, there is no more certain proof of elevated worth, than the impotent rage and opposition of the vicious. I never taught you to look with pride or arrogance on your equals or inferiors, but to be calm, self-possessed, and to maintain your ground, even against the great, much more against the rich! That is man's first duty; practise it, Friedemann, and no schoolmaster Kniff, or any one else, can make you dissatisfied with yourself or your efforts."

Caroline here interrupted the conversation, announcing a stranger, who wished to speak with her father.

"Who is it?" asked Sebastian.

"He will not tell his name, but says he is a friend of yours."

"Bring him in, then," answered the old man, and Caroline left the chamber.

"*Bon soir!*" cried the stranger, as he entered, in a sharp voice, while he hastened towards Sebastian, and held out his hand; "*bon soir, mon cher papa!* Do you not know me?"

Sebastian could not immediately recollect the face. Friedemann recognized him at once, and said—

"Ah! Monsieur Scherbitz! good evening."

"Ha! ha!" cried Scherbitz, laughing, "is not this our ex-court-organist? Exactly! there is the same ill-boding frown between the brows as in 1737. You are but little changed, my friend, with being thirteen years older. I am still the same, except that at fifty-three I am grown to be First Lieutenant."

"You proved yourself a friend to my son in time of misfortune," said Sebastian, "and are therefore ever welcome to me and mine. To what lucky chance am I indebted for the pleasure of welcoming you in my quiet home?"

"To the most unlucky, my good sir! I was so careless, at the Prime Minister's last court, as to tread on the left fore-paw of his lady-consort's lap-dog. The beast cried out; the Countess demanded satisfaction; and in punishment for my misdeed I am marched as first lieutenant to Poland, in the body-guard of his Excellency."

Friedemann laughed. Sebastian, who felt a horror creep over him at his sarcastic, misanthropic wit, sought to change the conversation, but in vain; Scherbitz went on jesting in his bitter way about his tragical destiny. He concluded his account with the information—that he had come over to Leipzig simply and solely to see Papa Bach once more in his life, for, on the word of a first lieutenant, he had ever loved and honored him since the first time he beheld him, thirteen years ago.

The next morning, von Scherbitz was walking in the little garden behind Thomas school, which afforded but a narrow view, being bounded by the high wall on one side, when he saw at the other end Caroline, occupied in fastening the branches of a vine to an espalier. He approached and saluted the young lady; she turned and replied with the same cordiality.

"You are very early at work, Mademoiselle Bach," said Scherbitz, after a pause, during which she was arranging her vines.

"My father takes great pleasure in cultivating vines," answered Caroline.

"Do they flourish here?"

"Oh, yes! sometimes."

"I heard some charming singing, early this morning; it was a woman's voice. Faustina never sang clearer! Were you the singer, Mademoiselle Bach?"

Caroline blushed, and said—"Not I—it was my mother."

"Your mamma! *C'est vrai!* Friedemann told me she sings admirably. But you sing too, mademoiselle?"

"I hum a little, sometimes, like all girls when they are cheerful—but none of my father's daughters are musical—and he says we have neither taste nor talent to learn it properly."

"Perhaps you understand it by intuition, already."

Caroline looked at the lieutenant, and replied with a smile—"you are a good guesser, M. Scherbitz."

"No great guessing is required; there are many young ladies, who do not sing or play according to rules, yet who, nevertheless, are by no means unmusical."

"Oh! I love music I love it dearly! Brother Friedemann knows that—and it is therefore we are so dear to each other. But it is a very peculiar kind of music that I mean."

"You mean church music?"

"No!"

"Or concert music?"

"Nor that."

"Or dancing music?"

"No—no!"

"*Eh bien!* then you are fond of the Opera?"

"Not I—indeed!"

"What sort of music then will you have?"

Caroline laughed, but immediately after replied with a gentle sigh—"The music that I mean is not to be had here in Leipzig."

"What does that mean? Leipzig is the musical capital of all Europe!"

"Yes—it is very strange—but quite true! I find little or nothing of it here, admirably as my father, my brothers and their scholars execute their parts. Something is still wanting."

"Mademoiselle Bach, you must have studied in Professor Gottsched's college, since you are not satisfied even with your father and your brothers!"

"Ah! you must understand me!" cried Caroline, eagerly. "If I would enjoy my music in perfection, all around me must harmonize, and that is not possible here. But in a wood, surrounded by high mountains, the summits glowing in the morning or evening light, while it is yet twilight below; or when only a ray here and there streams down upon the foliage; while above, in the deep blue heaven, clouds are moving, white, rosy and golden—that is a charming accord. And the tops of the trees waving and whispering—the bushes answering in sighs—the brook singing its constant, yet ever new melody—the flowers moving like magic bells—the wild bird trilling his song! And when the sun is set, and the moon climbs the rocky verge and pours her soft silvery light on the scene,—or when dark clouds gather in the heavens, and hissing lightnings dart through them, and echo reverberates the thunder, and the swollen stream roars, and foams over the rocks and the crushed trees—all is to me, music!"

Scherbitz looked a moment in astonishment at the young lady, then answered—"Mademoiselle, it is possible you are not a singer, but you are a *poet!*" And he left her, to communicate his discovery to his friend.

Friedemann, with a bitter smile, replied—"It is as you say, von Scherbitz, and that it is so, is reason enough to drive me mad, if there were none other! I love this child, as my own soul. I have seen her grow up, and ripen into bloom—I shall see her die—for the fairest gifts of heaven are only lent to poor unhappy man, that their loss may add to his misery."

"True, and false, *mon ami*! as we take it. Do you know in what lies your fault and mine? We philosophize too much! Do not laugh; *parole d'honneur*—I speak in earnest! It is true, each of us in his way; we should have done better by acting, instead of thinking so deeply; instead of mocking at, and saying all possible evil of this miserable world—we should have acted. Not the will, but action, removes mountains. There lies a paradox in the truth that the greatest thinker, when it comes to the deed, can do absolutely nothing; a paradox, but it manifests at the same time the wisdom of the Creator; for wo to the system of the world, if the mightiest thoughts and designs were deeds! Satan, who revolted, cannot be dangerous to heaven. Man, whom the Maker created after his own image, could, if he possessed the power to do what he imagines in the moments of his exstacy—"

"Cease, von Scherbitz!" cried Friedemann; "I see the abyss before me!"

"*Va!* we are safe, *cher ami*! for as I said, we are but philosophers. Had not the minister played the spy on you and his pretty niece, had not I, malheureusement, stepped upon the foot of the Countess' lap dog, we should be perhaps at this moment both sitting quietly in Dresden—you as Natalie's fireside friend, bewitching her, yourself, and the world—I, as a merry page of fifty-three, jesting and enduring—and, *morbleu!* am I not enduring even now?"

"Do you know," asked Friedemann, and as he spoke his countenance assumed a strange expression—"do you know I have often fervently prayed that I might be mad—for a time—not for ever!" in a quick and vehement tone—"no, no! for all the world not for ever! but for a time I would be mad, that I might forget; and again, I feel the memory of what I have experienced would even then cling to me." He pressed his hand with a wild gesture before his eyes.

The lieutenant started, and said, soothingly—"Give not so much heed to my idle talk, my friend! I am *old*, melancholy—have no hope of a brighter future; but you, you are young, can yet do much—so much—"

"What can I do?" cried Friedemann, with harrowing laughter. "Nothing—nothing—nothing! With me at five and thirty, all is dead! All— more than with you at fifty! Ha! mark you not, where *madness* lurks yonder, behind the door, and makes ready to spring upon my neck, as I go out? He dares not seize on me when my father is near; but shrinks up, till he is little, very little, then hides himself in an old spider's web over the window. But he shall not get hold of me so easily! ha, ha, ha! I am cunning! I will not leave the chamber without my father! Look you, old page, I understand a feint as well as you!"

"*Mon ami! mon ami!* what *is* the matter?" cried the lieutenant, and seizing his friend by the shoulders, he shook him vehemently. "Friedemann Bach, do you not hear me?"

Friedemann stared at him vacantly a moment. At length his face lost its unnatural expression, his eyes looked like living eyes again, and he asked softly—"What would M. Scherbitz?"

"What would I? man! what makes you such an idiot? Recollect yourself."

"Eh!" said Friedemann, smiling; "Eh, M. Scherbitz, who takes a jest so deeply? And you really believe, that I am sometimes mad? Ah! not yet; I am rational, more rational than ever!"

"Well, well! *mon ami*, it was your jest, but one should not paint Satan on the wall. Pry'thee, sit you down, and play me something, that I may recover myself; you acted your part so naturally."

Friedemann sat down in silence to the instrument and began to play.

"I dreamt not of this!" muttered the lieutenant, while Friedemann, after having played half an hour, suddenly let his hands drop down, sank back, and fell fast asleep.

On the morning of the 21st July, 1750, the church-bells rang a solemn, yet cheerful peal, inviting the pious inhabitants of the city to the house of God. The sky was perfectly cloudless; the glad Sabbath sun shone brightly, and the pious heart felt strengthened anew in faith and devotion. Into Friedemann's heart also this day penetrated a beam of comfort, of joy, of love. He had spent a part of the preceding night in studying a masterpiece of his father's—the great Passions Music. Full of the grandeur of the work, his face animated with serene delight, he was walking to and fro in the chamber of the old man, pondering in his mind a similar work, which he had thought of undertaking.

Sebastian sat in his arm-chair, with folded arms, dressed ready for church, and followed with his eyes, smiling affectionately, the movements of his son. After a while he said—

"I am glad the Passions Music pleases you so well; I have a work of quite another kind finished, the first idea of which I got from your *Fughetten.* And you are the first after me that shall see it."

He went to his desk, opened it, took out a sealed packet and gave it to his son. It bore the inscription—"To my son Friedemann."

"In case I had died without seeing you again," observed the old man. "I am rejoiced it has happened otherwise; you may break the seal."

Friedemann did so, and on opening the package, his eyes fell on that nobly conceived, that admirably executed work, which, from the day of its first appearance to the latest time, has commanded the admiration and reverence of all the initiated—"*The Art of Fugues, by Johann Sebastian Bach.*"

Friedemann looked over the manuscript with sparkling eyes, and said—"Then I have not lived in vain! *my* poor attempt has suggested a work which, or I must be deceived, is destined to immortalize the name of its author! Receive my thanks, father; you have given me *much* to-day!"

"I know, Friedemann, you at least appreciate and honor my design; so that I receive much from you. Such appreciation is most gratifying to us from those we love, and is the highest reward earth can bestow."

"And you, father, have understood me?"

"Yes—grieve not over the judgment of others; yet while you endeavor to deserve the appreciation, the regard of your equals, labor to instruct those who cannot repay you thus. Will man assume more than higher powers— and only show to the best, that he belongs to the best! Are you skilful and faithful, let your light shine, else you degrade yourself and rebel against the Being who gave you power and inclination to be so."

Here the chime of the bells, which had ceased for some time, began anew; the door opened, and Madame Bach, her three daughters, the boy Christian, and von Scherbitz, entered, all ready for church. Madame Bach gave her husband a prayer-book and a bunch of flowers; Caroline handed him his hat.

Sebastian rose, gave his arm to his wife, and walked to the door, accompanied by his children and his friend. Turning back an instant, he glanced at the window shaded with vine-leaves, on which the sunlight glistened, and said—

"What a lovely morning!"

He was about quitting the room, when he stopped suddenly! prayer-book and flowers fell from his hands: the females shrieked; he struggled to regain his strength a moment, then sank back lifeless into the arms of his son.

Thus died Johann Sebastian Bach, by a stroke of apoplexy, the 21st of July, 1750.

Three years after, Baron von Globig was celebrating the feast of the vintage at his splendid villa at Loschwitz, some distance from Dresden.

Richly gilded gondolas, with long and many colored pennants, were gliding to and fro over the bosom of the Elbe, landing the distinguished guests invited by the proprietor of the villa. The splendor, nay, profusion, that marked all the preparations, was not unworthy of the favorite and confidant of the Count von Brühl. Nothing was wanting which the most refined and fastidious taste could suggest.

The host fatigued himself by exuberant efforts to do the honors suitably; this appeared the more singular, as no one took particular notice of him; all observation being directed to his lady, who, though dignified and courteous in her demeanor, manifested little interest in anything that passed.

As twilight came on, colored lamps were lighted in the garden walks, and gorgeous illuminations were displayed before the entrance. Bands of musicians alternated with each other, and joined in full bursts of harmony; brilliant and stately figures whirled through the merry mazes of the dance; all was hilarity and joy, and care was banished.

When the company reassembled in the saloon, the Prussian ambassador presented to the lady of the house a young but distinguished-looking man, as Philip Emanuel, the second son of the great Sebastian Bach.

The Baroness blushed slightly, and after a few words of salutation had passed, asked — "Where is your elder brother, now?"

"We do not know," replied Philip, sadly; "Friedemann disappeared from Leipzig the day of our father's death, and none of us have seen him since."

The Baroness turned away without speaking again. The Baron came up and said in his bland tone — "Will you have the kindness, most honored sir, to let us hear before supper a little, if but a little piece from you? My guests will be delighted to listen to the celebrated Monsieur Bach; and to enhance the effect of your divine playing, I have, by way of fun, permitted a poor half crazy musician from the Prague choir, who plays dances in the villages, to give us a tune in the ante-chamber. The doors may be opened, but he must not come into the light, for his dress is soiled and disordered."

Meanwhile a full accord sounded from the ante-room; a servant threw open the doors, and in the imperfect light the guests had a glimpse of a meanly dressed man, sitting at the piano, with his back turned towards the door.

The company had anticipated a joke, for the Baron had privately informed every body of his purpose: but it was quite otherwise, when they had heard the wonderful, entrancing harmony, now towering into passion, now sinking to a melodious plaint, which the poor unknown musician drew from the instrument. All were touched; but the Baroness and Philip stood, pale as death, and looked inquiringly, yet doubtingly, upon each other. Suddenly, at a bold turn in the music, the Baroness whispered—"'Tis he!"— and Philip cried aloud—"'Tis he! 'tis my brother—Friedemann!"

The musician turned round, sprang up, and rushed into Philip's arms. But at sight of the Baroness, he started back with the exclamation—"Natalie!"

The Baroness fell back in a swoon. Friedemann, forcing himself a way through the crowd, rushed from the house.

THE OLD MUSICIAN

In a room in the upper story of a house in the Friedrichstadt of Berlin, sat an old man, reading musical notes that lay on a table before him. From time to time he made observations with a pencil upon the margin; and seemed so intently occupied that he noticed nothing around him. The room was poorly furnished, and lighted only by a small lamp that flared in the currents of wind, flinging gloom and fitful shadows on the wall. A few coals glimmered in the grate; the loose panes clattered in the window, shaken by the storm without; the weather-cocks creaked as they swung on the roof, and the moaning blast uttered a melancholy sound. It was a night of cold and tempest, and the last of the old year.

The figure of the old man was tall and stately, but emaciated; and his pale and furrowed visage showed the ravages of age and disease. His thin snow-white locks fell back from his temples; but his eyes were large and bright, and flashing with more than youthful enthusiasm, as he read the music.

The bell struck midnight. From the streets could be heard festive music and shouts of mirth, blended in wild confusion; and the wind bore the chant of the Te Deum from a neighboring church.

The old man looked up from his occupation, and listened earnestly. Presently the door was opened, and a young man entered the apartment. The paleness of his face appeared striking in contrast with his dark hair; his expression was that of deep melancholy, and his form was even more emaciated than that of his companion.

"Did you hear the hour strike?" asked the old man.

"I heard it; it was midnight."

"Indeed!"

"You had better go to rest."

"To sleep, mean you? I do not need it. I have been reading this legacy of my father. Would that you had had such a father, poor Theodore! What is the New year?"

"Eighty-four."

"Eighty-four! when it was thirty-seven—we will not speak of that!"

"You always talk thus," said the young man. "Am I never to know who you are?"

"You might have asked that the day we first met; the day I found you—a madman—who had placed the deadly weapon against his own breast. I pulled it away; I said to you, Live! even if life hath nothing but wo to offer! Live, if thou canst believe and hope; if not, bid defiance to thy fate; but live!"

"You saved me; you see I live, old even in youth."

"You have many years to number yet."

"Perhaps not; I suffer too much! But tell me your name, perverse old man!"

"He who composed that noble work," said the old man, pointing to the music, "was my father."

"And have you not torn out the first leaf, on which was the title and name? You know I can guess nothing from the notes; they speak a language unknown to me. Speak, old friend; who are you?"

"The Old Musician."

"Thus you are called by the few who know you in this great city. But you have another name. Why not tell it me?"

"Let me be silent," entreated the old man. "I have sworn to reveal my name only to one initiated, if I meet such."

The youth answered with a bitter smile. There was a pause of a few moments; the old man looked anxiously at him, as if noticing for the first time his sunken cheek, and other evidences of extreme ill health. At length he said—

"And have you no better fortune, Theodore, for the New year?"

"Oh yes, fortune comes when we have no longer need of her."

He drew a roll of money from his vest pocket, and threw it upon the table.

"Gold!" exclaimed the old man.

Theodore produced a flask from the pocket of his cloak. "You have drunk no wine," he said, "in a long while! Here is some, the best of Johannisberger! Let us greet the New year with revel!"

The old man turned away with a shudder, for recollections of pain were associated with the time.

The youth took a couple of glasses from the cupboard, drew another chair to the table, and sat down while he uncorked the flask. As he filled the glasses, a rich fragrance floated through the room.

He drank to the old man, who responded; and the glasses were replenished.

"Ha, ha! you seem used to it!" cried Theodore, laughing. "It is good for you. Wine is better than Lethe; it teaches us not to forget pain, but to know it the frivolous thing it really is. What a pity that we find the philosopher's stone only in the bottom of the cup!"

"And how, I pray, came you by such luck?"

"I sold my work to a spendthrift lord, travelling through the city."

"It is a pity you had not a *replico*, for your work will never become known, thus disposed of."

"Ay, but how much is lost that deserves to remain! Those sketches cost me seven years of more than labor; all I have thought, lived, suffered; the first dream of youth; the stern repose after the struggle with fate! I sacrificed all—I spared not even the spark of life; and I thought, when the work was finished, the laurel would at least deck the brow of the dead. Dreams, fantasies! Wherever I offered my work, I was repulsed. The publishers thought the undertaking too expensive; some said I might draw scenes from the Seven years' war, like M. Chadowiski; others shook their heads, and called my sketches wild and fantastic."

"Yes, yes!" murmured the old man, musingly. "Lessing, who died three years ago, was right when he said to me, 'All the artist accomplishes beyond the appreciation of the multitude brings him neither profit nor honor.' Believe me, Theodore, I know well by experience what is meant by the saying 'The highest must grovel with the worm.'"

"And I must grovel on, old friend! As long as I can remember, I have had but one passion—for my art! The beauty of woman moved me with but the artist's rapture! Yet must I degrade my art to the vain rabble; must paint apish faces, while visions of divine loveliness float before me; must feel the genius within me comprehended by none; must be driven to despair of myself! Gifted as few are, free from guilt, I must ask myself, at five and twenty, wherefore have I lived?"

"Live;—you will find the answer."

"Have you found it—at seventy-four? You cannot evade the question; it presses even on the happy. Had I obtained what I sought, the answer might be—I have lived, and wrought, to win the prize; to shine a clear star in the horizon. So shines Raphael to me; and to you, some old master of your art; and we are doomed to insignificance and disappointment."

"Be silent!" exclaimed the old man; "that leads to madness, and madness is terrible! They tell me I was thus a long while."

"Have no fear of that, old friend! We are both too near a sure harbor! Come, finish the wine; welcome the New year! Hark! to the music and the revelry below in the streets; and we are exalted like the ancient gods on the top of Olympus, sipping the precious nectar, and laughing at the fools who rejoice in their being. Drink, as I do! Well, yonder is your bed, and here is mine. I am weary, and wish you a good night!"

The old man also retired to rest; the storm ceased to rage without. The music and ringing of bells continued throughout the night.

The first beams of the sun poured into the chamber, and awoke the old man. It was a clear and cold morning; the air was keen and bracing, the sky blue and cloudless, and the frost had wrought delicate tracery on the panes.

The old man looked out of the window awhile, then went to awaken his young companion. Alas! the hand that lay upon the bed-clothes was cold and stiff. Theodore's sorrows were ended. The spirit so nobly endowed had broken in the struggle with destiny.

Long did the old man gaze upon the pale remains, his features working with intense emotion. His last stay was broken; his only friend had departed; he was alone and forsaken in the world.

He sat down by the body, and remained motionless the whole day. As night came on, the woman who kept the house came to deliver a message to Theodore, and found the old man sitting by the corpse, exhausted and shivering with the cold. She led him into a warmer room, and gave him food.

The Old Musician and Theodore had lived together nearly two years. The youth supplied their wants by his small earnings as a portrait painter, and by his receipts now and then for a drawing. The old man had nothing; and the landlady, who saw that what Theodore had left would not last long, urged him to go to the overseer of the poor-house and seek an asylum. He repelled the idea, and answered, "No, I will go to Hamburg."

"To Hamburg!" repeated the woman. "That you cannot do. Hamburg is a long way from Berlin, and before you reach there you would be on another journey."

But the next day the old man seemed to have forgotten his purpose. According to his custom before he met with his young friend, he wandered through the streets of Berlin, stopping to listen wherever he heard music. Sometimes he would go into the houses, being seldom prevented; for many remembered the Old Musician, whom they had concluded dead, and were glad to see him once more.

As he wandered one evening through the streets, he stopped in front of a palace brilliantly illuminated, from which came the sound of music. He was about to enter, according to his wont, but the Swiss porter pushed him rudely back; so he stood without and listened, and, in spite of the cutting night wind, continued to stand and listen, murmuring often expressions of pleasure and admiration.

A lacquey in rich livery, running down the steps, encountered the old man, and cried in surprise, "Ha! is that you again, Old Musician? It is long since I have seen you. But why do you stand there shaking in the cold?"

"The Swiss would not let me pass," answered the old man.

"The Swiss is a shallow-pate. Never heed, old friend, but come in with me, and I will bring you a glass of wine to thaw your old limbs. My lord gives a grand concert!" And he led the old man up the steps, saying to the porter, "You must never hinder him from coming in; it is no beggar, but the Old Musician. He comes to hear the music, and my lord has given orders that he shall always be admitted."

The lacquey led the old man to a seat near the fire in the ante-room, and drew a folding screen before him. "Keep yourself quiet, my good friend," he said; "You are out of view here, and yet can hear everything. I will fetch you a glass of wine presently."

The old man sat still and listened to the music in the saloon; it thrilled through his inmost heart. He remained there many hours, till the lacquey, who had frequently visited him in his corner, came and said:

"It is time now to go, my friend; the company are dispersing; I will send my boy home with you."

"That was admirable music!" cried the old man, drawing a deep breath.

"I am glad you were pleased," replied the lacquey. "All you heard to-night was composed by the same master, who is now the guest of my lord."

"Who is he?"

"Master Naumann, chapel-master to the Elector of Saxony."

"A Saxon!" cried the old man. "Naumann! that is well; where is he?"

"Here, in the house."

"Let me speak with him."

"Certainly, if you want to ask anything."

"No, not to ask; I want to thank him."

"Well, you may come to-morrow morning."

"I will come!"

Naumann was not a little surprised when the servant, the next morning, announced his strange visitor. To the question, who was the Old Musician? the man could give no other answer than—"He is the Old Musician, and nobody in Berlin knows his name. He is sometimes half crazy, but is said to have a thorough knowledge of music."

"Let him come in," said Naumann; and the lacquey opened the door for the old man.

Naumann rose when he saw him, for in spite of his mean apparel, he had a dignity of mien that inspired with involuntary respect. Advancing to meet him, he said:

"You are welcome, my good sir, though I know not by what name to address you. But you are a lover of the art, and that is enough. Be seated, I pray you."

The old man, still standing, answered, "I come to thank you, sir chapel-master, for the pleasure of yesterday evening. I was privately a listener to the concert, in which were performed your latest compositions. I will not conceal from you my name; I am Friedemann Bach!"

Naumann stood petrified with astonishment. "Friedemann Bach!" he repeated at length, in a tone of deep and melancholy interest; "the great son of the great Sebastian Bach! It is strange, indeed! Only last year I saw your brother Philip Emanuel at Hamburg. The excellent old man mourns you as dead."

"Let him do so," was the reply, "and all who knew me in better days; for the knowledge of my life, as it is, would make them unhappy. Even in Berlin none know that Friedemann Bach yet lives; not even Mendelssohn, the friend of Lessing, to whom I owed, that while he lived, I needed not to starve."

"What can I do for you?" asked Naumann. "Your brother told me your history. How shall I tell you all the admiration, the affection, the sorrow I have felt, and still feel for you? Tell me, what can I do?"

"Nothing," answered Bach; "you have done everything for me, in showing me what I could and should have done. I strove after that which you have accomplished. You know wherefore I failed, how my life was wasted, why I fell short in all my bold and burning schemes. But you need not the warning of my history. You walk securely and cheerfully in the right path, and I can only thank you for your magnificent works. The blessing of God be with you! and now I feel that I have nothing more to do in this world."

The Old Musician departed, and Naumann, when he had collected his thoughts, inquired in vain where he could be found. Friedemann had not suffered the boy who went home with him the preceding evening to go to his door. At length Naumann happened to meet with Moses Mendelssohn, and mentioned what had occurred. Mendelssohn was amazed to hear that Friedemann Bach was yet living, and in Berlin. The two made an appointment to go the next morning to the ancient abode of Lessing, where the Old Musician had lived.

They went together to the house of Lessing in the Friedrichstadt. The landlady opened the door.

"Does M. Friedemann Bach live here yet?" asked Mendelssohn.

"Ah, pardon me!" cried the woman, wiping her eyes with her apron; "just at this time yesterday they carried away my poor Old Musician! He died exactly three weeks after his young friend the painter, whom he loved so well." Her voice was interrupted by tears.

Mendelssohn and Naumann left the house in silence.

MOZART

FIRST VISIT TO PARIS

One morning, in the month of November, 1763, a middle aged man, with two children, was seen standing at the door of a small hotel in the Rue St. Honoré. When the servant in livery opened the door in answer to his knock, he inquired if M. Grimm lived there, and presented a letter to be given to him. By his dress, he was evidently a stranger, and as his accent proved, a German. Some minutes passed, while the valet went to deliver the letter; he then returned, and ushered the visitors into his master's presence.

Mᶜ Rae, sc.

MOZART.

M. Grimm, the celebrated critic, was reclining in a large arm-chair, close to the fire-place, in a splendid apartment, occupied in reading a new tragedy. He held in his hands the letter he had just received, and glanced over its contents, while the two younger visitors, although uninvited, drew near the fire and spread out their little hands to feel the warmth.

The letter was from one Frederic Boëmer, a fellow-student of M. Grimm at the University of Leipzig, and Secretary to the Prince Archbishop of Saltzburg; less favored however by the gifts of fortune than M. Grimm, who, having come to Paris as the preceptor of the Count von Schomberg's sons, had risen to be the oracle of literature and art. The letter was filled with reminiscences of the past life of the two friends; and only at the close did the writer remember the purpose of his missive. This was to introduce M. Mozart, the sub-director of the chapel of the Archbishop, who found the small salary he received insufficient for the support of his family, and had determined to travel with his children, and endeavor to earn a maintenance by the exhibition of their astonishing musical talents. They were recommended to the attentions of M. Grimm, whose good word could not fail to excite interest in their behalf.

"You are M. Mozart, of Saltzburg, and these are your children?" asked the critic of the stranger, when he had finished reading the letter.

"Yes, Monsieur."

"And you are come to Paris to exhibit these young artists? I fear I cannot promise you the success I could wish, and for which you hope. The French, with all their pretensions to taste in music, commonly judge of it as deaf people would do. They are in love with the screaming of their actors, and fancy the more noise the finer harmony. Your only chance of success here is to pique the public curiosity by proving the remarkably precocious genius of your children; moreover, the people of the court give the tone to the rest of society, and it will be necessary to secure their favor. I may do something for you with those I can influence; I will try what I can do. Let me see you again in a few days."

With this scanty encouragement, the father of Wolfgang Mozart was fain to quit the magnificent dwelling of the correspondent of princes.

Leopold Mozart had some reason, founded on experience, to hope for success in his enterprise. He had been, with his wife and two children, in the principal cities of Germany. At Munich, the first place visited by him, his reception by the Elector was encouraging. At Vienna the children were admitted to play before the Emperor. After their return from this first expedition to Saltzburg, the youthful Wolfgang devoted himself, with more ardor than ever, to his musical studies. It was in the month of July, 1763, that this marvellous child, then eight years old, began his journey to Paris, passing through the cities of Augsburg, Manheim, Frankfort, Coblentz and Brussels, and stopping in all of them to give concerts.

Arrived in Paris, without patrons or friends, and but imperfectly acquainted with the language, the father no longer felt the confidence he had before. His first care was to find out the residence of M. Grimm, and to deliver his letter. The splendor that surrounded that distinguished person, was astonishing to him; and contrasting it with the simple home of the Archbishop's secretary, he did not wonder at finding himself dismissed with a vague promise of protection.

As the little family walked through the streets, they found everything new and wonderful. The beauty of the buildings, the richness of the equipages, the splendor of the shops, delighted the youthful travellers, accustomed to the quiet and plain exterior of the smaller German cities. Now they stopped to admire some extraordinary display of magnificence in the shops; now to hear the singers, or those who performed on musical instruments in the streets.

"Sister," said the little Wolfgang, after they had listened for some time to a man playing the violin in the court of a hotel, "if they have no better music than this in Paris, I shall wish we had stayed in Vienna."

The father smiled on the infant connoisseur, and called their attention to different objects as they walked on. They had now reached the Place Louis XV., between the court and garden of the Tuilleries,—where the new equestrian statue of that monarch, executed by Bouchardon, had just been erected. A great crowd was assembled here. Some one had discovered, affixed to the pedestal of the monument, a placard with the words "*Statua Statuæ*." Very little was necessary, then as now, to bring together a crowd among the population of Paris. Considerable excitement was evinced in the multitude. It was by no means allayed when the police arrested several, whom, from their wild behavior, they judged to be disturbers of the public peace.

Leopold, holding his children by the hand, continued to advance, curious to see the cause of the tumult, yet obliged frequently to draw his little ones close to him, to protect them from the rude jostling of the passers by. Suddenly he felt a hand laid in a kindly manner on his arm.

"My friend," said the person who stopped him, "I perceive you are a stranger here. Let me advise you to go no farther; you may be taken up by the police."

"Can you tell me," asked Leopold Mozart, "the cause of all this confusion?"

"Not a whit; but I can do better—advise you to get off while you may," returned the other. "It would be a pity those pretty children should spend the night in prison! This way—this way!" And giving a hand to the boy, the friendly speaker assisted the Germans to escape from the throng. When they were in safety, he replied to the father's thanks by a courteous adieu, and departed in another direction from that in which they were going.

Our little party lost no time in hastening to the Hotel des Trois Turcs, Rue Saint Martin, where they had fixed their temporary home. It was already past their customary dinner-hour. As they took their places at the table, a servant handed a small package to the elder Mozart. It contained tickets of admission to the opera, sent by M. Grimm. It was the second representation in the new hall of the Tuilleries. The bills promised an entertainment that would be likely to draw a considerable audience.

Here was delight in store for the inexperienced inhabitants of Saltzburg! They talked of nothing else. They dined in haste, and scarce gave themselves time afterwards to make the requisite change in their dress; so great was their impatience and fear of losing, by delay, the smallest portion of their expected enjoyment. They were soon on the way to the theatre, where they arrived full two hours before the commencement of the performance.

By good fortune, while they were looking about in search of some amusement to occupy the time, they lighted upon the gentleman who had warned them to escape from the crowd in the Place of Louis XV. He appeared to have plenty of leisure and joined their party. The singular circumstance that the opera should be performed in the Hall of the Tuilleries, excited the curiosity of Leopold Mozart. His new acquaintance gave him in detail an account of the removal, its consequences, etc., which in brief were somewhat as follows:

A fire broke out in the theatre of the opera, April 6th, 1763, supposed to have originated from the negligence of the workmen employed there. The alarm was not given till too late to save the building, and the flames spread to the buildings of the Palais Royal, the wing of the first court being soon destroyed. No lives were lost, though about two thousand persons were at work in extinguishing the fire. In Paris the people are always disposed to laugh at the most lamentable occurrences, and there was no lack of jokes on this occasion. When the talk was of choosing a location for the new hall, they spoke of the Carousel, the Louvre, and several other places. An abbé, who was well known to hate French music, observed that the opera ought to be located opposite the place where bull-fights were held — "because your great noises should be heard without the city."

The Duc d'Orleans was anxious that the opera should remain in his neighborhood. He requested of the king that the building should be reconstructed on the same spot, offering many facilities, as well as promising to provide all the means that could be devised for the future safety of the edifice. Louis consented, and the work was commenced. Meantime the French comedians generously offered to give up their theatre gratuitously three times a week for the performances of the opera. The locality however was not convenient; and the managers could not agree to the conditions on which the theatre occupied by the *Comédie-Italienne* was offered. One immense hall in the Tuilleries was suitable for the purpose; and the king gave permission that it should be appropriated for the opera. At the first concert, on the 29th of April, a great crowd attended. The female singers were Arnould, Lemiére and Dubois; the chief male performers, Gelin, Larrivé and Magnet. The wags said the concerts were the ointments for the burning. The singers were loudly applauded, and it was observed that the orchestra was fuller and performed better than that of the opera.

While these and other pieces of information were given with true French volubility to M. Mozart, the children listening with great attention, the crowd assembled and before long began to chafe and murmur because the doors were not yet opened. The appointed hour struck from the great clock of the Tuilleries, and the impatient multitude pressed with violence against the barriers erected. Our Germans were beginning to be alarmed for their own safety, when the doors were thrown open, and they were borne with the foremost comers into the theatre. They took seats in the pit; the two rows of boxes being occupied by the aristocratic part of the audience.

The admiration of the youthful Mozart was excited by the proportions and splendor of the hall, the luxury of the decorations, and the magnificence of the ladies in the dress circles. Here were the most gorgeous accompaniments to music. He gazed about him wonder-struck till the overture began.

With more than a father's interest, Leopold watched the countenance of his son. How would a mere child, whose musical taste was not an acquirement, but a gift—an inspiration—judge of what he heard? This orchestra was celebrated throughout Europe, solely on the faith of French judgment. Leopold saw the shade of disappointment on the boy's speaking face.

"Father," whispered he, when there was a pause in the music, "they do better than this in our chapel!"

And so in Leopold's estimation they did; but he dared not to set his own opinion against that of the Parisians; he dared not speak with the boldness of his son.

The overture seemed a long punishment to Wolfgang; at last the curtain rose, amidst an uproar of applause that for some time prevented the actors from being heard. None of the performers were known to the Mozart family. By good luck, however, their acquaintance of the outside obtained a seat near them, and had something to say about every one.

"That is Sophie Arnould," he remarked of one of them; "she is a delicious actress; there is none more exquisite upon the stage."

"And is she the first singer in the opera?" asked Wolfgang, after having heard her grand air.

"Certainly," replied the complaisant cicerone, "you may see that by the applause she calls forth. She plays better than she sings, I confess; her voice has not power enough for the place; but she makes amends for all that by her spirit in acting—by her gestures, and the expression of her eyes, which I defy you to resist. Our young gentlemen are enchanted with her wit; her conversation furnishes the most piquant sauce to their suppers. If in song she only equalled M'lle. Antier, a great actress who retired from the opera twenty years ago! M'lle. Antier was for twenty years the chief ornament of the first theatre in the world. The queen presented her, on her marriage, with a snuff-box of gold, containing the portrait of her majesty; M. and Mme. de Toulouse also made her beautiful presents. She had the honor of filling the first parts in the ballets danced before the king. M'lle. Arnould has not obtained the like favors; but it must be owned that the court is less liberal than formerly. Meanwhile, she is the idol of the public, and her reign promises to be of long duration."

The youthful artist could not echo these praises. He shook his head and remained silent.

"Or do you like better M'lle. Chevalier, the actress now on the stage? Her *fort*, they say, is in the grand, the tragic; you need not say to her with Despreaux—

"To move my tears, your own eyes must be wet."

"I defy you to remain cold while she is declaiming some great scene. But she has not the grace of Sophie Arnould, and there is something of hardness in her tones. Nevertheless, she has her partisans. One of our poets has written some verses to be put at the base of her portrait, to the effect that she bewitches by her voice the hearts that have stood proof against her face."

Neither in this instance could young Mozart share the enthusiasm of his neighbor. He had no experience, but he was endowed with an intuitive and delicate apprehension in music, which taught him that with their great voices these artists of the opera were not great singers. He became restless with his discontent. The performance went on. The male singers, Pillot and Zelin, were below mediocrity.

"We should have M. Chasse in this part," cried the cicerone; "he had a most imposing voice, and noble action; but alas! he retired six years ago! His place has not yet been filled."

The only part of the representation that pleased little Wolfgang, was the dancing. Vestris was not there, but the celebrated Lany performed a *pas de deux* with her brother. This actress had also received the homage of poetry. The last ballet was admirably executed. It restored the good humor of the young critic.

"After all, my father," said Wolfgang, as they returned home, "it was not worth while to come from Vienna to Paris to hear such music." Leopold pressed his boy's hand, as he thought that this fresh impulse of genius made him a better judge than all the educated and schooled connoisseurs of Paris.

Returning to the hotel of the Trois Turcs, they found an invitation from the Baron d'Holback to a soirée the next evening. But this, and how young Mozart played the organ in the royal chapel, and by his performance and his sonatas, gave the first intimation of that wonderful genius that was to work a revolution in music, it belongs not to our present task to describe.

"DON GIOVANNI"

THE ARRIVAL

A light travelling carriage stopped before the hotel of the Three Lions, in Prague. A drove of servants poured out of the house; one opened the carriage door, and assisted an elegant young lady to alight; she sprang out, and was followed by a young man, humming a cheerful tune.

"St. Nepumuck!" cried the host, who had come to the door; "do I see aright? Herr von Mozart?"

"You see, I keep my word!" replied Mozart, saluting him cordially. "Yes! here I am once more, and you may keep me till after harvest; and as a surety for my wise behavior, I have brought my wife along with me."

The host bowed low to the fair lady, and began a set speech with the words—"Most honored Madam von Mozart—"

"Leave your speechifying, man!" cried Mozart, interrupting him, "and show us our quarters; and let us have some refreshments; and send a servant to Guardasoni, to inform him that I am here." He gave his arm to his lady, and stepped into the house, followed with alacrity by the host, and the servants with trunks and band-boxes, which they had unpacked from the carriage. A handsome young man, who just then crossed the market, when he heard from a footman the name of the newly arrived guest, rushed up the steps, and into Mozart's chamber, and threw himself into his arms with an exclamation of joy.

"Ho, ho! my wild fellow!" cried Mozart, "you were near giving me a fright!" and turning to his wife, he presented the young stranger to her. "Well, how do you like him? this is he—Luigi Bassi, I mean."

THE LIBRETTO

"I sing this evening the Count in your Figaro, Master Mozart!" said Bassi.

"Very well!" replied Mozart. "What say your Prague people to the opera?"

"Come to-night to the theatre, and you shall hear for yourself! This is the twelfth representation in sixteen days; and this evening it is performed at the wish of Duke Antony of Saxony."

"Ho, ho! and what says Strobach?"

"He and the whole orchestra say every night after the performance, that they would be glad to begin it over again, though it is a difficult piece."

Mozart rubbed his hands with pleasure, and said to his wife—

"You remember, I told you, the excellent people of Prague would drive out of my head the vexation I endured at Vienna! And I will write them an opera, such as one does not hear every day! I have a capital libretto, Bassi, a bold, wild thing, full of spirit and fire, which Da Ponte composed for me. He says he would have done it for no one else; for none else would have had the courage for it. It was just the thing for me! The music has long run in my head; only I knew not to what I should set it, for no other poem would suit! In Idomeneo and Figaro you find sounds—but not exactly of the right sort; in short—it was with me, as when the spring should and would come—but cannot; on bush and tree hang myriads of buds, but they are closed; then comes the tempest, and the thunder cries, 'burst forth!' and the warm rain streams down, and leaf and blossom burst into sudden and bright luxuriance! The deuce take me, if it was not so in my mind, when

Da Ponte brought me the libretto! You shall take the principal part; and the deuce take you!"

Bassi wanted to know more of the opera; but Mozart assumed an air of mystery, and laughing, put him off, exhorting the impatient to patience.

FIN CHAN DAL VINO

In the evening, when Mozart appeared in the theatre, in the box of Count Thurn, he was greeted by the audience with three rounds of applause; and during the representation this testimony of delight was repeated after every scene. This was the more pleasing to the composer, as his Figaro had been very indifferently received in Vienna. Through the ill offices of Salieri, the piece had been badly cast and worse performed; so that Mozart had sworn an oath never to write another opera for the Viennese.

Loud and prolonged "vivats!" accompanied his carriage to the hotel; there he found his friends—Duscheck, the leader Strobach, and the Impressario of the opera company, Guardasoni, who had ordered a splendid supper; afterwards came Bassi, Bondini with his wife, and the fair and lively Saporitti. Much pleasant discourse about art, and sportive wit enlivened the meal; the gaiety of the company, even when the champagne was uncorked, never once passing, however, the bounds of decorum.

In his festive humor, Mozart was not so reserved to the curiosity of the impetuous Bassi, as he had been in the morning; but was prevailed on to give him a sketch of his part, of which three airs were already finished.

"Very good, Master Amadeus!" said Bassi, "but these airs are, with deference, rather insignificant for me."

"How?" asked Mozart, looking at him with laughing eyes.

"I mean," answered Bassi—"there is too little difficulty in them; they are all too easy!"

"Do you think so?"

"Yes—exactly so—Master? You must write me some very grand, difficult airs, or give me some you have ready! eh? will you do so?"

"No!" replied Mozart with a smile; "no, my good Bassi! that I will not do." Bassi's face visibly lengthened, but Mozart continued good humoredly, "Look you, tesoro! that the airs are not *long*, is true; but they are as long as they should be, and neither more nor less. But as to the great, too great facility, of which you complain, let that pass; I assure you, you will have plenty to do, if you sing them as they should be sung."

"Ha?" mused Bassi.

"For example, sing me this air—'*Fin chan dal vino!*'"

He stepped to the piano; Bassi followed him somewhat unwillingly; and just glancing at the notes, began hurriedly and with not too gentle a touch.

"Gently—gently!" cried Mozart, laughing, and interrupting his playing; "not so *con furio* over hedge and stone! Can you not wait, to keep pace with my music? Where I have written *presto*, must you sing *prestissimo*, and pay no heed at all to *forte* and *piano*? Eh? who sings there? a drunken beast of a landlord, or a merry Spanish cavalier, who thinks more of his gentle love, than of the wine? I pray you—drink a glass of champagne, think of your beloved, and, mark me! when it begins to hum in your ears—in the softest, most ærial tempo, *piano, piano! crescendo forte piano!* till at the last all crashes together in the loud, wild jubilation—that is what I mean."

And Bassi, inspired by the exhortation of the master, sprang up, drank a glass of champagne, snatched a kiss from the lovely cheek of Saporitti, began the air anew, and completed it this time with such effect, that the whole company were electrified and encored the song with shouts of applause.

"Well!" cried Mozart with a smile, after Bassi had three times rehearsed it, "said I not so? does it not go off pleasantly!" Before he could prevent it, Bassi seized his hand, kissed it, and said modestly—

"I will do my best—to have you *satisfied* with me!"

HERR VON NEPUMUCK

At Duscheck's urgent request, Mozart quitted his abode in the city, and removed to Kosohirz to the country-seat of his friend. He came there on a lovely morning in September. Duscheck had quietly arranged a little fête, and the composer was not a little surprised and delighted to find himself welcomed to his new abode by his assembled friends and acquaintances. To crown his joy, Duscheck handed him a written request, signed by many of the most distinguished citizens of Prague, that he would very soon give a concert! For this purpose the theatre was placed freely at his disposal, and Count Johann von Thurn had offered to bear the expenses. Mozart, with a heart full, observed—

"The Viennese did not *this* to me."

"It seems, my friend," said Duscheck, "that your good Viennese, as you always call them, knew not rightly what they had in you, and less what they should do with you! The Emperor left you without a place, and made the sneak, Salieri, master of the musical band; while he well knew who you were and who Salieri was;—and the people of Vienna looked on quietly—O, fie!"

"Nay," replied Mozart to his zealous friend; "think not so ill of him; Joseph has more important affairs than mine to think about; and then, you know, he has counsellors, on whom he depends, and who know how to get the right side of him. As to the Viennese, I always maintain that they are brave fellows. When I came from Salzburg, where my lord the Prince Bishop had treated me like a dog, and the Viennese received me so cordially—I felt as if I had stepped into paradise! For that I shall remember them now and ever! In truth, they are often a little stupid, and always willing to be told that they are magnanimous, and connoisseurs, and the like; yet if one tells them the truth to their face—they will hear, and will applaud him, and grant him all he asks. But that I cannot do; I would rather bear a blow than thrust my praises into any body's face. I have held a wheedler, all my lifelong, for a shabby fellow, and shall I myself become one? Salieri makes nothing of it—but it is not so bad with him, for he is an Italian, and they bepraise each other even to plastering. Bah! let the Viennese prefer him to me! let them stuff him with sweetmeats! Give me a glass of Burgundy!"

Before Duscheck could turn round to hand the glass to his friend, a tall corpulent man, having a red shining visage, with a friendly simper and low obeisance, offered the master a goblet full of the dark sparkling liquor.

Mozart took the cup, and drank a long draught, and repeated the following lines with a comic air of seriousness, looking the colossal Ganymede in the face:

"Johann von Nepomucken

Musst springen von der Prager Brucken,

Weils dem Wenzel nit wollt glucken,

Der Königin Beicht ihm zu entrucken."

"The master recollects me, then?" asked the stout man with sparkling eyes; Mozart replied smiling—

"How could I have forgotten my excellent trumpeter, Nepomuck Stradetzky?"

"Herr *von* Nepomuck!" growled the trumpeter, correctingly; but immediately added in his blandest tone, and with an air of humility—"Pray, pray, Herr von Mozart—*von!*" The master nodded obligingly and reached out his hand to him.

When the company reassembled in the evening, they were unexpectedly entertained with pieces from "The Marriage of Figaro," by a chorus of Prague musicians. Mozart listened well-pleased, and thanked them cordially when they ceased.

"But, if you would do me a very great pleasure, gentlemen," said he, "I beg you to indulge us by playing and singing the fine old song of the Prague Musicians. You know which I mean!"

Highly honored and pleased at this request, the musicians began:—

"The Prague musicians' band,
Wandering in every land,
A welcome still have they!
They wear no clothing rich,
Nor boast of courtly speech,
Yet fiddling,
And blowing,
Still welcome greets their way.

"How youth and maiden round,
When horn and fiddle sound,
Whirl in the dance so light!

To the old toper's eyes
The sparkling goblet flies,
With fiddling,
And blowing,
In beauty doubly bright!

"And when the song is done,
And the dances through are run,
And quiet every guest—
Then sounds the thankful hymn
For joy filled to the brim,
Ascending,
Soft breathing
From every honest breast.

"Then let us onward ever,
Cheerful and gay for ever,

With us St. Nepomuck!
Till with full pockets, we,
And empty flasks—you see,
Still singing,
And blowing,
Stand on the Prager Bruck."

Still playing, the musicians receded, the sound growing softer and fainter every moment; the moon rose above the mountains, the Moldau uttered its low mysterious murmur;—and deeply moved, Mozart rose, wished his friends a heart-felt good night, and betook himself to his chamber, where till near morning he continued playing on the piano.

THE DISTRIBUTION

Mozart gave his concert, and reaped therefrom not only rich store of applause, but no contemptible gain. As Duscheck wished him happiness with the latter, and added—

"I know indeed, that you write more for the sake of fame than of gold—particularly in Vienna—"

"For what should I write?" muttered the master; "for fame? for gold? Certainly not! for generally I fail to get either. I write for love of *Art*—I would have you know!"

Meanwhile Mozart had worked assiduously at his Don Giovanni; and on the fourth of October, 1787, showed it to the Impressario complete, except the Overture, and a few breaks in the instrumentation.

Guardasoni was greatly rejoiced—and immediately counted out to the master the stipulated ducats;—but when Mozart began to speak of the distribution of the parts, the poor Impressario confessed with grief, that he had for the last month anticipated trouble in this business; for that there was always a ferment among the singers, male and female—every she and every he laying claim to a principal part.

"My people, I thank fortune," he concluded, "are none of the worst, and Bassi is good nature itself; but in certain points they can manage to give a poor Impressario enough to do; and in particular, the fair Saporitti and the little Bondini are possessed with a spirit of tormenting, when they are in their odd humors."

"Take care only, not to let them perceive your apprehension," said Mozart; "they are friendly to me, that I know, and you shall soon see how I will bring them all under my thumb."

"Between you and me," observed Guardasoni with a sly smile, "I expect the greatest condescension from Saporitti; for, proud as she is, she is not only friendly to you, but, I imagine, something more than friendly!"

"Eh! that may be!' cried the master, rubbing his hands with delight; for much as he honored and loved his wife, he did not disdain a little flirtation now and then. Guardasoni continued innocently—

"As I tell you—for she said to me the other day—"I could fall in love with the Signor Amadeo, for he is a great man, and I should not mind his insignificant figure."

"The master was crest-fallen! It was not a little mortifying to hear that the fair Saporitti had made mention of his small and insignificant figure, especially to such a tall man as Guardasoni. He colored, but merely said with nonchalance—

"Call them together for me, Signor Guardasoni, and I will read them the text they are to sing."

Guardasoni went away, and the next day assembled all the singers in the green-room of the theatre. Mozart came in, dressed in rich sables, a martial hat adorned with gold lace on his head, the director's staff in his hand. He ascended a platform, and began his address at first in a formal and earnest manner; but gradually sliding off into a good humored, sportive tone, for he never could belie his harmless character.

MOZART'S SPEECH

"Honored ladies and gentlemen—

"It is known to you that long ago I received from your Impressario, Signor Guardasoni, the flattering commission, to compose an opera for *his* company. I undertook it the more gladly, as I have the pleasure of knowing you all, and therefore the certainty of laboring for true artists.

"My work is finished; 'Don Giovanni, *ossia il dissoluto punito*.' I can assure you, I have honestly endeavored to study carefully the peculiar character of each of the honored members of Guardasoni's present company, and have had particular regard to this in every part in my opera.

"I have thus succeeded in composing a work, which forms not only of itself a harmonious whole, but in each separate part promises the artists for whom it was intended, the fairest success. An opera, which I believe will please even in future times; which will be perhaps pronounced my best work, as I myself esteem it such. But one thing I know; that a representation so perfect as I hope for it through you, is not to be procured hereafter.

"Where could we find a Don Giovanni, like my young friend Luigi Bassi? his noble figure, his wonderful voice, his manner, his wit, his unstudied fire, when he bends in homage to beauty,—qualify him eminently for the hero of my opera. Of the profligate he can assume just so much as is necessary; for my hero is no rude butcher, nor a common mischievous villain, but a hot-headed, passionate youth.

"Could I point out for him a more perfect Donna Anna, than the beautiful, stately, virtuous Saporitti? All conflicting feelings of love, hate, sympathy, revenge, she will depict, in song and in action—as I conceived them when I composed the work.

"And who could represent the faithful, delicate, resentful, yet ever forgiving and loving Elvira, more consummately than the charming, gentle, pensive Catarina Micelli? She is Don Giovanni's warning angel, forsaking him only in the last moment. Ah! such an angel should convert *me*, for I also am a great sinner, *spite of my insignificant figure*! And now for the little, impatient, mischievous, inexperienced and curious Zerlina.

"*O, la ci darem la mano, Signorella Bondini!* sweet little one! you are too tempting! and if my stanzerl were to sing her "vedrai carino" to me, like *you*, by Jupiter! it were all over with me!"

"That the good Felice Ponziani is satisfied with his Leporello, and the excellent primo tenoro, Antonio Baglioni, with his Don Ottavio, rejoices my very heart. Signor Guiseppo Lolli has, out of friendship for me, undertaken the part of Massetto, besides that of the Comthur, because he would have all the parts *well* performed. I have already thanked him for his kind attention, and thank him now again.

> "And thus I close my speech so meet;
> With joy the evening will I greet,
> When my beloved opera
> Through you appears in gloria!
> If author and singers are agreed,
> Of toil for the rest there is no need!
> And you shall see with what delight
> I will direct and set you right;
> I will pay diligent heed to all,
> That neither in time nor touch you fall.
> Let every one but do his best—
> We of success assured may rest;

So tells you from his candid heart

Wolfgang Amadeus Mozart."

The master ended his speech; his audience clapped approbation, and they separated in good humor and mutual satisfaction.

THE REHEARSAL

On the twenty-eighth day of October, Don Giovanni being complete except the overture, the rehearsals began. On the morning of the first rehearsal, before Mozart went to the opera-house, he walked for recreation in the public garden. Before him he saw the well known figure of the trumpeter, Nepomuck Stradetzky, absorbed, as it seemed, in meditation. Mozart walked faster, overtook him and tapped him gently on the shoulder. Nepomuck turned quickly, growling out—

"Ha, what do you want?" but bowed almost to the ground as he recognised the master, and said: "Ah! I beg a thousand pardons, worthy Herr von Mozart! I was deep in revery, and thought it some knave who wanted to play a trick upon me! I beg your pardon—"

"For what?" replied Mozart. "Nobody is pleased at being disturbed in a revery—not I, at least! But what were you thinking about, Herr von Stradetzky?"

Nepomuck answered with a clear brow, "Ay, of what but your opera, most excellent Herr von Mozart? Is not all Prague full of expectation of the miracle that is to appear? Wherever I go, I am asked, "Herr von Nepomuck, when is the first representation? You play the tenor-trumpet, eh, Herr von Nepomuck?"

"No." I answer, "the bass-trumpet!"

"So, so!" they say—"the bass-trumpet, eh, Herr von Nepomuck?"

"Have you tried your notes through, Herr von Nepomuck?"

"Yes, indeed! Herr von Mozart! and I am delighted with the long full tones; but in the two choruses are a few hard notes."

"Pah! you will get through with them, Herr von Nepomuck!"

"I hope so, Herr von Mozart, and will do my best."

They walked a little longer, chatting, in the shaded avenue, and then betook themselves to the theatre.

The rehearsal began; Mozart was everywhere! now in the orchestra, now on the stage, directing or improving the scenic arrangements. In the ball scene of the first act, where Bassi did not dance to please him, he himself joined the circle and danced a minuet with Zerlina with so much grace, that he did all credit to his master Noverre. So by a bold stroke he amended the shriek of Zerlina, which after repeated 'Da capos' did not suit him; creeping behind her at the moment she was about to repeat the cry for the fourth time, he suddenly seized her with such violence that, really frightened, she screamed in good earnest; whereupon he cried laughing, "bravo! that is what I want! you must shriek in that way at the representation."

The good-humored little Bondini forgave him her fright; but an instruction in the second act was not so well received. Here, in the church-yard scene, to strengthen the effect of both adagios, which the statue has to sing, he had placed the three trumpeters behind the monument. In the second adagio the trumpeters blew wrong; Mozart cried, "Da capo!" it was repeated and this time the bass only failed. The master went to the desk, and patiently showed Nepomuck how he wanted the notes played; but even after the third repetition Nepomuck made the same blunder.

"What the mischief, Stradetzky!" cried Mozart, with vexation, and stamping his foot; "you must play correctly!"

Nepomuck, offended, grumbled out, "Herr von Stradetzky is my name, and I play what is possible to play with the trumpet! what you have written *there*, the devil himself could not play."

"No, indeed!" said Mozart gently; "if what I have written suits not the instrument, I must by all means alter it!" He immediately made the alteration and added to the original instrumentation both bassoons as well as two double basses. Finally, he let the chorus of Furies sing *under* the scene, and would not permit visible demons to drag Don Giovanni into the abyss.

With this the rehearsal ended. Mozart, on the whole, was satisfied with the singers and the orchestra; and the performers promised themselves the most brilliant success. As the master went home from the theatre, Nepomuck Stradetzky came behind him, took hold of the skirt of his coat, and said earnestly—

"Do not be angry with me, Herr von Mozart, because I have been a little bearish! That is often my way, and you know I mean well!"

Mozart replied cordially, "Nay, Herr von Nepomuck, I ought to be grateful to you, for having pointed out to me the error in my notes for the trumpet. Nevertheless, it is true, faults may be pointed out in a pleasant manner! Well, in future we will observe more courtesy!"

Nepomuck promised, and they parted in friendship.

THE OVERTURE

The lovely Saporitti endeavored sedulously to efface from the memory of the little Master Amadeo, the unintentional offence her remark had given him. Mozart speedily forgave and forgot it, and was unwearied in giving her assistance in the study of her part, not hesitating to find fault where it was necessary, but likewise liberally bestowing encouraging praise.

The Signora one morning took occasion to praise the serenade of Don Giovanni, as peculiarly happy, and commended its bland southern coloring; observing that *such* soft persuasive love tones were foreign to the rude northern speech. Mozart replied with a smile—

"We Germans speak out indeed more honestly; yet it often-times sounds not ill!" And the evening of the same day, the master sang a serenade, charming indeed, but quite in the taste of the bagpipe-playing Prague musicians, under the window of the Signora Saporitti.

Meantime the day appointed for the first representation of 'Don Giovanni,' the third of November, was just at hand, and Mozart had never yet written the overture! Guardasoni urged—the master's friends were anxious—Mozart only laughed, and said, "I will write it this afternoon." But he did not write it; he went on an excursion of pleasure with his wife. Guardasoni was now really in despair.

"You see, it never will do!" he cried repeatedly, and sent messengers in every direction in vain; Mozart was no where to be found; and Strobach was obliged to promise that in case of extreme necessity he would adopt the overture to Idomeneo.

It was midnight when Mozart's carriage stopped before his dwelling; and his friends, Guardasoni at their head, immediately surrounded him with complaints and reproaches. The master sprung out of his carriage, crying—

"Leave me to myself; now I will go to work in good earnest!" He went into the house, shut the door behind him, threw himself on his seat at the writing table, and began to write. In a few minutes, however, he started up, and cried laughing to his wife—"It will not come right yet! I will go to bed for an hour; wake me up at that time, and make me some punch!" And without undressing he flung himself on the bed. Constance prepared the punch, and in an hour's time went to awaken her husband; but Mozart slept so sweetly, she could not find it in her heart to disturb him. She let him lie another hour; then, as time pressed, she awakened him.

Mozart rubbed his eyes, collected his thoughts, shook himself, and without further ado began his work. Constance sat by him, gave him the punch, and to keep him in good spirits, began to tell him all manner of funny and horrible stories—of the Prince-fish, of Blue Beard, of the Princess with swine's snout, etc., etc. till Mozart, still writing, laughed till the tears ran down his cheeks. At two o'clock in the morning he began his wonderful work; at six it lay on the desk finished. The master started up; he could hardly stand upright. "Done for this time!" he muttered; "but I shall not soon try it again!" And he laid himself down again to sleep.

At seven the copyist came for the notes, in the utmost hurry to write them out, which he could not accomplish before half-past seven in the evening; so that the performance, instead of commencing at seven was postponed to eight o'clock. Still wet, and covered with sand, the hastily copied parts were brought in and arranged in the orchestra.

The strange story of the composition of the overture soon spread among the audience. When Mozart came into the orchestra, he was greeted with thundering 'Bravos!' from an overflowing house. He bowed low, and turning to the performers in the orchestra, said—

"Gentlemen, we have not been able to have a rehearsal of the overture; but I know what I can venture with you. So, quick! to work!" He took up the time-staff, gave the signal, and like a thunder burst, with the clang of trumpets, sounded the first accord of the awful andante; which, as well as the succeeding allegro, was executed by the orchestra with admirable spirit. When the overture was at an end, the storm of applause seemed as if it would never cease.

"There were indeed a few notes dropped under the desk," observed Mozart, smiling, to Strobach during the introduction; "but on the whole it went off splendidly! I am greatly indebted to these gentlemen."

How during the remainder of the opera the applause rose from scene to scene—how from its first representation to the present day, on every occasion, the *'Fin chan dal vino,'* called and still calls forth enthusiastic encores, is well known, not only to the brave people of Prague, but to the whole civilized world.

This little circle of scenes may prove a pleasant memorial of the first production of a noble work, destined through all future time to command the admiration of feeling hearts.

LAST VISIT TO DOLES

It was a holiday in the year 1789; and the venerable cantor of Saint Thomas' church, Leipzig, after morning service was over, made ready to take a walk about the city, in company with a few of his friends.

The month was May, and the morning was lovely; the old gentleman had smoothed the immaculate ruffles of his shirt-bosom, placed his three-cornered hat on his head a little over the left ear, and taken his Spanish gold-headed walking stick in his hand, ready for his promenade—when a sudden idea darted into his head. The music he had partly composed early that morning, while engaged about the church-service, and which he had thought would turn out nobly, came to him all at once; and fearful of losing it, he turned immediately back, with his customary ejaculation, "To Him alone be the glory!" and entered his own house, where were already arrived his faithful wife and his beloved daughter, Lena.

The good dame asked with some anxiety, wherefore he had returned so soon; and Lena looked as if she feared she would next have to run for the doctor. But Father Doles, (it was no less a person,) soon dissipated their fears by informing them that nothing but a new musical thought had brought him back. The women laughed at this; Lena took his hat and stick, and while her mother helped him to pull off his brown over-coat, and to put on his flowered silk dressing-gown, not forgetting the little black silk cap, she arranged the writing-table, and placed on it some fresh paper for his notes. Next she brought him a bowl of soup, with a bottle of old Rhenish wine, a cask of which had been given her father by the gracious Elector, in token of approbation of his services.

When all was ready, Father Doles embraced his wife, kissed the white forehead of his daughter, and they both left him to his labors. He sat down and commenced his work, not without an inward prayer for success, as was his pious custom.

He had not been writing very long, when the door was opened more hastily than usual, without much ceremony. A tall, stately man strode in, and across the room to where Doles was quietly sitting. It was Jacobus Freigang, a merchant and highly respected magistrate. He came near the table, and struck the floor hard with his cane. Doles looked up from his work, nodded with a cordial smile, and said, reaching his hand to his friend, "Salve!"

His friend did not take his offered hand, but cried rather angrily—"Tell me, I entreat you, are you going to behave like a vain fellow in your old days, and treat your friends as if they were not deserving of civility? There we all are—Weisse, Hiller, and I, and Friedrich, and another person; there we all are, waiting and waiting for you, and running to the door to see if you were coming, and thinking how we should enjoy your surprise at sight of our newly arrived guest. At last, Breitkopf comes to ask after you, and you are not come—though you promised me in the choir you would speedily join us! The company are impatient; Hiller grows surly; I stand there like a fool; at last Friedrich says you must have gone home—so here I come and find you sitting quietly at work! In the name of decency! what are we to make of you?"

Doles laughed heartily at his friend's comical anger, and then good-naturedly apologised for his neglect. "Do not be angry with me, old friend; I had to write down my thema! Bethink you, I am seventy-two, and any day may be my last. I must use what time I have, and when Heaven sends me a good musical idea, make haste and write down what my old head cannot long retain. Now I have just finished my thema, and if you wish it, I will go with you; though, after all, I am but dull company for younger ones, and they must have dined already."

"You must not dine at home to-day!" cried his visitor, "our friends are waiting—you must go to Breitkopf's this moment."

"Nay, Freigang, now I think of it, 'tis a holiday—and my wife and daughter must not sit down alone to table."

"They know you are going with me; and as for leaving them alone, I have sent Friedrich to them. He will eat enough for two! So, off with your dressing-gown, and on with your coat."

"But—"

"But me no buts! I will fetch you a valet who will make you bestir yourself!" so saying, Freigang stepped to the door, opened it, and cried—"Come in!"

A young man, small of stature, and elegantly dressed, of pale complexion, large, dark, flashing eyes, a handsome, aquiline nose, and a mouth that seemed made for music, entered quickly. The voice in which he gave cheerful greeting to Father Doles, as he sprang to his side, was music itself.

Doles started from his seat with an exclamation of joy: his grey eyes sparkled, his cheeks flushed, and as he embraced the young man, tears of delight rolled down them.

"My Wolfgang!" he cried, "my dear, good son! I am rejoiced to see you once more!"

Freigang laughed, as much as to say, "See, my point is gained now!"

Lena and her mother came in at that moment, and ran to welcome the stranger. As soon as her father had released him, the lively girl clapped her hands over his eyes, standing behind him, and cried—

"Who is this, Wolfgang—can you tell?"

"A lovely, mischievous little girl!" answered Mozart, laughing, "who calls herself Lena, and shall give me a kiss!" and turning round, he caught her in his arms, and took his revenge.

"Is your wife with you this time?" asked Madame Doles.

"No, I have not brought her with me," answered Mozart, while he assisted Doles to arrange his dress. "She is not fully recovered from her last winter's illness. Ah! how often she wishes for you, good mother; you would hardly believe we could feel so lonely and desolate in so large a city as Vienna!"

"Why do you not come and live here?" asked Lena impatiently, "where we all love you so much. We would never let you feel lonely or desolate. Your wife should like us all, and I would keep your boys with me. Be advised, Mozart, and come to live in Leipzig."

"You are always *couleur de rose*, Lena," said the composer, laughing; "but I should find it harder to get away than you imagine. In the first place I could not leave my Emperor, and in the next, as far as art is concerned, one can do in Vienna as he cannot well elsewhere."

"Hem," muttered Freigang, "we are not badly off as to music, here."

"By no means," said Mozart, earnestly, "and most excellent music. Your church music and your concerts are unrivalled—may I never live to see the day when they shall be talked of as a thing that is past! But you know, father," he turned to Doles, "while your artists and connoisseurs stand among the first, as regards the public and the popular taste, you cannot compete even with the Viennese, much less with mine excellent friends of Prague and Munich. I hope and trust these matters will change for the better in time; just at present, I at least find it my interest to prefer Vienna, Munich, or Prague."

"It is as you say, dear Wolfgang," replied Doles; "they call our Leipzig a little Paris; but we must plead guilty to some northern coldness and caution, and this excessive prudence it is which hinders us from following immediately in the new path you have opened for us."

"And yet I have reason to quarrel with the Viennese," interrupted Mozart. "My Giovanni can testify to that."

"Shall I confess to you," said Doles, "that as much as I have heard of this opera, though it surprises, astonishes, charms me, it does not, to say the truth, quite *satisfy* me?"

The composer smiled; his old friend began to criticise, when he interrupted him—

"Why have you heard the opera *piecemeal* in this way? After Idomeneo, Don Giovanni is my favorite—I might say my masterpiece! But you must not hear it piecemeal; you cannot judge of it except as a whole."

"For my part, I am delighted with your Figaro," said Lena; "it is sung and played everywhere here; you may hear it in the streets on every barrel organ. I sing it myself on the piano;" and therewith she began carelessly to sing—

"And my glass still flattering, tells me

That I am not such a fright!"

"Lena! Lena!" said her mother, shaking her head. But Mozart cried— "Bravo! go on, little one!" and going to the piano, he began to play. They went through the duet, and at the end Freigang applauded heartily. Then he took Father Doles under one arm, and the composer, still humming, under the other, and bidding the ladies a friendly "Adieu!" departed.

"What a charming man is Mozart!" exclaimed Lena, and still singing her favorite tune, accompanied her mother to the dining room, where they found Friedrich just arrived.

After a social dinner at the house of the hospitable Breitkopf, Mozart's publisher, the friends adjourned to the celebrated Rosenthal, where Goëthe, as a student, used to amuse himself. The pretty Swiss cottage was not then built; but on the place where it now stands, was pitched, in the summer months, a tent or pavillion, spacious enough to accommodate a large party of ladies and gentlemen in case of a sudden shower, or when they sought refreshment from the heat.

Madame Doles and Lena, Madame Freigang and her daughter Cecilia, went early to Rosenthal, accompanied by Friedrich, and prepared for the arrival of the gentlemen. It was a pleasant little party; the guests were all in high spirits; even the stern Hiller, who sometimes appeared something of the cynic, was heard to burst into frequent laughter at Mozart's sallies of humor and impromptu verses. Friedrich, a lad of about eighteen, the favorite pupil of Doles, stood near the composer, and listened smiling, though now and then he looked grave when Mozart's gayety seemed about to overstep the bounds of decorum.

In the midst of their talk Hiller became suddenly serious, then turned about quickly, as if he had a mind to go back, before they entered the tent. Freigang caught his arm, and cried—

"What is the matter with you, Hiller? Right about, you do not part from us till after sunset."

"Let me alone!" answered the stern old man. "I cannot bear to look at the good-for-nothing fellow!"

"At whom?" Freigang followed the direction of his friend's finger, and burst out a laughing. "Ha! Mozart!" he cried, "look yonder; there comes Hiller's favorite!"

A man was coming towards the company; he approached with very unsteady steps, but did not perceive them till he stood directly before them. He seemed about thirty years of age, perhaps older; was slender and well formed, but his features were sharpened and pallid, and his whole person bore the marks of excessive dissipation. His oiled-cloth cap was placed sideways on his uncombed head; his coat had once been a fine one, but lacked much of the lace belonging to it, and several buttons here and there; his satin vest was frayed and torn; his rumpled collar, (the cravat was entirely wanting,) as well as the rest of his attire, bespoke a slovenly disregard to comfort or cleanliness.

"Bon jour, monsieur?" cried Freigang, as this disgusting object came near.

The man stood still, rolled up his meaningless eyes, contracted his brows, and at length shading off the sun with his hand, looked inquisitively at the speaker. After a few moments he recognized him, and with a low, ceremonious bow, from which he found it difficult to recover himself—"Most worthy sir!" he said, "at your service—I am your humble—servant!"

"You seem to be in deep thought," observed Freigang, laughing.

"He is drunk, the wretched dog!" muttered Hiller, greatly disgusted.

"If I am not mistaken," stammered the man, "I have the honor—to salute—the most excellent Director of music—Monsieur Hiller—yes—I am right—it is he! I am happy—to speak with your excellency! I am highly pleased at the—unexpected—pleasure of this meeting!"

"I am *not*," retorted Hiller, angrily; "I would have walked a mile out of the way to avoid it. I do not feel honored at being in such company."

"Nay, Hiller," remonstrated Mozart.

"Let the excellent Director scold as much as he likes," said the stranger, indifferently, and speaking more fluently than at first; "what is in the heart, must come out of the lips; and after all, I must allow, Monsieur Hiller has indeed some little cause to be vexed with me! You must all know I ran away with his foster-daughter! I am the famous violoncellist, Mara, the husband of the famous singer—"

"Is it possible?" cried Mozart, astonished and grieved; "can this be Mara?"

"At your service, most worthy master—eh? what is the little man called?" said he, addressing Doles.

Doles answered—"It is the chapel-master, Mozart, from Vienna."

Mara lifted up both hands in amazement. "The little"—he cried, "the *great* Mozart—who has composed such splendid quartettos! who has composed Don Giovanni, and I know not what!"

"The same!" answered Weisse; and Freigang advised Mara to look at him straight, for he was worth taking some pains to see.

Mara seemed overpowered with his respect; he took off his soiled hat, and making a low bow, said to Mozart, "I have the honor to be—your—servant! You see me to-day for the first time *en canaille*; I need not apologise to you, for you know how apt good resolutions are to melt away in a bowl of liquor!" The composer colored slightly. "Another time," continued the tippler, "you shall see me with my best face, and hear how I can handle my instrument; till then, I have the honor to commend myself to your friendly remembrance!" He went on past the company, but on a second thought turned back for an instant and addressed Hiller. "Before we part, most worshipful music-director—I know you have had much uneasiness on the score of Gertrude; her running away from you was to be excused, as you were only her foster-father! but you would be quite shocked to learn in what a manner she has behaved to me, as Madame Mara, and what I have had to bear on her account! I wish not to insinuate that she has not her good qualities or is altogether an ill-disposed person—*au contraire!* She paid my debts once in Berlin, but what did that help me? did not the great Frederick—may he rest in peace—keep me a quarter of a year among his soldiers, and had not the brutal corporal the impudence to beat me! Sir, I assure you, such treatment soured my feelings, and to this day, when I am playing, I often think of my wife and the King, and the corporal with his heavy cane! Excuse me then, sir, for if I do take a drop too much now and then, 'tis to drown my sorrows at Gertrude's scandalous behavior! Let us part good friends, old gentleman; mind not trifles. I shall be happy to see you at any time at my house in Windmill Street, No. 857. I am sober every day, till eight o'clock; come and see me, and if you like a dance I will play for you; my violincello is a capital old instrument, a veritable Cremonese, full toned and strong. Your servant, sir." Therewith the drunken musician walked on, leaving Hiller undecided whether to laugh or be angry.

The company sat down to a collation under the tent. Mozart was astonished to find Cecilia grown so much. The last time he had seen her was at Berlin, five years before. She was then a pretty child, but now a very beautiful girl. It is not for words to paint that fresh, innocent beauty, the pledge of an unsullied soul. She had grown a woman, and her manner was changed from girlish vivacity and frankness, to womanly dignity and reserve. Mozart did not, however, like her dropping the familiar "*Du*," (Thou,) and "Wolfgang!" in conversation with him.

"Why do you not still call me Wolfgang?" asked he. "Lena, calls me so, and is she not of the same age with yourself?"

But Cecilia said "Mozart," so prettily, it sounded like music from her lips. The composer soon learned to reverence her as the gifted and cultivated woman, as well as to admire her as the lovely girl. Nor had he reason to complain of coldness or constraint when once she became interested in the conversation. The hours flew swiftly to that social party of friends, and twilight came too soon upon them.

As they went forth, Cecilia took Lena's arm and whispered—

"How charming he is, Lena! do you not love him?"

"Ah, Cecilia!" answered her friend, gravely, and shaking her head, "take care you do not love him too much—you know he is sometimes fond of playing the flirt."

Cecilia blushed, and smiled incredulously, but said nothing. The gentlemen accompanied the ladies to the house of Doles, and then went to supper at Breitkopf's.

The next day Mozart was showing his friends an autograph letter of King Frederick William II., of Prussia, and a royal present of a gold watch, set round with rich jewels. The composer, on his last visit to Berlin, had played in the King's presence, and this had been sent as a token of approbation. Lena clapped her hands with delight at seeing it, and called her mother to admire its magnificence, and Doles expressed equal wonder at its splendor, and the liberality of the King.

"Are you pleased with it, father?" cried Mozart, "well, I will make it a present to you," and would have pressed the watch upon him, but Doles firmly refused, saying it was not treating the King with proper respect to give away his gift. Mozart was really vexed that he should decline it, and would not take back the watch without a grave reproof from Madame Doles. A year after, the same watch was stolen from him by a dissolute musician, Stadeler by name, whom he had permitted to lodge in his house several months, furnished him with supplies, and even composed for him a clarionet concert.

After this little matter was adjusted, and the usual skirmish between the composer and Lena at an end, he and Doles accompanied by Friedrich went to the rehearsal of his concert.

Many persons are living in Leipzig who are so happy as to remember having listened to that last concert of Mozart. I have seen their eyes sparkle, and their cheeks glow, in speaking of it. It recalled to their bosoms the enthusiasm of youth.

Mozart was not wholly satisfied with the musicians, and he drilled them thoroughly. Once he stamped on the floor so emphatically, that he shattered a costly shoe-buckle. The performers were vexed, and played prestissimo; he cried "Bravo!" and said to an old friend, when he saw him shaking his head—"Nay, nay, do not disturb yourself about my strange behavior this morning. These people are old and slow: their work to-night will be a drag, unless I put some fire into them by scolding them out of patience. I think now all will go off admirably."

And all did go off admirably that night. The boundless applause of the audience, and Mozart's cheerful commendations and thanks, put the orchestra once more in high good humor.

Cecilia, who had already much reputation as a singer, sang two airs from Idomeneo. Mozart was delighted with her. The true feeling of her singing showed that she was possessed of genius, that rare and precious gift of heaven; thus he whispered to her father while she was singing, and at the end conducted her from the stage himself. Cecilia thought the master's approval worth more than the noisy applause of the audience, and went home proud and happy.

Some of the wealthy connoisseurs had ordered a splendid supper to be prepared at the principal hotel, in honor of the distinguished composer. When the concert was over, they carried him off in triumph. Freigang was of the party. Doles relished not scenes of mirth, and went home with his wife and daughter, and Cecilia.

The ladies could not give up talking of the pleasures of the evening, till a late hour; and just as Cecilia was taking leave of her friends, a servant came from the hotel with a message to Father Doles that the chapel-master begged they would not wait up for him, as he should not return home that night. The messenger added, by way of comment—

"They are very merry yonder; I do not think for a year past we have opened so many bottles of champagne as for the party to-night—"

"Very well!" said Doles, interrupting him, and dismissed the servant.

"I am sorry for Mozart, indeed," whispered Cecilia, as she bade Lena good night.

"Never mind," returned that lively girl, "be quiet about it, and I will read him a lesson to-morrow, the like of which he has not heard for a long time."

The next morning Mozart made his appearance at breakfast, pale and haggard-looking; confused in his discourse and looking much ashamed. Neither Doles nor his wife made any allusion to his dissipation of the preceding night, and Lena did not venture to show her displeasure in the presence of her parents. Yet Mozart felt that things were not exactly as they should be, and all frankness and openness as he was, he could not long disguise his real feelings. He began to lament what had passed, half in jest and half in earnest; "It had been," he said, "too wild a night for him, and to say truth, he would have much preferred a quiet evening after the concert," adding, "but you know, once is not always."

"True, my dear son," replied Father Doles, with a smile, "and if you really enjoyed yourself, the gayety of last night could do you no harm. Only, I beg of you in future, to leave off in time, and carry nothing to excess! Your health is feeble, and will not bear much: take good care of it, for the powers of body and mind are but too easily exhausted. Remember poor Mara!"

Mozart looked very grave, and said, somewhat sadly, "Ah! there are the ruins of a noble creature! Let me die, rather than fall thus! No, I shall remember last night—the mischief take *such* hospitality!"

"Why, what happened?" asked Doles, anxiously.

"You know, father, the invitation was given by the friends of *art*," said Mozart, with an emphasis of some bitterness; "I accepted it as such; the concert elevated my spirits, and I went with them. All was well at first—we were a set of rational men, met together in the spirit of social enjoyment. When the toasts were going round, one of the company went out and returned with Mara, already half drunk, and set him up to make sport for the rest. The poor wretch made me a very ridiculous speech, and when he was animated by a few more glasses of champagne, they brought him a violincello, and invited him to play. I wished for some cotton in my ears, for I thought nothing else but that I was to suffer torture; but it was far otherwise; indeed I cannot describe to you my sensations, when he began to play—I never heard the like before. It was music to stir the inmost soul. I could not refrain from tears through the adagio, and thought of the witch-music Tartini heard in his dreams—so moving, so entrancing! At the wild concluding allegro, I could have embraced the performer. I did not attempt to conceal what I felt." The composer stopped suddenly, as if even the recollection moved him.

"Well, and what then?" asked Doles, at length.

Mozart bit his lips. "Mara then played the variations in my duet from Don Giovanni—'La ci darem la mano!' I assure you, even had I not heard his previous splendid performance, these variations, played in such a manner as showed the most thorough appreciation of the whole work, would have convinced me of his being a perfect master of his art, and of his instrument, and led me to reverence him as such. But how did the friends of art take it?" here Mozart sprang up highly excited, his eyes flashing fire, though his face was paler than ever, "how did they applaud his playing? with huzzas and toasts! and when he ceased, they plied him with more and more wine, till he was beastly drunk and beside himself, and then they set him upon all sorts of foolery, and made him imitate on his instrument, from which he had just drawn such matchless tones, the mewing of cats, the braying of an ass, the crowing of a cock, and the like, and they laughed to see him degrade himself. Oh, shame! shame! And they laughed the more when Mara, unable to stand any longer on his feet, fell on the floor—and then I, like the rest, drank till I was reeling," concluded he, with a bitter expression of self-contempt.

"Do you not think, my dear son," asked Doles, mildly, after a pause, "that the time will come when the true artist's worth will be estimated properly, and he assume the dignity he deserves?"

"It is possible," answered Mozart, gloomily, "but the artist will never live to feel it."

"You certainly do, Wolfgang?"

The composer shook his head with a melancholy smile—"You are mistaken, my dear friend, I do *not*. But I am satisfied that some few appreciate and are faithful to me, and I can depend upon them; you for example, father, and my fair friends here!"

Lena wiped her eyes, and said—"Nay, Mozart, you should not talk so, as if you had but few friends."

Here Friedrich joined them.

"Here comes another," said the master, smiling, "one who understands me also. May you ever have the consolation of real friends, my good lad, and keep your spirit free and uncontaminated! Aim at that above all things, and do not forget *me*, Friedrich, when I am—gone!"

"Never, never!" cried the youth, clasping the master's hand and pressing it to his heart. They then bade the ladies good morning, and went out for a walk.

Lena forgave her friend from her heart, and resolved to spare him the lesson she had intended to inflict on him.

"I leave it all to you. Do what I told you and be silent," said Mozart, in the street, to the lad Friedrich, giving him at the same time a well-filled purse.

Friedrich took the purse, promised secrecy, and hastened to the dwelling of the unhappy Mara. Mozart went on to pay a visit at the house of his friend, Freigang.

"My father is asleep yet," said Cecilia, as she came into the parlor to meet him. "If you will wait a few moments, I will awaken him."

"By no means!" said Mozart, detaining her; "Let your father sleep on. I will pay my visit to you, with your permission. I wish to thank you for your admirable singing last evening. Indeed, Cecilia, I was delighted with the simplicity and taste of your performance. I detest the airs and graces so many young women of the present day introduce into their songs. I have been so disgusted in Vienna, that I would not hear the singers again in my pieces."

"How were you amused, last night, after the concert?" asked the young lady.

"Very badly."

"How was that?"

Here Mozart told her what he had related to Doles. Cecilia colored, and he saw tears in her eyes as he concluded.

"How cruel," she said, with noble indignation, "thus to take advantage of the weakness, say the vices of a man in whose breast, notwithstanding all his faults, the fire of genius is still inextinguishable."

"Cruel indeed!" echoed Mozart.

"But you must not fancy all the world selfish and regardless of the artist's high claims, because some are so, who indeed are incapable of appreciating what they pretend to admire. Shun such men, dear Mozart— shun them utterly! there is no safety in their companionship."

"You mean to warn me?" asked the composer.

"I only entreat you," said Cecilia, earnestly; "such associations can never profit, but must disturb you. What need have I to say anything? Have not you yourself learned by experience how hard it is to help being drawn down in the vortex?"

Mozart confessed that such was the truth; but desirous of removing any unfavorable opinion of his discretion that his fair friend might have conceived from his recent act of folly, he entered into an argument to show her why she need never fear his falling into such snares. This led to reminiscences of his days of enthusiasm, and the raptures of his past successes.

Mozart received, as a parting present from Doles, a collection of church pieces by the elder Bach. These he prized highly, and laid them carefully in his portmanteau. The day was passed in quiet conversation with his venerable friend; in the evening a few came in to bid the master adieu, for he was going to start for Vienna with the evening post, and that went at nine.

It was half-past eight; the faces of all the company began to grow sad, but Mozart seemed gayer than ever. Indeed, those who remember this his farewell interview with his friends, say they never knew him in such high spirits. Excitement, even of a painful kind, sometimes produces such effects upon ardent natures; and besides, the composer wished to keep up the spirits of the rest.

"If we should never meet again!" whispered Cecilia, sadly, and Father Doles responded to her melancholy foreboding.

"Let's have no whimpering!" cried Mozart, laughing. "I will not hear it. I will give you a toast—Long life, and a happy meeting next year!"

The glasses were filled, and rang as they brought them together. Some one observed the sound was like a knell. Mozart brought his down impatiently on the table and shivered it; he laughed again, and hoped their friendship would prove more durable than the fragile glass.

"Master Mozart!" said Hiller, "will you not write us some little piece before you go, just to bring you to our thoughts sometimes, and remind us of this hour? It *is* possible that we shall never *all* meet again in this world."

"Oh, willingly," answered Mozart. He paused a few moments thoughtfully, and then called to Friedrich to bring him paper and writing materials.

Friedrich obeyed with alacrity, and the master wrote a piece impromptu, while the others were looking on, wondering at him, and exchanging glances.

When he had finished, he tore the paper into five pieces, and keeping one part for himself, divided the others; to Doles, *basso primo*, to Hiller, *basso secondo*; Friedrich, *tenore primo*, Weisse, *tenore secondo*.

"Now," he cried, "we have no time to lose; *allons*—begin!"

They sang the farewell song of Mozart! Never was farewell sung with deeper feeling or with better execution. When it was at an end, they all sat silent and sad. Mozart was first to recover himself; he started up, bade a hasty adieu to all present, and seizing his hat, with another broken "farewell," rushed from the room.

His friends still sat, as if stupified by their grief. Presently the post-horn sounded, and the coach rolled past the window. Their beloved companion was gone.

In the autumn of that same year they buried the venerable Father Doles.

It was just before the Christmas festival, in the year 1791, that Lena, now a happy wife and mother, busied at home in preparing Christmas gifts, was surprised by her friend, Cecilia, who rushed into the room pale as death, without hat or mantle.

"Cecilia!" cried Lena, much alarmed, "what ails you—what has happened?"

"Read it—read it!" faltered the breathless girl, and putting a newspaper into her friend's hand, she burst into tears, and sank on a seat.

"The Vienna Gazette," said Lena, and trembling with indefinite apprehension, she looked over a column or two, before her eyes lighted on the paragraph:

> "Vienna, December 6th.—Died yesterday evening, the celebrated musician and composer, Wolfgang Amadeus Mozart, Chapel-Master, Knight of the Golden Spurs, etc., etc., in the thirty-sixth year of his age."

The genius of Cecilia was not destined to ripen on earth. In another year the weeping Lena followed her bier to the grave. She was buried near the resting-place of Father Doles.

THE ARTIST'S LESSON

In a room meanly furnished, of a small house, No. 857 Windmill street, Leipzig, a man in the beginning of middle age was reclining on a seat, one morning in 1789. He was well built and slender, and his features were rather handsome than otherwise; but they were sharpened and bleached by dissipation, and his whole person bore the marks of excess. He wore a flowered silk dressing-gown, torn and frayed in various places; his collar was open and soiled, though it displayed the whitest of necks; and a dirty velvet cap had just been removed from a head that seemed as if it had not in many days known the discipline of a comb. This individual was leaning on a table, turning over some pages of music carelessly; a violoncello lay beside him.

The sun was high in heaven, the day cloudless and beautiful; a soft and balmy air came in at the open window and door, and stirred the disordered locks of the student, if such he might be called. He seemed now occupied in thought, and pushed away the music; anon he heaved a deep sigh, shook his head and began once more to pore over the notes.

"Bon jour, mon cher!" cried a merry voice, and looking up, the student recognized Heinrich Ferren, one of his neighbors and boon companions, and briefly returned his salutation.

"What the mischief are you about here?" asked Heinrich.

"Ah, mon ami," replied the other, "if I could only hold it fast! But it flies and whirls about my head—worse than the fumes of the champagne, and is gone as quickly."

"What do you mean?"

"I had a dream last night—such a dream! I and my fellow there," pointing to the violoncello, "were alone together in the woods; and so glorious an air came to me—so graceful—so moving—so entrancing! Tartini's witch music was nothing to it! and it seemed that a spirit voice said to me, 'Do this—Mara—you can!' Oh, Heinrich! I have been striving ever since I waked to catch it, but in vain; and I was looking over these notes to find something that might recall it."

"Pshaw—'twas but the wine we drank last night."

"No, no, Heinrich—but I'll tell you what it was; the voice of my genius"—

"You make me laugh, Mara!"

"Then what think you of this?" and catching up the instrument, the musician ran over the strings several times, bringing forth snatches of melody so exquisite that Heinrich himself started; but melody broken and incoherent, mingling the wildest and most touching harmony with what was frequently commonplace and harsh.

"Ah! 'tis not that yet! I cannot catch it!" and throwing down the instrument with a gesture of despair, the disappointed artist buried his face in his hands.

"Come, do not take it so," cried the friend; 'twill come to you to-night! Who thinks, ha! of work in the morning? and you, Mara, of all others, whose inspiration is always in the bottom of your glass!"

"True, true, Heinrich! and we will dive for it, eh!" and rising, the artist went to a closet and brought out a couple of flasks and two tumblers. "Here's what will drive away melancholy." He poured out the wine and they pledged each other.

"Come, I have a thought," cried the violoncellist. "It was at Rosenthal, in my dream, that I heard the witch music. I will go there to-day, with my good fellow, and perhaps it will come back to me. I cannot compose in this house, but in the green vale and under the blue sky—ah, Heinrich!"

"I suppose Madame Mara favors you with an accompaniment sometimes—ha! ha!" cried the friend, laughing.

Mara held up his finger significantly and shook his head. "The public are enchanted with Gertrude's singing, but 'tis anything rather than *adagio* with me! Ah, mine is a sad lot! And what think you? she will give me no more furniture to my room, though I have had to part with piece after piece to pay for our suppers, Heinrich! You see to what I am reduced! but two chairs and a bench and table, and my fellow here," hugging his instrument, "which I will die rather than pawn. And Madame Mara rides in her carriage and dresses like a queen at the concerts, and wins all hearts, and gives me nothing of all the money she has paid her! It all goes to the bank, laid up for her luxury, while I have to sell the furniture for this"—pointing to the wine. "But I'll outwit her. I have a jewelled brooch she thinks lost, and mean to sell it to-morrow; 'twill keep us in good liquor for a month, and then I know where to find more of the same plunder!"

The degraded artist chuckled over the idea of robbing his wife; his *friend* laughed with him, but observed that were he blessed with a wife who could make money, he would know how to obtain it without stratagem.

"Oh, as to that, mon ami, remember her foster-father—Hiller, the music director; 'tis he encourages her obstinacy, and I should not like to break with him altogether. As to Gertrude, she thinks she acts for my good. Did she not quarrel for my sake with the King at Berlin? Did she not give up her appointment, worth two thousand a year, at the court of Frederick the Great, because the King and I could not pull together? Then, after all, I am not fit, as she says, to be my own master; and I would rather submit to her than the monarch who shut me up three months, or the corporal who thrashed me! 'Sdeath! that corporal with his stout cane! it makes me foam to think of it! But I'll pay him back some day or other." And with hand already tremulous from drunkenness, Mara filled and emptied his glass again, signing to his companion to do the same, with a ludicrous expression of hilarious hospitality.

At this moment the clock struck, and a door opened opposite the one leading into the street. A lady of fine figure, and elegantly dressed in a riding habit, came into the room. She stopped as if about to speak, but seeing the wine on the table and the condition of both the tipplers, she cast on them a look of profound and withering contempt, and passed on to the outer door without saying a word.

"Bravo, Madame Mara!" cried Heinrich, when he had recovered from his surprise after she had gone out. "Her ladyship likes not to find us drinking so early. Where goes she? ah! to the rehearsal; and that reminds me, Mara, of what I had nearly forgotten. We must go also; so no more wine till supper time!"

"I will not go!" said Mara, doggedly.

"Yes you will. Do you know who is to be there? The chapel-master from Vienna!"

"What do you say—Mozart?" cried the violoncellist, springing up, half sobered by surprise.

"The very same, mon cher."

"To-day—at rehearsal?"

"Exactly; Father Doles, Hiller, Weisse and others have arranged a concert for the chapel-master, and it is to take place to-night. Master Wolfgang arrived yesterday. You must go with me to rehearsal and see him."

"That I will, Heinrich. Do you know it has been the desire of my life to know the great Mozart? Oh, to think of his quartettes! I have painted him before me as I played the music—grand, noble, of towering form, dark, flashing eyes and trumpet voice"—

"Hold, Mara, you are out there," interrupted Heinrich, laughing heartily. "The little Master Wolfgang never sat for such a picture! In the first place, he is not towering, but low of stature and insignificant in appearance."

"But no less the *great* Mozart!" cried Mara, with enthusiasm. "The creator of Idomeneo, of Don Giovanni! I must know him, if only to tell him how I adore his music. Allons—mon ami; but stay; I must put on my coat."

And pulling off his dressing-gown, assisted by Heinrich, the musician in trembling haste put on a coat that had once been a fine one, though it lacked now much of its lace and several buttons; and clapping his cap on his head, and taking up his stick, after locking up his violoncello, the two worthy companions made their way to the theatre.

Almost all the distinguished musical characters in Leipzig were at the rehearsal of Mozart's last concert, for it was the last he ever gave in that musical capital of Europe. There was the venerable Father Doles, whose guest Mozart was; there was the cynical director Hiller, whose sternness was not proof against the gayety of the chapel-master; there were pupils of his and Doles, and many other connoisseurs. When our two tipplers arrived, the music and the company seemed to bewilder the brain of the violoncellist, already fuddled by the wine he had drunk. He walked unsteadily to one of the side scenes and looked on. The performers were rehearsing a scene from Don Giovanni; a little, pale, thin man stood on the stage and seemed much interested, for he stopped them several times and forced them to go over what they had sung. Several times he stamped violently on the floor, and once he seized one of the singers by the shoulders and shook him, crying "Prestissimo! I will not have my music dragged out in that way!"

His friends laughed, and the singers looked angry; Mozart cried "Da capo!" and they went on sullenly, but with more spirit than before. Then he encouraged them with "Bravo, friends, I have you now!" and clapped his hands.

Through the rehearsal he continued to play the same part; running hither and thither, stopping one, correcting another and swearing at another, till the performers at last caught his spirit and excelled themselves to please him.

"Is that the man?" asked Mara of his companion when the rehearsal was at an end; and being told that it was Mozart, he took off his cap, went up to him and made a low, ceremonious bow, rolling his red eyes and stammering an expression of his sense of the honor of standing in the presence of so distinguished a person.

"Eh, who is this?" inquired the composer, turning to Hiller.

"One whose company does *us* no honor," replied the director, angrily surveying the slovenly figure before him. "I wonder he dares intrude himself here."

"Who is he, then?"

"Mara, at your service—Mara, the violoncellist," answered the tippler, with another scraping bow; "I would thank you, sir, for your excellent music."

"Mara? I have heard of you; you are a famous player. I am happy to make your acquaintance."

"I thank you, Master Mozart; I am most honored and happy to make yours; I have long wished for this good fortune. I am aware, sir," with a glance at Hiller, "that I have enemies who misrepresent me; and that is easy, too, for I sometimes misrepresent myself. But I would have *you* appreciate me. I should like to hear your judgment on my playing; I should hold it an honor, sir, to be permitted to play before you. I should esteem it a favor if you would visit me. I live at 857 Windmill street, and shall be happy to see you at any time—before noon. It would give me great pleasure" —

"I will certainly visit you," said Mozart.

"You—visit this drunken wretch?" exclaimed Hiller in unfeigned surprise. "No, he is not worthy of your acquaintance." Just then Madame Mara passed out and descended to her carriage. "He is the torment of his excellent wife, who has made sacrifices enough for him, and now that he is wholly lost and there is no hope of his reformation, she allows to him the necessaries of life, even while she leaves him forever."

"How?—Gertrude—my wife—" stammered Mara.

"Yes, your injured wife;" repeated the music-director. "You have outraged her feelings by your miserable excesses; you have destroyed her rest by your midnight orgies; she is weary of you. She will return no more to your house; she will see you no more. To-morrow she departs for Paris."

"Bravo, Heinrich, what fun we shall have!" cried the violoncellist, with a flourish of his stick. "*Eh bien*, foster father—"

"In pity, to you, degraded wretch," continued Hiller, "she has directed me to supply you with provisions as you need, but with no money to minister to your depraved passion for drinking. Now you know what you have to depend upon."

"Your most obedient, my lord," said Mara, bowing with a flourish almost to the ground, from which obeisance he recovered himself with great difficulty, amidst the laughter of the bystanders. "I am wholly at your service, most excellent director of music—at your excellency's service! But I shall not draw on my banker. I am beholden to Madame Mara, but I can play the violoncello as well as she. You should hear me play," turning to Mozart. "These gentlemen here, can tell you something of my taste in music."

"Oh, yes," cried several in a breath; "Monsieur Mara is a first rate player on the violoncello. You are too severe with him, Monsieur Hiller."

"Oh, much too severe!" repeated others. "Mara is a good fellow—an excellent fellow—and the best of company. What should we do without him? He is the life of our suppers." Hiller, in disgust, drew Mozart away; Doles and his party had already gone. They left the theatre while the inebriated musician was making a grateful speech to his "good friends," and gesticulating in a manner to kill them with laughter.

We change the scene to the celebrated Rosenthal, the beautiful retreat where Goëthe passed so many hours of leisure when a student. It was indeed a valley of roses; for the season was early summer, when flowers are most abundant and the tender green of the rich foliage is freshest and brightest. It was a lovely afternoon, but not sultry; a large awning was spread for temporary use; and just in the shade of a group of trees was set out a table with refreshments. There were not more than a dozen seats arranged round it, evidently for a small and select company. Ere long carriages drove up and some ladies alighted and began to arrange the collation. Two of them were the wife and daughter of Doles; they brought flowers which they had gathered, and decorated the table, placing a wreath of roses and laurels over the seat destined to be occupied by their honored guest. The rest of the company soon joined them, and it would be interesting, had we space, to relate the conversation that formed the most delightful part of their entertainment. They were a few choice spirits, met to enjoy the society of Mozart in an hour sacred to friendship. There was no lack of humor and mirth; indeed the composer would have acted at variance with his character had he not beguiled even the gravest by his amusing sallies; but the themes of their discourse were the musical masters of the world and the state and prospects of their art.

"You have in truth some reason to quarrel with our good Leipzig," said one of the company to Mozart. "We are slow and cold; we hang back from what they call your innovations, but time will bring us along; and you must not, meantime, judge us incapable of appreciating the wonders you have made known to the world."

"Far from it," replied the composer; "or if I should be vexed at the caution of your public taste, unwilling to admire at once what is new, I should be rebuked by your eminence in concerts and church music. You are unrivalled in your artists, and to please your connoisseurs I should esteem the highest triumph in my life."

"But could we only entice you to live here" —

"No, the atmosphere does not suit me; the reserve would chill my efforts, for I live upon the love of those who suffer me to do as I please. Some other time, perhaps, I may come to Leipzig; just now Vienna is the place for me. By the way, what think you of Bonn?"

"You cannot think of Bonn for a residence?"

"Not I; but never despair! Had you asked me where art had the least chance of spreading her wings for a bold flight — where she was most securely chained down and forbidden to soar, I should have answered, 'Bonn.' But that unpromising city has produced one of the greatest geniuses of our day."

"Who — who?" eagerly demanded several among the company.

"A lad — a mere lad — who has been under the tutelage of the Elector's masters, and shocked them all by his musical eccentricities. They were ready to give him up in disgust. He came to me just before I left Vienna; modest, abashed, doubting his own genius, but eager to learn his fate from my lips. I gave him one of my most difficult pieces; he executed it in a manner so spirited, so admirable — carried away by the music, which entered his very soul — forgetful of his faintheartedness — full of inspiration! 'Twas an artist, I assure you; a true and noble one, and I told him so."

"His name?"

"Louis von Beethoven."

"I know his father well," said Hiller.

"Then you know one who has given the world a treasure! For mark me; railed at as he may be for refusing to follow in the beaten path, decried for his contempt of ordinary rules, the lad Beethoven will rise to a splendid fame! But his forte will be sacred music."

The conversation turned to the works of Bach and Händel.

As the sun declined westward the company rose and returned to the city. When they had left the grounds, a figure came forward from the concealment of the foliage and walked pensively to and fro. He had heard most of the conversation unobserved; it was the artist Mara.

"Well, well," he said to himself, "I have heard and know him now. His taste is the same with mine; he glories in Händel and old Sebastian; and yet how much may still be done! Ah, that music in my dream!" He struck his forehead. "But I can keep nothing in my head; Mara—Mara—*non e piu com era prima!* If 'twere not for this vertigo, this throbbing that I feel whenever I strive to collect my thoughts and fix them on an idea; if I could but grasp the conception, oh, 'twould be glorious!"

The spirit of art had not yet left the degraded being it had once inspired; but how sad were the struggles of the soul against her painful and contaminating bonds!

"Why," resumed the soliloquist, "why was I not invited to make one among the company assembled here to welcome the great chapel-master? I too am a famous artist; I can appreciate music; the public have pronounced me entitled to rank among the first. But nobody will associate with Mara in the day time! It is only at night, at the midnight revels, where such grave ones as the director scorn to appear, that Mara, like a bird of evil omen, is permitted to show his face. Then they shout and clap for me and call me a merry fellow; and I *am* the merriest of them all! But I do not like such welcome; I would rather be reasonable if I could, and the wine would let me—the wine—am I a slave to that? Ha, a slave! Alas! it is so; wine is my master, and he is jealous of every other, and beats me when I rebel, till I cry mercy and crouch at his feet again. Oh, if I had a friend strong enough to get me out of his clutches! but I have no friends—none—not even Gertrude. She has left me, and there is no one at home now, even to reproach me when I come back drunk, or make a noise in the house over the table with a companion or two. Heinrich—no—he laughs and makes game of me like the rest. I am sick of this miserable life; I am tired of being laughed at and shunned; I will put an end to it all, and then they will say once again, 'Poor Mara!'"

With a sudden start the wretched man rushed away and was presently hid among the branches of the trees. A whistle was heard just then, and a lad, walking briskly, followed, hallooing after him. He came just in time. A stream, a branch of the Pleysse, watered the bottom of the valley; Mara was about to throw himself into it in the deepest spot, when his arm was caught by his pursuer.

"What the mischief are you about?"

"Let me alone!" cried Mara, struggling.

"Do you mean to be drowned?"

"Yes; that is just what I want. I came here for that purpose. And what have you to say against it, Friedrich?"

"Nothing, if your fancy runs that way," replied the lad, laughing. "Only you have plenty of leisure for it hereafter, and just now you are wanted."

"Wanted?"

"Yes; I came to look for you."

"Who wants the poor drunkard, Mara?"

"They want you at Breithoff's to-night, at the supper given to Mozart after the concert, and you must bring your instrument; we are to have some rare fun. Come, if you are obedient, you shall go with me to the concert."

Mozart's concert! Surprised and pleased that some of his acquaintance had remembered him, Mara suffered himself to be led away by his companion.

The concert was a splendid one and attended by all the taste and fashion of Leipzig. The orchestra was admirable, the singers were full of spirit and good humor, the audience delighted, the composer gratified and thankful. The good effect of his drilling at rehearsal was evident; but those who listened to the noble music and rewarded the performers by frequent bursts of tumultuous applause, knew not the source of their unusual animation and gave them all the credit. Mozart thanked them in a brief speech, and as soon as the concert was at an end was led off in triumph by the connoisseurs, his friends.

Magnificent beyond expectation was the entertainment prepared, and attended by many among the wealthy and the noble, as well as the most distinguished artists. The votaries of art had indeed superior claims, for the feast was in honor of Art and her noblest son. The revelry was prolonged beyond midnight, and as the guests became warmed with good cheer, we are bound to record that the conversation lost its rational tone, and that comical sallies and uproarious laughter began to usurp the place of critical discourse. They had songs from all who were musical; Mara, among the rest, was brought in, dressed in a fantastic but slovenly manner, and made to play for the amusement of the company. When he had played several pieces, the younger guests began to put their practical jokes upon him and provoke him to imitate the noises of different animals on his violoncello. Mara entered into all their fun, convulsing them with his grotesque speeches and gestures, drinking glass after glass, till at last he fell back quite overpowered and insensible. Then his juvenile tormentors painted his face and clipped his mustaches and tricked him out in finery that gave him the look of a candidate for Bedlam, and had him carried to his own house, laughing to imagine what his sensations would be next morning, when he should discover how ludicrously he had been disfigured. In short, the whole party were considerably beyond the bounds of propriety and sound judgment. Mozart also— —

It was considerably after noon the next day, that poor Mara, the victim of those merciless revellers, might be seen sitting disconsolately in his deserted home. He had no heart even to be enraged at the cruelties practised on him. Pale as death, his eyes sunken and bloodshot, his limbs shivering, sat this miserable wretch, dressed in the same mockery of finery which had been heaped upon him in wicked sport.

The door opened and Mozart entered.

At sight of the composer Mara rose and mechanically returned his salutation. Mozart looked grave and sad.

"You are much the worse for last night's dissipation, my good fellow," said he.

"Ah, Master Mozart," said the violoncellist, with a faint smile, "it is too good of you to visit such a dog as poor Mara."

"I have something to say to you, friend," answered the composer in a voice of emotion. "In the first place, let me thank you for your music last night."

The bewildered artist passed his hand across his forehead.

"I say, let me thank you. It is long since I have heard such music."

"You were pleased with it?" asked Mara, looking up, while a beam of joy shot into the darkness of his soul.

"Pleased? it was noble—heart-stirring! I must own I did not expect such from you. I expected to be shocked, but I was charmed. And when you played the air from Idomeneo—sacré! but it went to my soul. I have *never* had my music so thoroughly appreciated—so admirably executed. Mara, you are a master of your art! I reverence you!"

"You?" repeated the artist, drawing his breath quickly.

"Yes; I own you for my brother, and so I told them all last night."

The poor man gave a leap and seized the master by both hands; rapture had penetrated his inmost heart. "Oh, you make me very happy!" faltered he.

"I am glad of it; for now I am going to say something painful." Mara hung his head. "Nay, I reproach myself as much as you. We both behaved ill last night; we both forgot the dignity of the artist and the man."

Again the poor violoncellist looked bewildered.

"We forgot that such as we, are set up for an example to the uninitiated, and yielded to the tempter, wine! Art—our mother—has reason to blush for us."

"For me," cried Mara, deeply moved. "But not for you."

"Yes, for me," repeated Mozart; "and for all who were there. It was a shameful scene. What," he continued, with rising indignation, "what would the true friends of art have thought of such beastly orgies, celebrated in her name? Why, they would have said, perhaps, 'these men are wild fellows, but we must let them have their way; we owe the fine music they give us to their free living; they must have stimulus to compose or play well.' No, no, no! it is base to malign the holy science we love. Such excesses but unfit us for work. I have never owed a good thought to the bottle. I tell you I hate myself for last night's foolery."

"Ah, master; you who are so far above me!" sighed Mara.

"And lo, here, the wreck of a noble being!" said the composer, in a low voice and with much bitterness; then resuming, "Listen to me, Mara. You have been your own enemy; but your fall is not wholly your own work. You are wondrously gifted; you can be, you shall be, snatched from ruin. You can, you shall, rise above those who would trample on you now; become renowned and beloved and leave an honored name to posterity. You have given me a lesson, Mara—a lesson which I shall remember my lifelong— which I shall teach to others. You have done me good—I will do something for you. Come with me to Vienna."

The poor violoncellist had eagerly listened to the words of him he so venerated—whom he looked on as a superior being. While he talked to him as an equal, while he acknowledged his genius, lamented his faults and gave him hope that all was not yet lost, the spirit of the degraded creature revived within him. It was the waking of his mind's energies; the struggle of the soul for life against the lethargy of a mortal malady. Life triumphed! Mara was once more a man; but overcome by the conflict and by the last generous offer, he sank back, bowed his face upon his hands and wept aloud.

"Come," cried Mozart, after a pause, during which his own eyes were moistened, "come, we have no time to lose. I go out to-night by the evening post for Vienna; you must accompany me. Take this purse, put your dress

in order and make haste. I will call for you at eight. Be ready then. Not
word more."

And forcing a well filled purse into his trembling hands, the maste
hastened away too quickly to hear a word of thanks from the man he had
saved from worse than death.

The great composer was early summoned from this and many othe
works of mercy and benevolence. But if his noble design was unaccomplished
at least good seed was sown, and Mara placed once more within view o
the goal of virtuous hope. Rescued from the mire of degradation, he might
by perseverance, have won the prize; if he did not, the fault was this time
wholly his own. Whatever the termination of his career, the moral lesson is
for us the same.

GLUCK IN PARIS

In the street St. Honoré, opposite the principal entrance of the Palais Royal, on a clear evening in the autumn of the year 1779, stood two young officers engaged in a zealous dispute. Suddenly one of them sprang backward a few paces, and, after a pause of an instant, the swords of both flew from their scabbards, and flashed in the lamp-light as they crossed each other.

"*Mort de ma vie!*" cried another voice, and a powerful stroke forced asunder the weapons of the combatants; "a duel in the open streets, and at night, without seconds? Put up your swords, gentlemen, till to-morrow; then I will second you. My name is St. Val, Captain of Hussars in the Body-guard."

"St. Val?" was the exclamation that burst from both the young men, and St. Val, recognising them, cried laughing—"How? Montespan! Arnaut? Orestes and Pylades fighting? By Jupiter! that is amazing. What may be your quarrel?"

"Ah!" replied the young Arnaut, "talk not of quarrels. My friend and I were only settling a small difference of opinion with regard to the composers of 'Iphigenia in Tauris.' My friend gives his voice for the Chevalier Gluck; I for the admirable Piccini;" and therewith the young men prepared to begin the fight anew.

"Put up your swords!" exclaimed St. Val, once more interfering; "Is that the whole cause of your duel?"

"Does it seem to you insignificant?" asked M. de Montespan.

"Why—not exactly"—replied the peacemaker; "I am aware that the citizens of Paris are at present divided into Gluckists and Piccinists; but Monsieur Arnaut, if you are going to fight the Gluckists, you must first begin with your own uncle, and your idol Jean Jacques.—Follow my advice, Messieurs; put up your swords and come with me to the Palais Royal, where you can cool your blood with a few glasses of orangeade in the Café du Feu. This, by my life, is the first time I ever interfered to stop a duel. But in this case, it seems to me not the silliest thing I could do."

During the captain's speech, the rage for fighting had evaporated in the breasts of the young officers. They shook hands cordially, returned their swords to the sheath, and followed St. Val.

The brilliantly illuminated saloon of the Café du Feu was at that time the place of resort for the Parisian *bel esprits*; every evening they repaired thither, and with them many young gentlemen of the higher classes — amateurs, connoisseurs, and artists who had come to Paris to admire, or if possible to be admired.

Thus, when our friends entered, they found a various company. Many young men of the nobility resident in Paris, were to be seen there, scattered about the several tables, surrounded by a crowd of followers, admirers, critics, &c. From every group was heard a confused clamor of argument, declamation, and dispute; in short, there was a perfect war of tongues, and the battle cry here, as all over Paris, was 'Gluck' and 'Piccini.' Though true Parisians, and used to all this uproar of a café salon, the newly arrived thought it best to secure for the present a place rather more quiet. They caught one of the flying garçons, held him fast, questioned him, and were soon seated in a snug side room.

Three men, besides themselves, were occupants of the room. One, somewhat advanced in years, sat in a corner opposite the entrance, by a table furnished only for one person. He was deep in the shadow of a pillar, so that no one could discern his features; comfortably ensconced in an arm-chair, he drummed lightly on the table with the fingers of his right hand; his head leaning back, and his eyes fixed on the ceiling. He seemed to take no notice of those who entered, and was to all appearance equally indifferent to what passed afterwards.

Nearer the door, and on the other side from the table at which our friends took their place, the other two were seated. The youngest was scarce twenty years of age; a handsome, animated Frenchman, well made, though not tall; the glance of his deep blue eyes, shaded by dark, heavy lashes, was free and unembarrassed. The outline of his features was expressive, his mouth and chin were classically formed, his complexion was of that rich brown which belongs to the native of Provence; his voice was agreeable, his manner easy and spirited without being assuming, and his dress poor, though decent and clean. His prepossessing exterior formed a strange contrast with that of his companion. The latter was a man of about twenty-nine; and answered tolerably to the description which Diderot drew of Rameau's nephew, except that he was not so long and thin. There was something expressive of mental weakness in his movements; and the air of discontent and spite in his whole manner was not to be mistaken. A rough, bristling, unpowdered peruke, of a pale brown color, covered his head; his features were heavy and might have passed for unmeaning, but for a pair of keen, squinting eyes, and a peevish twist about his mouth, which showed at once the disposition of the man. His pronunciation of French was shocking, and betrayed him for a Saxon.

"You must pardon me, sir," said the young man, ingenuously, "if I trouble you with my numerous questions; but you are a German, and you must be assured that we French know how to value your great countryman, who has shown us new paths, hitherto undreamed of, to the temple of fame. [7] You are yourself a musician—a composer; you can feel what we owe to the illustrious master! Tell me, what know you of him? And would he not disdain to be the friend and guide of a youth who aspires after the best?"

His companion slowly passed his broad hand over his face, with an oblique glance at the enthusiastic speaker, twisted his mouth into a tragical smile, and answered maliciously; "Hem! yes! would you have me speak of M. Gluck? Indeed, very willingly! I do not exactly understand what a people so accomplished, of so much judgment and taste as the French, find so grand and splendid in this man!"

"How, sir? Speak you of the creator of Armida, of Iphigenia, of Orpheus?"

"Hem, yes; the same. To say truth, he is not thought much of among us in Germany, for we know that of genuine art, I mean of the rules, he understands little or nothing; as the learned Herr Forkel in Gottingen, and many other distinguished critics have satisfactorily proved."

The handsome youth looked astonished at the speaker for a moment, then answered modestly; "I am myself far from being so learned in the rules of art, as to be able to judge how correct may be the severe reproach his countrymen cast upon the Chevalier Gluck; but—" with rising warmth, "of one thing I am fully and firmly convinced, that his is a noble and powerful spirit. All I have ever heard of his music, awakens high feelings in me; no low or grovelling—nay, *no common* thought, can come near me while I listen to it; and even when spiritless and dejected by untoward circumstances, my despondency takes instant flight before the lofty enjoyment I experience in Gluck's creations."

"And think you," cried young Arnaut, who with his friend had drawn nearer, "think you, sir German, the celebrated Piccini would condescend to enter into a contest with the chevalier, were he not convinced that he was to strive with a worthy adversary?"

The other was visibly nettled at this question, asked in an animated tone. With a furtive look at the young man standing over him, he muttered in broken phrases,

"Hem! I suppose not! how could I presume to think so? I have all due respect for M. Gluck, even though I have no cause to boast of his friendship towards me; *but* it does not follow that he is the best composer. We have men very different, as the learned Herr Forkel has clearly proved; and it is certain that M. Gluck, with regard to a church style—"

"But *ma foi!*" interrupted the brown youth, with vivacity, "we are not talking of church styles, but of a grand opera style! Would your German musical critics have Gluck's Armida made a nun's hymn, or his wild motets of Tauris sung in the style of Palestrina?"

"Not exactly," replied the squinter; "but as the learned Forkel has proved, the Chevalier Gluck understands nothing of songs."

All present, except the man in the corner, exclaimed in amazement at this—"Nothing of songs?"

"As I remarked," he continued, "Gluck understands nothing of songs; for he cannot carry through an ordinary melody according to rule, and in the old established way; his song, so called, is nothing more than an extravagant declamation."

The brown youth started up, his gentle kindliness changed into glowing indignation, and with vehemence replied—"Sir, you are not worthy to be a German, if what you say of your great countryman is said in earnest. That Gluck is really a mighty artist, we are all agreed in Paris; the dispute is only to whom the palm of superior greatness shall be yielded, to him or Piccini. We all acknowledge that Gluck, equally far from the cold constraint of rules, and from capricious innovation, seeks to convey the truest expression of feeling and passion; and sets himself the only true aim that exists for the opera-composer. Church and concert music present a different object for the master; whether Gluck could reach that—whether he attempts it—you—I—the multitude know not! He has set himself *one* task, pursuing that, however, with all his strength, according to the mission of the free-born spirit!"

"What is your name, young man?" asked a sonorous voice behind the speaker. All looked in that direction; the man in the corner stood up, the light of the candles shining full on his face.

"The Chevalier Gluck!" cried they all, in astonishment.

"The same!" replied Gluck, smiling; and then turning to the young enthusiast, he repeated his question. The youth trembled with delight, and bowing low to the master, answered—

"My name is Etienne Mehul, and I am a musician."

"That I heard," said Gluck; "I shall be glad if you will visit me; here is my address." He handed it to him, then turned to the squinter, who sat without daring to look up, by turns red and pale. Gluck enjoyed his embarrassment a few moments, then addressed him with a mixture of indignation and contempt; "Mr. Elias Hegrin! I am rejoiced to meet you so unexpectedly in Paris, in order to tell you once more out of my honest heart, what a miserable rascal you are. So, sir! I understand nothing of music and of songs; and yet you went the whole year in Vienna in and out of my house at your pleasure, and received instruction from me how to correct your works, and took without a scruple of conscience what I gave you out of my own pocket, as well as what I procured you through patrons. Truly, your stupid arrogance must take umbrage, because I candidly told you, you can master only the lifeless form, not the spirit. You seek what you can never obtain, not for the sake of art, but for your own temporary advantage; and you would do better to be an honest tailor or shoemaker, than a mean musician.—*That* is what you could never forgive me; and so you go off and abuse me for money in Gottingen! You are pardoned, sir, for I bear no malice. Go hence in peace, and grow better, if you can; but that, I think, will be difficult; for he who blasphemes the pure and sacred maiden Art, because she repels his degrading embraces, will be likely to remain a rascal as long as he lives.—Adieu, Messieurs!"

And Gluck walked out of the room, nodding courteously once more to young Mehul.

A gay group was assembled in the apartment of the young queen Marie Antoinette. The Comte d'Artois, the favorite of the Parisian world of fashion, had just returned to the capital from his hunting-castle, and had come this morning in company with his brother, the Comte of Provence, to pay his homage to his lovely sister-in-law.

The queen received the youthful count with great kindness; Provence presenting him as Grand Master of the chase. D'Artois asked with vivacity, "What is there new in Paris? how many balls have they danced without me? how many flirtations have begun and ended without me? who has served my brother of Provence as accoucheur, at the birth of a new piece of wit? what is the newest spectacle? and what are the good Parisians quarrelling about?"

"A good many questions in a breath!" replied Antoinette, with a smile; "I will answer the last, since we are all warmly interested therein. The newest spectacle we are looking for, is the contest between Gluck and Piccini. Both have composed a piece on the same subject; and it is now to be decided which of the two shall keep the field. This is what the Parisians are disputing about."

"I am for Gluck!" cried D'Artois, "for by my faith, madame, your countryman is a noble fellow!—He was on the chase with me, and made five shots one after the other. As to the Italians, they do not know how to hold a gun."

"Despite that," said Provence, "I like better the music of the Italian, than the German, which can only be recited, but to which one cannot well either sing or dance, as our Noverre very justly observes."

"Oh! Noverre has been obliged to dance to it," interrupted the queen, and began in her lively manner to tell how Noverre had gone one morning to the Chevalier Gluck, and told him his music was worth nothing, and that no dancer in the grand opera could dance to his Scythian dances: and how Gluck in a rage had seized the little man, and danced him through the whole house, upstairs and down stairs, singing the Scythian ballets the while;—and had asked him at last, "Well, sir! now think you, a dancer in the grand opera can dance to my music?" To which Noverre, panting and blowing, replied, "Excellent! sir, and the ballet corps *shall* dance!"

All laughed, and thought such a dancing master just the thing for the gentlemen and ladies of the grand opera, who were all growing every day more arrogant and insufferable in their behavior.

A page announced the Chevalier Gluck, who came to give her Majesty a lesson on the piano.

"Let him come in"—said the queen, and Gluck entered.—"We were just speaking of you," said the Princess Elizabeth to him; "and the queen praised you for a good dancing master."

"And my brother bears witness to your expertness in the chase, for on that account he belongs to your party," said Provence.

"Ah! let him alone," cried the queen, "do not vex him with your idle talk. He will have enough to do, not to lose his patience with me."

"Because you do not play half so well as queen, as when you were archduchess, Antoinette," replied Gluck gravely, speaking in German.

Antoinette replied, laughing, in the same language, "Wait a little, Christophe; your ears shall ring presently.—Be quiet, ladies and gentlemen!" she added in French, and went to open the piano. In her haste she seemed to have made a mistake; for when she tried the key, she could not open the instrument. At length she started up impatiently, and cried—"Come hither, Gluck, and help me!"

Gluck tried his hand in vain; the others followed, but equally fruitless were their efforts.

"This is vexatious!" said the queen; and Gluck exclaimed—"What fool can have made such a lock?"

"Take care what you say, chevalier," said Provence; "the king himself made the lock, and I believe it is of a new-fangled sort."

D'Artois now went out and returned with the king. Louis XVI., in his short jacket, his head covered with an unsightly leathern cap, his face glowing, and begrimed with soot, with rough hands and a bundle of keys and picklocks at his girdle, looked, in truth, more like an industrious locksmith than a king of France.—He went and busied himself at the instrument; examined the lock with the earnest air of an artisan, and tried several keys in vain; shook his head dissatisfied, and tried others; at length he hit upon the right one. The lock yielded, and with a mien of triumph, as if he had won a battle, he cried—"Look there! it is open! Now madame, you can play."

But the hour was over, and the queen had lost the inclination to play. Gluck waited for the sign of his dismissal; and the Princess Elizabeth begged that he would entertain them with something new from his Iphigenia. The master of sixty-five seated himself at the instrument and began the frenzy scene of Orestes. All were silent and attentive, particularly Louis, who, when the piece was ended, went up to Gluck, and said, with downcast eyes, in broken sentences—"Excellent, chevalier—most excellent! I am charmed—delighted; I will have your opera produced first—with all care— with all splendor—just as you please! and I hope the success will be such as to gratify you."

The Chevalier Noverre and the Signor Piccini were here announced and admitted. They came in together. Noverre started when he saw Gluck, and it was evident that he was embarrassed at his presence, though his pride prevented him from betraying such a feeling more than an instant. Piccini was easy and unembarrassed; and when the king commanded him to salute his adversary, he did so with dignity and cordiality. Gluck returned the greeting in like manner.

"What do you bring us new, gentlemen?" asked Antoinette. Noverre answered, with solemn gravity, "Your Majesty was pleased to grant Signor Piccini permission to play you his last notes out of the opera of Iphigenia in Tauris."

"Very well!" replied the queen; and turning to Piccini, she asked, graciously, "What selection have you made, Signor?"

Piccini bowed and replied—"The Chevalier Noverre wished that your Majesty would permit me to play before you the Scythian dance, number one."

The Comte d'Artois burst into a peal of laughter; and even the other aristocratic personages, except the king, who shared the embarrassment of Piccini and Noverre, had some difficulty in restraining their mirth.

"You have my ready permission," said Antoinette. Piccini seated himself at the piano, and began to play his Scythian dance, to which the Comte of Provence and Noverre kept time. The others confessed that Piccini's dance was far more pleasing, melodious, and adapted to the grace of motion, than that of Gluck. But D'Artois whispered to the king, that he thought the dance, considered by itself, admirable; but beyond dispute, better fitted for a masqued ball, in the salon of the grand opera, than for a private abode in Tauris.

Louis did not reply; Gluck stood listening earnestly and attentively; his sense of the merit of his opponent was visible in his countenance, except that now and then a light curl played about his mouth, when Piccini indulged too much in his pretty quaverings and tinklings. Noverre responded with his foot, by a natural impulse, to the music.

Great applause rewarded Piccini when he ceased; and Noverre neglected not to explain, with an air of great importance, that in the music they had just heard, was displayed that inspiriting rhythmus, which alone had power to charm the dancer's feet, so that he could give soul and expression to his pirouettes and entrechats.

"Very good, Monsieur Noverre," said the king, interrupting the current of the dancing master's speech; "I agree with you that the music of Signor Piccini is admirable, but I hope also, that you will make yourself acquainted with the music of the Chevalier Gluck."

"Sire," lisped Noverre in reply, "we, the Chevalier Gluck and I, *are* on the most friendly terms." A deep sigh followed these words, but Louis took no notice of it, and after a while permitted the artists to depart.

Going out of the Tuilleries, after Gluck and Piccini had taken a courteous, though cold leave of each other, Gluck said mischievously to the ballet-master—"Take care, chevalier, not to forget what the king commanded you. If you have complained of me to his majesty, because I made you dance against your will, I must take the liberty to assure you, that you have no cause to be ashamed of having gone through a dance with me; for granted I am not—and a pity it is!—such a proficient in the art of dancing as yourself, yet I am, as well as you, chevalier of the order de l'Esprit, in which character I have the honor to wish your worship a good morning."

And stepping into his carriage, he drove homeward. Noverre looked after him much vexed. Piccini laughed.

The rehearsals and preparations for the representations of the two Iphigenias were nearly finished, and the day was already appointed when the masterpiece of Gluck was to receive the sentence of the Parisians. It was to be performed first, for the precedence was yielded to him as the oldest of the two champions.

"When kings build, cartmen have work;"—the truth of that saying was proved. Men who knew little or nothing of music wrote, for the advantage of their party, treatises, learned and superficial, upon Gluck and Piccini, upon the differences in their style, and upon the operas in question, in a tone as assured and confident as if they had diligently studied the compositions of the masters. The partisans of both received the treatises with satisfaction, reading all that were presented with as much edification as if they had been the productions of Rameau or Rousseau; perhaps with even more eagerness, as the zest of scandal was added.

There was also much dissension among the performers; and poor Piccini had not a little to do, by a thousand attentions, flatteries and favors, to propitiate those of them who were opposed to him, and induce them to promise not to spoil his work purposely. Gluck behaved differently; he resorted to threats, and compelled his enemies at least to conceal their ill designs, for they feared him. As for the rest, he trusted to the excellence of his work, and his motto—"Truth makes its way through all things;" and even in anticipation of the most unfavorable event, consoled himself by the reflection—"Well! the worst success does not make a good work a bad one!" [8]

He sat in his chamber the morning of the day before the representation of his Iphigenia, preparing for the final rehearsal, when the servant announced young Mehul.—"Come in, my dear friend!" cried Gluck cheerfully, as he rose and went to the door to meet his visitor. "I am rejoiced to see you, and have expected you before this."

"I ventured not to disturb you before," replied Mehul, "but to-day—"

"Well—to-day—"

"My anxiety brought me hither."

"Anxiety!—and wherefore?"

"To-morrow your new opera is to be performed for the first time—you have so many enemies.—Ah! should the success of your noble creation no be answerable to its worth!"

"Then let it be so," said Gluck, smiling.

"Can you say that with so much calmness?"

"Why not?—Do you think of devoting yourself to dramatic composition?"

"I wish with all my heart to do so, and should be very unhappy should I find my powers inadequate."

"Prove them, young man! Go boldly to work: do not deliberate long; but what reveals itself to you lay hold on with glowing inspiration; plan and complete it with earnest heed. It will soon be shown, what you can do, now or in future. And if I judge you rightly, I think it will not go wrong with *you*! Yes—that is the great matter, that we deviate not from the way. But it is hard in itself; and men and the world make it yet harder for the artist. Many, of whom better things might have been hoped, fall in the conflict.

"You remain victor!"

"Hem—that is as one takes it. Nothing is perfect upon earth; and even if I have gone through life neither a fool nor a knave, still am I not without faults. Each, for good or evil, must be experienced before he can truly value the better part. To the generality, the All Benevolent has granted to know but little, till either what they have is irremediably wasted, or they are in danger of losing it. Happy he, who quickly apprehends, and holds it fast, nor lets it go, though his heart should be torn in the struggle. What will you say when I confess to you, that perception of the highest, the *only* good, came late, fearfully late, to me. When I look back on my earlier days, I am often astonished. Music was all to me from earliest youth. When a boy, in my home, in lovely Bohemia, I heard her voice, as a divine voice, in all that surrounded me—in the dense forest, in the gloomy ravine, the romantic valley—on the bold, stark cliff—in the cheerful hunter's call, or the hoarse song of stream and torrent, her voice thrilled to my heart, like a sweet and glorious prophecy. All was clear to my youthful vision. Love commanded— and there was light! Then I thought there was nothing so great and god-like, that man, impotent man, could not achieve it. Too soon I learned that something was impossible. The royal eagle soars upward toward the sun; yet can he never reach the orb; and how soon are clipped the spirit's wings! Then come harassing doubts, false ambition, thirst of gain, envy, disappointed vanity, worldly cares—the hateful gnomes of earth—that cling to you, and drag you downward, when you would soar like the eagle. So is it with the boy—the youth—with manhood—with old age. One perhaps redeems himself from folly; discerns and appreciates the right, and might create the beautiful. But with folly flies also youth, its ardor and its vigor; and there remains to him enthusiasm, passion for the sublime—and—a grave!"

"Oh, no, no!" cried Mehul, with emotion; "much more remains to *you!*"

"Think you so?" asked Gluck, and after a pause continued; "Well—perhaps something better—it is true; for when I freed myself from the fetters of the unworthy and the base, there came to me a radiant and lovely vision, from the pure bright *Grecian age.* But, believe me, the work of holding it fast, and shaping it in the external world, is my last. And melancholy it is, that a whole vigorous, blooming lifetime could not be consecrated alone to such a theme. But I submit, for I could not do otherwise; and I will bear it, whether these Parisian bawlers adjudge me fame and wealth for my work, or hiss me down."

The hour struck for the rehearsal; Gluck broke off the discourse, and accompanied by his young friend, went to the Royal Academy of music.

Meanwhile Nicolo Piccini, morose and out of humor, was walking up and down his chamber, from time to time casting a discontented look at the notes of his opera, that lay open on the desk. At times he would walk hastily to the desk as if a lucky thought had struck him, to insert something in the work; but he would let fall the pen before he had touched the paper, shake his head with a dissatisfied and melancholy air, and begin again to walk the room.

There was a knock at the door; Piccini heeded it not; there was a second—a third! At length he went to the door, opened it, and Elias Hegrin entered. Piccini seemed disturbed at sight of him, and asked ungraciously—"What do you want? Why are you here again?"

With his usual sullen smile Elias replied—"The Chevalier Noverre sent me; he said Signor Piccini wished to speak with me."

Piccini remained a few moments in gloomy silence, as if struggling inwardly; at length he said with a sigh—"It is true; I wished to see you."

"And in what can I serve my honored patron?"

"By speaking the *truth!*" replied Piccini, regarding him sternly. "Confess it, Elias Hegrin, you uttered a falsehood, when you told me Gluck stirred up all his friends and acquaintances to make a party against me."

Elias Hegrin changed color, but he collected himself, and answered—"I spoke the truth."

"It is *false*, Elias! and you spoke a falsehood when you told me you had read the manuscript of my adversary, and that the work scarce deserved the honors of mediocrity!"

"It was the truth, Signor Piccini, and I can only repeat my opinion of the opera of the Chevalier Gluck."

"So much the worse for your judgment of art, for now, after having heard five rehearsals, I must, aye, and *will*, declare before all the world, that Gluck's Iphigenia is the greatest of all operas I know, and that in its author I acknowledge my master."

Elias stared.

"I believed I had accomplished something worthy in my own work," continued Piccini, speaking half to himself; "and indeed, my design was pure; *that* I can say; nor is what I have done altogether without merit;—but oh! how void and cold, how weak and insignificant does it seem to me, compared with Gluck's gigantic creation! Yes—creation! mine is only a work! A human work, which will soon vanish without a trace—while Gluck's Iphigenia will endure so long as feeling for the grand and the beautiful is not dead in the hearts of men."

"But—Signor Piccini"—stammered Elias.

"Be silent!" interrupted Piccini, in displeasure. "Wherefore have you lied? wherefore have you slandered the noble master, and toiled to bring down his works and his character to your own level in the dust? Are you not ashamed of your pitiful behavior? I have never fully trusted you, spite of Noverre's recommendation; for well I know that Noverre hates the great master for having wounded his ridiculous vanity; but I never thought you capable of such meanness as I now find you guilty of. Gluck stir up his friends, to make a party against me!—There! look at these letters in Gluck's own hand, written to Arnaud, Rollet, Maurepas, wherein he judges my work thoroughly, dwelling upon the best parts, and entreats them to listen to my opera impartially, as to his own, and to give an impartial judgment, for that he is anxious only for the truth. Through my patron, the Count of Provence, I obtained these letters from those gentlemen, whom he persuaded to send them to me, thereby to remove my groundless suspicions. How mortified am I now for having descended to make common cause with you! I have been deceived; but you—tell me, man, what has induced you to act in this dishonorable and malicious manner towards your benefactor?"

While Piccini was speaking, Elias had shrunk more and more into himself. Humbled, and in a lachrymose voice he replied, "Ah, my dearest patron, you misapprehend me. Yes—I will confess, I have spoken falsely—I have acted meanly—shamefully! But I am not so bad as you think me. If you but knew all! Ah! I am an unhappy man, and deserve not your anger, but rather your sympathy. When a boy, I heard it daily repeated by my parents and family, that I had extraordinary talent for music; that I should become a great composer, and one day acquire both wealth and reputation. In this hope I applied myself zealously to art, hard as it was to me. My first work of importance was looked on as a miracle in the town where I lived; this strengthened me in the opinion of my abilities, and I thought I had only to go to a great city, to reap renown and gold without measure. I went to Vienna; but gained neither."

"I know it; but there Gluck took you by the hand, supported you, gave you instruction, corrected your works."

"He did so, indeed; but he likewise told me I had no genius, and that I never could be a great composer."

"And did he deceive you? what have you proved yourself? Can you for this, hate and maliciously slander him, because he honestly advised you to desist from useless efforts, to limit yourself to a small circle in our art, or rather to become an honest tailor or shoemaker?"

Elias shrugged his shoulders with vexation, squinted sullenly at the speaker, and answered in a fierce tone: "Yes—I hate him! I shall always hate him! what need was there of telling me so? Even if I was in error—I dreamed of fame and gold—and have had neither! Curse him! He has embittered my life; and I will embitter his, whenever it is in my power."

"Go—wretch!" cried Piccini, full of horror. "Go, we have nothing more in common. The divinity of man is honor; your gods are selfishness— vanity—envy—cowardly malice! Such as you deserve no sympathy— away!" And gnashing his teeth with spite and impotent rage, Elias Hegrin left Piccini's house.

Piccini's opera was greatly admired, but that of his adversary obtained a complete victory, and awakened an enthusiasm till then unknown even in Paris.

Followed by the acclamations of the enraptured multitude, after the third representation of his work, Gluck left the opera-house on his way to his quiet home. He was accompanied only by his favorite Mehul, who was to be his guest for the evening, and aid him to celebrate his victory.— Arrived at Gluck's house, they both entered the room where the collation was prepared, but started with surprise as they entered; for a man, wrapped in his mantle, stood at the window, looking out upon the clear starry night. At the rustling behind him he turned round.

"Signor Piccini!" cried Gluck, surprised.

"Not unwelcome, I hope?" said Piccini, smiling.

"Most welcome, by my troth!" answered Gluck, taking and cordially shaking the offered hand. "Yes, I honor so noble an adversary."

"Talk no more of adversaries!" cried Piccini earnestly; "our strife is at an end; I acknowledge you for my master, and will be happy and proud to call you my friend! Let the Gluckists and the Piccinists dispute as long as they like; Gluck and Piccini understand each other!"

"And esteem each other!" exclaimed Gluck with vivacity; "Indeed, Piccini, it shall be so!"

FOOTNOTES

[7] Gluck has been called the Michael Angelo of music.

[8] Gluck's own words to Rousseau.

BEETHOVEN

If, dear reader, you have never been so happy as to travel through the beautiful country of the Rhine, I wish from my heart you may speedily have that pleasure; for truly, he who has not seen that unrivalled land, with its pretty villages and its noble cities, its smiling villas and vineyards, and romantic ruined castles—its lordly Rhine, the father of all—nor heard the cheerful songs of its peasants, laboring in the vineyards, cannot know how dear and lovely is our native Germany!

If you have been at Bonn, dear reader, it follows as a matter of course, that you left not unvisited the venerable cathedral. And how solemn and strange the feeling that filled your heart, when entering, for the first time, beneath the shadow of those lofty, twilight arches! An awful stillness prevailed around, and speaking pictures looked forth upon you; then as you advanced, streams of softened light came downward from the arched windows of the gigantic nave! The organ was heard; a low, distant murmur, swelling louder and higher, till, rising into powerful harmony, the "Gloria" burst forth; then, overpowered by emotion, rapt in contemplation of the unspeakable greatness of Deity—conscious of the feebleness of man—you could but kneel and adore!

Mc Rae, sc.

BEETHOVEN.

At least, so it was with me—and often so—when a youth. I have listened to that music, heard it from beginning to end, then rushed down from the choir, to throw myself prostrate on the marble pavement, and weep tears of joy! Were not heaven and earth my own? Did I not see them in their holiest loveliness? Heard I not enraptured, their thousand thousand voices—from the sweet murmuring of the flowers, to the awe-inspiring thunder-peal? Understood I not the mysterious harmony of all I saw and heard?

Alas! those years of enthusiasm are flown; the harmony is broken! The flowers that mark the coming of spring, have no longer a voice for me; the startling thunder, that once spoke of the sunshine and beauty about to succeed the short-lived storm—has no significance; even the tones of the magnificent music fail to lift my soul to the height of devotion, inspiring her to mingle her adoration with the world-wide hymn of praise! My heart is hard and cold; but seldom roused, and relapsing into deadness when the brief excitement is over. I am older even in feeling than in years. I shun the merry company of men; I shudder at their jests—their careless hearts—their jovial faces; for they seem to me like shadows—gibbering forms—that mockingly repeat the tones of life. Enough of myself; how prone are we to run into egotism! Let me rather amuse the reader by some reminiscences of a gifted individual, whose fame is linked with the scenes I have spoken of.

THE BOY

It was a mild October afternoon, in the year 1784. A boat was coming down the Rhine, close to that point where the fair city of Bonn sits on its left shore. The company on board consisted of old and young persons of both sexes, returning from an excursion of pleasure.

The sun was sinking in the west, and touched the mountain summits, castle-crowned, with gold and purple, as the boat came to the shore not far from the city. The company landed, full of gaiety and mirth, the young people walking on before, while their seniors followed, as happy as they, though more thoughtful and less noisy. They adjourned to a public garden, close on the river side, to finish the day of social enjoyment by partaking of a collation. Old and young were seated, ere long, around the stone table set under the large trees. The crimson faded in the west; the moon poured her soft light, glimmering through the leafy canopy above them, and was reflected in full beauty in the waters of the Rhine.

The merriment of the guests was at its height; the wine sparkled, and lively toasts were drunk, in which the youngsters joined as gleefully as their elders.

"Your boys are right merry fellows," said a benevolent-looking old gentleman, addressing Herr von Beethoven, a tenor singer in the Electoral chapel; pointing, at the same time, to his two sons—lads of ten and fourteen years of age. "They will certainly turn out something clever," he continued, laughing, as he watched their pranks; "but tell me, Beethoven, why do you not take Louis with you, when you indulge the children with a party of pleasure?"

"Because," answered the person he addressed, "because Louis is a stubborn, dogged, stupid boy, whose troublesome behavior would only spoil our mirth."

"Ah!" returned the old gentleman, "you are always finding fault with the poor lad, and perhaps impose too hard tasks upon him! I see you are more indulgent to the others. It is no wonder he becomes dull and obstinate; nay, I am only surprised that he has not, ere this, broken loose from your sharp control."

"My dear Simrock," replied Beethoven, laughing, "I have a remedy at hand for such humors—my good Spanish cane, which, you see, is of the toughest! Louis is well acquainted with its excellent properties, and stands in wholesome awe thereof! And trust me, neighbor, I know best what is for the boy's good. He has talent, and must be taught to cultivate it; but he will never go to work properly, unless I drive out some of his capricious notions, and set his head right."

"Ah, Johann!" interposed Madame von Beethoven, "you do not know the boy! He has the best and most docile of dispositions, if you only manage him in the proper way."

"The proper way!" repeated the father; "and so I must coax and cajole him, and ask his leave humbly to give him a word of instruction!"

"No, certainly; only grant him the same indulgences you allow to his brothers."

"He is not like Carl and Johann," was the muttered answer; "they ought not to be treated alike."

"Nay, nay, neighbor," said Simrock, earnestly.

"Let us talk no more about it," interrupted Beethoven; "I know well what I am doing; and my reasons are satisfactory to myself. *These* boys are a comfort to me; a couple of fine lads; I need hardly ever speak to them, for they are ready to spring at a glance; they always obey me with alacrity and affection. Louis, on the other hand, has been bearish from his infancy. I have never sought to rule him by fear, but only to drive out a little of his sulkiness now and then; yet nothing avails. When his brothers joke with him, as all boys will sometimes, he usually quits the room murmuring; and it is easy to see he would fain beat them if he were not afraid of me. As to his studies, music is the only thing he will learn—I mean with good will; or if he consents to apply himself to anything else, I must first knock it into him that it has something to do with music. *Then* he will go to work, but it is his humor not to do it otherwise! If I give him a commission to execute for me, the most arrant clodpole could not be more stupid about it."

"Let him alone, then, to live for his favorite art," said Herr Simrock. "It is often the case that the true artist is a fool in matters of every-day life."

"Those are silly fancies," answered Beethoven, again laughing. "Helen is always talking so. The true artist is as much a man as others, and proves himself so; will thrive like the rest of the world, and take care of his family. I know all about it; money—money's the thing! I mean Louis to do well; and that he may learn to do well, I spare not trouble—nor the rod either, when it is necessary! The boy will live to thank me for my pains."

Here the conversation was interrupted, and the subject was not resumed. The hours flew lightly by; it struck nine, and the festive company separated, to return to their homes.

Carl and Johann were in high glee as they went home; they sprang up the steps before their father, and pulled the door bell. The door was opened, and a boy about twelve years old stood in the entry, with a lamp in his hand. He was short and stout for his age; but a sickly paleness, more strongly marked by the contrast of his thick black hair, was observable on his face. His small grey eyes were quick and restless in their movement, very piercing when he fixed them on any object, but softened by the shade of his long dark lashes; his mouth was delicately formed, and the compression of the lips betrayed both pride and sorrow. It was Louis Beethoven.

"Where are my father and mother?" asked he.

"Hallo, nightcap!" cried Carl, laughing, "is it you? Cannot you open your eyes? They are just behind us!"

Without answering his brother, Louis came to meet his parents, and bade them "good evening."

His mother greeted him affectionately; his father said, while the boy busied himself fastening the door—"Well, Louis, I hope you have finished your task?"

"I have, father."

"Very good; to-morrow I will look and see if you have earned your breakfast." So saying, the elder Beethoven went into his chamber; his wife followed him, after bidding her sons good night, Louis more tenderly than any of them. Carl and Johann withdrew with their brother to their common sleeping apartment, entertaining him with a description of their day of festivity. "Now, Louis," said little Johann, as they finished their account, "if you had not been such a dunce, our father would have taken you along; but he says he thinks that you will be little better than a dunce all the days of your life—and self-willed and stubborn besides."

"Don't talk about that any more!" answered Louis, "but come to bed!"

"Yes, you are always a sleepy head!" cried they both, laughing; but in a few moments after getting into bed, both were asleep, and snoring heartily.

Louis took the lamp from the table, left the apartment softly, and went up stairs to an attic chamber, where he was wont to retire when he wished to be out of the way of his teasing brothers. He had fitted up the little room for himself as well as his means permitted. A table with three legs, a leathern chair, the bottom partly out, and an old piano, which he had rescued from the possession of rats and mice, made up the furniture; and here, in company with his beloved violin, he was accustomed to pass his happiest hours. He was passionately fond of solitude, and nothing would have better pleased him, than permission to take long walks in the country, where he could hear the murmur of streams and the rustling of foliage, and the surging of the winds on the mountains. But he had not that liberty. His only recreation was to pass a few hours here in his favorite pursuit, indulging his fantasies and reveries, undisturbed by his noisy brothers, or his strict father's reproof.

The boy felt, young as he was, that he was not understood by one of his family, not even excepting his mother. She loved him tenderly, and always took his part when his father found fault with him; but she never knew what was passing in his mind, because he never uttered it. How could he, shy and inexperienced, clothe in words what was burning in his bosom—what was perpetually striving after a language more intense and expressive than human speech? But his genius was not long to be unappreciated.

The next morning a messenger came from the Elector to Beethoven's house, bringing an order for him to repair immediately to the palace, and fetch with him his son Louis. The father was surprised; not more so than the boy, whose heart beat with undefined apprehension as they entered the princely mansion. A servant was in waiting, and conducted them without delay, or further announcement, to the presence of the Elector, who was attended by two gentlemen.

The Elector received old Beethoven with great kindness, and said, "We have heard much, recently, of the extraordinary musical talent of your son Louis. Have you brought him along with you?" Beethoven replied in the affirmative, stepped back to the door, and bade the boy come in.

"Come nearer, my little lad!" cried the Elector, graciously; "do not be shy. This gentleman here, is our new court organist—Herr Neefe; the other is the famous composer, Herr Yunker, from Cologne. We promised them both they should hear you play something; and think you may venture upon a tune before them. The late Master von Eden always spoke well of you."

"Yes, he was pleased with me!" murmured the boy, softly. The Prince smiled, and bade him take his seat and begin. He sat down himself in a large easy chair. Louis went to the piano, and without examining the pile of notes that lay awaiting his selection, played a short piece; then a light and graceful melody, which he executed with such ease and spirit—nay, in so admirable a manner, that his distinguished auditors could not forbear expressing their surprise; and even his father was struck. When he left off playing, the Elector arose, came up to him, laid his hand on his head, and said encouragingly—

"Well done, my boy! we are pleased with you! Now, Master Yunker," turning to the gentleman on his right hand, "what say you?"

"Your Highness!" answered the composer, "I will venture to say the lad has had considerable practice with that last air, to execute it so well."

Louis burst into a laugh at this remark; the others looked surprised and grave; his father darted an angry glance at him, and the boy, conscious that he had done something wrong, became instantly silent.

The Elector himself laughed at the comical scene. "And pray what are you laughing at, my little fellow?" asked he.

The boy colored and looked down as he replied, "Because Herr Yunker thinks I have learned the air by heart, when it occurred to me but just now while I was playing."

"Then," returned the composer, "if you really improvised that piece, you ought to go through at sight a motiv I will give you presently."

"Let me try," answered Louis.

"If his Gracious Highness will permit me," said the composer.

Permission was granted. Yunker wrote down on paper a difficult motiv, and handed it to the boy. Louis read it over carefully, and immediately began to play it according to the rules of counterpoint. The composer listened attentively—his astonishment increasing at every turn in the music; and when at last it was finished in a manner so spirited as to surpass his expectations, his eyes sparkled, and he looked on the lad with keen interest, as the possessor of a genius rarely to be found.

"If he goes on in this way," said he in a low tone to the Elector, "I can assure your Highness that a very great counterpointist may be made out of him."

Neefe observed with a smile, "I agree with the master; but it seems to me the boy's style inclines rather too much to the gloomy and melancholy."

"It is well," replied his Highness, smiling, "be it your care that it does not become too much so. Herr von Beethoven," he continued, addressing the father; "we take an interest in your son; and it is our pleasure that he complete the studies commenced under your tuition, under that of Herr Neefe. He may come to live with him after to-day. We will take care that he wants for nothing; and his further advancement, also, shall be cared for. You are willing, Louis, to come and live with this gentleman?"

The boy's eyes were fixed on the ground; he raised them, and glanced first at Neefe and then at his father. The offer was a tempting one; he would fare better and have more liberty in his new abode. But there was his *father!* whom he had always loved; who, spite of his severity, had doubtless loved him, and now stood looking upon him earnestly and sadly. He hesitated no longer, but seizing Beethoven's hand and pressing it to his heart, he cried, "No! no! I cannot leave my father."

"You are a good and dutiful lad," said his Highness. "Well, I will not ask you to leave your father, who must be very fond of you. You shall live with him and come and take your lessons of Herr Neefe; that is our will. Adieu! Herr von Beethoven."

From this time Louis lived a new life. His father treated him no longer with harshness, and even reproved his brothers when they tried to tease him. Carl and Johann grew shy of him, however, when they saw what a favorite he had become. Louis found himself no longer restrained, but came and went as he pleased; he took frequent excursions in the country, which he enjoyed with more than youthful pleasure, when the lessons were over.

His worthy master was astonished at the rapid progress of his pupil in his beloved art. "But, Louis," said he, one day, "if you would become a great musician, you must not neglect every thing besides music. You must acquire foreign languages, particularly Latin, Italian, and French. These are all necessary, that you may know what learned men have said and written upon the art. You must not fancy all this knowledge is to come to you of itself; you must be diligent and devote yourself to study, and be sure of being well repaid in the end. For without such cultivation you can never excel in music; nay, even genius, left to itself, is but little better than blind impulse. Would you leave your name to posterity as a true artist, make your own all that bears relation to your art."

Louis promised, and kept his word. In the midst of his playing he would leave off, however much it cost him, if the hour struck for his lessons in the languages. So closely he applied himself, that in a year's time he was tolerably well acquainted, not only with Latin, French, and Italian, but also with the English. His father marvelled at his progress not a little; for years he had labored in vain, with starvation and blows, to make the boy learn the first principles of those languages. He had never, indeed, taken the trouble to explain to him their use in the acquisition of the science of music.

In 1785 appeared Louis's first sonatas. They displayed uncommon talent, and gave promise that the youthful artist would in future accomplish something great, though scarcely yet could be found in them a trace of that gigantic genius, whose death forty years afterward filled all Europe with sorrow.

The best understanding was now established between father and son, and the lad's natural generosity and warmth of heart being unchecked by undue severity, his kindly feelings overflowed upon all around him. This disposition to love his friends, and to enjoy life, remained with the artist to the end of his days. The benevolent Master Simrock was much pleased at his good fortune, and withal somewhat surprised, for spite of his compassionate espousal of the boy's cause, he looked upon Louis rather as a dull fellow. Now, his opinion was quite changed; and to show his good will he sent him several presents, and insisted on his coming frequently to his lodgings, to drink a glass of Rhenish in company with his old friend.

"We were both mistaken in the lad," he would say to old Beethoven, "he abounds in wit and odd fancies, but I do not altogether like his mixing up in his music all sorts of strange conceits; the best way, to my notion, is a plain one. Let him follow the great Mozart, step by step; after all, he is the only one, and there is none to come up to him—none!" And Louis's father, who also idolized Mozart, always agreed with his neighbor in his judgment, and echoed—"None!"

Thus the summer flew by; the foliage grew yellow and began to fall. Our young hero delighted—as what poetical soul does not?—in communion with nature. He wandered often in the woods, and welcomed the autumn breezes that scattered the yellow leaves at his feet. I have always found a pleasant melancholy in my walks at this season, when the slant rays of the sun gleam upon dismantled trees, and the wealth of summer lies on the ground; when the winds sigh through the desolate branches, or the ear is startled by the woodman's stroke, or perhaps the winding of the hunter's horn.

Let none despair of himself to whom Heaven has granted the power of enjoying the beauty of Nature! In her maternal bosom is consolation for every wo! He is her favored child. Doth he weep over blighted hopes or crushed affections—unreproved his tears flow, and amid silence and solitude, in the calm wood, he hears angel voices that mourn with him, while from the stars far up in heaven comes down a whisper of consolation; "Life is brief, and frail and changeful is the heart of man; but Love is infinite—eternal; thou hast friends that know no change; look above, and hope!" And with the coming sun that wakes to life such myriads of happy creatures, shall new strength and hope visit his soul. But alas for thee! child of sorrow, if thou hearest not that kind healing voice; if night is starless to thine eyes—ere ceases thy heart to beat! Could life arise for thee from the dead, thou wouldst still be wretched, wouldst still stand alone and uncared for—kept but by Divine compassion from despair.

Enjoy while thou canst, oh, youthful enthusiast! the luxury of thy being—the beauty around thee! Think'st thou 'tis but after all a lovely dream? No—'tis a fair reality, still more fleeting than a dream! Dreams may return to enchant us; realities that are past, never!

The first lasting sorrow that befel Louis was the loss of his father. Beethoven's health failed at the beginning of winter. Ere long his physician pronounced him beyond hope. By his own request his family were informed that his end was near. Helen and her two sons, Carl and Johann, received the intelligence with loud lamentations; Louis said not a word, but his grief was no less acute.

At night the afflicted family gathered round the bed of the dying. "My Louis!" said Beethoven, faintly. The boy was kneeling by the bed, pale as the sick man himself. He clasped his father's cold hand and pressed it to his lips, but could not speak for tears.

"God's best blessings be upon you, my son!" said his parent. "Promise me that throughout life you will never forsake your brothers; I know they have not loved you as they ought; that is partly my fault; promise me that whatever may happen, you will continue to regard and cherish them."

"I will—I will, dear father!" cried Louis, sobbing. Beethoven pressed his hand in token of satisfaction. The same night he expired. The grief of Louis was unbounded. It was a bitter thing thus to lose a parent just as the ties of nature were strengthened by mutual appreciation and confidence; but it was necessary that he should rouse himself to minister support and comfo to his suffering mother.

The first keenness of his sorrow was blunted by time; and he returne with renewed diligence to his studies. His mother often remonstrated again his pursuit of them with such absorbing eagerness. "You will injure you health, my beloved son," she would say. But he would answer cheerfull "Be not uneasy, dear mother; the winter will soon be past, and when sprin comes I will relax my labors."

Louis was now in his eighteenth year; and the period was memorable i his life. A young kinswoman of his mother, whose parents lived in Cologn came on a visit to Bonn. Adelaide was a beautiful, sprightly girl. Louis sa her, and it seemed to him that all his previous existence was but a voic and that his real being had but just begun. He was conscious of a thousan new perceptions, and thought he had never before felt or seen what was i the world. Nature had new charms for him; he had capacities for joy befor undreamed of. As for music, till now, it seemed to him the spirit of art ha slumbered within him. How magnificent was her awakening! The magi name of Adelaide, her voice, her smile, called his genius into full life, an he felt that he had power to do as he had never done.

First love! Is it not a misnomer? for but *once* can the heart bow to th all-subduing influence! Once cold can it ever be warmed again to that brigh luxuriance of life and feeling? And how soon does the tender flower born o fantasy, wither in the breath of reality—never to bloom again! Memory o the lost paradise alone remains; it is well if there remain not also the saddes fruit of disappointment—a sceptical scorn of all that seems winning anc lovely. Happy he whom fate deprives of the object of his love before th sweet illusion is over! No words can paint his heartfelt anguish at the loss But one bliss is left him; the image of the beloved is still robed in its magic charms; his faith in his ideal is still unshaken. His heart has never proved the bitterest pang.

For a time our youthful hero was the happiest of the happy, for he yielded his soul to the sway of love, and music was its appropriate language. But Adelaide understood him not; how could she? His eyes indeed spoke a passion deeper than words could reveal; his melodies were of a bolder and higher, yet a tenderer cast; but it was only in the silence of his own apartment, when he sat playing alone, that these signs of emotion might have been discovered. In her presence he sought not to paint in language his devoted love; it was enough for him to look upon her, to watch her graceful movements, to listen to her voice. That was inspiration enough; he wished not for more.

The fair sex are not usually pleased with this species of mute homage; all maidens are not Cecilias; most of them prefer a lover bold enough to venture on an open confession of their power to charm. The fair dream Louis indulged was ere long to be rudely broken. I am not going to give the reader a melancholy love tale; suffice it to say the boy's passion became known to his brother, Carl, and one evening he chanced to overhear a conversation between him and Adelaide. Carl was telling his cousin of Louis's love for her, and laughing at his simplicity in never dreaming of declaring it. Adelaide laughed heartily at her "unsophisticated lover," as she called him, saying she had never suspected such a thing—that she could not help pitying the poor boy—yet was half inclined to draw him out, it was such a capital joke! Carl joined in her merriment, and the two concerted a scheme for their own amusement at the expense of poor Louis.

Pale and trembling, while he leaned against the window-seat concealed by the folds of a curtain, Louis listened to this colloquy. As his brother and cousin left the room, he rushed past them to his own apartment, locked himself in, and did not come forth that night. Afterwards he took pains to shun the company of the heartless fair one; and was always out alone on his walks, or in his own room, where he worked every night till quite exhausted.

"The lad has found us out," said Carl to his pretty cousin.

"What a pity!" answered Adelaide; "I should like to have brought him to reason in my own way, I confess. Such an excellent joke! It is really a pity!"

THE YOUTH

The first emotions of chagrin and mortification soon passed away in the bosom of young Beethoven, but he did not soon recover his vivacity. His warmest feelings had been cruelly outraged; the spring of love was never again to bloom for him; and it seemed, too, that the fair blossoms of genius also were nipped in the bud. His self-confidence, so necessary to the development of the artist, was shaken—nay, had nearly deserted him.

The wings of his spirit had unfolded joyously in the sunshine of love, and were spread for a bold flight into the upper regions of Art, where the every-day world could not follow him. As in after life, he was entirely indifferent to the applause of the multitude, and never sought it. What he thought and felt he expressed in his enthusiastic inspiration; his best reward was the consciousness of having aimed at the best, and deserved the approbation of true artists.

If, however, the cultivated taste of the present day fails fully to appreciat him, it will not be wondered at that the critics of the time, fettered as the were to the established form, should have been shocked at his departur from their rules. Even Mozart, whose fame stood so high, whose nam was pronounced with such enthusiastic admiration, what struggles ha he not been forced into with those who would not approve his so calle innovations!

The youth of nineteen had struck out a bolder path! What marve then, that instead of encouragement, nothing but censures awaited him His master, Neefe, who was accustomed to boast of him as his pride an joy, now said coldly and bitterly, his pupil had not fulfilled his cherishe expectations—nay, was so taken up with his new-fangled conceits, that h feared he was forever lost to real art.

"Is it so, indeed?" asked Louis of himself in his moments of misgiving and dejection. "Is all a delusion? have I lived till now in a false dream? Oh where is truth on earth? I wish I were dead, since my life is worse thar useless!"

Young Beethoven sat in his chamber, leaning his head on his hand, looking gloomily out of the vine-shaded window. There was a knock at the door: *piano—pianissimo; crescendo,—forte,—fortissimo!* Still, wrapped in his deep despondency, he heard it not, nor answered with a "come in."

The door was opened softly a little way, and in the crevice appeared a long and very red nose, and a pair of small, twinkling eyes, overshadowed by coal-black bushy eye-brows. Gradually became visible the whole withered, sallow, comical, yet good-humored face of Master Peter Pirad.

Peter Pirad was a famous kettle-drummer, and was much ridiculed on account of his partiality for that instrument, though he also excelled on many others. He always insisted that the kettle-drum was the most melodious, grand, and expressive instrument, and he would play it alone in the orchestra, *partoutement*, as he said. But he was one of the best-hearted persons in the world. It was quite impossible to look upon his tall, gaunt, clumsy figure, which, year in and year out, appeared in the well-worn yellow woolen coat, siskin colored breeches, and dark worsted stockings, with his peculiar fashioned felt cap, without a strong inclination to laugh; yet ludicrous as was his outward man, none remained long unconvinced that spite of his exterior, spite of his numerous eccentricities, Peter Pirad was one of the most amiable of men. [9]

From his childhood, Louis had been attached to Pirad; in later years they had been much together. Pirad, who had been absent several months from Bonn, and had just returned, was surprised beyond measure to find his favorite so changed. He entered the room, and walking up quietly, touched the youth on the shoulder, saying, in a tone as gentle as he could assume, "Why, Louis! what the mischief has got into your head, that you would not hear me?"

Louis started, turned round, and recognising his old friend, reached him his hand.

"You see," continued Pirad, "you see I have returned safely and happily from my visit to Vienna. Ah! Louis! Louis! that's a city for you! May I be hanged if 'tis not a noble city! Something new every day; something to please all tastes. Such living! Oh! 'twas admirable! and as for taste in art, you would go mad with the Viennese! As for artists, there are Albrechtsberger and Haydn, Mozart and Salieri,—my dear fellow, you *must* go to Vienna." With that Pirad threw up his arms as if beating the kettle-drum, (he always did so when excited) and made such comical faces, that his young companion, spite of his sorrow, could not help bursting out a laughing.

"Saker!" cried Pirad, "that is clever; I like to see that you can laugh yet; it is a good sign; and you shall soon give care and trouble to the winds. Ay, ay, where old Peter comes, he banishes despondency; and now, Louis, pluck up like a man, and tell me what all this means. Why do I find you in such a bad humor, as if you had a hole in your skin, or the drums were broken? You know me, lad, for a capital kettle-drummer; there is not another such in the land. I warrant you there are plenty of ninnies who fancy they can beat me; but everybody who is a judge laughs at them. You know, too, I have always wished you well; so out with it, my brave boy, what is the matter with you?"

"Ah!" replied Beethoven, "much more than I can say; I have lost all hope, all trust in myself. You, perhaps, will not understand me, Pirad; you will censure me if I have been doing wrong; yet you have always been a kind friend to me, and I will tell you all my troubles, for indeed, I cannot keep them to myself any longer!" So the melancholy youth told all to his attentive auditor: his unhappy passion for his cousin; his master's dissatisfaction with him, and his own sad misgivings.

When he had ended, Pirad remained silent awhile, his forefinger laid on his long nose, in an attitude of thoughtfulness. At length, raising his head, he gave his advice as follows:

"This is a sad story, Louis! but it convinces me of the truth of what I used to say: your late excellent father—I say it with all respect for his memory—and your other friends, never knew what was really in you. As for your disappointment in love, that is always a business that brings much trouble and little profit. Women are capricious creatures at best, and no man who has a respect for himself will be a slave to their humors. was a little touched in that way, myself, when I was something more than your age, but the kettle-drum soon put such nonsense out of my head. M advice is, that you stick to your music, and let her go; my friendship will be a truer accompaniment for you; and that, I need not assure you, will never fail. For what concerns the court-organist, Neefe, I am more vexed his absurdity is what I did not precisely expect. I will say nothing of Her Yunker; he forgets music in his zeal for counterpoint; as if he should say he could not see the wood for the tall trees, or the city for the houses! Have I not heard him assert, ay, with my own living ears, slanderously assert that the kettle-drum was a superfluous instrument? Only think, Louis, the kettle-drum a superfluous instrument! Donner and —. Did not the great Haydn—bless him for it!—undertake a noble symphony expressly with reference to the kettle-drum? What could you do with "*Dies iræ—dies illa,*" without the kettle-drum? I played it at Vienna in Don Giovanni, the chapel master Mozart himself directing. In the spirit scene, Louis, where the statue has ended his first speech, and Don Giovanni in consternation speaks to his attendants, while the anxious heart of the appalled sinner is throbbing the kettle-drum thundering away—" Here Pirad began to sing with tragical gesticulation. "Yes, Louis, I beat the kettle-drum with a witness, while an icy thrill crept through my bones: and for all that, the kettle-drum is a useless instrument! What blockheads there are in the world! To return to your master,—I wonder at his stupidity, and yet I have no cause to wonder. You are perhaps aware that many wise and sensible people take me for a fool and a ridiculous fellow, because I disagree with them on certain subjects; nevertheless, I know much that wise and sensible people do not know. Now my creed is, that Art is a noble inheritance left us by our ancestors, which it is our duty to enlarge and increase by all honest and honorable means. There are those among the heirs who think the capital already large enough; talk of the impossibility of bettering it—a bird in the hand being worth two in the bush, etc. But such spiritless persons only waste what they know not how to use to advantage. He who has a soul for art will not spare his labor, but consider how he may best do justice to the testator, and render useful the good gift of the Almighty, surely not bestowed for nought! No, my dear boy, I tell you I hold you for an honest heir, who would not waste your substance; who has not only power, but will, to perform his duty. So take courage; be not cast down at trifles; and take my advice and go to Vienna. *Himmeltausend!* whom have you here above yourself? but there you will find your masters: Mozart, Haydn, Albrechtsberger, and others not so well known, but well worthy your emulation. One year, nay, a few months in Vienna will do more for you than ten years vegetating in this good city. You can soon learn, then, what you are capable of, and what not; only mind what Mozart says, when you are playing in his hearing."

The young man started up, his eyes sparkling, his cheeks glowing with new enthusiasm, and embraced Pirad warmly. "You are right, my good friend!" he cried, "I will go to Vienna; and shame on any one who despises your counsel! Yes, I will go to Vienna."

When he told his mother of his resolution she looked grave, and wept when all was ready for his departure. But Pirad, with a sympathizing distortion of countenance, said to her, "Be not disturbed, my good Madame von Beethoven! Louis shall come back to you much livelier than he is now; and even if he does not, why, the lot of the artist is always to suffer some privation, that he may cling more closely to his science. And, madam, you may comfort yourself with the hope that your son *will* become a great artist!"

Young Beethoven visited Vienna for the first time in the spring of the year 1792. He experienced strange emotions as he entered that great city; perhaps a dim presentiment of what he was in future years to accomplish and to suffer. He was not so fortunate this time as to find Haydn there; that artist had set out for London but a little before. He was disappointed, but the more anxious to make the acquaintance of Mozart.

Albrechtsberger, Haydn's intimate friend, undertook to introduce him. "But we must not be out of patience, Beethoven," said he, good humoredly, "if we have to go frequently to the master's house without finding him. Schickaneder has got him in his clutches at present—for Mozart has written an opera for his company. There are some new and difficult scenes in the piece which the manager wants to arrange, and he gives our friend the master no rest, with his suggestions and contrivances. It is a shame that Mozart has to work for such a man; but he must live, you know, with his wife and children; and I heard Haydn say his place here has only brought him in eight hundred guilders for the last year."

They went several times, in fact, to Mozart's house before they found him at home. At last, on a rainy day, one that suited not for an excursion with the Impressario, they were so fortunate as to find him. They heard him from the street, playing; our young hero's heart beat wildly as they went up the steps, for he looked on that dwelling as the temple of art.

When they were in the hall, they saw through a side door that stood open, Mozart sitting playing the piano; close by him sat a short, fat man, with a shining red face; and at the window Madame Mozart, holding her youngest son, Wolfgang, on her lap, while the eldest was sitting on the floor at her feet.

"Stop, my good sir," cried the fat man, seizing Mozart's hand, "I do no altogether like the last! You must alter it, you must indeed! Look you, thi is what occurs to me: that slow adagio may stand, if you like; the people d not care about listening to it; they lean back in their seats and gaze at th doors swinging; but that allegro, it does not suit—"

"I believe you are a fool outright, besides having no conscience! interrupted Mozart, rising angrily from the piano. "I have yielded you fa too much, but the overture you have nothing to do with; and I wish I ma be hanged if I alter a single note in it for you! I would rather take back th whole opera and throw it into the fire!"

"If you will not write popular music," grunted the other, "you canno expect me to have your pieces represented."

"Very well," said the master, decidedly, "then we owe each othe nothing, and I need plague myself no more about it."

"Nay, nay," pursued the fat man, who changed his ground when he saw the composer was really in earnest, "you may leave the overture as it is it is all the same to me; I only wanted to give you my ideas on the subject."

"I would not give much for your ideas," muttered the master; and he turned to receive his new visitors. His face soon brightened up; he greeted Albrechtsberger cordially, and looked inquiringly on his young companion

"Herr von Beethoven from Bonn," said Albrechtsberger, presenting his friend; "an excellent composer and skilful musician, who is desirous of making your acquaintance."

"You are heartily welcome, both of you, and I shall expect you to remain and dine with me to day," said Mozart; and taking Louis by the hand he led him to the window where his wife sat. "This is my Constance," he continued; "and these are my boys; this little fellow is but three months old"—and throwing his arm round Constance's neck, he stooped and kissed the smiling infant.

Louis looked with surprise on the great artist! He had fancied him quite different in his exterior; a tall man, of powerful frame, like Händel. He saw a slight, low figure, wrapped in a furred coat, notwithstanding the warmth of the season; his pale face showed the evidences of long continued ill health; his large, bright, speaking eyes alone reminded one of the genius that had created Idomeneus and Don Giovanni.

"So you, too, are a composer?" asked the fat man, coming up to Beethoven; "Look you, sir, I will tell you what to do; lay yourself out for the opera; the opera is the great thing!"

Louis looked at him in surprise and silence.

"Master Emanuel Schickaneder, the famous Impressario," said Albrechtsberger, scarcely controlling his disposition to laugh.

"Yes," continued the fat man, assuming an air of importance, "I tell you I know the public, and know how to get the weak side of it; if Mozart would only be led by me he could do well! I say, if you will compose me something,—(I have written half-a-dozen operas myself)—by the way, here is a season ticket; I shall be happy if you will visit my theatre; to-morrow night we shall perform the Magic Flute; it is an admirable piece, some of the music is first rate, some not so good, and I myself play the Papageno."

"You ought to do something in that line," said Mozart, laughing, "Your singing puts one in mind of an unoiled door-hinge."

The Impressario took a pinch of snuff, and answered with an important air, "I can tell you, sir, the singing is quite a secondary thing in the opera, for I know the public; however, I have some good singers; and as for myself, even you, Mozart, will acknowledge my merit one of these days." And he went on to tell them of an ingenious and comical arrangement he had devised in the dress of the new part.

They were all much amused with it; and the Impressario continued to repeat, "I can tell you, I know the public."

Here several persons, invited guests of the composer, came in; among them Mozart's pupils, Sutzmayr and Wolfl, with the Abbe Stadler and the excellent tenorist, Peyerl. After an hour or so spent in agreeable conversation, enlivened by an air from Mozart, they went to the dinner table. Schickaneder here played his part well, doing ample justice to the viands and wine. The dinner was really excellent; and the host, notwithstanding his appearance of feeble health, was in first rate spirits, abounding in gayety, which soon communicated itself to the rest of the company.

After they had dined, and the coffee had been brought in, Mozart took his new acquaintance to the window, apart from the others, and asked, "Did you come through Leipzig?"

Beethoven replied in the affirmative.

"Did you remain long there?"

"I merely passed through."

"That is a pity! I love Leipzig; I have many dear friends there; the dearest, my good old Doles, is dead some time since; yet I have others, and when you return thither you may stay longer; I will give you letters to them.

But now, I beg of you, tell me how it stands with yourself, and what you have learned? If I can be of any service to you, command me."

Louis pressed the master's hand, which was cordially extended to him, and without hesitation gave his history, and informed him of his plans, concluding by asking his advice.

Mozart listened with a benevolent smile; and when he had ended, said, "Come, you must let me hear you play." With that he led him to an admirable instrument in another apartment; opened it, and invited him to select a piece of music.

"Will you give me a thema?" asked Louis.

The master looked surprised; but without reply wrote some lines on a leaf of paper and handed it to the young man. Beethoven looked over it; it was a difficult chromatic fuguetheme, the intricacy of which demanded much skill and experience. But without being discouraged, he collected all his powers and began to execute it.

Mozart did not conceal the surprise and pleasure he felt when Louis first began to play. The youth perceived the impression he had made, and was stimulated to more spirited efforts. As he proceeded the master's pale cheeks flushed; his eyes sparkled; and stepping on tiptoe to the open door, he whispered to his guests, "Listen, I beg of you! you shall have something worth hearing."

That moment rewarded all the pains, and banished the apprehensions of the young aspirant after excellence. Louis went through his trial piece with admirable spirit, sprang up, and went to Mozart; seizing both his hands and pressing them to his throbbing heart, he murmured, "I also am an artist!"

"You are, indeed!" cried Mozart, "and no common one! And what may be wanting, you will not fail to find, and make your own. The grand thing, the living spirit, you bore within you from the beginning, as all do who possess it. Come back soon to Vienna, my young friend—very soon! Father Haydn, Albrechtsberger, friend Stadler and I will receive you with open arms; and if you need advice or assistance, we will give it you to the best of our ability."

The other guests crowded round Beethoven, and hailed him as a worthy pupil of art! even the silly Impressario looked at him with vastly increased respect, and said, "I can tell you, I know the public,—well, we will talk more of the matter this evening over a glass of wine."

"I also am an artist!" repeated Louis to himself, when he returned late to his lodgings. Much improved in spirits, and re-inspired with confidence in himself, he returned to Bonn; and ere long put in practice his scheme of paying Vienna a second visit.

This he accomplished at the Elector's expense, being sent by him. He did not, indeed, see Mozart again, nor could he even find the grave of his deceased friend. But the spirit of the illustrious master was with him; and the world knows well, how Father Haydn honored the last request of his friend.

And thus I close this brief account of the early years of the greatest master of modern times. His boyhood was not free from care and suffering; his youth was troubled; and we who are familiar with the events of his life, know how much he endured as a man, even while his hours were passed in preparing "joy, pure, spiritual joy" for us all. But he was a true artist; he fulfilled his noble mission; and that consciousness, and his earnest longings after the pure and the good, gave him strength to bear the woes of life, strength to pass through the dark valley of death, whither he went down rejoicing, as a conqueror to victory.

His first disappointment is immortalized in his song of "Adelaide." In his opera "Leonore," he has loved to remember Truth, while forgetting the deserts of Faithlessness; and while his great symphonies paint the strifes of humanity, does not his "Egmont" proclaim the victory of the falling hero? But to still deeper and higher feelings has he appealed—exalted devotion, joy heaven-born; hope eternal; faith in Infinite Love. Never shall his sacred compositions cease to awaken the purest and loftiest emotions that can sway the human heart.

FOOTNOTES

[9] It may be interesting to the readers of the above sketch to know something of this remarkable individual. Peter Pirad was born in Hamburg; his father was a dealer in grain and distiller; his business, though coarse, was lucrative, and Peter, his youngest son, was destined to follow the same. The son had, however, little inclination thereto; his whole heart and mind were bent to the science of music; and his father resolved, when he was but eight years old, to bind him apprentice to a town musician, since he was firmly persuaded that "nothing better could be done with the young rascal."

His master soon discovered Peter was not so dull as seemed at first; and after a course of instruction, when Telemann, a director of music in the city, heard him play on the viol and horn, and beat the kettle-drum, he became so much interested in the boy that he devoted several hours to giving him lessons, in recompense for which kindness Peter assisted whenever Telemann's compositions were performed, playing the kettle-drum in a manner that astonished all who heard him.

When Telemann died, Peter was about twenty-four. He remained a year longer in Hamburg, and prosecuted his higher studies under Philip Emanuel Bach. His father died in 1768; he had buried his mother a year before. He now left Hamburg for the first time in his life, to obtain a knowledge of the world. After some adventures he turned his course to Vienna, thence to Saltzburg, where he became acquainted with the court trumpeter, an intimate friend of Mozart's family. Schachtner was master not only of the trumpet, but also of the *viola di gamba*, a now forgotten instrument. Pirad became warmly attached to him; without doubt the excellence of Schachtner stimulated him to higher proficiency as a kettle-drummer, for he ascribed his enthusiasm on that instrument to the impressions received during his stay in Saltzburg. From Saltzburg he went to Vienna; from Vienna to Prague, Dresden, and Berlin, where he made himself personally acquainted with all the great masters then living. The year 1788 found him at Bonn, where he beat the kettle-drum in the electoral chapel. He always looked upon Bonn as his home, till the outbreak of the French Revolution, when he became alarmed, and then there was no rest for the sole of his foot. In the later years of his life he used to speak with great emphasis of a bedstead, painted red, in which he had been often frightened from sleep for the space of half a year, because it reminded him of the guillotine.

In Copenhagen, where he drew breath quietly after his terror, he applied himself to his favorite science. Naumann's Orpheus so moved him that he was obliged to keep his bed several days. Except Hoffmann, and the excellent violin player, Rolla, in Dresden, I know of no artist on whose physical constitution the hearing of delightful music produced such violent, even pernicious effects, as on that of Peter Pirad.

Till this time Peter had known little or nothing of love; here he became enamored of his landlady, the widow of a

Danish ship lieutenant, a dame of goodly proportions, being about as tall and twice as thick as himself. He married this colossal fair one. His first son, even in his sixteenth year, was taller than his father. If I am not mistaken, he is yet living, a painter, in Riga.

In the last years of his life Pirad settled at Hamburg, whence he made frequent and long excursions. At length his journeyings ceased at Flensburg, where, in 1822, he died, peaceful, happy, and full of years. As a performer on the kettle-drum, he has seldom or never been surpassed. He had also the most thorough knowledge of counterpoint; played on many instruments with skill and precision; and was perfect on the organ and double bass. But his kettle-drum was everything to him. He was incessantly occupied with it. He kept it in as perfect tune as the most devoted violin virtuoso ever kept his instrument. Not an indent was to be seen in it; the parchment was so fine and transparent it looked as though it would burst at every stroke, and yet Pirad would play without injuring it from the highest pianissimo to the deepest forte. He suffered none else, however, to meddle with it; and I verily believe, notwithstanding his characteristic timidity and gentleness, would have murdered any body outright, who should have spoiled his instrument.

It may readily be conceived that his peculiarities caused him many vexations. He lived continually in disputes with his landlord and neighbors; for it was not unusual with him when, in the middle of the night, a new idea came into his head, to spring out of bed and beat his kettle-drum till the whole neighborhood was in an uproar.

His language was a mangled mixture of almost all the different German dialects, varied with broken phrases of Italian, French, and Latin. With his wife he murdered Danish, which he understood as imperfectly as she did German; so that each seldom comprehended all that the other meant to say; yet they always agreed.

Many amusing anecdotes might be related of Pirad, but the space allotted to a note is already filled up with this brief account of the leading incidents of his life.

THE MISSION OF GENIUS

It was a lovely summer afternoon about 1787; one of those days late in the season, when the luxuriant beauty of summer is the more precious because it must soon depart. The serenity of the skies, the blandness of the atmosphere, deepening to a refreshing coolness as the day drew near its close, the bright green of the foliage, and the clear blue of the waters, added joyousness to the wonted cheerfulness of a holiday in the fair city of Bonn and its neighborhood. Numerous boats, with parties of pleasure on board were passing up and down the Rhine; numerous companies of old and young were assembled under the trees in the public gardens, or along the banks of the river, enjoying the scene and each other's conversation, or partaking of the rural banquet. But we have nought to do with any of these.

At some distance from the city, a wood bordered the river; this wood was threaded by a small sparkling stream, that flung itself over a ledge of rocks, and tumbled into the most romantic and quiet dell imaginable, for it was too narrow to be called a valley. The sides, almost precipitous, were richly lined with verdure; the trees overhung it so closely that at noon-day this sweet nook was dark as twilight; and the profound silence was only broken by the monotonous murmur of the stream. A winding path led down to the secluded spot.

Close by the stream half sat, half reclined, a youth just emerging from childhood. In fact, he could hardly be called more than a boy; for his frame showed but little development of strength, and his regular features, combined with an excessive paleness, the result of confinement, gave the impression that he was even of tender years. His eyes would alone have given him the credit of uncommon beauty; they were large, dark, and so bright that it seemed the effect of disease, especially in a face that rarely or never smiled.

A most unusual thing was a holiday for the melancholy lad. His home was an unhappy one. He had been treated from infancy with harshness by his father. His brothers received hourly indulgences; Louis had none. They were praised for their application to study, or pardoned when they played truant; Louis was called a dunce, and punished severely for the slightest neglect. His brothers jeered and rallied him continually; he responded by sullen silence. The father boasted of them as his pride, and denounced Louis as an ungrateful blockhead, who had no aptitude nor taste for learning.

Besides that this cruel partiality sank deep into the boy's heart, and nourished a feeling of jealousy and discontent, Louis felt within himself that he in some degree deserved the charge of neglecting his lessons. His general studies were utterly distasteful and disgusting to him: and he found application to them impossible. His whole soul was given up to one passion—the love of music.

Oh, how precious to him were the moments of solitude! He lived for this—even his poor garret room, meanly furnished, but rich in the possession of one or two musical instruments, whither he would retire at night when released from irksome labor, and spend hours of delight stolen from slumber, till nature yielded to exhaustion. But to be alone with nature—in her grand woods—under the blue sky—with no human voice to mar the infinite harmony! how did his heart pant for this communion! Welcome, thrice welcome, the permission given to spend this holiday as he pleased; and while others of his age joined lively parties of their friends, he stole forth from the busy city, and wandered far as he dared, in search of solitude.—His breast seemed to expand, and fill with the grandeur, the beauty, of all around him. The light breeze rustling in the leaves came to his ear laden with a thousand melodies; the very grass and flowers under his feet had a language for him. His spirit, long depressed and saddened, sprang into new life, and rejoiced with unutterable joy. Yes—the lonely— friendless boy, to whom no father's heart was open, was happy—beyond measure happy!

Blessed is the poet; for him there is an inner life, more glowing, more radiant, more intense than the life of other men! For him there is a voice in nature, mute to others, that whispers of peace and love, and immortal joy. To him the visible enshrines the invisible: the earthly is but the shell of the god-like, with which his spirit claims kindred. Wo to him, if he, the appointed interpreter of Heaven, do not reveal to men less favored the utterings of that mysterious voice; if he suffer not the light within him to radiate a glory, that it may enlighten the earth!

The hours wore on, a dusky shadow fell over foliage and stream, and the solitary lad rose to leave his chosen retreat. As he ascended the narrow winding path, he was startled by hearing his own name; and presently a man apparently middle-aged, and dressed plainly, stood just in front of him.

"Come back, Louis," said the stranger; "it is not so dark as it seems here: you have time enough this hour, to return to the city."

The stranger's voice had a thrilling, though melancholy sweetness; and Louis suffered him to take his hand and lead him back. They seated themselves in the shade beside the water.

"I have watched you for a long while," said the stranger.

"You might have done better," returned the lad, reddening at the thought of having been subjected to espionage.

"Peace—boy," said his companion: "I love you, and have done all for your good."

"You love me?" repeated Louis, surprised. "I have never met you before."

"Yet I know you well. Does that surprise you? I know your thoughts also. You love music better than aught else in the world; but you despair of excellence—because you cannot follow the rules prescribed."

Louis looked at the speaker with open eyes.

"Your masters, also, despair of you. The court organist accuses you of conceit and obstinacy; your father reproaches you; and all your acquaintance pronounce you a boy of tolerable abilities, spoiled by an ill disposition."

The lad sighed.

"The gloom of your condition increases your distaste to all studies not directly connected with music, for you feel the need of her consolations. Your compositions, wild, melancholy as they are, embody your own feelings, and are understood by none of the connoisseurs."

"Who are you?" cried Louis—in deep emotion.

"No matter who I am; I come to give you a little advice, my boy. I compassionate, yet I revere you. I revere your heaven-imparted genius; I commisserate the woes those very gifts must bring upon you through life!"

The boy lifted his eyes again; those of the speaker seemed so bright, yet withal so melancholy, that he was possessed with a strange fear. "I see you," continued the unknown solemnly, "exalted above homage, but lonely and unblessed in your elevation. Yet the lot of such is fixed by fate; and 'tis better, perhaps, that one should consume in the sacred fire, than that the many should lack illumination."

"I do not understand you;" said Louis—wishing to put an end to the interview.

"That is not strange, since you do not understand yourself," said the stranger. "As for me—I pay homage to a future sovereign!" and he suddenly snatched up the boy's hand and kissed it. Louis was convinced of his insanity.

"A sovereign in art"—continued the unknown. "The sceptre that Haydn and Mozart have held, shall pass without interregnum to your hands. When you are acknowledged in all Germany for the worthy successor of these great masters—when all Europe wonders at the name of Beethoven—remember me."

What a prediction to the obscure lad, whom his father, a tenor singer in the Elector's chapel, almost daily called a blockhead!

"But you have much ground to pass over," resumed the stranger, "ere you reach that glorious summit. Reject not the aid of science; of literature; there are studies now disagreeable, that still may prove serious helps to you in the cultivation of music. Contemn not *any* learning; for Art is a coy damsel, and would have her votaries all-accomplished! Above all—*trust yourself*. Whatever may happen, give no place to despondency. They blame you for your disregard of rules; make for yourself higher and vaster rules! You will not be appreciated here; but there are other places in the world: in Vienna"—

"Oh, if I could only go to Vienna;" sighed the lad.

"You *shall* go there, and remain;" said the stranger, "and there too you shall see me, or hear from me. Adieu now—*auf wiedersehen*." ("To meet again.")

And before the boy could recover from his astonishment, the stranger was gone. It was nearly dark, and he could see nothing of him as he walked through the wood. He could not, however, spend much time in search; for he dreaded the reproaches of his father for having stayed out so late.

All the way home he was trying to remember where he had seen the unknown, whose features, though he could not say to whom they belonged, were not unfamiliar to him. It occurred to him at last, that while playing before the Elector one day, a countenance similar in benevolent expression, had looked upon him from the circle surrounding the sovereign. But known or unknown, the "auf wiedersehen" of his late companion rang in his ears, while the friendly counsel sank deep in his heart.

Traversing rapidly the streets of Bonn, young Beethoven was soon at his own door. An unusual bustle within attracted his attention. To his eager questions the servants replied that their master was dying. Louis had ever loved his father, notwithstanding his harshness; and shocked to hear of his danger, he flew to his apartment. His brothers were there, also his mother, weeping; and the physician supported his father, who seemed in great pain.

The elder Beethoven lingered long enough to know, and to be touched by, the filial attentions of his son; when he died, it was with affectionate regret that Louis closed his eyes.

Much needed, and of incalculable use, were the counsel and comfort of the unknown friend. They sustained the youthful composer amid the railleries, the reproaches, the anger of all who knew him in his native city, excited by what they termed his scorn of the laws of harmony; they sustained him against discouragement and self-distrust, nourished by continual censure in a character naturally gloomy and eccentric; against temptations to gain popularity by humoring the prevalent taste; against the desire of triumphing at once over his enemies by showing them that he could be great, even on their own ground. Still more—they sustained him amidst the anguish of a first and unhappy love; the only passion that ever divided with Art the empire over his soul. Most of all, they sustained him under the want of appreciation where he had confidently looked for it. When the Elector, having promised him after Neefe the place of court organist, sent him to Vienna to complete his studies under the direction of Haydn, that great man failed to perceive how fine a genius had been entrusted to him. Nature had endowed them with opposite qualities; the inspiration of Haydn was under the dominion of order and method; that of Beethoven sported with both, and set both at defiance. When Haydn was questioned of the merits of his pupil he would answer with a shrug of the shoulders—"He executes extremely well." If his early productions were cited as giving evidence of talent and fire, he would reply—"He touches the instrument admirably." To Mozart belonged the praise of having recognized at once, and proclaimed to his friends, the wonderful powers of the young composer.

Years passed on, and Beethoven continued to reside at Vienna with his two brothers, who had followed him thither, and took the charge of his domestic establishment, so as to leave him entirely at leisure for composition. His reputation had advanced gradually but surely, and he now stood high, if not highest, among living masters. The prediction was beginning to be accomplished.

It was a mild evening in the latter part of September, and a large company was assembled at the charming villa of the Baron Raimond von Wetzlar, situated near Schœnbrunn. They had been invited to be present at a musical contest between the celebrated Wolff and Beethoven. The part of Wolff was espoused with great enthusiasm by the Baron; that of Beethoven by the Prince de Lichnowsky; and, as in all such matters, partisans swarmed on either side. The popular talk among the music-loving Viennese was everywhere discussion of the merits of the rival candidates for fame.

Our hero was walking in one of the avenues of the illuminated garden, accompanied by his pupil, Ferdinand Ries. The melancholy that marked the composer's temperament, seemed more than ever to have the ascendency over him.

"I confess to you, Ferdinand," said he—apparently in continuation of some previous conversation, "I regret my engagement with Sonnleithner."

"And yet you have written the opera?"

"I have completed it, but not to my own satisfaction. And I shall object to its being produced first at Vienna."

"Why so? The Viennese are your friends."

"For that very reason I will not appeal to their judgment; I want an impartial one. I distrust my genius for the opera."

"How can that be possible?"

"It is my intimacy with Salieri that has inclined me that way; nature did not suggest it; I can never feel at home there. Ferdinand, I am self-upbraided, and should be, were the applause of a thousand spectators sounding in my ears."

"Nay," said the student, "the artist assumes too much who judges himself."

"But I have not judged myself."

"Who then has dared insinuate a doubt of your success?"

Beethoven hesitated; his impressions, his convictions, would seem superstition to his companion, and he was not prepared to encounter either raillery or ridicule. Just then, the host with a party of the guests met them, exclaiming that they had been everywhere sought; that the company was all assembled in the saloon, and everything ready for the exhibition.

"You are bent on making a gladiator of me, dear Baron," cried the composer, "in order that I may be mangled and torn to pieces for the popular amusement by your favorite Wolff."

"Heaven forbid that I should prejudge either combatant," cried von Wetzlar. "The lists are open; the prize is to be awarded not by me."

"But your good wishes—your hopes—"

"Oh, as to that, I must frankly own, I prefer the good old school to your new-fangled conceits and innovations. But come—the audience waits."

Each in turn the two rivals played a piece composed by himself, accompanied by select performers. Then each improvised a short piece. The delight of the spectators was called forth in different ways. In the production of Wolff, a sustained elevation, clearness and brilliancy recalled the glories of Mozart's school, and moved the audience to repeated bursts of admiration. In that of Beethoven there was a startling boldness, an impetuous rush of emotion, a frequency of abrupt contrasts—and withal a certain wildness and mystery—that irresistibly enthralled the feelings, while it outraged at the same time their sense of musical propriety. There was little applause, but the deep silence, prolonged even after the notes had ceased, told how intensely all had been interested.

The victory remained undecided. There was a clamor of eager voices among the spectators, but no one could collect the suffrages, nor determine which was the successful champion in the contest. The Prince Lichnowsky, however, stood up, and boldly claimed it for his favorite.

"Nay," interrupted Beethoven, advancing, "my dear Prince, there has been no contest." He offered his hand to his opponent. "We may still esteem each other, Wolff, for we are not rivals. Our style is essentially different; I yield to you the palm of excellence in the qualities that distinguish you."

"You are right, my friend!" cried Wolff; "henceforth let there be no more talk of championship between us. I will hold him for my enemy who ventures to compare me with you; you, so superior in the path you have chosen. It is a higher path than mine, an original one; I follow contentedly in the course marked out by others."

"But our paths lead to the same goal," said Beethoven. "We will speed each other with good wishes; and embrace cordially when we meet there at last."

There was unusual solemnity in the composer's last words, and it put an end at once to the discussion. All responded warmly to his sentiment. But amidst the general murmur of approbation one voice was heard, that seemed strangely to startle Beethoven. His face grew pale, then flushed deeply; and the next moment he pressed his way hastily through the crowd, and seized by the arm a retreating figure.

"You shall see me in Vienna," whispered the stranger in his ear.

"Yet a word with you. You shall not escape me thus."

"*Auf wiedersehen!*" And shaking off the grasp, the stranger disappeared.

No one had observed his entrance: the host knew him not, and though most of the company remarked the composer's singular emotion, none could inform him whither the unbidden guest had gone. Beethoven remained abstracted during the rest of the evening.

The opera of "*Leonore*" was represented at Prague; it met with but indifferent success. At Vienna, however, it commanded unbounded applause. Several alterations had been made in it; the composer had written a new overture, and the finale of the first act; he had suppressed a duo and trio of some importance, and made other improvements and retrenchments. Not small was his triumph at the favorable decision of the Viennese public. A new turn seemed to be given to his mind; he revolved thoughts of future conquests over the same portion of the realm of art; he no longer questioned his own spirit. It was a crisis in the artist's life, and might have resulted in his choice of a different career from that in which he has won undying fame.

Beethoven sat alone in his study; there was a light knock at the door. He replied with a careless "come in," without looking up from his work. He was engaged in revising the last scenes of his opera.

The visitor walked to the table, and stood there a few minutes unobserved. Probably the artist mistook him for one of his brothers; but on looking up, he started with indescribable surprise. The unknown friend of his youth stood beside him.

"So, you have kept your word," said the composer, when he had recovered from his first astonishment; "and now, I pray you, sit down, and tell me with whom I have the honor of having formed acquaintance in so remarkable a manner."

"My name is of no importance, as it may or may not prove known to you," replied the stranger. "I am your good genius, if my counsel does you good; if not, I would prefer to take an obscure place among your disappointed friends."

There was a tone of grave rebuke in what his visitor said, that perplexed and annoyed the artist. It struck him that there was affectation in this assumption of mystery; and he observed coldly —

"I shall not attempt, of course, to deprive you of your incognito: but if you assume it for the sake of effect, I would merely give you to understand that I am not prone to listen to anonymous advice."

"Oh that you would listen," said the stranger, sorrowfully shaking his head, "to the pleadings of your better nature!"

"What do you mean?" demanded Beethoven, starting up.

"Ask your own heart. If that acquit you, I have nothing to say. I leave you then, to the glories of your new career; to the popular applause — to your triumphs — to your remorse."

The composer was silent a few moments, and appeared agitated. At last he said: "I know not your reasons for this mystery; but whatever they may be, I will honor them. I entreat you to speak frankly. You do not approve my present undertaking?"

"Frankly, I do not. Your genius lies not this way;" and he raised some of the leaves of the opera music.

"How know you that?" asked the artist, a little mortified. "You, perhaps, despise the opera?"

"I do not. I love it; I honor it; I honor the noble creations of those great masters who have excelled in it. But you, my friend, are beckoned to a higher, a holier path."

"How know you that?" repeated Beethoven; and this time his voice faltered.

"Because I know you; because I know the aspirations of your genius; because I know the misgivings that pursue you in the midst of success; the self-reproach that you suffer to be stifled in the clamor of popular praise. Even now, in the midst of your triumph, you are haunted by the consciousness that you are not fulfilling the true mission of the artist."

His piercing words were winged with truth itself. Beethoven buried his face in his hands.

"Wo to you," cried the unknown, "if you suppress, till they are wholly dead, your once earnest longings after the pure and the good! Wo to you, if, charmed by the siren song of vanity, you close your ears against the cry of a despairing world! Wo to you, if you resign unfulfilled the trust God committed to your hands; to sustain the weak and faltering soul, to give it strength to bear the ills of life, strength to battle against evil, to face the last enemy!"

"You are right—you are right?" exclaimed Beethoven, clasping his hands.

"I once predicted your elevation, your world-wide fame," continued the stranger, "for I saw you sunk in despondency, and knew that your spirit must be aroused—to bear up against trial. You stand now on the verge of a more dreadful abyss. You are in danger of making the gratification of your own pride, instead of the fulfilment of Heaven's will, the aim—the goal of your life's efforts."

"Oh, never!" cried the artist; "with you to guide me——"

"We shall meet no more. I watched over you in boyhood; I have now come from retirement to give you my last warning; henceforth I shall observe your course in silence. And I shall not go unrewarded. I know too well the noble spirit that burns in your breast! You will—yes—you will fulfil your mission; your glory from this time shall rest on a basis of immortality. You shall be hailed the benefactor of humanity; and the spiritual joy you prepare for others shall return to you in full measure, pressed down, and running over!"

The artist's kindling features showed that he responded to the enthusiasm of his visitor; but he answered not.

"And now farewell. But remember, before you can accomplish this lofty mission, you must be baptised with a baptism of fire. The tones that are to agitate and stir up to revolution the powers of the human soul, come not forth from an unruffled breast, but from the depths of a sorely wrung and tried spirit. You must steal the triple flame from heaven; and it will first consume the peace of your own being. Remember this—and droop not when the hour of trial comes! Farewell!"

The stranger crossed his hands over Beethoven's head, as if mentally invoking a blessing—folded him in his embrace, and departed. The artist made no effort to follow him. Deep and bitter were the thoughts that moved within him; and he remained leaning his head on the table in silent revery, or walking the room with rapid and irregular steps, for many hours. At length the struggle was over; pale, but composed, he took up the sheets of his opera and threw them carelessly into his desk. His next work, "*Christ in the Mount of Olives*," attested the high and firm resolve of his mind, sustained by its self-reliance, and independent of popular applause or disapprobation. His great symphonies, which carried the fame of the composer to its highest point, displayed the same triumph of religious principle.

Once more we find Beethoven, in the extreme decline of life. In one of the most obscure and narrow streets of Vienna, on the third floor of a gloomy-looking house, was now the abode of the gifted artist. For many weary and wasting years he had been the prey of a cruel malady, that defied the power of medicine for its cure, and had reduced him to a state of utter helplessness. His ears had been long closed to the music that owed its birth to his genius; it was long since he had heard the sound of a human voice.

In the melancholy solitude to which he now condemned himself, he received visits from but few of his friends, and those at rare intervals. Society seemed a burthen to him. Yet he persisted in his labors, and continued to compose, notwithstanding his deafness, those undying works which commanded for him the homage of Europe.

Proofs of this feeling, and of the unforgotten affection of those who knew his worth, reached him in his retreat from time to time. Now it was a medal struck at Paris, and bearing his features; now it was a new piano, the gift of some amateurs in London; at another time, some honorary title decreed him by the authorities of Vienna, or a diploma of membership of some distinguished musical society. All these moved him not, for he had quite outlived his taste for the honors of man's bestowing. What could they—what could even the certainty that he had won immortal fame, do to soften the anguish of his malady, from which he looked alone to death as a relief?

"They wrong me who call me stern or misanthropic," said he to his brother, who came in March, 1827, to pay him a visit. "God knoweth how I love my fellow-men! Has not my life been theirs? Have I not struggled with temptation, trial and suffering from my boyhood till now, for their sakes? and now, if I no longer mingle among them, is it not because my cruel infirmity unfits me for their companionship? When my fearful doom of separation from the rest of the human race is forced on my heart, do I not writhe with terrible agony, and wish that my end were come? And why, brother, have I lived, to drag out so wretched an existence? Why have I not succumbed ere now?

"I will tell you, brother. A soft and gentle hand—it was that of Art—held me back from the abyss. I could not quit the world before I had produced all—*had done all that I was appointed to do!* When my mission is accomplished, then thrice welcome death! I have been guided through life by Patience, the handmaid of Truth; I will go with her even to the footstool of the Eternal."

The servant of the house entered, and gave Beethoven a large sealed package directed to himself. He opened it; it contained a magnificent collection of the works of Händel, with a few lines stating that it was a dying bequest to the composer, from the Count di N— —. He it was who had been the unknown counsellor of Beethoven's youth and manhood; and the arrival of this posthumous present seemed to assure the artist that his own close of life was crowned with the approval of his friend. It was as if a seal had been set on that approbation, and the friendship of two noble spirits. It seemed like the dismissal of Beethoven from all further toil. Could it be that nothing more remained for him to accomplish on earth?

The old man stooped his face over the papers; tears fell upon them, and he breathed a silent prayer. After a few moments he arose, and said, somewhat wildly, "We have not walked to-day, Carl. Let us go forth. This confined air suffocates me."

The wind was howling violently without; the rain beat in gusts against the windows; it was a bitter night. The brother wrote on a slip of paper, and handed it to Beethoven.

"A storm?—well—I have walked in many a storm, and I like it better than the biting melancholy that preys upon me here in my solitary room. Oh, how I loved the storm once; my spirit danced with joy when the winds blew fiercely, and the tall trees rocked, and the sea lashed itself into fury. It was all music to me. Alas! there is no music now so loud that I can hear it.

"Do you remember the last time I led the orchestra in the concert at Von——'s? Ah! you were not there; but I heard—yes—by leaning my breast against the instrument. When some one asked me how I heard, I replied, '*J'entends avec mes entrailles.*'" [10]

Disturbed by his nervous restlessness, the aged composer went to the window, and opened it with trembling hands. The wind blew aside his white locks, and cooled his feverish forehead.

"I have one fear," he said, turning to his brother, and slightly shuddering, "that haunts me at times. It is the fear of poverty. Look at this meanly-furnished room, that single lamp, my meager fare; and yet, all these cost money, and my little wealth is daily consumed. Think of the misery of an old man, helpless and deaf, without the means of subsistence!"

"Have you not your pension secure?"

"It depends on the bounty of those who bestowed it; and the favor of princes is capricious. Then, again, it was given on condition I remained in the territory of Austria, at the time the King of Westphalia offered me the place of chapel-master at Cassel. Alas! I cannot bear the restriction. I must travel, brother; I must leave this city."

"You—leave Vienna?" exclaimed his brother in utter amazement, looking at the feeble old man whose limbs could scarcely bear him from one street to another. Then recollecting himself, he wrote down his question.

"Why? Because I am restless and unhappy. I have no peace, Carl! is it not the chafing of the unchained spirit, that pants to be free, and to wander through God's limitless universe? Alas! she is built up in a wall of clay, and not a sound can penetrate her gloomy dungeon!"

Overcome by his feelings, the old man bowed his head on his brother's shoulder, and wept bitterly. Carl saw that the delirium which sometimes accompanied his paroxysms of illness had clouded his faculties.

The malady increased. The sufferer's eyes were glazed; he grasped his brother's hand with a tremulous pressure.

"Carl! Carl! I pardon you the evil you did me in childhood; I have pardoned all. Pray for me, brother!" cried the failing voice of the artist.

His brother supported him to the sofa, and called for assistance. In an hour the room was filled with the neighbors and friends of the dying man. He seemed gradually sinking into insensibility.

Suddenly he revived; a bright smile illumined his whole face; his sunken eyes sparkled. "I shall *hear* in heaven!" he murmured softly, and then sang in a low but distinct voice the lines from a hymn of his own:—

> "Brüder!—über 'm Sternenzelt,
>
> Muss ein lieber Vater wohnen."

In the last faint tone of the music his gentle spirit passed away.

Thus died Beethoven, a true artist, a good and generous man. Simple, frank, loyal to his principles, his life was spent in working out what he conceived his duty; and though his task was wrought in privation, in solitude and distress, though happiness was not his lot in this world, doth there not remain for him an eternal reward?

The Viennese gave him a magnificent funeral. More than thirty thousand persons attended; the first musicians of the city executed the celebrated funeral march composed by him, and placed in his heroic symphony; the most famous poets and artists were pall-bearers, or carried the torches; Hummel, who had come from Weimar expressly to see him, placed a laurel crown upon his tomb. Prague, Berlin, and all the principal cities of Germany paid honors to his memory, and solemnized with pomp the anniversary of his death. Such was the distinction heaped on the dust of him whose life had been one of suffering, and whose last years had been solitary, because he felt that his infirmities excluded him from human brotherhood.

FOOTNOTES

[10] Fact.

PALESTRINA

"Ha!" cried Alexander, as he entered the apartment of his friend Johann, and found him in a melancholy mood, sitting at his table, "ha, my dear fellow! what is the matter? Depending on your promise, if the weather was fair, to walk with me in the country, I have been sitting all the morning in best dandy trim—in my new-fashioned uncomfortable coat, waiting for you! but in vain; so I got up, at last, and came in search of you; and lo! find you undressed, or, at least, not in holiday trim as I am—at your desk, studying old yellow music, and not, as it seems, in humor exactly *couleur de rose!*"

"Yes, I am out of tune!" replied Johann, "and all I do to get the better of my humor, goes ill with me. So, at last, as always when all other means fail, I betake me to some good old master in music. To-day, however, my study has only made me more melancholy, instead of bettering my spirits. The excellence of old times serves but to remind me of the present low state of our art, and the mediocrity of our artists!"

"Hold, friend; go not too far! Think upon the old proverb—'All is not gold that glitters.' All are not artists who please to call themselves such."

"Sound advice!" exclaimed Johann, "as if it occurred not of itself to every reasonable man who visited Leipzig after a few years' absence! *One* I sought here—Mendelsohn Bartholdy! He is absent. The others, with their insufferable pretension, and their worthlessness, only disgust me."

"Yet I know one, who could do well, if he would only endeavor earnestly—our little fat friend, Stegmayer; a nature truly Mozartesque! Pity only he is not really enthusiastic in his art—but on the contrary, too much devoted to gay living!"

"Truly, a pity! he is the only one I can think on with satisfaction, for his really noble talents! all the rest, I repeat it, disgust me with their labored ingeniousness their extraordinary self-complacency—their current coin of praise—paid from hand to hand."

"You should not take it so tragically! It is too much the case now, from the highest to the lowest, that art is shockingly abused."

"My friend, it would be melancholy, indeed, if better spirits could look on *calmly*; it is my firm conviction, that indifference towards the good and the beautiful, is more worthy of condemnation than open hostility. I should be ashamed to be ignorant of bad authors, and bad works; because I hold it my duty to battle for the good, against the common and the mean, with all the weapons at my command. Chide me for a Don Quixotte—I care not. I fight, like him, not alone against windmills! and spite of his craziness, esteem the Knight of the Rueful Countenance an honest, worthy—yea, an admirable character."

Alexander laughed at his friend's singular notion; but said, good-humoredly—"No, my dear fellow, I do not compare you to the Knight of the Rueful Countenance; though sooth, as I observed a while ago, you show little, to-day, of your wonted cheerfulness. For the rest, I entirely agree with you as to the arrogance of our composers. I read, for example, some time ago, in the Mitternachtsblatt, an essay of a Mr. T., in Berlin. Mr. T., himself a composer, liberally plasters his friend, C.B., and forgets not himself at the end. This might pass, and his praise—for somewhat is allowed to friendship—and as a composer of songs, C.B. has real merit, even though he cannot equal, much less rival a Schubert, a B. Klein, a Spohr, or a Löwe! But Mr. T. repeats some very silly remark of B's upon Peter von Winter, and particularly his 'Opferfest,' and calls it a just, solid, spirited judgment! Now neither T. nor B. have ever written any thing which could come nigh that cavatina of Myrrha, 'Ich war, wenn ich erwachte,' or the duet, 'Wenn mir dein Auge strahlet.' To a quartette like the droll, pathetic one, 'Kind, willst du ruhig schlafen,' neither of the two gentlemen can aspire. But they believe they can do better. I would give them simply this advice; to write off the dramatic text of the opera, and then compose it. All Germany will thank them if they make it better than good old departed Winter."

"Of such vanity *my* old master knows nothing," observed Johann, as he showed his friend the title-page of the music lying before him; "the good *Giovanni Pierluigi* was as simple and excellent a man as a great and admirable artist. He confirmed the old truth, that to be a worthy artist, one must first be a worthy man. This saying has been oft repeated; but, to my mind, can never be repeated often enough! If it cannot help the ordinary and the mean to self-knowledge and improvement, it will sustain the good, when outward circumstances threaten to overpower them; for he who means most honestly with art, has ever the most opposition from without to struggle against.

"It was not easy for Giovanni Pierluigi to come forth as the creator of a new style in church music. Born in Palestrina, 1524, he found no contemporary exemplar in his art, who could have guided him in the right way. Music—I mean church music—was near utter extinction! Soft tinklings—not unfrequently pieces from operas, and amorous canzonets joined together, were heard in the sanctuaries. Consequently, it was music the most remote from sacred, which, from his childhood Palestrina not only heard, but helped to produce, for he had been sent to Rome as chorister, to study music.

"But in his youthful breast glowed a spark of the god-like, which soon rose to a flame that illumined the night around him! Palestrina discovered what, in a time of universal degeneration, may not be taught; he discovered what was wanting—what must be done; and yet more—the means to remove the evil! In himself he bore from the beginning, the good and the beautiful, which he was to set up in place of the corrupt and the repulsive. Thus equipped, courageous, but without presumption, conscious, but void of self-complacent vanity—he entered the arena of contest; thus he ventured to gainsay Pope Marcellus II. and his cardinals, who wished all music banished from the church; and through his *Missa Papae Marcelli*, he not only reformed music, but gave the first inducement to make it a substantial part of the Romish service.

"His efforts, his work found appreciation; yet for a long and melancholy time, the reward seemed uncertain. Palestrina had been singer in the Popish chapel; he lost this place; for, following his human, honorable heart—he married. His marriage, as appears from his letters, was so displeasing to the Holy Father, that Palestrina was on the point of quitting Rome, having lost, with his place, the means of subsistence. Fortunately, some true friends of art espoused his cause; he obtained another situation in Saint John Lateran; at a later period he was chapel-master at Santa Maria Maggiore. He founded an excellent school, produced immortal works, and ended the fair labor of a useful life as chapel-master at Saint Peter's, the second of February, 1594.

"The simple, quiet life of this great man, has always possessed deep interest for me; and it has often occurred to me to represent to the public, in the form of a Tale of Art, that important period in which he saved Music from the ban which hung over her. But I have relinquished the idea; for in Palestrina's life, as in his works, there seems nothing *made up*. All lies before us so simple, so noble, so sun-like clear, that it would be quite impossible by aid of the most ingenious fiction, to paint it more lovely and elevated than is the plain reality. The greatest poets, Goëthe particularly, have felt this at times powerfully; and have often given unadorned, the simple relation of facts, touching enough, indeed, to dispute the pre-eminence with all their fictions.

"In Palestrina's works, reigns the purest church-style; no other master has come nigh him, in this respect. Loftiness, strength, and wildness, form the character of his music, which fills the heart with devotion, and bears it upward to God, free from the chains of earth, and all that claims earthly emotion.

"It is undeniable that all church-music should have this only aim—to lift the spirit to devotion—to God; according to the word of holy writ— which commands all those who come into the presence of the Lord, to come with a pure heart and holy thoughts.

"The more recent church-composers have not followed this noble aim. Latterly, even in Italy, the pure style has declined, and how much may be shown by the circumstance that the Italians, even towards the close of the last century, admired Jomelli as a *great* church-composer! The German style was never so pure as Palestrina's, because it was not so natural and unconstrained. Palestrina's simplicity was harshness with Sebastian Bach; the strict German rules point out, now and then, by far more what is prohibited, than what is permitted, and even demanded. Händel, in his Messiah, Mozart, in his Requiem, broke the fetters, and soared upward, powerful eagles, towards the sun; yet without losing sight of the laws they acknowledged as just and necessary. Haydn, in his *Messen*, is less conscientious; his *creation* belongs, beyond dispute, only to the concert hall. But in the most recent times, what appears written for the church, can only fulfil the smallest part of those claims justly advanced by the restorer of church music. And in this point of view, I regard as quite objectionable, those oratorios of Friedrich Schneider, in which the 'God be with us,' has the principal part, and is accompanied by flageolet, kettle-drum, trumpet, and bass trumpet."

"They will cry out against this judgment of yours, my dear Johann," said Alexander, "but you are right! and it is abominable, that in our most stirring, grand, spiritual music, Satan has the word! But that is the mischief of imitation among the Germans! I am sure Friedrich Schneider would, in every respect, have done something excellent, as he has really done in so many respects, had not his first appearance been at the time when the people were all enthusiasm about Weber's 'Volks Oper.' As highly as I honor Schneider's great talent, much as I esteem him for a worthy man, I must blame him severely, that he has suffered himself to be carried away by the intoxication of a theatrical public, and led to produce works which, in spite of splendid things in them, can yet be regarded on the whole, (as well in an artistical view, as if we look upon their tendency,) only as *changelings*! Nay, I scarce suppress the wish—unkind enough! that Schneider might be, for once, condemned to hear, from beginning to end, the oratorio of a certain Mr.

H——, 'Christus der Erlöser.' This H——, inspired by the laudable wish of becoming, in the shortest possible time, a rich man and a famous composer, set himself to work and patched together this affair; in which he not only pilfered to his heart's content from poor Schneider, but imitated and twisted him so after his fashion, that his oratorio seems a horrible caricature of all Schneider's oratorios. Where Schneider employed one bass trumpet, master H—— would have *three*! Satan tunes up—the flageolets fall screeching in, and the tutti of the infernal chorus follows with frightful clamor. In 1833 the composer brought his astonishing work to Leipzig to be represented, to the great delight of the assembled auditory!"

"No more," said Johann; "no more of the man and his pitiful efforts! let us turn to nobler, more exalted objects! How much I regret that I could not be present at the representation of the 'Paulus' of Mendelsohn Bartholdy! I am assured by a connoisseur, that Felix has here followed the path by which Händel reached the crown of immortality; nor could he praise sufficiently the wise moderation with which the youthful master, spite of his enthusiasm, has shunned all exaggeration in his work. Mendelsohn Bartholdy," concluded he, "is able and sound to the core; so that we have ground to hope that a true man shall arise in him, to show us the path by which we may return, through the ancient simplicity, to the ancient glory!"

"Heaven grant it!" cried Alexander, fervently; "it cannot well be worse with us! Yet a life-impulse, too fresh and glad, is stirring in Art, for us to fear her death. She will not die! and let it only happen that the young aftergrowth may find a model not too far removed from them; for youth ever joins himself most willingly to the nearest.

"Will Felix become this model? I know not; but I hope so, as I wish it; and wish, also, that no young artist may ever forget—'*That he who would become a great artist, must first be a pure and true man.'*"

Alexander shook his friend cordially by the hand, and they parted.

THREE LEAVES FROM THE
DIARY OF A TRAVELER

I.

Milan, *4th May, 1811.*

Am I dreaming?—or do I still tread the earth? Scarce two days have passed, and yet I have lived through events that might occupy a year. On the second of May, at eight in the evening, I arrived at this place. My road brought me first to the cathedral. The slender sickle of the new moon hung in the violet expanse; the western sky was yet crimson with the last rays of the sun; a range of lamps just lighted, threw a red glare on the streets. The lofty obelisk of the Gothic temple, surmounted with its bronze statue, rose in the clear blue ether; a holy silence seemed to wrap its summit, that contrasted with the crowd and excitement below, of people hastening to the theatre. I stood long absorbed in mute admiration. Suddenly two figures stepped out from the shadow of a large pillar; they were, like myself, in traveling gear. As they were passing, I heard familiar voices, and sprang forward to greet Hermann and Adolph, two intimate friends, whom I had not seen for several years. How joyful this unexpected meeting!

We repaired to the nearest café and took seats at a table near the door, to enjoy the fresh breath of evening. While the lights flared in the breeze, and flasks of the Lombard champagne—the foaming wine of Asti—stood before us, each told what had befallen him since the current of time had carried us in different directions after our last separation. Necessity had sundered us, not only from each other, but from our fatherland. My friends were just from the Tyrol; they had visited the ever-memorable scene of that *holy* strife which those true-hearted sons of the mountains, trusting in justice human and divine, maintained against the over-bearing power of France. Our conversation, more earnest than was altogether prudent, naturally turned to these events, so interesting to the heart of the patriot. "We visited, also," said Adolph, "the dwelling of Hofer—that noble hero. Let me read you"—here he drew out his tablets, and turned to me—"a poem which I composed on this sacred spot." Here he read me some verses on Andreas Hofer's dwelling, a copy of which I took, and have placed in my journal.

We remained in conversation till midnight, when the people came back from the theatre; then separated with promises of seeing each other again. I had gone but a few hundred steps on the way to my lodgings, when I became aware that the heavy jingling tread of a French gend'arme was closely following me. To see if I was the object of his pursuit, I suddenly turned and crossed towards a side street. He followed. I glanced at him; he seized me by the arm. "*Monsieur, votre portefeuille,*" said he. I gave it up. "*Vous me suivrez.*" I obeyed. I now understood all.

He led me to a lofty old building, which I had never before seen; a huge door, fastened with heavy bolts, was opened: within were French soldiers on guard. My conductor spoke a few words to the officer, apart. I was then led away by two soldiers, preceded by a turnkey with a lamp. We mounted some steps, then passed through a dark gallery. The turnkey stopped at a door strongly secured with iron bars, and I found myself in a narrow cell, ventilated only by a small grated window, through which glimmered a ray of starlight. The gend'arme entered after me, and I was subjected to a rigorous search. My papers were all taken away, but my watch and purse were courteously handed back. The jailer asked if I wanted anything; I laughed bitterly. "Well, to-morrow morning," said he, and went out. I remained alone in the darkness.

For an hour or more I lay on the straw matting, and pictured to myself the horrors of my fate. Only twenty-one, and full of hope—ready to serve and save my country, to perform great deeds! What was now before me? Was I ever again to see my parents, my sisters, my beloved? A prisoner, perhaps to be led forth to-morrow to kneel on the ground and receive the bullets of the soldiers—for my love to my native land. Thoughts on these subjects filled my tortured brain. But suddenly my attention was arrested; the stillness of night was broken by a tone of melody so soft, so exquisite, so melancholy, that it pierced my inmost heart, and tears sprang to my eyes. Was it a song? No; there was no voice, but a melody such as was never heard before—such as Orpheus might have drawn forth! It was—yes, let the cold-hearted laugh—it was the sound of a violin!

How shall I describe that music? Sunk in despair as I was—the dungeon, the galleys, death before my eyes—it raised me to the height of rapture; it filled me with the joy of freedom, and yet, strangest of all, with feelings solemn and profound! On the silence of night it stole like magic; the light breeze wafted it through the bars of my window; clear, softly swelling like the sigh of the mourner's breast—plaintive and imploring, like the accents of love—gently yielding, like the timid bride—that wondrous harmony took possession of my care-fraught soul. Then the player, as it seemed, improvised airs on his instrument; now glided the tones along; now he rose into energy and power, now melted in the most seducing melody; yet the notes were ever clear, as if they had been drops of pearl. After these rhapsodical strain, he passed, by a strange but charming transition, into a melody of wonderful pathos. Never can I forget the effect of this music, so sweet and exquisite yet full of sadness; now swelling into silvery richness, now dying gently away. It was like the noble, melancholy plaint of an imprisoned king. The thought entered my bosom—how much have those who are better than we oft to suffer!—and in the midst of misfortune I felt a calmness and a trust which I could never have obtained through the pleadings of reason. The player continued his music, and I knew not whether to wonder most at his compositions or his execution. He seemed at length under the influence of inspiration; his music was full of fire; he passed into stranger combinations, into bolder and wilder flights, yet surpassing harmony was in all; and he appeared to create difficulties only to triumph over them. Friends who read my journal, you will say, perhaps, the imagination of the prisoner deceived him. No, I have myself played the violin, (I do it now no more,) and could never have conceived aught like what I heard. The music at last ceased, but it lingered unforgotten in my soul—ay, I longed more to hear it again than to recover freedom.

It was day; I heard the beating of a drum: I climbed to my window and looked out. A company of soldiers marched into the court; three prisoners stood in front of them. At a sign from the officer, they marched away. The jailer opened my door; I asked him about them. "In an hour," he replied, "they are to die; they are suspected of treason—of having favored the insurrection among the Tyrolese."

These words were my death-warrant. I heard them shuddering, but with composure. The jailer continued—"It is now the hour when the prisoners are allowed to take the air in the court. Will you go down?"

We went. I saw in the court a rough, vagabond crowd, ruffians whom the energy of the French government had collected out of all Lombardy, to shut them up here. Leaning against a pillar, his eyes fixed on the sun, which had just risen, I observed a young man about twenty-five, who seemed worn out with suffering. He was pale and emaciated; his eyes were sunken; a prominent, bent nose, a high forehead, black masses of hair, and a long beard, gave him a wild appearance. But the expression of deep sorrow in the sharp lines of his chiseled mouth, and his pale, attenuated cheeks, imparted a touching interest to his face. I looked long at this singular person; he seemed not to see any one, but continued to gaze upwards towards the sun.

All at once he perceived the jailer, and hastily went to him. "I entreat you," he said, speaking earnestly, in Italian; "can I not move you?"

"No," replied the old man, sternly, "you cannot; and if you are not quiet o' nights, I will even cut your last string for you."

This, then, is the player, thought I; and I was hastening to speak to him when I heard my name pronounced behind me. It was the gend'arme who had arrested me. "*Suivez moi, monsieur*," he said, sternly. I was compelled to obey. Before the door stood a coach; we entered, drove off and stopped before a handsome house. My companion was silent as the grave. We alighted, and he led me up the steps and into the house. We waited some time in the hall. At last the door of a side room opened, and a voice cried, "*Entrez.*" Joyful surprise! I stood before General K——, who, four years before, had been brought wounded to the house of my parents in Berlin; and although an enemy, had received generous attention and nursing.

"My young friend," he cried, grasping my hand, "how imprudent you have been! Had I not, by mere chance, occupied this post, nothing could have saved you. You are free."

"And my friends?"

"They are also at liberty."

"A thousand thanks—"

"Silence; I am *yet* in your debt. Be my guest to-day, with your friends. To-morrow you must depart, for I leave Milan with my troops, and your adventure here might still have serious consequences for you. Your passports to Germany are already made out."

II

Paris, *13th April, 1814.*

I received from M. —— the following note:—

"Your story of the musician in the dungeon, and your longing to hear him again, form a pretty romance; but, like other romances, it savors strongly of imagination. I told it to Lafont to-day; he laughed, and said, 'I pledge myself to cure this feverish enthusiasm: I must give him a violin concert.' I have taken him at his word. This evening his promise is to be fulfilled; and, to put you down completely, Baillot, Kreuzer and Rode are also invited! Can you desire more? I shall expect you this evening."

I cannot describe what I felt at this invitation. For the last four years I had heard all the violin players in the different cities where I had been, yet nothing in the smallest degree approached what I remembered. Now I was to hear the four most famous masters the world knew. I trembled for my ideal.

With a beating heart, I found myself in the brilliantly lighted saloon. Ah, the splendor of the scene, the elegant dresses of the ladies, were displeasing to me; I thought of my dungeon in Milan, and the melody that seemed wafted from another sphere.

The concert began. Lafont played first. The most perfect polish, a tone of silvery clearness—in andante, as in allegro, grace itself—were his; but it was as a finely wrought miniature beside the nameless charm of that glorious picture before my mind's vision.

Next I heard Kreuzer. Brilliant as a string of diamonds were his passages, full and clear were his tones, and of surpassing boldness and strength; but his was the brilliancy of pure metal, or of jewels—not the living beam that penetrates the soul.

Baillot now came forward. The full, energetic harmony he drew from the instrument, roused memory in my breast. A noble fire glowed in his work; he ruled like a monarch over the realm of sound. But my prisoner ruled like a god!

At last appeared Rode. His noble, expressive features, his air of graceful, manly dignity, influenced me in his favor. He began. I started involuntarily; he brought back to me powerfully the recollection of the player who had so deeply moved my heart. His representation appeared like the sculptured image that pictures forth the very form of a loved being. The same fervor breathed in his music, the same fire, restrained by kindred power. At the moment, I almost fancied he equaled the mysterious stranger; but as he proceeded, I felt that what seemed in him so wonderful, so finished an effort, would have been accomplished at once and with ease by my prisoner. *His* chainless spirit would have soared upward and onward still, seeking more distant heights, more fathomless depths;—*him* the bounds of earth could never have contained. He swept the empyrean towards the confines of other worlds, and the harmonies heard there he gave back to men in tones of unrivaled melody.

Thus I felt during the remainder of the concert. After it was over, M. —— introduced me to the celebrated artists. Courtesy required that I should praise their performance—and who would not have praised it? Of my prisoner I was silent; but Lafont, to whom M. —— had told the story, began himself to question me. I endeavored to avoid speaking on the subject, in vain; at last I related the occurrence. All except Rode smiled; and when I mentioned and described some peculiar difficulties which I had heard overcome in a wonderful manner, Lafont exclaimed, "Oh, you are joking with us!" In short, it was plain they did not believe me. I was vexed, and soon after took my leave. Hardly was I out of the door when I perceived some one following me hastily; it was Rode.

"Sir," said he, "your narration has deeply affected me. Is it true—upon your honor?"

I assured him it was.

"Yes," he answered, "I believe you; but I am convinced there lives only one man on earth who can be your mysterious prisoner. Fifteen years since, when I was a young man, I chanced to be in Genoa. Going home late one evening, I heard the sound of a violin. The playing filled me with astonishment. At first I could not perceive whence came this enchanting music; but I soon discovered the performer to be a youth hardly grown out of boyhood, who stood on a garden wall not very high, and, looking towards a dimly-lighted window, drew from his instrument those heavenly sounds. I stood rooted to the ground. At that time I was myself a performer; but never had I dreamed of such mysteries in music as were here revealed to me. Hidden in the shadow, I remained listening. The moon came from behind a cloud, and shone full on the figure of the youthful player. His features were like those you have described, but softened, probably, from his extreme youth.

"He ended his playing; the window opened, and a female figure appeared and threw something down. An instant after, a harsh voice cried, 'Traditore, pel diavolo!' At this outcry, the boy sprang down from the wall into the street, plunged into a side alley, and disappeared before I could recover from my surprise. At the same time I perceived a head peering over the wall, and oaths and menaces were poured forth without stint. The light in the window was extinguished. Evidently it was some love affair. After some minutes, I came out from my concealment, and as I passed along the wall, I trod upon something which proved a violin bow. The lad must have lost it as he leaped from the wall. I have this bow yet: it is marked with a P. I hoped by means of it to discover the young musician, but the troubled state of the times compelled me in a day or two to leave the city. Since then I have heard nothing of my unknown artist. But I owe him much. The impression his magical performance left with me was deeper than I could express; by it I have modeled and improved my own. Yes, I am indebted to this strange appearance—this revelation, I might call it—for perhaps the greatest part of my fame!"

I heard this relation of the great artist with astonishment. Then I owned to him that I had found in his playing some resemblance to that of the unfortunate stranger. It seemed as if Rode had apprehended and followed the *first* flights of that wild spirit.

We parted. I have hope still so mighty a genius must one day sway th world. If tyrant fate have not already crushed him, that spirit must one da be crowned sovereign over all hearts!

III

Berlin, *30th March, 1829.*

After long residence in the north, I arrived here at half-past eight in th evening.

"What is there at the theatre to-night?" said I to the butler.

"Nothing of consequence. But you should go to the concert, *mein Herr* A violin player—"

"I have had enough of violin players."

"But this one is a wonder. The critic, Rellstab, writes his pen to the stump in praises of him. Look here, in the paper."

"Very well. What is the name of the wonderful performer so praised by the critic?"

"His name? I will tell you in a moment. It has just escaped me. An Italian—"

"An Italian?"

"Yes. It begins with a P."

"A P? I must go instantly to the concert. Where will I find a ticket?"

"Over the way. I do not think you can procure any now elsewhere."

I hastened to get one.

The concert hall was so crowded that I could not get in, but was forced to remain outside with many others. The tutti of the last composition was ended; the solo—a pollacca—began.

"'Tis he, or none!" cried I. "I have heard those tones before; they are unforgotten, deep in my heart. But what a miracle! Do two play, or three? *That* I have never heard. I will not trust my ear. If I might but see him—only one look! In vain: the crowd presses the door too closely. I will, at least, lose not one note."

The performer ceased. A thunderburst of applause shook the building. I pressed forward and strove to get a sight of him; others, equally eager, pushed before me: I was again disappointed. What thoughts swelled in my heart! I waited with impatience to hear him begin once more. At last— —.

"Now he plays on the G string," said some one near me. He began. Is it possible? That was the very melody I heard in prison! Those were the self-same tones that once—calming, elevating, faith-inspiring, as if sent down from heaven—shed light into my gloomy soul!

I forced my way forward through the multitude. I saw once more the pale, melancholy brow, the sunken eyes, the long dark hair, the same feeble aspect of the whole person. It was he! The mystery of nineteen years was at length solved. The stranger who had filled my youthful breast with feelings wonderful, unutterable, who had ceaselessly accompanied me since, like a veiled apparition, familiar, yet from which I could not tear the covering, stood before me. I heard, I saw——Paganini!

THE YOUNG TRAGEDIAN

One morning in the summer of 1812, the busy manager of an Italian theatrical company returned to his lodgings in a hotel in one of the principal streets of Naples. His brow was contracted, and an air of disquietude spread over his whole countenance. He announced to the landlord that he was in an hour to leave the city with his company. Mine host divined that he would not depart in the sunniest of humors.

"So, you have not been successful in your search, Master Benevolo," he asked.

"Mille diavoli! there never was such luck!" was the petulant reply. "Here I have stayed three days beyond my time, in the hope of finding what Naples, it seems, does not afford; and now I must begone to play at Salerno, without an actor of tragedy in my company!"

"And such a company!" echoed Boniface.

"Such a one, indeed! though I say it, it is the pride of Italy! a magnificent princess! Did not the Duke of Anhalt—swear she was as ravishing in beauty as exquisite in performance—with eyes like diamonds, and a figure superb as that of Juno herself!"

"Enough to make the fortune of a whole troop!" cried the landlord.

"Well—and then such an admirable comic actor; with a figure that is all one laugh, and a wit like Sancho Panza's! A genius, too, for the pathetic; he will make you sigh an instant after a convulsion of mirth; and he weeps to enchantment. He is Heraclitus and Democritus in one."

"He is an angel!" cried the landlord with enthusiasm.

"An unrivalled troop—a perfect coronet of gems—with but one wanting:—the tragic. Ah, me! what shall I do without a Geronimo, or a Falerio?" and the Impressario wrung his hands.

"Do not despair, maestro," said the good-natured host; "you may find one yet to your mind."

"And whence is he to come? from the clouds! He must fall directly; for in two hours I must be on my way to Salerno. Some of my friends are there already; and the performance has been twice postponed, waiting for me. I might have made such sums of money! Saint Antonio! how provoking to think of it!"

"You are disturbed, Signor Impressario," said the fat hostess, who had stood in the door during the preceding conversation, and now waddled forward, her hands placed on her hips, with an air of importance,—"because you have not been able to find a tragedian for your excellent company?"

"Assuredly, buona mia donna."

"And you have tired yourself out with running about the city in search of one; and now are going to leave us disappointed, in hopes that one will drop from the clouds for you on the way!"

"Ah! there is no hope of that."

"No—for the heavens do not rain such good things at Salerno. But here—Signore—here is one already fallen for you; and a capital fellow he is."

"Who!—what do you mean?" exclaimed both manager and landlord in a breath.

"Ah, there is a secret about it that I know, but shall tell no one!" cried the hostess, with looks of triumph. "You must not even know his name. But you shall have your tragedian."

"My tragedian?"

"Yes. He is a young man of prodigious genius. He came to us last night. Oh, if you had but heard and seen him! All the maids were in tears. If he had only a robe and poignard, he would be absolutely terrific. Then he sang droll songs, and made us laugh till my sides ached. I should have brought him to you before, but you went out so early."

"Whence did he come?—at what theatres has he appeared?"

"Oh, as to practice, he has had none of it; he has never been on the stage; but he has a genius and passion for it. He has left his home and friends to become an actor."

"Hem"—mused the Impressario. "Let us see him. Perhaps—"

The landlady had already quitted the room. She returned in a few minutes, leading, or rather pulling forward a lad apparently sixteen or seventeen years of age. He was tall and stout for his years; but his beardless face and boyish features, together with a shuffling bashfulness in his gait, caused the hopes of the manager to fall to the ground more rapidly than they had risen.

"Him!" he exclaimed in utter astonishment; "him!—why, he is a child!"

"A child!" repeated the landlady;—"and must not everything have a beginning? He is a child that will make his own way in the world, I promise you."

"But he is not fit for an actor," said the director, surveying, with a look of disappointment, the youth who aspired to represent the Emperors of Rome and the Tribunes of the Italian republics.

"Have a little patience," persisted the dame. "When you see his gestures—his action, you will sing another song. Come forward, Louis, my boy, and show the Signore what you can do."

The overgrown lad cast his great eyes to the ground, and hung his head; but on further urging from his patroness, he advanced a pace or two, threw over his arms the somewhat frayed skirt of his great coat to serve as a drapery, and recited some tragic verses of Dante.

"That is not bad!"—cried the Impressario, drawing his breath. "What is your name, my lad?"

"Luigi," was the reply, with a not ungraceful bow.

"What else?"

"He is called simply Luigi," interposed the hostess, with an air of mystery; "he has reasons at present for concealing his family name; for you see—he has broken bounds—"

"Exactly, I comprehend; and the runaway would fare hardly, if he were caught again. But I should like to hear him in Otello."

Thus encouraged, Luigi recited a brilliant tragic scene from Otello. The eyes of the director kindled; he followed with hands and head the motions of the youthful performer, as if carried away by sympathetic emotion, and applauded loudly when he had ended.

"Bravo—bravissimo!" he exclaimed, rubbing his hands; "that is something like—it is just the thing! You will make a capital Moor, when you are set in shape a little. Come, my fine fellow, I will engage you at once, and you shall not find me a bad master. I will give you fifteen ducats a month, and here is the first month's pay in advance, to furnish your outfit. You must appear like a gentleman, and your clothes are shabby. Go now, make your purchases, pack up, and let us be gone. I will have a mule ready for you."

The hostess led off her *protégé* in triumph, while the Impressario busied himself in preparations for immediate departure. Poor Luigi, being new to the city and its pleasures, had contracted sundry debts the day before, which honor bade him pay before he made other use of his money. By the time these demands were satisfied, a round bill paid to the hostess, and a new coat, with change of linen, provided for himself, not a fraction was remaining of his fifteen ducats. But it was no less with a light heart and smiling face that he joined his employer, and the whole troop was soon on the road out of Naples.

On their arrival at Salerno, the Impressario had advertisements struck off, announcing that a young tragic actor would appear in an extremely popular part. He presented him to the public as a *phenomenon*—as an example of the most wonderful genius, developed at a tender age.

The Impressario was walking briskly about giving directions, in the happiest mood imaginable, rubbing his hands, and congratulating himself on the possession of such a prize. Visions of wealth in prospect rose before his eyes, as he saw the treasurer counting out the piles of gold just received. But alas, for the deceptions of the world, his present joy and bright anticipations for the future! Fate breathed on his magic castle, and the fabric melted into thin air.

Luigi was behind the scenes, arrayed in an imperial costume of the middle ages, endeavoring, by the practice of action and gesture, to habituate himself to the feeling that he was sustaining the part of a sovereign. He was partly encouraged, partly abashed by the comments of one of the chorus, a young and lovely creature, whose expanding talents gave promise of future eminence. The name of Rosina, though not her own, will suit here as well as any other.

"That will not do, your majesty!" she cried, correcting an awkward movement Luigi had just made. "Only think of such an Emperor!" and she began to mimic his gestures with the prettiest air of mock dignity in the world—so saucy and provoking at the same time, that the lad vowed he would have his revenge in a kiss; and presently the little maid was chased around the scenes by Luigi, to the great disorder of his imperial robes and the discomfiture of his dignity.

Suddenly there was an unusual bustle, and the sound of steps and voices without. "The curtain is going to rise!" cried Luigi in consternation. "Give me my sword, quick!" But the noise came nearer, and was in the direction opposite to the audience. What was his astonishment and dismay when he saw advancing towards him the vice-rector, followed by six *sbirri*, with the manager giving expression to the utmost grief and despair. The young *débutant* stood petrified, till the vice-rector advanced, and laying his hand on his shoulder, arrested him by virtue of an order from His Majesty the King of Naples. It was his business—so he proclaimed to the astonished bystanders—the whole company having rushed together at the news of this intrusion—to secure the person of the fugitive Luigi, and carry him back to the *Conservatorio della Pietá de' Turchini*, where he would be remanded to his musical studies under the direction of the famous master, Marcello Perrino.

The disappointment was too much for the dignity of the Emperor *in petto*. Luigi burst into tears, and blubbered sadly; the pretty Rosina cried out of sympathy, and there was a general murmur of dissatisfaction.

"Signore,—Signore—" remonstrated the Impressario,—"such a genius—he must not be restrained; tragedy is his vocation!"

"His vocation just now is to go back to school," returned the vice-rector, gruffly.

"But, Signore, you are robbing the public; you are robbing me!"

"Has not the worthless boy been robbing His Majesty, who was graciously pleased to send him to the Conservatorio after his father's death? How has he repaid His Majesty's protection?"

"He is engaged in my service. I have advanced him a month's pay."

"You should have thought twice before employing a raw youth, whom you knew to have run away from his guardians. Come, boy."

The *sbirri* laid hold of Luigi, and somewhat roughly disencumbered him of his imperial robes. The audience without the curtain at the same time manifested unequivocal symptoms of impatience. The manager was in absolute despair.

"Let him only remain, and play in this piece."

"Not a moment," said the vice-rector; "we have no time to lose."

"Dear Master Benevolo," entreated Luigi, who had dried his tears: "be not troubled about me; I will have my revenge yet. I will be a tragedian in spite of them."

"But my losses?"

"I will make them up—I pledge you my word."

"My fifteen ducats paid in advance?"

"You shall have them again."

"If not in this world"—added the vice-rector, with a sullen laugh—"you may keep your account open for another."

"Stay, Luigi;" cried little Rosina, as the men led him off, "here is your handkerchief," and she put hers into his hands. The lad understood her, and pressed the keepsake to his lips.

"At least," said the manager, recovering a little from his disappointment, "I have not lost everything. The vagabond has left his trunk behind," and he went to make his peace with his impatient audience.

Next morning he ordered the trunk brought to him. It was very large, and so heavy that the servants who carried it imagined it to be filled with gold. The Impressario, having called together some of his friends to make an inventory of its contents, caused the lock to be broken. It was found filled with—sand. The young debutant, anxious to make a favorable impression, and not being in possession of a wardrobe, had had recourse to this piece of deception in order to command respect and attention at the inns where they stopped on the way from Naples.

Words cannot describe the rage of the manager. He vented it in execrations against Luigi, whom he denounced as a cheat, an impostor, and a thief. And his fifteen ducats—they had been thrown away! The only retaliation in his power was to write a letter full of violent abuse to the shameless offender, ending his invectives with the assurance that so base a fellow need never aspire to the honors of tragedy. Luigi said not a word when he read this missive. From that time he applied himself with so much diligence to his studies, that his masters had no reason to complain of him. He bade fair, they all said, to rival Bohrer on the violoncello, and Tulon on the flute. And for his encouragement and that of his comrades, a hall of representation was constructed in the interior of the Conservatorio, where those who desired might gratify a passion for the stage.

Late in the autumn of 1830, it was announced that a new artist, of great reputation in Italy, would appear at the *Théâtre Italien* in Paris. Great expectation was excited; as his progress through the cities beyond the Alps had been a continued triumph. The immense audience was hushed in suspense. Even after the curtain had risen, the connoisseurs seemed resolved that their applause should not be bestowed till it was fairly earned. But when the debutant appeared, there was a hum of admiration at sight of his majestic, imposing figure and noble countenance, expressive not only of power, but of frank good humor; and the first tones of that magnificent voice, swelling above the orchestra in lordly music, "like thunder amid a tempest," yet piercing to the very depths of pathos, called forth a burst of rapturous applause. At the close of the piece the spectators vied with each other in his praises, and voted him by acclamation the first *bassetaile* of the age.

The tragic opera of Otello was announced for representation, amidst the shouts of admiring thousands.

"I will go to hear Otello, since you bid me, madonna," said the ex-manager of an Italian opera company to the fair Rosina, now an admired singer, but in the midst of fortune and fame retaining the same excellent heart; "but I have no pleasure in listening to these French actors. They do not fill my idea of tragedy. Ah! the best days of the art are gone by!"

"But, Master Benevolo, you have not seen the new artist?"

"No, nor do I care to see him. I should not like what pleases these fantastical Parisians."

"But you must hear him. He is an Italian. I have an invitation for you, written in his own hand."

"Ah! that is courteous and attentive, seeing I am a stranger in Paris. How came he to send it to me?"

"He knew you to be a friend of mine," answered the lady rather embarrassed.

"*Ebbene*, I will attend you, my lady." And at the appointed time the ex-manager escorted the fair singer to the theatre.

"There is a figure for tragedy!" cried he in involuntary admiration, as the colossal form of the actor moved across the stage, and he bowed in dignified acknowledgement of the applause of the audience. "Ha! I should like him for the tyrant in Anna Bolena!" But when his powerful voice was heard in the part—when its superb tones, terrible yet exquisitely harmonious, carried the senses, as it were, captive, the Italian gave up his prejudices, and joined in the general enthusiasm. And at the point where the father of Desdemona curses his daughter, Benevolo uttered a cry, into which the very soul of emotion seemed to have passed.

"Wonderful! *stupendo! tragico?*" he exclaimed, wiping his eyes, when the curtain had fallen, and he rose to offer his arm to his fair companion.

"But you must see him," persisted she, and led the ex-impressario behind the scenes.

The wonder of the Parisian connoisseurs advanced to meet them. Benevolo gazed in awe on the person whose performance had moved him so deeply, and thought he saw the impress of majesty in his features. Clasping his hands, he saluted him as the king of tragedy!

"Ah, my good Master Benevolo! I am rejoiced to see you at last! It has been my evil fortune that we have not met before! Now, tell me if you have been pleased. Think you I will ever make a tragic actor?"

"You are the first in the world!" cried the Italian. "I am proud of my countryman."

"Ah, *mio fratello!* but you had once not so good an opinion of me. Ha! you do not recognize your old acquaintance—the runaway Luigi!"

The ex-impressario stared, in silent astonishment.

"I have grown somewhat larger since the affair at Salerno;" said the artist, laughing and clapping his sides. "But I forgot; I was under a cloud when we parted. Ah! I see you have a *heavy* recollection of that trunk of mine, and the fifteen ducats. I always meant to ransom that unlucky trunk; but only, you understand, with my pay as a tragedian, to make you unsay your prediction. Here is an order for twelve hundred francs."

The ex-manager drew back. "I cannot receive so much," he said.

"Nonsense, friend; you are too scrupulous. Bethink you; my fortune has grown apace with my *embonpoint.*"

Benevolo grasped his hand. "You are a noble fellow!" cried he; "and now, as a last favor, you must tell me your name. You act under an assumed one, I suppose?"

"Not at all; the same——Lablache."

"Lablache! are you, then, a Frenchman?"

"My father was one; he fled from Marseilles at the time of the Revolution; but I was born in Naples. Does that satisfy you?"

"I always took you for a nobleman in disguise," said Benevolo; "but now I know you for one of the nobility of artists."

"That is better than the first," said Lablache; "and now you must come home and sup with me, in the Rue Richelieu. I shall have a few friends there, and *la belle* Rosina will honor us."

FRANCIS LISZT

It is especially desirable that the materials for the biography of a man of genius—a great artist, poet or scholar, should be ample, embracing even the most trivial details. We often remain in ignorance of the real character of a celebrated person, because we cannot possess ourselves of any faithful history of those circumstances of his life, which always exert a vast influence, and have perhaps chiefly contributed to render him what he is.

The position now occupied by Liszt, makes a notice of his life particularly interesting. In the prime of manhood, he is already acknowledged to be the first pianist of the age. Europe, in all its length and breadth, is filled with his fame. He belongs to the whole world. Who takes so little interest in the progress of art, in our day, as to be inattentive to the note of triumph borne on the winds through Germany, France, and England? But it is not enough for the heedful listener that all is now light and enthusiasm; he would look back into years past, and catch the dull echo of the murmurings of envy and jealousy. He would admire and bless the artist's firmness and constancy, the energy of soul that persevered against all discouragements—that bore with the toil of study—and struggled onward, though burdened and weary, till the goal at last was reached, and labor crowned by success. To all who sympathize with him, it will be interesting briefly to observe his progress.

Mc Rae, sc.
FRANCIS LISZT.

Francis Liszt was born on the twenty-second of October, 1811, in Reiding, a village not far from Oedenburg, in Hungary. The year of his birth was remarkable for the appearance of a comet; a fact which did not fail to impress the mind of his father, Adam Liszt. He looked upon the phenomenon as a sign of his son's future eminence. This superstition of a fond parent may meet with some indulgence, when it is recollected how Goëthe himself, who seemed in general most at home on earth, commenced his confessions of "Poetry and Truth."

Adam Liszt was in the service of Prince Esterhazy; and was so excellent a musician, that he could rank high as a virtuoso among the connoisseurs. His instrument also was the piano: and with his splendid execution, had he come forward, he might have obtained no small reputation. But he preferred to remain unknown, having no desire to acquire celebrity for himself. All his ambition and his hopes centered in his son. Often, when he had been playing, while the boy listened, absorbed profoundly, to the melody he drew from the instrument, he would seize the happy moment to impress the young listener with his counsels. "My son," he would say, "you are destined to realize the glorious ideal that has shone in vain before my youth. In you *that* is to reach its fulfilment, which I have myself but faintly conceived. In you shall my genius grow up, and bear fruit; I shall renew my youth in you, even after I am laid in the grave."

Such prophetic words call to recollection the poor woman in Genoa, who held her son upon her knees, and talked to him of heavenly visions. "Nicolo," said she to the boy, "an angel came to me last night, and told me thou should't be one of the greatest performers of thy time." That boy was Paganini. How wonderfully has the prophecy been fulfilled—both in Paganini and Liszt!

Before it bursts forth in its full splendor, genius shows itself in gleams and at intervals, revealed often by a word or look. The observing father, the tender mother, are usually first to discern it while unrecognized by others; and to anticipate, from slight intimations, the future greatness of the child.

With more than a parent's joy did Adam Liszt observe the first germ of his boy's talent. He placed the small fingers on the keys; played simple tunes—which were readily imitated; he saw that all would be according to his wish! These exercises were commenced when the little Francis was six years old; at the age of nine he played for the first time in public at Oedenburg, Ries' Concerto, in three flats; and at the conclusion extemporized a *fantaisie*. The boy improvised without difficulty the most striking *rhythmen*, the most surprising cadences. The spectators were struck with surprise and admiration, and tears of joy bedewed the happy father's cheeks. All wondered at the genius of the young performer; his friends embraced and praised him; Prince Esterhazy put fifty ducats into his little hand, and gave him a warm recommendation to all the noble patrons of music in Hungary. This was the *first* step in his career; but one so important that he could no more go back.

The high commendations he received, were far from encouraging idleness in the young artist. On the contrary, they caused him to look into himself, and to contemplate earnestly the steep height he had to climb, if he would justify all these large expectations. The youth of Francis, therefore, was laborious and full of trouble. That noble ambition, which fills every great soul, was often a torment to him. The struggles of the spirit weakened the body; and sickness interrupted his exertions. This state of things brought about in him that delicate, nervous sensibility which renders the artist susceptible to all impressions; so that his excitable fancy is wrought upon by every idea or object. Vague religious feelings, sometimes pleasing, sometimes melancholy, took possession of him; his soul was divided between study and prayer. As the boy Goëthe, in his naive devotion, kindled pastilles on his father's desk, and watched the incense rise heavenward, the boy Liszt was absorbed in the mystical philosophy of a Jacob Böhme, and walked with his imagination among apocalyptical visions. He thought he grew thereby stronger for his art, and more susceptible to the impression and power of dreams. He wandered, uncertain in religion as in art, often starting back shudderingly as he hovered over the infinite abyss.

These boyish visions—he was then from ten to twelve years old—were not without influence upon his genius in after life. Let us trace in some measure the poetry of his progress, striving to throw the torch of fancy over his moments of romance. It is a task of importance, to analyze such a mind!

After the concert in Oedenburg, Adam Liszt proceeded with his son to Presburg. His success was the same, or even greater; for by means of the Counts Amaden and Zapary, the father obtained for six years a salary of six hundred florins, to enable him to give the boy suitable instruction and cultivation. A journey to Vienna, and a residence there for the purpose of study, were now in his power. This was soon accomplished. Both father and son went to Vienna; and Carl Czerny conducted the boy's lessons on the piano. Nothing better could have been done to perfect him in the *technik*. Those who know what skilful pianists have come forth from that school, and that a Liszt was now the pupil, if they bear in mind the merits of the teacher and those of the scholar, will know how to estimate the result.

Here were added also his higher studies under Salieri; his diligent exercise in counterpoint; in the strict compositions of church music; of partition and reading. Eighteen months passed in such labors. Francis often knew not if it was night or day, so absorbed was he in his studies. He never shrank from the most tedious labors, nor from any task requiring the most intense application: ever anxious to win a smile of pleasure from his grave though gentle master, though he could not satisfy himself. It might indeed be said that he pursued music with a species of obstinacy. By way of recreation and encouragement amidst such exertions, his father arranged in Vienna a concert, in which the product, as it were, of eighteen toilsome months was to be exhibited.

At this concert, all the nobility and the musical *élite*, of Vienna were present; among them Beethoven. For that hour, Beethoven forgot his own sad lot, his own abiding sorrow, and in his earnest, laconic manner gave his encouragement and applause to the youthful artist. How happy would the great man have felt, with what delight would he have pressed that young artist to his wildly throbbing heart, could he have foreseen that Francis Liszt would be the most earnest worshipper of his lofty genius, the most admirable and judicious interpreter of his ideas!

In truth, the deep veneration Liszt now cherishes for Beethoven and his works, is the best and most certain evidence of his own spiritual depth. The history of all time has proved that a great mind can only be discerned and estimated at its full value by a kindred one. Liszt's appreciation of Beethoven is an indication of his own superiority as an artist. It may truly be said, this admiration and love are without parallel. Where is to be found one like him, whose whole being, productive, creative, combining—forming—expansive—has so passed into that of his exemplar, and lives on, not in slavish imitation, but with free and kindred impulse—working with the same will?

But to return to Vienna. We see our young artist for the first time in this old imperial musical capital; we hear repeated and stunning applauses poured in his ears, and see him return modest and astonished to the quiet chamber where he pursues his studies. For him an important period had come; and he looked abroad on the new world that opened upon him, not in hope of gaining praise or gold, but amidst incitements to strive after the full development of his genius. At last he tore himself from the arms of his kind, parental friend, Salieri; closed in his loving heart a solemn, melancholy farewell look from Beethoven, and hastened to his father at Paris.

It was to be expected, the *Conservatoire* would receive one so gifted with open arms; would rejoice to number him among its pupils. But Francis Liszt was a stranger: Cherubini therefore treated him with chilling neglect, though he himself had been received in a foreign land! While the

Conservatoire shut the door against the wonderful boy, all the saloons of Paris opened theirs to him with enthusiastic welcome. Everywhere he was fêted, caressed, applauded. All the world was mad about the fair blue-eyed lad, on whose high forehead already began to appear the impress of inspiration. He played in the Palais Royal before the Duke of Orleans, and became the rage! A dangerous rock was before the youthful adventurer; ask we if he sailed safely past it, in spite of the storms of court-favor, and the shoals of self-love? Scholars, artists, wealth, beauty, aristocracy, all did homage to him; no soirée was complete without him; the gifted, proud boy was the idol of the day. The world flattered; his father admonished; and Francis obeyed the warning parental voice. He pursued the path his own energy had opened, with unwearied zeal. After a year's residence in Paris, he went over to London, where he was received with the same enthusiasm, expressed according to the national temperament of the English.

In the year 1824, both father and son returned to Paris, and the energies of Francis were particularly employed upon an opera—"Don Sancho, or the Palace of Love," which was produced in 1825 in the Royal Academy of music, with great applause, and highly esteemed by the connoisseurs. Our artist was then fourteen years old. Adolph Nourrit led him upon the stage, at the call for his appearance, amid thunders of applause. Rudolph Kreutzer, then director of the orchestra, embraced him with transport.

After these exertions and excitements, a time came again when Francis gave himself up to religious enthusiasm. In order to divert his thoughts by new objects, his father resolved upon short excursions into the Departments, and even a longer one to England; but the lad's indisposition gained the upper hand, and they were obliged to take refuge in Boulogne for the sea-bathing. Here Francis lost his father. This mournful event, which caused the affectionate boy such deep affliction, naturally had a depressing influence upon his genius. He indulged freely his melancholy visions and sad fancies, which now presented themselves under the solemn aspect of religion, now assumed the colors of romance. He longed continually for some remote solitude, in which without interruption he might nurse his fantastic musings.

Probably never poet or artist was called upon thus to suffer. But the vigor of his mind was shown in his gradual self-recovery even after such wanderings; only by much discipline could he be restored to repose and serenity. And by an acquaintance with literature, and the philosophical sciences of the day, his views in art were enlarged, no less than those of life and the world. New wants, new claims, new inquiries opened upon him. He sought as it were a back-ground, against which he could appoint the true place and dimensions of art.

While his mind thus improved, and his conceptions enlarged—while step by step he advanced—his spirit more and more cleared—purified—exalted—the worst that can happen to a man earnest to fulfil his duty befel him also; enemies rose up; he became the object of envy; and their hate began to work its purposes in secret. But of this we will be silent. The murmurs of enmity have long been hushed, and an artist, particularly, is born to endure such things. Let us turn rather to those other days which exercised a singular influence on his excitable mind.

When absorbed in his religious enthusiasm, Liszt composed only Masses; being unable, in the tumult of his feelings, to attain to anything like self-possession or a calm activity. From the dominion of this kind of madness he was delivered by another——love. He loved a lady of high rank—loved with the same ardor with which his soul embraced everything, and yielded himself wholly to the new passion. His love was unhappy; what suffering must it not have caused him! He became misanthropical. He shut himself up for weeks together, confiding his complaints and his pains only to the keys of his instrument. Those only who have thus suffered, can fully understand his condition at this time.

His personal history at this period is almost as obscure and involved as his genius itself; but it is said that he composed nothing except plans of Masses. Ere long, however, the elasticity of his temperament not only bore him out of his depression, but carried him to the opposite extreme; and he became for a time the votary of sense. St. Simonian sentiments took root and budded in his breast; to ripen all—came the Revolution. Liszt was carried away by the excitement of the people; by the visions of Freedom. He was animated by enthusiastic admiration of what he beheld; he felt an impulse *musico-political*, if so it might be called. He longed to produce in art all that he saw of stirring importance in the world; to fix the experience of those tumultuous days in the expression of music; to concentrate the feelings of many hearts, and give the people a Revolutionary Symphony, in the same manner as Beethoven had conceived and represented his battle of Vittoria. Does some narrow mind ask why he did not execute this grand thought? Those who know what were the circumstances—what repose, and abstraction from exciting scenes without, were necessary for the conception and creation of such a work, will wonder at the artist for having imagined it; will admire him for the thought, and not condemn him because it was not completed. Had the requisite rest and leisure been his, he would *then* also, undoubtedly, have realized the lofty ideal at which he aimed.

After this, the writings of George Sand, or Madame Dudevant, took complete hold of his fancy. Not less wholly did he yield his soul to Paganini, by whom he was quite carried into enthusiasm. He used to say to Madame

Sand, as to his other intimate friends, that he found in Paganini's playing on the violin something indefinite, inexpressible, which he always sought to attain on the piano.

We must take occasion here to speak of Liszt's relations to some modern pianists; and for this purpose avail ourselves of the criticism of the celebrated Fétis, in the "Revue Musicale Belge." As an illustration of some remarks on the subject of art and artists, he mentions Clementi, the first who introduced an elegant and brilliant style on the piano, the model of a thoroughly cultivated *technik*,—of natural and spirited combination; of rounded periods. We see that he drew the attention of his contemporaries upon himself, that he exhibited himself to them as an exemplar, and prescribed the classic form of the bravour sonata, as Joseph Haydn had invented that of the harmonious sonata. If we view him in this splendor, when his fame spread everywhere without bounds, and the best pianists of his time were laid under the necessity of imitating him, we must regard him as the inventor; and yet he only perfected the ideas of others, and has displayed taste rather than genius. The proper inventor was Emanuel Bach, who presented Germany with sixty concertos. He gave to the sonata a harmonious as well as a brilliant side, which was particularly cultivated by Haydn and Clementi. Emanuel Bach appeared with this accomplishment before 1740; sixty years later it was exercised, not originated, by Dussek, Cramer, and Steibelt; and Clementi's manner improved it while he added modifications of his own.

The art of those worthy men exercised itself in the circle of the softer feelings. Their only aim was to please the ear and move the heart. They sought not to paint the vehement emotions; the forms of art were to possess rather a soothing and restraining power.

These ideas took another direction, when Mozart gave to instrumental music a character of passionate, dramatic expression. The ultimate object of this new path was not understood at first, and it met the disapprobation of those accustomed to the old way, who saw in this mingling of changeful feelings more matter for blame than praise. Mozart's composition for the piano, full of expression, energy, and harmony, had to struggle long in rivalship with the light and elegant style of Clementi; then came to his aid the passionate fiery imagination—owning no rule but that of genius—of Beethoven, and the adherents of the new school increased from day to day. This powerful imagination, for the first time, showed the untenableness of stereotype forms in the new path. Beethoven, full of deep admiration for the glorious creations of Mozart, at first followed in the steps of that great master; but he soon indulged himself in freer and bolder flights. He gave new turns to the accustomed passages, bestowing much care on the completeness of harmony; greatly increased the dissonances, and hesitated not to introduce unions of accords and transitions till then unheard of, yet which at this day appear to us so simple and natural.

The issue of these combinations was an entire change in the fingering, which was many times assailed by the scholars of Cramer and Clementi. Only the Viennese school adopted the alteration, and therefore took, in this respect, the first place in art. To this we owe the progress and the present elevation of piano music. Beethoven's works were still regarded by the pianists as too grave for a large and mixed public, and were given up to professed connoisseurs. They—the players—attained their end more readily by pleasing compositions, in the execution of which Hummel gave them a new study. A *virtuoso* of the first rank in that day, he stood also high as a composer; yet can he in no way be compared with Beethoven, either in boldness or originality; he was only a man of taste and of solid attainment. Under his hands a certain fine manner was cultivated, in which he knew how to introduce brilliant figures with singular effect.

We find it necessary to explain the history and progress of piano music as early as 1807, to enable us to determine the position and work of Liszt. Fifteen years had passed since Mozart's death, and already we see his form and method three times changed. For ten years Hummel governed the manner of playing. In the course of this time, C. M. von Weber gave new movements of dramatic expression. In his piano music, he showed a glowing but wild and ill-regulated genius. Both artists and publishers were afraid to produce his compositions. Only his "Freischutz" snatched his name from the oblivion into which it had fallen.

In 1817, arose a new composer for the piano, of great merit, a *virtuoso*, who seemed born to give piano-playing a new direction. It was Moscheles. Bolder and more brilliant, more general and energetic in passages and figures than Hummel, he introduced new and tasteful embellishments; his variations on the "Alexander March" were examples in this kind for many skilful pianists. Afterwards he enlarged his style, and gave it more scope and elevation; for example, in his "Fantasies" upon Irish songs. Not less praise did he win in his graver compositions; his concertos showed a deep knowledge of harmony, as well as of dramatic feeling. These gradually rose to his "Concert Fantastique" and "Pathétique," two works as remarkable for groundwork as for expression. The "Etudes" begun with Cramer, were enlarged with Moscheles. He gave them a higher and more refined form, and may therefore be regarded as having given in those "Etudes" the first impulse of importance. Moscheles was at this height of his fame, when, as has been mentioned, the boy Francis Liszt came to Paris, and was received with so much enthusiasm in all circles. He stood, indeed, remarks Fétis, beyond gainsaying, high in his technical cultivation; but he wanted that, which, besides his remarkable and interesting *personnel*, could be produced to the world as an abiding and decisive mark; in a word, his wild, fiery, eccentric genius wanted the peculiar school which exhibited itself and him as a definite epoch in the history of art. His early compositions were full of difficulties; from all the figures shone the fire that blazed around the productions of the youthful artist. Those who asked for schools and industry in this wildly luxuriant natural garden, were sure to be disappointed.

At this time suddenly appeared Thalberg in Paris, and produced such an impression as no pianist had before him. Not that in playing he could have surpassed, or even equalled Liszt; but he had the tact to seize upon a happy idea, which was at once understood. This related to the filling up of the keys in the space between the hands. (*See Revue, etc.*)

This innovation was not altogether suffered to pass as such; it was asserted that Beethoven had already availed himself of these means in his sonatas; and blame was now cast upon the very exaggeration which gave a certain uniformity, perhaps more, to the structure and effect of his compositions. This view is only made prominent in order to obtain for Liszt the proper point of sight, from which to measure his reaction, and the gigantic height he gained.

Liszt had already left Paris, when Thalberg appeared there, but the rumor of his success and triumph reached his ears. It caused him sleepless nights. Let us imagine the feelings of an artist, conscious of his own power, knowing himself without a rival, yet seeing another suddenly elevated in popular opinion to an equality with him—perhaps generally judged to be his superior! Liszt felt that wrong had been done him, and hastened back to Paris. Thalberg was no longer there; but there was a division of opinion and judgment among the Parisians, as once there had been between the Gluckists and Piccinists. The talk was now of Lisztians and Thalbergians; strife ran high between the parties; and to observe it and hear their disputes was the most interesting amusement of the fashionable world. Liszt did not this time go before the public, to become acquainted, perhaps, only with his own enthusiastic partisans; but indulged his speculations in solitude. His clear spirit could discover the folly and worthlessness of popular idolatry, and scorn to win it by means he felt to be unworthy his genius.

Three years passed, in which the name of Liszt was but seldom, and at intervals, heard. The lives of gifted men seem to need such pauses to prepare for a full development of what is within them. The electric fluid must be gathered in secret, before the lightning of genius can break on the dazzled eyes of men, and its thunder amaze the world.

What he did during this interval, says Fétis, few know, notwithstanding the enthusiasm he everywhere excited. The charming *"Lucia fantaisie,"* and the wonderful combination of *fantasies* upon "Robert the Devil" — give but incomplete evidence of his employment. Even those who heard him improvise at the concert at Liege an admirable capriccio on a thema to all appearance barren, given him by the audience; those who heard his performance, *prima vista,* of the most difficult passages in accumulated pieces from illegible manuscripts, which he executed with so much readiness as to astonish the authors themselves, and with infinite ease; those who know how many great compositions are impressed on his memory, so that he can execute any one of them at any moment; those who know him for the most complete musician of our time, and the most gifted in his way; even they have no idea of the thorough change which took place in his creative power during the three years spent by him in retirement.

Fétis goes on, in his philosophical manner, to explain how the doings of Thalberg, suggesting new combinations to the mind of our artist, already busy with improvements, wrought a change in him, and impelled him upon a path that was quite his own. The victory was accomplished; and triumphantly could the question now be answered—"Is Liszt also distinguished as a composer?"

Liszt has recorded his new views, and the forms invented by him, in an immense work, entitled "Three years of wandering." The first part contains recollections of Switzerland, the second recollections of Italy, the third of Germany. Fétis says, "I was indulged by the artist with a hearing of some portions of it; and must do him the justice to say, that these displayed most uncommon attainments in art. Perhaps it will be said, when the work appears, that the composer has had the orchestra more in view than the piano—yet I know not if this objection is not praise rather than blame. However it may be, I will not forestall the judgment of competent critics by recording my simple impressions. I merely quote the *'Etudes d'execution transcendante,'* which have particularly led me to this long exposition," &c.

We have found it necessary to follow this writer so far, because his remarks help to develop the personal history of Liszt, and to place his individuality with regard to art in a strong light. Fétis is, besides, such a well known and universally respected authority in the higher musical studies, that he will be gladly listened to in his observations on a genius so remarkable.

Those who venture to deny Liszt a general talent for composition, will find they have measured him by false and inapplicable rules. The foundation of composition is Imagination, the living, powerful creative faculty. Let us take only those works which show most clearly Liszt's art, and the subtlety of his spirit—the Transpositions [11] of Beethoven's symphonies, and the songs of Schubert. It cannot be doubted that a power of imagination has here been displayed by him, such as would not be needed for another original work.

Liszt in these has not merely copied; he has emulated with creative power; and so successfully that there is a second birth. These transpositions, grand in the symphonies, tender in the songs—are the culminating point of musical plastic power. It is impossible to particularize the expression with more subtlety; to express the spirit more accurately and fully. Therein lies a brilliant conception of harmonious completeness, that fills the heart and soul alike, when those spiritual graces press upon them. In truth, one should only hear that genesis of pastoral symphony—those wonderful pictures, called into life by the powerful and magic touch of Liszt. Any other virtuoso, were he the most accomplished and excellent of players, would have given us, instead of divine poetry, only massive, or at best, tasteful prose!

In 1837, Liszt felt the earnest desire of poetical spirits, to visit the great world. The swan also spreads her silver wings, and sails southward, towards the land of beauty and song; of art and antiquity—towards Italy. That is peculiarly the land of song; it is well known how the heart there opens to, and welcomes all that bears the name of music. From Milan to Venice, from Florence to Naples, a dazzling flame of enthusiasm surrounded the artist. In all these places Liszt gave concerts, which were attended by crowded audiences. He abode some time in Rome, to the delight of the people; and the walls of the Engelsburgh resounded to the echo of his renown. External nature seemed to smile upon him: he himself says, he was wonderfully benefited by the pure air and the cloudless sky. He had not in a long time enjoyed such health and serenity. And his compositions have the same purity and clearness as the atmosphere. There originated those grand and marvellous transpositions, of which mention is made above; there were written his "*Nuits de Pausilippe.*" One may ask himself, if out of all these does not breathe a kind of classic repose—elevating the feelings and inspiring a calm delight, like the pure beauty of a moonlight heaven in that lovely land! Our artist confesses that he, at this period, passed beyond the time of wild exuberance in feeling—of stormy restlessness, of mystical fantasy; and that he owed the clearing up of his spirit to the country and nature around him. Thus composed, he went to Germany, Carlsruhe, Munich, Stuttgart; in short, all the principal cities of southern Germany heard his magical performance with astonishment. All the journals and papers held but one language respecting him—that of enthusiastic admiration. But in the midst of this appreciation and these honors, the longing to revisit home was awakened in his breast. One morning he sprang suddenly out of bed, and ordered his horse to be got ready. What to him was the applause, the homage of strangers! he longed to be again where he had been first seen and heard. "For Hungary!" This impatience was the pure desire of a grateful heart.

Liszt did not deceive himself. How he was received, how he was valued, all Hungary can witness. It is impossible to describe the joy with which he was welcomed by old and young, high and low; by artists and critics, even to the highest in the land. He was the loved theme of all tongues. Mothers told their children how the "little Francis" had become another Emperor Francis in the kingdom of art; how he had made himself so great and famous; and how he could play a whole book full of strange and beautiful stories on the piano. He gave concerts—first in Vienna, then in Pesth—not to promote his own interest, but for the benefit of the poor, who had met with severe losses by the inundation; and for young artists, to enable them to prosecute their studies.

The noble and generous philanthropy of this conduct made a proper impression upon his countrymen. Two cities, Pesth and Oedenburg, created him an honorary citizen; a patent of nobility was solicited for him by the Comitat of Oedenburg; and the "Sword of Honor," according to Hungarian custom, was presented to him with due solemnities. This episode deserves particularly to be noticed. The following account is taken from an authentic journal:

"The national feeling of the *Magyars* is well known; and proud are they of that star of the first magnitude, which arose out of their nation. Over the countries of Germany the fame of the Hungarian Liszt came to them, before they had as yet an opportunity of admiring him. The Danube was swelled by rains; Pesth was inundated; thousands were mourning the loss of friends and relations, or of all their property. During his absence in Milan, Liszt learned that many of his countrymen were suffering from want. His resolution was taken. The smiling heaven of Italy—the *dolce far niente* of southern life—could not detain him. The following morning he had quitted Milan, and was on his way to Vienna. He performed for the benefit of those who had suffered by the inundation of Pesth. His art was the horn of plenty, from which streamed blessings for the unfortunate. Eighteen months afterwards he came to Pesth—not as the artist in search of pecuniary advantage—but as a Magyar. He played for the Hungarian National Theatre; for the Musical Society; for the poor of Pesth, and the poor in Oedenburg; always before crowded houses; and the proceeds, full 100,000 francs, were appropriated to those purposes and those institutions. Who can wonder that admiration and pride should rise to enthusiasm in the breasts of his grateful countrymen?

The distinguished artist—the noble-hearted man—deserved it all! In the theatre, in the street—Liszt was everywhere greeted with acclamations and vivats. He was complimented by serenades; garlands were thrown to him; in short, the population of Pesth neglected nothing to manifest their respect, gratitude, and affection.

"But these honors, which might have been paid to any other artist of high distinction, did not satisfy them. They resolved to bind him forever to the Hungarian nation, from which he had sprung. He was therefore made an honorary citizen of Pesth and Oedenburg, and a deputation of persons of consideration informed him that a patent of nobility had been asked for him from the Emperor and King. A still closer bond, however, was desired. The token of manly honor in Hungary is the sword; every Magyar has the right to wear a sword, and avails himself of that right. It was determined that their celebrated countryman should be presented with the Hungarian sword of honor. The noblemen appeared at the theatre in the rich costume they usually wear before the Emperor, and presented Liszt, amid thunders of applause from the whole assembled people, with a costly sword of honor. In receiving this, he was expected to enter into a solemn engagement *to bind himself forever to the Hungarian people, and to reside in Hungary.*"

In the autumn of 1840, Liszt went from Paris, where he had been for some time, to the north of Germany, and particularly to Hamburg. Here also, where the people are colder and less impulsive, his reception was the same as it had been elsewhere, wherever his admirable performance had been heard. He saw even adversaries silenced and ashamed; and enemies converted into the warmest friends, who were loudest in his praise. To show Liszt's power of memory and his intimate knowledge of the best pieces of music, it is only necessary to mention one instance among many. One evening in public he was requested to select and perform one of Beethoven's sonatas. He announced his willingness to play, and desired that the piece might be chosen. "*Sonata quasi fantasia,*" cried some one. Liszt consented; did he go to fetch the work? No—he played it at once from memory!

From Hamburg Liszt went to London. Enthusiasm, applause, sympathy, met him everywhere; he was courted by all. In fourteen days he gave nine concerts. He spared no exertion to fulfil expectation and satisfy his friends. Here a misfortune overtook him; he lost, through the carelessness of an agent, the proceeds of three hundred concerts. Imagine the feelings of the artist, exhausted both in mind and body, at the receipt of this disastrous news! But he knew that his true riches lay in his art; and that it was his best support. With a cheerful spirit, notwithstanding his reverses, he left the British Islands, to return to the banks of the Seine. From Paris, where he played for the Beethoven monument, and won universal applause by his

Robert-fantaisies, he went a second time to Hamburg, to shine the brightest star in the north German firmament. The deepest admiration, the silent throb of heartfelt enjoyment, greeted his appearance. Thence he went to Kiel; where, immediately on his arrival, and as it were on the wing, he gave a concert, proceeding to embark for Copenhagen. He played not less than seven times before the court: and here, as among the Parisians, commanded unbounded admiration. The citizens thronged to the concerts, impelled by curiosity, and returned home full of enthusiasm for the great performer. Once more he went back to Hamburg, and thence to the Rhine. What an agreeable entertainment was prepared for him, under the purple clusters of those vineyards, the reader may presently judge.

After Liszt, with his wonted kindness, had offered to give a concert in Cologne, the proceeds of which were to be appropriated to the completion of the Cathedral, the Rhenish *"Liedertafel,"* [12] resolved to bring him with due pomp from the island of Nonnenwerth, near Bonn, where he had been for some days. This was on the twenty-second of August, 1841. A steamboat was hired expressly for this purpose, and conveyed a numerous company to Nonnenwerth at eleven in the morning. The "Liedertafel" then greeted the artist, who stood on the shore, by singing a morning salute, accompanied by the firing of cannon, and loud huzzas. They then marched, with wind instruments in advance, to the now empty chapel of the cloister of Nonnenwerth, where again they sang; and thence to Rolandseck, where an elegant dinner was prepared for the company. All eyes were fixed upon Liszt; all hearts were turned to him. He proposed a toast in honor of his entertainers, and at the conclusion of his speech observed with justice that nowhere in the world could any club be found like the "Liedertafel" in Germany. When the banquet was over they returned to Nonnenwerth, where a crowd of people from the surrounding country was assembled. The universal wish to hear Liszt was so evident that he was induced to send for a piano, to be brought into the chapel: and to gratify the assembly—listening, and rapt with delight—by a display of his transcendan powers. The desolate halls of the chapel once more resounded with the stir and voices of life. Not even the nuns, we will venture to say, who in former times used here to send up prayers to heaven, were impressed with a deeper sense of the heavenly, than was this somewhat worldly assembly by the magnificent music of Liszt, that seemed indeed to disclose things beyond this earth. At seven o'clock, the "Liedertafel," with Liszt at their head, marched on their return, and went on board the steamboat, which was decorated with colored flags, amid peals of cannon. It was nine, and quite dark, when they approached their landing. Rockets were sent up from the boat, and a continual stream of colored fireworks; so that as the city rose before them from the bosom of the Rhine, the boat seemed enveloped in a circle of brilliant flame, which threw its reflection far over the waters. Music and huzzas greeted our artist on shore; and all Cologne was assembled to give him the splendid welcome, which in other times only monarchs received. Slowly the procession of the "Liedertafel" moved through the multitude to the hotel, where again and again, shouts and cheers testified the joy of the people at the arrival of their distinguished guest.

With the above illustration of the enthusiasm with which Liszt is received among those who know how to appreciate him, we end this brief sketch of his life.

In the personal conversation of Liszt, there is nothing eccentric or bizarre, as is often found with celebrated artists. He is attentive, cordial, takes an interest in general subjects of conversation, and is affable to all. Only where his dignity as an artist is concerned, does he show that imposing manner, of earnestness bordering on severity or gloom, which has been noticed as belonging to him. He speaks with a measured propriety of his own performances; hears every opinion respecting it with careful attention, but will never depart from what tends to the development of his own ideas in art. He yields as much as justice requires to the critics, but will never permit them to mould him by their judgment. "As I have begun, and carried on thus far, I will complete," said he once. The original artist must live out his own system.

Liszt commonly speaks quickly, rapidly, and abruptly; he often hesitates in his speech, from the want of words. His mind is so active, his perceptions so quick, that it is difficult to find ready expression; and while thus embarrassed, his countenance assumes a fixed, stern look, the brow contracted as if in anger. But when any one helps him out with a word, he smiles, and nodding his head, replies "yes—yes"—moving his head while listening, and waiting for what the other will say. In social intercourse he is thoroughly at his ease, and seems to forget that he is at all distinguished. He always shows himself ready to comply with the most timidly expressed wish that he should play for a dance; but it pleases him well when his wild, original *Galoppe chromatique* cannot be danced by. "It will not do;" he will say. "It will not give up the place where it belongs."

Liszt's whole physiognomy is of the Hungarian character; his thick fair brown hair falls in masses on his neck, where it is cut off short; his features are all strongly marked; his eyes rather long than large, bright and deepset, shadowed by dark eyebrows. His look is penetrating, and has something in it of conscious superiority; yet though it may occasion uneasiness to the object, it has too much mildness to inspire fear. All the portraits represent him too strong and stout. Liszt is of a slight and thin figure; his shoulders are drawn up from constant playing, but his hands are delicate and well proportioned; seeing them, one can hardly understand how he can play such things as the Symphonies and the Robert-Fantaisies. In this respect, he has something that might be called *Paganinish*; unbounded energy of spirit, and indomitable strength of will—developed in the most delicate physical organization. In short, the whole appearance of Liszt betokens, to the most casual observer, the indwelling of that high and wonderful genius, before which the world has bowed in reverential acknowledgment. His entrance into the concert-room generally draws from the assembly—particularly from the ladies—the exclamation, "Ah! what an interesting man! What an interesting figure!"

FOOTNOTES

[11] Uebertragungen.
[12] A musical club.

TAMBURINI

It was rather late in the evening of a day in autumn, 182-, that two well dressed persons were seen standing before a small house in one of the principal streets of Milan. They leaned against the railing at the foot of the steps, and were listening with such apparent attention, that their attitude and employment might have excited observation, but that a certain high-bred air indicated them to be above suspicion, and the delicious music heard from the house fully justified them in pausing to listen.

The music was low, plaintive and touching, and accompanied by a clear and melodious male voice. Now and then it swelled into deeper pathos, the voice being evidently interrupted by sobs; and one of the listeners, deeply moved, turned aside to brush a tear from his eyes. After it had continued some time with these alternations of harmonious complaint, it was suddenly broken off, and a dead silence succeeded.

"Poor Antonio!" said one of the gentlemen, with a deep sigh; "this affliction will kill him."

"Nay," answered his companion, "I have no fear. He has youth, health, ambition, to sustain him; and though I know he feels——"

"But you know not Antonio as I do, Ronza," rejoined the other. "It is the exquisite sensibility of his nature, the deep and passionate feeling hid under his graceful and composed exterior, that, even more than qualities merely professional, has contributed to his fame as the first of modern singers. And this exquisitely toned instrument, that yields such melody to the lightest touch, may be as easily shattered."

"He loved his mother devotedly; but—*cielo*—did he expect to survive her?"

"Ah! she was more than mother to him; he owed her his intellectual, his spiritual being. She directed his pure soul to the enjoyments alone fitted for him; she led him to the shrine of Art. No, Ronza, do not blame his grief."

"I do not blame it. I only say that the deepest wound, even in natures like his, may the sooner be healed! But let us go in."

The two friends ascended the steps, and knocked. They were admitted, and as they anticipated, found the person they had come to seek, plunged in a grief that defied all consolation—the more to be dreaded, as his outward manner was cold and calm. It was the snow upon the mountain, whose breast was consuming in volcanic fires.

"And yet I am grateful for your coming," he said, after every commonplace source of consolation had been exhausted in their kind efforts to divert his mind from the contemplation of the calamity that had crushed him. "I cannot now say how grateful, but you will forgive my lack of words. Will you pardon, also, Count Albert, my entreating you to take charge of these papers?"

And opening a drawer, he took out several letters and handed them to the count.

"How—you do not now think of leaving Milan?"

"No—but I retire from the world. To-morrow I enter the Convent di — —."

Count Albert di Gaëta and the Marchese di Ronza exchanged looks of dismay.

"So sudden a project— —."

"It is not sudden. My resolution has been formed since the day of my mother's death, and my application was forwarded immediately. I expect a reply to it every hour."

"You have been imprudent, my friend," said the Marchese. "You will regret the precipitation of this step."

"And what have I now to live for?" asked the mourner, bitterly.

"For fame," replied di Ronza.

"For art," said Count Albert.

The bereaved artist shook his head.

"When, at eighteen years of age," he said, "I met with my first triumph at Bologna; when the public far and near were pleased to applaud me, what, think you, was my joy in the enthusiasm I awakened? That *she* rejoiced in my success; that *she* encouraged me to persevering effort; that I was earning honor and competence for her enjoyment in old age. Now I have lost my only stimulus to exertion; I have lost my love of art; my faculties are paralyzed."

"This is not natural," observed the Marchese, gravely.

"But it is truth. The world is a desert to me; I leave it. The church offers me an asylum. I accept it as a refuge where I can bear with me her memory for whom alone I wished to live!"

"Your friends," said di Ronza, somewhat haughtily, "may not thank you for your exclusion of them. You have many to whom your success is a part of their daily joy. And yet, gifted with health, beauty, genius, not yet twenty-five, you would hide yourself in the cowl and scapulary from the admiration of men—the love of woman——."

The mourner gave an involuntary and impatient gesture. The Marchese saw that his brow was crimson, and a new light seemed to break on Ronza's mind, for a meaning smile played for an instant on his lip. It was gone before either of his companions perceived it.

"Before we part," asked he, "will you sing us this air from the Cenerentola?" and he took up a leaf of music.

"Nay," interposed Count Albert, "it is wrong to ask this. How unsuitable this song to the gloom of his feelings!"

"The better, that the power of music may for an instant dispel his melancholy thoughts. Come, Antonio, I will join you."

Antonio complied, and seated himself at the piano to sing. Ronza accompanied him, watching him closely all the while, and nodded his head with an expression of satisfaction when the air was concluded.

There was a knock at the door; Antonio arose from the instrument. The *portiere* entered, and handed him a letter. He begged pardon of his friends, and broke the seal; glanced over the contents, and buried his face in his hands.

The friends sat in silent sympathy. At length, in obedience to a sign from the mourner, Count Albert took the letter up and read it. It was an answer from the superiors of the Convent di ——. His application was rejected; their doors were closed against "an actor."

Courteously as the denial was expressed, it was evident that Antonio felt the implied insult to his profession; and indignation for the moment rose above his grief.

"The creed is indeed exclusive," he said, bitterly, "that refuses an actor space for repentance and preparation for death."

"They are right," said the Marchese, somewhat abruptly. "What sort of a monk would you make, *Antonio mio*? Your sorrow is profound, but it must in time abate; your heart will rise from its depression; you will feel once again the impulse of genius and ambition."

"Never!" interrupted the artist.

"I tell you, you will. I am old in the world, and therefore a true prophet. You will, and the time is not far distant. In the convent, your eyes would be opened, only that you might see the gloom surrounding you; your wings would expand, only that you might feel the weight that chained them to earth—forever! For I know you well enough to know that once fettered by the vows, you would die ere fling them off! They are right; they foresee the result. Be warned in time!"

"My resolution is unalterable," said Antonio. "Milan is not the world. In four days I shall leave it, and seek elsewhere the asylum I cannot obtain here. I am heart-broken and wretched; I cannot live among the scenes and associations of my past life. Better for me the grave of the suicide!"

"This must be remedied, and speedily," said Count Albert to his companion, after they had quitted their friend, whose sufferings seemed in no degree alleviated by their sympathy, "or nature will give way. That wild look of anguish; that fevered flush; the hurried and abrupt movement; the visible emaciation of his whole frame; all these make me shudder. An organization so susceptible, so delicate, cannot withstand so mighty a shock. Suffer this grief to prey upon him, and in three months he will fall its victim."

"You are right," replied di Ronza. "There is danger, and it must be averted. The world has no overplus of genius and worth, that we can afford to lose a Tamburini."

"But the means——."

"I have thought, and still think of them. Join me at my lodgings at ten. For the present I have an engagement. _A rivederci._"

And the friends separated.

The scene was a handsomely furnished drawing-room in the house of Madame Gioja. This lady—French by birth, celebrated for her many graces and accomplishments,—was the daughter of the Count Gaëtani, and wedded in early youth to the Marquis de Miriallia. His jealous love for the beautiful creature he had espoused prompted his last will, which made the forfeiture of his fortune the penalty of her second marriage. Surrounded by luxury and admiration, moving in the most exalted circles, the lovely widow cast her eyes upon a young artist, dependent on his profession for support. Love proved stronger than ambition, and she gave up splendor to share the lot of the poor man whom her heart had chosen. Her friends were indignant; she was deprived of her liberty; but being afterwards released from imprisonment, she left her native country to lead a wandering life, consoled for all her sacrifices by the love of her husband and children.

Madame Gioja was reading by a small table in the centre of the room. A young girl of exquisite beauty was playing at the piano, sometimes accompanying the music with her voice; and ever and anon the elder lady would look up from her book with a glance so full of tenderness and pride, that the spectator needed not to have observed the striking resemblance between the two to be certain of their relationship. The looks were such as only beam from a mother's eyes upon a beloved and only daughter.

"The Marchese di Ronza," said the portiere, throwing open the door.

Madame Gioja rose to receive her guest. The visit was unusual for one of rank so high; for the lady, be it remembered, had descended in marrying to the condition of her husband, and he was no associate of nobles. But she had in youth been familiar with courts and princes, and in grace and dignity she was not changed; so that though surprised at the visit, no princess could have received it with greater self-possession and composure.

The Marchese paid his respects to the lady, then turned to her daughter, who had risen from the piano, and fixed on her so prolonged a gaze, that the mother was startled and somewhat offended. She replied very gravely to some casual remark of her guest, and the young girl, who seemed aware that there was an embarrassment, blushed deeply. Ronza saw he had committed an error, and said with a serious air to Madame Gioja—

"May I crave the favor, madam, of a few moments' conversation with you on business?"

"Certainly," answered the lady; and turning to her daughter, "You may retire, my dear Marietta."

The young lady left the room. The Marchese remained a few moments silent, as if considering how he should introduce what he had to say. At length he said, abruptly—

"My business concerns the Signorina, as well as yourself. It is for your permission for her to sing in part of a new piece by Mercadante, to be immediately produced."

Madame Gioja hesitated.

"I have cultivated my daughter's talent for music to the utmost," said she, "and yet I tremble to decide on her choice of the art as a profession. She is so young, so sensitive, so ill able to sustain herself against the many trials of an artiste— —"

"And is it you who talk thus?" asked the Marchese, surprised. "You, who sacrificed opulence, rank, friends, for the love of art—to share the fortunes of a votary of music!"

"I am the better able," said the lady, smiling, "to judge of its consolations. Of its triumphs I say nothing; for I would not have Marietta influenced by the least whisper of vanity in her choice for life!"

"You are then undetermined as to your daughter's embracing the profession of music?" cried Ronza, astonished. "You have perhaps, other views—other designs for her?"

"Signore?" said the mother, evidently not understanding the drift of the question.

"Nay," said the Marchese, recovering himself, "it is not right to ask such questions, at least, without confiding our whole project to you, madam. And first, have no fears as to granting my request. It is only before a select audience that I wish your daughter to sing."

"Then my permission is freely granted," replied the lady.

"A word more. You are aware, madam, of the recent misfortune of our friend Tamburini?"

"The death of his mother? Ah! it was a terrible blow. I am told he bears it not with resignation."

"Alas! madam, the blow may cost him his life. Driven by grief to despair, he has already applied for admission into the Convent — —."

"This is dreadful!" exclaimed the lady; and Ronza saw that her cheek grew pale.

"His application," he continued, "has been refused, as it ought to be, and he is now resolved on quitting Milan. You know Antonio; you know him to be one of those fiery spirits, impatient of suffering, ready to plunge into imprudence, and obstinate against opposition. The only hope of saving him is to re-awaken his ambition—his impulse for art."

"And how can that be done?"

"By a master stroke, if at all; and in this I crave your aid. Your daughter—I have seen it—has much influence over our spoiled artist. I have seen his emotion when she sang, at your private concerts."

"You overrate her powers," said the mother, reservedly. "But her aid and mine shall be cheerfully given to any enterprise that promises to divert the grief of our valued friend. Your wish is— —"

"Simply, that she will take a part in the *Posto Abbandonato*, in an act of which he will appear. A few select friends are to be the audience. I will have the piece sent to her immediately."

"I promise for her."

"I thank you, madam, and the world will thank you," cried the Marchese, as he paid his parting salutations and hastened to his rendezvous with the count.

But the mother found opposition where she had not counted upon it—from the young lady herself. Marietta seemed the more averse to the proposition, the more she was reasoned with about it; and her own reasons for her reluctance were, as a petted young girl's are sometimes apt to be, so frivolous, that they vexed Madame Gioja. Was it obstinacy or coquetry? thought she; but her daughter was ever wont to be complying, and above all artifice. She told Marietta there was no receding from her word pledged for her compliance; and then, though with not a little pouting, the young lady set about learning the part assigned to her.

The preparations of Tamburini for leaving Milan were complete. The amateurs of the city were in despair; but no entreaties could move his determination. Count Albert passed with him the afternoon of the last day, to be crowned, according to the earnest solicitation of numerous friends, by a private concert, in which the already famous singer was to gratify them for the last time. It was to be his adieu to them, to music and the world.

"You will have the goodness also, dear count, to have this package delivered after my departure. It is a selection of the best pieces of opera music in my collection, with the great works of Gluck. Ah! he was once my favorite master."

"Have you lost your taste for his compositions?"

"No; but I can no longer do them justice. I am an ingrate, for if I ever had aught of energy, fire or force, I owe it to him. What strength, what soul there is in his creations! how they task the noblest faculties! Passion they have, but more than passion; it is the very mind, the genius of tragedy."

The count read the direction on the package—it was addressed "To Mademoiselle Marietta Gioja."

"There is another of my lost divinities," said Antonio, with a melancholy smile. "I might"—and his face flushed deeply as he spoke—"had I risen to the summit I once hoped to attain, to an eminence that would have conferred distinction on those I loved, I might have dared to offer her the homage of my heart. Beautiful as she is, the perfections of her person are surpassed by her mental loveliness, and oh, what angelic goodness! But I must not speak of her; it makes me bitter to think in what a delusion I have indulged."

"Believe it, believe it yet!" cried Albert, grasping his friend's hand.

"No; I am now fully awakened. What a mockery to think of one elevated so far above me! Her aristocratic descent, the pride of her mother's family,—the claims of these might have been satisfied, had I lived to realize my lofty visions! But they are dispelled, and I have resigned this sweetest hope of all; cherishing only the thought that she will not perhaps disdain my last gift; that these noble and glorious works may sometimes recall to her mind the memory of one who, had he proved worthy, would have dared to love her."

"This is folly!" exclaimed the count. "You are depressed, and the world seems dark to you. With time, the soother of sorrow——"

"You mistake, my dear friend. It is not the pressure of grief alone that weighs me down, and has crushed my energies. I were not a man had I not within me a principle that could bear up against the heaviest calamity. But," and he laid his hand impressively on Albert's arm, "heard you never of the *death of enthusiasm?*"

His friend sighed deeply.

"It is thus with me. I have nothing now to offer at the shrine of art. Shall I present her with a cold and soulless votary, rifled of his treasure of youth, and faith, and hope? Shall I, whose spirit has flagged in the race, long ere the goal was won, pluck at inferior honors? Shall I cumber the arena to dishearten others, when I can obtain no prize? How am I to inspire the public with confidence when I have lost it in myself? How can I kindle passion in others, who am dead to its fires? No, Count Albert, I have become insensible to the deepest, the highest wonders of music. I will not insult her by a dragging, desperate mediocrity. I will not impede the advance of better spirits. I have fallen in the battle—the honors of victory are not for me."

It was melancholy to see this paralysis, this prostration of a noble spirit! And yet, how to combat it? Argument was in vain, and the count rejoiced when this painful interview was at an end. It was already evening, and time to go to the concert; the carriage was at the door. He took his friend's arm and led him down. Not a word was exchanged as they drove on, till they drew up and alighted at their place of destination.

It was at the house of a distinguished amateur that this final concert was to take place, and the saloon had been fitted up as a small theatre. A select number of auditors—many more, however, than the performers had expected—were seated at the upper end of the room. The stage was brilliantly lighted, and the scenery so well painted and so admirably arranged as almost to bewilder the senses with illusion. All that taste and poetry could devise, lent their enchantment to the scene.

Those who have observed the effect of sudden excitement on minds long and deeply depressed,—that is, in temperaments highly susceptible,—may conceive the conflict of emotion in the breast of Antonio, as he found himself thus unexpectedly surrounded by the external splendor and beauty of scenic art. He had anticipated meeting with a few friends, to sing with them a farewell song. What meant these flowery wreaths, this blaze of light, this luxury of painting? The orchestra struck up; their music seemed to penetrate his inmost soul; the revulsion of feeling kindled a wild energy within him. He felt, and at once, almost the inspiration of early youth. Though convinced it was but momentary, he yielded to the impulse and advanced upon the stage.

His symmetrical and noble figure, the grace and expression of his movements, the mind beaming from his features, would at any time have prepossessed an audience in his favor. Under the present affecting circumstances, appealing to every heart, the welcome was tumultuous and long. Tamburini, as he acknowledged it, recovered his melancholy composure. It was destined soon to be overthrown.

At a little distance from him stood the heroine of the piece; like him, bewildered at the novelty of her position and the splendor of her reception, and blushing in much confusion. Could Antonio believe his eyes? It was Marietta Gioja!

With an involuntary exclamation of surprise, he hastened towards her. He did not perceive either pride or coquetry in her evident avoidance of him. But there was no time for explanations. The music played on, and both performed their parts to the rapturous delight of all who listened.

At last the curtain fell. The young debutante was standing upon the stage; she turned to go, but at the instant her hand was clasped by Antonio and covered with burning kisses.

"Marietta, dear Marietta, how can I thank you for this?"

She struggled to withdraw her hand; she repelled him haughtily. He saw that her face was bathed in tears.

"For pity's sake, Marietta, tell me how I have offended you!"

"Let me go, sir; it is all I ask!"

But love was stronger than reason or reserve. The torrent had burst its bounds, and it must overflow. In language impassioned as his own heart, irrepressible as the burning lava of a volcano, he poured forth the love so long nourished in secret. He told her of his hopes and fears—all,

all swallowed up in earnest, ardent devotion! The tide of feeling had swept down at once both memory and resolution.

The hues of the rose and lily chased each other rapidly across the cheek of the beautiful girl. Suddenly, at a rustling in the silken folds that veiled them from a view of the audience, she snatched her hands from her lover and rushed off the stage.

Antonio was about to follow her, when Madame Gioja appeared. She led by the hand her trembling and blushing daughter.

"My daughter came hither in obedience to my commands," said she. "And now, Marietta, that your bashful scruples are satisfied, and there is no danger that our friend can charge you with any unmaidenly project for storming his heart, you may as well tell him that you love him in sincerity, though in truth this scene is not the fittest for a real declaration. Since it must be, however, take my blessing, dear children!"

There was a continued clamor without, and frequent cries of "Tamburini." Presently a corner of the curtain was raised, and the Marchese di Ronza appeared, his face radiant with benevolent joy.

"I have the happiness to announce to you, my friends, that our distinguished and well beloved Antonio has concluded to defer, indefinitely, his departure from Milan. You will dispense, therefore, with his farewell at present. I have reason to hope that he will ere long favor us with his performance through the whole piece of the *Posto Abbandonato*, and congratulate you, as well as myself, upon the certainty that he has no idea of *abandoning his post!*"

Loud, heartfelt and rapturous was the cheering that greeted this announcement. Tamburini heard, and wondered in his new born happiness how he could ever have yielded to despair.

Thus was a great artist rescued from self-despondency and restored to the world. The disappointment of his first project of turning recluse, was made to bring forth wholesome fruit. But the Marchese, whose plan of a surprise had so admirably succeeded, was never willing to give love all the credit it deserved. As to Madame Gioja, she knew the human heart, and wondered not at the result.

A short time after, the nuptials of Marietta and Antonio were celebrated. Though he cherished with veneration to the end of his life the memory of his mother, yet never again did he yield to that self-distrust and despair, which in the true artist is burying the talent committed to him.

It was near sunset on a bright and warm day in September, 182-, that a gentleman and lady, dressed in travelling attire, might have been seen descending the steps of a palazzo fronting on one of the principal canals of Venice. They were followed by an attendant, another having gone before with their luggage, and deposited it in a plain looking gondola fastened at the foot of the steps. The travellers took their seats in this gondola, and as they pushed off, observed two gentlemen ascend the steps of the house they had just quitted, and ring at the door. While they were talking with the porter, a turn in the canal carried the gondola out of sight.

"Who knows what we have escaped, Marietta, *cara*?" said the male passenger. "If my eyes inform me rightly, one of yon cavaliers is Signor Bordoni, a friend of the Impressario here, come doubtless to tempt me with some new piece, and urge me to stay."

"I should not regret an accident that kept us longer in Venice," observed the lady. "You are, I know, well appreciated."

"We will return; oh, yes! We are not bidding a long adieu to the sea-born city. But I must not disappoint our friends at Trieste."

"How lovely a scene!" exclaimed the lady, after a pause of some length.

And in truth it was beautiful. The sun had set, but his beams yet lingered on the towers and cupolas of the palaces of Venice, and on the light clouds that overhung them like a canopy of gold. They had passed from the canal, where light boats were shooting to and fro in every direction, and the sound of footsteps and lively voices filled the air, into one of the lagunes, where a complete stillness prevailed, broken only by the plash of the water as the oars dipped, and the gentle ripple as the boat swept on, and the softened, distant murmur of human life and motion in a great city. The moon rose large, and round, and bright, in the east. There was a delicious mistiness in the atmosphere that mellowed every object; a dreamy and luxurious softening, like the languor that enhances the charms of an oriental beauty. At no great distance lay the vessel that was to convey the passengers to Trieste, waiting for them and the hour appointed to set sail.

"See that large gondola yonder!" said the lady, laying her hand suddenly on her husband's arm. "How gracefully it glides over the waters; and it seems to follow straight on our course."

It came onward, indeed, with almost incredible velocity; and was now near enough for them to observe that it was painted black, and moreover of a somewhat peculiar construction.

"It is a government boat," said the man.

"She has armed men on board," remarked their attendant. "She bears directly upon us."

"Antonio!" exclaimed the lady, pressing close to her husband with an expression of apprehension.

"Be not alarmed, Marietta mia; they mean us no harm—though sooth to say, it is somewhat discourteous to follow us so closely. Hold there," he cried to the gondolier; "let us rest a moment and see what they want with us."

The gondolier backed water with his oars so dexterously, that the course of the light vessel was checked in an instant, and she quivered on the water without making a foot's progress. At the same moment the other boat came along side, and also stopped. An officer wearing the imperial uniform stood up and signed to the gondolier as if forbidding him to proceed.

"May I ask, signore, what this means?" demanded the gentleman passenger. "We are in haste."

"And we also," replied the officer. "I am in search of a person called Antonio Tamburini."

"I am he."

"It is well. You will please accompany me."

"That is impossible. I am about to sail for Trieste. We are on our way to the vessel."

"You must return. I have an order for your arrest." And he exhibited an order, signed by the proper authorities, and made out in due form, for the arrest of Antonio Tamburini.

The lady uttered a half shriek, and clung to her husband.

"Here is some mistake, signor. I am the singer Tamburini. I have never interfered in politics; I have nothing to do with the government. I am but a chance passenger through Venice."

"My orders are positive," said the officer, with some appearance of impatience. "Make way there;" and while his armed attendants moved so as to allow seats for the prisoners, he offered his hand to the lady to assist her into the other boat.

Our hero was sufficiently vexed at this unexpected delay, but saw that it was inevitable. Offering his arm to his wife, he helped her to change her place, and gave directions for the transfer of his luggage. In a few minutes they were retracing their course across the lagune.

Not a word was spoken by any of the party, except that once the officer inquired if the lady's seat was commodious. Notwithstanding the silence, however, his manner and that of his men was respectful in the highest degree; and this circumstance somewhat encouraged the hopes of his prisoners that their unpleasant detention might be followed by no serious misfortune. But who could penetrate the mysteries of governmental policy, or the involutions of its suspicion?

Thus it was not without misgiving that Tamburini entered Venice on his compulsory return; and these apprehensions were strengthened when he saw it was not the intention of his guards to conduct him to his late residence. They passed the Palazzo di — —; the arcades of San Marco. They were not far from the ancient ducal palace. Thoughts of a prison, of secret denunciations, of unknown accusers, of trial and sentence, were busy in Antonio's brain, and caused him to move uneasily. As for the lady, she was pale as death, and hardly able to support herself upright. The more inexplicable seemed the danger the greater was her dread. Once she leaned towards her husband and whispered, in a touching tone of distress—"My mother—how will she feel when she knows what has befallen us!"

Gentle and generous instinct of woman! Her first thought under the severest pressure of calamity is always for the dear ones whom the blow that crushes her perchance may bruise!

At length the gondola stopped. The moon was shining so brightly, that the marble steps seemed almost to radiate light. There was a hum of voices at a distance, and tones of music at intervals floated on the air; but all was still immediately around them. Two of the guard took their places on either side of the prisoners; two followed; the officer walked before and led the way up a dark flight of steps that terminated in a wide corridor. This, too, was only lighted by a torch carried in the hand of one of the attendants.

"Antonio, whither are we going?" asked Madame Tamburini, in a feeble voice, and leaning heavily on her husband's arm, half fainting with affright.

"Courage, my beloved!" answered he, supporting her with his arm; "we shall soon know the worst."

Crossing the corridor, they entered another long gallery, and walked its whole length in silence, stopping before a massive door at the lower end. The officer directed the door to be opened. It swung on its hinges with a most dungeon-like grating, and the prisoners were ushered into the next apartment.

The sudden light, combined with the effect of overpowering surprise, nearly completed the work of terror on the lady's trembling frame; she would have fallen to the earth had not the officer supported her. Several persons came crowding round to offer their assistance. Tamburini thought himself fallen into a trance, and rubbed his eyes. They stood in the green-room of the opera house!

This, then, was their dungeon! And what meant this bold invasion of their liberty?—this marching them back as prisoners, under guard, and in fear of their lives? Was it the work of the Impressario? Apparently not—for he stood with open eyes and mouth, as much astonished as the rest at the unexpected apparition of the distinguished singer. He turned an inquiring look towards the officer.

"I know what you would ask, Signor Tamburini," replied the cool official, "and will give you all the satisfaction in my power. I have the honor to announce to you the commands of His Majesty the Emperor. It is his imperial will that you perform this night in the Marriage of Figaro. The Emperor himself, with His Majesty the Emperor of Russia, will honor the performance with his presence."

Who is there that had the happiness of being present on that memorable occasion, of witnessing the brilliant and graceful performance of Tamburini, that can forget it? The splendor of the scene, the countless number of spectators, comprising the beauty and aristocracy of the most aristocratic of Italian cities, assembled in the presence of two of the most powerful monarchs in Europe; the pomp of royalty; the enthusiasm of a people eager to do homage to genius; the gorgeous decorations of the theatre; the admirable aid of a well chosen orchestra—all these were but accessories to the triumph of the young and distinguished artist. It was for him this glorious pageant was devised—he was the power that set in motion this vast machinery! What wonder that human pride failed to withstand a tribute so splendid, and that Tamburini, as he trod the stage, and listened to the bursts of rapturous applause that shook the house like peals of thunder, and knew himself the cynosure of all eyes,—the idol of beauty, nobility and royalty,—felt within his breast an inspiration almost superhuman!

When the opera was over, he was called out to receive the bravos of the audience, and the wreaths that fell in showers at his feet. When, flushed with triumph, yet filled with gratitude, he returned behind the curtain, he was surprised to find himself still a prisoner. The guard was ready to conduct him accompanied by his wife to the lodging assigned them. They were treated, indeed, with courtesy and respect, like prisoners of state; but our hero felt uneasy under the restraint, of which he could obtain no explanation further than "he would know on the morrow."

The next day, a little after noon, Tamburini was conducted to the imperial presence. Surrounded by his court, by foreign nobles and visitors of distinction, the emperor entertained his illustrious guest, the Emperor of Russia, who sat at his right hand. There was silence throughout the courtly assembly when the artist was led in. He made a suitable obeisance when his name was announced, and stood with a respectful air to await the monarch's commands.

"Signor Tamburini," said the Emperor of Austria, "you stand before us a prisoner, and, we understand, plead ignorance as to the cause of your arrest."

"I am, indeed, ignorant, sire," replied the artist, "in what respect I have been so unfortunate as to transgress the laws or offend your majesty."

"We will tell you, then," said the emperor, gravely. "It was your treasonous design to pass through this noble city without stopping to perform at the opera house. Your plan was detected—you were taken in the very act of departure."

"Your majesty——," began the artist.

"Silence, sir; it is in vain to defend yourself. You are proved guilty not only of a conspiracy to defraud our good Venetians of their rights in refusing them the privilege of hearing you, but of *lese majesté* against ourself and our illustrious brother, the Emperor of Russia. You lie at our mercy; but you have many friends, and at their intercession we remit you other punishment than a few days' imprisonment. Meanwhile, we have ordered a sum to be paid you, in testimony of our approval of your last night's performance; and in addition, ask of us any favor you choose."

"Sire, my gratitude—your gracious condescension——"

Tamburini's voice faltered from emotion.

"Your boon, if you please!" cried the emperor, impatiently.

"Sire, it is simply this—permission to keep my word, pledged to my friends at Trieste, who are expecting me."

There was a murmur of surprise among the spectators. The monarch, after a pause, replied, with a gracious smile—

"You are a noble fellow, Tamburini, and your request shall be granted. Only to-night we must have you in *Lucia di Lammermoor*. We are told you are inimitable in that last adagio. And now, come nearer."

The artist knelt at the monarch's feet.

"Receive from our hands this medal *di nostro Salvatore*," [13] and the emperor flung the chain around his neck. "Learn thus how much we love to do honor to genius."

Thus loaded with distinction, the artist was presented to the Russian emperor, and received the compliments and congratulations of the nobility present. He was destined ere long to receive in other lands honors almost equal to those bestowed in his own; and to show how boundless and how absolute is the dominion Heaven has given the true artist over the human heart.

FOOTNOTES

[13] Wellington was the only foreigner who had received this compliment previously to Tamburini.

BELLINI

The hunting-castle of Moritzburg, in Saxony, a place noted as the locality of the tradition of the "Freischutzen," is situated a few hours' ride from Dresden. It was my custom to pass a week or two there in the harvesting season, with the worthy forester. He was always glad to see me, because I took pleasure in his pursuits; drew sketches of forest scenes, and composed hunting songs such as were sung in Saxony and Bohemia. There were jovial meetings, too, occasionally at the public house in the neighboring village of Eisenberg; where we had sometimes a dance with the merry country damsels, to the tunes played by the Bohemian fiddlers.

One afternoon in September of 1835, I was present at one of these gatherings, and had mingled freely in the sports. I was leading off my partner for a waltz, when the post-boy from Dresden came in, and distributed his letters among the guests. He recognized me at once, and coming forward with a "'Tis lucky, sir, I find you here," handed me a letter.

I broke the seal; it ran as follows:

> *La Sonnambula* is performed to-morrow night; and Francilla appears as Amina. She sends you her compliments. Come and see her!
>
> "Your friend,
"J. P. Pixis."

I called one of the servants and ordered my horse saddled immediately. After the waltz was over, I took a hasty leave, threw myself on my horse, and rode with all speed towards Dresden.

I arrived in time for the opera; of which I was glad, for I had determined not to call upon Francilla till after the representation of La Sonnambula. The next morning I went to her lodgings in Castle-street, and was admitted. As I entered the parlor, she came to meet me, looking unusually pale, and with eyes red, as with weeping. She held out her hand in silence; I was startled; the cheerful welcome died on my lips. I looked anxiously at her, but did not venture to speak.

At length she asked, with a pensive smile, if I had been the preceding night at the opera.

"Indeed I was, Francilla," I replied. "I saw you, and hardly know how I got home, so filled were head and heart with the music. I have much — so much to say to you! But I find you so altered — so — —"

"Dejected, you would say," interrupted the singer. "Ah yes! and well I may be so; and you too!"

"Why, Francilla! what has happened?"

"Alas! Bellini is dead!" she cried, and began to weep bitterly.

I was amazed. "Bellini dead!" the great master, whose noble creations had enchanted me but a few hours before! Sad news, indeed! and grievous it was to think how early he had been called from us; he, so admirable as an artist — so honored and beloved as a man! I felt even disposed to murmur at the painful dispensation.

After a few moments' indulgence of emotion, Francilla endeavored to compose herself. She pressed her handkerchief to her eyes, rose and went for her album, to show me the drawing I had sent her for the volume. The drawing was a sketch of herself as Romeo, in the moment that Juliet, awakening in the tomb, calls on his name, while he answers with uplifted eyes, thinking it the voice of an angel.

We turned over the leaves of the album, which she held on her lap, while I knelt beside her. It was a pleasure to observe the play of her expressive features, as this or that name presented itself, exhibiting different emotions in turn. When the bold, rude autograph of Judith Pasta was displayed, the soft and languishing eyes of Francilla kindled with a look of haughtiness; and Sontag herself never smiled more sweetly than she, pointing to the name of Countess Rossi.

When she came to the handwriting of her uncle Pixis, in Prague, she stopped to tell me of his wife and mother, and their quiet domestic life; charging me, in case I went again to Prague, with many messages. While running on thus, and turning over the leaves of the album, she suddenly paused. Two names were recorded, opposite each other, those of Vincenzo Bellini and Maria Malibran. Maria had written a few words of friendship; Bellini a passage from the Capuletti, — the beginning of Romeo's lamentation over Juliet, when he first discovers her death.

Without speaking, Francilla took from me a silver pencil she had sent me some time before, drew a cross under Bellini's signature, and gave me back the pencil with a look I shall never forget.

Al length, to break the painful silence, I said, "Tell me, Francilla, why, in the last act of the Capuletti, do you make use of Vaccai's music — not

Bellini's? No doubt, in detached portions, Vaccai is simpler and more expressive; but as a whole, Bellini's composition is far superior, and the close infinitely more touching. The passage, 'Padre crudel,' etc., in particular, is so moving, and at the same time so calm, I wonder, and so do others, that you have changed it for Vaccai's, which is so much tamer."

Francilla did not answer immediately, but looked earnestly at me. When she spoke, it was in a strangely solemn tone. "Listen, and I will tell you a history, which is indeed a romance in itself. You will then see what our poor friend has suffered: and why Maria and I could not sing his last act."

And with her eyes fixed upon the cross under Bellini's name, she continued:

"You know, mon ami, that Vincenzo was born at the foot of Etna. He looked not like it, indeed, for he was fair and blue-eyed, like your pretty women of Dresden; and to say truth, was a little effeminate, and rather foppish sometimes in his manners. Poor Vincenzo! I used to laugh, when you, in old times, described him to me as you thought him. In short, he was like any ordinary young gentleman, both in appearance and behavior. I tell my story after a crooked fashion?" she asked, interrupting herself, with a smile.

"No, no! dear Francilla," I cried, "go on, I pray you!"

"I will, then," she continued. "Though Bellini might have been taken for a fool or a fop at the first glance, it needed but little penetration to discover that he was a genuine son of Sicily; and that in spite of his gentleness and his weakness, all the warmth of the south glowed in his bosom. I can hardly tell how, in a few words, to give you a just and lively picture of the wonderful nature of Bellini! It was not like the volcano of his country, where you pass through luxuriant meadows, thick and stately woods, and fields of snow, before you reach—beyond a fearful lava waste, the brink of the fiery abyss; nor was it like the Hecla of your land, where eternal fire burns under eternal ice. It resembled rather an English garden, laid out with sentimental taste, with pretty shady walks and quiet streams, ornamented with shrubs and flowers, with sloping hills and fountains, and temples of delicate architecture. Ah me! I see him bodily before me. Such a garden—half-charming—half wearisome—with the abyss of fire beneath—was Bellini! And the fire burning in his breast was the love of Art—and of Maria."

"What do you mean, Francilla?"

"Yes—it is so; he loved Maria as he loved art. How could it be otherwise? Did she not surpass all others; did she not glorify sound? Was it not she who, herself inspired with a power that gave a charm irresistible to all she did—inspired the other singers who aided her in the representation of Bellini's works! With Bellini himself—in producing anything—the question was always—'What will Malibran say to it?' She was his muse, his ideal, his queen of art. He could not live without her; were I Malibran, I think I should not long survive him."

"Ah, a pretty romance, Amina! But you forget that Malibran married M. Beriot."

"How can I forget that, remembering the effect produced by the information on the good Vincenzo? He turned pale, trembled and faltered, and quitted the company without saying a word. Yet he could not have dreamed that Maria would wed him, for she had always treated him as if he were ten years younger, though he was in reality a year her senior. But he thought not of the possibility of her marrying again, after her divorce from that hateful Malibran; and surely M. Beriot, who was once on the point of shooting himself for the sake of Sontag, but on reflection concluded to live a little longer, was the last person he would have imagined likely to be chosen.

"After that, poor Bellini avoided Malibran as much as possible. If he caught a distant glimpse of M. Beriot, he would go quickly out of the way; not from fear of his rival, but lest he might be tempted to follow him—and after the good Sicilian fashion"—here Francilla, her eyes flashing, swung her arm with the gesture of one who gives a blow with a dagger—"do you comprehend?"

"Aye, my pretty Romeo! The pantomime is expressive enough; but surely your fancy—"

"I know a certain somebody," she interrupted, "who would have had no conscience in carrying the matter through, to be rid of a happy rival. May I be kept from such blood-thirsty lovers! But to my story. No one knows what *might* have happened, spite of the softness of heart of the good Bellini; but Malibran left Paris and went to Italy, accompanied by her husband.

"It is certain that Bellini never confided to any one the secret of his unhappy passion—thus I must call the feeling that swayed him at this time. Notwithstanding it became known ere long among his friends; and Maria must have guessed it; for from that hour she sang his pieces with reluctance. Still, she appeared in the part of Romeo; and it seemed as if she could not give it up. At the last representation of the Capuletti in Milan, it happened that, in the final act, when Romeo takes the poison, such a deathlike shuddering seized Maria's frame, that she could scarcely command herself to go through with her part. When the play was over, she declared no power on earth should compel her to sing again the Romeo of Bellini. From this time she sang that of Vaccai; but she had counted too much on her own self-denial; and at a later period returned to poor Vincenzo's music so far as to retain the first acts of his Capuletti, and to sing only the last act of Vaccai.

"When Vincenzo heard of this cruel conduct of his adored friend, he was so cast down that he would write nothing more—would think nothing more! He talked idle stuff, and would smile vacantly, if any one addressed him, or when he spoke; in short, he was quite insufferable.

"One day the giant, Lablache, entered his apartment. Vincenzo lay on the sofa, pale and listless, and only noticed his visitor by fixing upon him his half closed eyes. Lablache cried like a trumpet, opening his immense mouth: 'Holloa! there! what are you lying here for, like an idle lout of a lazzaroni on the Molo, wearying yourself to death with doing nothing? Up, Bellini—up and to work! Paris, France, all Europe, is full of expectation of what you are to bring forth after your Norma, which your adversaries silenced. Bellini! do you hear me?'

"'Indeed I do hear, my dear Lablache!' answered the composer in a lachrymose voice; 'you know my hearing is of the best; and if it were not, your excellent brazen bass pierces one through and through! But I pray, caro, think me not unkind, if I entreat you to leave me to myself; to tell the truth, I am really now fit for nothing better than the *dolce far niente!* I am indifferent to everything!'

"Lablache struck his hands together, and cried, in a tone that vibrated through the walls: 'Is it you, Bellini—you—who speak thus? you, who till now have pressed on towards the noblest goal, nor relaxed your efforts till you reached it!—Man!—Master—Friend! will you suffer yourself to be checked in your career of fame—to lose the magnificent prize glittering before you? Will you demean yourself like some cooing Damon who whines forth complaints of the cruelty of his Doris or Phyllis? For shame! away with these womanish pinings! I tell you—'

"'My good Lablache,' interrupted Bellini, very gently, but visibly embarrassed; 'you do me injustice. I know not why you suspect me of pining—I utter no complaints—'

"'Hold your tongue!' cried Lablache, much vexed. 'Will you deny it? I know where the shoe pinches, very well!'

"Bellini looked down without speaking.

"'And you look at this moment,' continued Lablache, 'like an apprehended schoolboy. Bellini! have you nothing to say?'

"'Since you know all,' said Vincenzo, with a deep sigh, 'you know then that *she* sings nothing more of mine.'

"Lablache came up, laid his powerful grasp on the young master's shoulders, lifted him from the soft cushions of the sofa to his feet, shook him well, and with flashing eyes, exclaimed: '*I* will sing something for you!'

"With stentorian voice, like a martial shout, he began the allegro to that famous duet from 'I Puritani:'—'*Suoni la tromba e intrepido*'. Bellini's pale cheeks flushed; tears started from his eyes; at length, throwing himself into Lablache's arms, he joined his voice in the song. When it was ended, he pledged his word to his friend that in a few weeks he would finish the composition of the whole opera.

"Vincenzo did as he promised. Before many weeks had passed, he gave 'I Puritani' complete into the hands of Lablache, who in great delight, promised that the work should be worthily represented.

"The opera was cast; the rehearsals began. After the first rehearsal, Bellini went to his country seat at Puteaux, not far from Paris. He could not be present at the second rehearsal, on account of indisposition. It was on the night of its first representation, just at the time when that famous duet was repeated amidst thunders of applause from the enraptured audience, that the news was spread through the theatre: 'Bellini died an hour ago at his country seat.'"

Francilla closed the album, rose quickly, and went to the window. I thought it best to leave the room quietly; but she turned as I was going, and saying in a low tone: "Stay, mon ami, I have not sung you anything to-day!" seated herself at the piano. The song was a melancholy one, and might have been composed for the farewell of him who had so lately gone from earth. She sang with wonderful expression and feeling.

"The sun's last beam has paled away—

The quiet night is near;

And stars far off and numberless

Are shining still and clear.

The flowers their leaves in odors steep,

Soft whispers on the breezes sleep.

So light my bosom's throbbings—I,

Too blest, might deem mine angel nigh!

"He is—my spirit tells me so,

That soon shall quit this clay;

Freed from the load of earthly wo,
He bears my soul away.

The wo that pierces here my breast
In yonder world shall make me blest;
That for which here in vain I long,
In that pure sphere shall swell my song!

"Then, O thou Genius bright—draw near,
And bid me quickly come;
Give me the consecrating kiss—
I follow to thy home!
And she, to whom myself I gave,
Shall seek the singer's lonely grave;
There let the flower that greets her, say—
'He loves thee still—though passed away!'"

When she had ended, Pixis came into the room. "What is all this?" he cried, as he saw the traces of emotion on her countenance.

"Francilla," I replied, "has been telling me of Bellini's unhappy love for Malibran."

"Do not believe a word of it!" [14] cried Pixis, laughing. "If you get her on that chapter, she will go on romancing like any poet in the world."

The conversation was broken off by the entrance of the pretty Maschinka Schneider. Francilla welcomed her friend with joy; and the two ladies talked of the representation of the Capuleti, which was to be repeated in a few days. I was consulted respecting the arrangements in the burial vault, and had many thanks for my excellent advice about the Romeo of Francilla and the Giulietta of Maschinka.

When, in taking leave, I kissed the hand of my little friend, she whispered me earnestly that I must think of what she had told me. I did think of it when, a year afterwards, I read in the newspapers that Malibran had died on the 23d of September at Manchester; the same day on which, a year before, the death of Bellini had taken place.

FOOTNOTES

[14] The reader is advised to follow the counsel of Pixis. Bellini was always in love, it is true; but we have no reason to believe Malibran was ever the object of his passion.—*Trans.*

LOVE VERSUS TASTE[15]

CHAPTER I

In the summer of 1825, it happened that a young man, whom we shall simply call Louis, a musician by profession, arrived in Berlin. He had long wished to visit this city; its advancement in art, its gifted men, the cultivation and taste of its citizens generally, were no slight attractions for the artist and student. It was his rule to neglect no opportunity of hearing anything good; so that he usually visited the opera every evening.

One day soon after his arrival in Berlin, passing the opera house, he saw a man fastening a fresh bill to a column of the building. He waited to read it; it announced the sudden illness of one of the singers, on which account the evening's entertainment was to be changed. Instead of the Otello of Rossini, Don Giovanni was to be performed.

While Louis stood, attentively reading the bill, he heard a soft female voice close to him say, "Ah! I am so glad of that!" He turned quickly, and saw a beautiful young girl, who had noticed the bill in passing by. When she caught the young man's look, she blushed, and turning away her head, walked hastily on. Louis stood gazing after her; the tones of her rich voice had charmed him, but much more her slender, elegant, and graceful figure, and the lovely face of which he had caught a brief glimpse. Unacquainted with the ways of young men in large cities, he did not follow her, but stood looking till she vanished from his sight, and then went thoughtfully towards his lodgings.

Suddenly the idea struck him, she will of course be at the opera to-night! and he resolved to do what he had never done before, observe the ladies particularly.

The hour came for the opera; carriages rolled along the streets; Louis sat in the pit where he could see over the house, and looked eagerly around for his unknown fair one. In vain; she was nowhere to be seen!

The magnificent overture began; Louis was now in despair. She would not be at the opera; for who would miss the overture to Don Giovanni! He was disappointed, and felt only half roused to his wonted enthusiasm. The grief of Donna Anna, Elvira's tears, Zerlina's witchery, Don Giovanni's bold wickedness, failed to excite him as they had been used to do. In fact, he only half listened to the music.

The performance was at an end. Discontented and vexed with himself, Louis stood in the vestibule while the crowd was passing out. Just then he caught the tones of a remembered voice—"To the left, dear father, the carriage is at the other door!" He started, and pressing forward, saw what appeared to be the same dark silk scarf he had seen in the morning. It was worn by a young lady, who leaned on the arm of an elderly man; and both were going towards the side door. Louis was about to follow them, when he felt a hand laid on his shoulder, and at the same moment his arm was grasped by some one in the crowd. "Good evening, friend!" cried a rough voice. "Whither, in such haste? I have been looking for you everywhere. Quick, come with me! We shall sup together!" The speaker was Heissenheimer, an old merchant; an excellent man, and a passionate admirer of music. Louis had brought a letter to him; and thus he found it impossible to decline his friendly invitation, unwelcome as it was just at this moment. Mechanically he suffered himself to be led away, wishing, however, the old gentleman and his supper at the bottom of the sea, and looking back more than once, to see if he could catch a glimpse of his beautiful unknown. Nothing could be seen but a throng of strange faces, and his companion hurried him out of the nearest side door, to escape the confusion.

While they made their way through the crowd without, Heissenheimer did not observe the abstraction of his young companion. They soon emerged into a clear space, where the moon shone brightly on noble buildings; and the old man suddenly cried—"But have you nothing, friend, to say? I have been waiting for the expression of your delight, and hardly kept my own within bounds. What is the meaning of this? Is anything the matter?"

"Nay, Mr. Heissenheimer," returned the young man, smiling, "I have felt the beauty of the work none the less, that I have enjoyed it in silence."

"But," cried the other petulantly, "that is not the way with young people! I like not this dullness, and grave looks, when the heart should be full of joy. You have youthful spirits, love, fire in your breast, and should give them vent! Be cheerful, I tell you; be delighted, be frolicsome, be half mad with enthusiasm; or I warn you, you have old Heissenheimer for an enemy! But stop; here we are at the place already!"

They stood under some linden trees, in front of a house whose lower story was brilliantly lighted. The light fell full upon the street through the windows. Before they entered, both turned to look at some passers-by. What was the astonishment of Louis to recognize his fair unknown, leaning on the arm of the elderly man he had seen at the opera! The lamplight shone upon her face; it was the very same! He started forward; nothing now would have withheld him; but Heissenheimer sprang also towards them, exclaiming— "Ha! Signor Ricco! Maestro! whither away! Good even to you, pretty Nina!"

Both stopped at this salutation. While Heissenheimer was speaking with them, Louis stood in some embarrassment; till his friend recollected himself, and presented him. "Ecco—Maestro—here is a young musician, who will give you something to do: he will dispute with you about Sebastian Bach and Rossini, Master Louis——the chapel-master, Signor Ricco, and his daughter Nina!" Louis bowed, coloring deeply, and murmured some indefinite words about pleasure and honor. His companion interrupted them with "My good friends, may I beg the favor of your company with us? Will you sup in the *Café Royal*, fair Nina?" Nina declined the invitation gracefully, but begged her father not to lose the pleasure. Their home was only two doors off, and she could go there without escort. "We will all escort you," said the old merchant, "hurt as I am that you will not go with us." Two or three more gallant speeches passed, and the three accompanied the young lady to the chapel-master's house. After a polite acknowledgment of their courtesy, Nina disappeared; the gentlemen went to the café, where an excellent supper was prepared, with the best wines; and Heissenheimer played the merry host to his heart's content.

CHAPTER II

After Signor Ricco had explained the mystery of his daughter and himself going home on foot, their carriage having disappointed them, the conversation turned on the opera they had just seen. The chapel-master declared, with a half comic distortion of face, that he wished he had stayed away.

"And why, maestro?" asked Heissenheimer.

"I hoped to have heard Rossini's magnificent *Otello*; and was compelled to take instead that confounded Don Giovanni."

"Ricco," said the old merchant, "you are certainly skilled in the black art, and have wrought magic upon me; else I know not what prevents me from throwing this empty champagne flask at your head! Butler—some more wine! and have done, chapel-master, with your nonsense about Rossini, for whom I know you care as little as I! and tell us truly, were you not enraptured with the glorious masterpiece of to-night?"

"O Germans—where are your ears? Caro Heissenheimer, I will tell you the truth; but shall I criticise as an Italian or a German?"

"What do you mean by the distinction?" asked Louis.

"What a question! Young man, can you be so ignorant? As Italian, I complain that this opera gives me no rest; that I must be kept on the stretch from beginning to end; that I forget the singers in the orchestra; that I feel more fear and horror than delight; in short, I complain that the devil, instead of Don Giovanni, has not taken the composer, who forces me to *labor*, where I expected only *pleasure*. But I can also complain as a German. Do you think I know not what you wish? *Per Bacco!* the misfortune is, you only *half* wish! An opera should be a whole; connected from beginning to end; each impression on the mind should be a stone added to the dramatic structure, strengthened by the music. Is it not so?"

"I should think a reasonable person would desire nothing less," answered Louis.

"Well then—have you that in Don Giovanni?"

"You will drive me crazy!" cried Heissenheimer impatiently.

"Nay—rather you me—senseless Germans!" returned Ricco. "You can devise a theory that leaves nothing to be wished. But place a work of art before you, you have no eyes nor ears—much less a judgment. You fit on your theory; do they agree in a few points—well; the work is a masterpiece, though it may differ in all essentials from your own principles; thenceforth you *believe* blindly, and each adopts the other's opinion. Do they not agree—you have not independence enough to yield to an impression of nature, and judge thereby that the thing is worthless. If a German is dying with rapture, he is to blame if not enraptured according to rule! Corpo di Bacco! I have more gall in me than wine! Fill my glass!"

"You are leaving the subject—Signor Ricco," said Louis; "you were to complain of Don Giovanni as a German. I confess, I am curious to hear you."

"I also," added the merchant. "But it will come to nothing; for I see he is treating us to one of his accustomed jokes."

"Nay—it is my ardor that leads me to digression. To return to Don Giovanni. At first—and then the Germans were reasonable, for they had in their theatres chiefly the works of Italian composers or their pupils—at first, I say—the thing was not popular, and with reason."

"Stupid slanderer!" exclaimed Heissenheimer.

"There were in it a few good musical touches, and the Germans thought it a pity the work should be lost. They fitted on a skilful theory; they found that Don Giovanni stabs the commendatore, and commits other crimes, and is finally carried off by the devil: the thing is complete, and has a capital moral! Why should it not please? So its nonsense and folly are passed over. A single wise head has seen through it, who really understands more of the opera than your thirty millions of Germans besides. This was your late Hoffmann. He marked well where the thing halted: but he admired the music, and put a good face on it for his countrymen, quieting the last murmurs of their consciences. How he must have laughed over their fond delusion!"

"As well as I can gather your meaning," said the young artist, "you seem to think there is a want of unity of idea in the action and music of Don Giovanni?"

"I should be blind and deaf if I thought otherwise."

"And thus, as a German, you would find fault with the work?"

"Exactly."

"I entreat you, then, to dispense with your oracular ambiguity, and passing by a few improbabilities and other trifling defects—to show us where is the vulnerable heel of this Achilles."

"Ha, maestro!" cried the merchant, "you have but shallow water for the war-ship with which you mean to manœuvre round this walled and fortified citadel of art! You will be aground presently."

"On the contrary—I will make you a breach, so that the enemy shall march in with all his forces."

"Triumph not too soon!" cried Louis—"for we shall fight to the last man in its defence."

"Right, my young friend!" added Heissenheimer; and Ricco proceeded, after a digression or two, from which he was called back by his two challengers—

"Is it not true, friends, that in a drama each principal person should contribute substantially to the progress of the action? You assent; well— in Don Giovanni there are five—the Commendatore, Giovanni, Octavio, Donna Anna, and Elvira. I have nothing against the old man, nor Giovanni. Your Hoffmann has cunningly rescued Donna Anna from criticism; Octavio may be considered to have a sort of right to his place. He is, so to speak, the earthly hostage for the elevated Anna, or rather the stake to which she is bound. Now for Donna Elvira. Many have felt that this fifth person is the fifth wheel to the wagon; and in many ways they have sought to justify her appearance. But it has not succeeded. Your Hoffmann does best, who says as good as nothing of her."

"I thought," observed Louis, "she was to be regarded as an avenging goddess; at least, so the great composer conceived her, even if the poet assigned her a somewhat doubtful place."

"Excellent!" cried the merchant. "What have you to say to that, Ricco?"

"That it is not true. An avenging goddess—who whimpers rather than implores for love, and at last would snatch from justice the object of her revenge!—The kneeling in the last finale, or ante-finale (for you would have a battle also about this double close) looks like revenge!—Look you, this Elvira could be borne, or not observed, if she did not so lower herself in the middle of the piece. And here the composer is even more in fault than the poet. The terzetto in A major I will let pass; I will believe she can forgive her repentant betrayer, and love him again. But the sestetto! Have you borne in mind what wickedness has been committed towards her? I am an Italian, and we look over some things more easily than you Germans. But a Chinese, or a barbarian, must revolt at this! The trusting, confiding, forgiving, loving Elvira is exposed to the deepest disgrace—the most crushing insult! Has she a spark of womanly pride or Castilian spirit in her breast, it must burst into a flame that will consume the guilty betrayer, or sweep the wretched victim to destruction. What has she suffered? The most horrible injury that can be inflicted on a woman! Why does she not snatch a dagger, to plunge it into the breast of the slave who has been employed against her—or that of the fiend Don Giovanni, the author of the outrage, or those who behold her dishonor—or, Lucretia-like, into her own? Go—you Germans, and boast of your passion for completeness! You feel not where a work of art strikes the heart. When Leporello's mask is fallen, and Elvira, who should sink back in despair, or rise in the invincible might of revenge, sings so passionately with the other five voices—as if nothing more had happened to her than Zerlina,—I feel my blood boil! Would our Rossini have done the like? In his polonaises you feel the dolor of love: could you only understand the heavenly melodies as the maestro himself conceived them! The notes are not—indeed—but he dreamed of a singer such as your wooden German never thought of; a singer, the charm of whose expression could ennoble the most insignificant passages into a moving plaint of the heart! Have you never heard that the English Garrick could so repeat the alphabet as to move his audience to tears? So it is with Rossini's music. He sacrifices himself; he wants not to shine; but that his performers should. But your German hears from paper; and thus writes tolerably. And you trouble not yourselves, if your singers misrepresent the best your master has furnished. The performance of to-night—but I am speaking only of Don Giovanni. What say you to my criticism on Elvira? why do I not hear reproaches?"

"You are a clever critic," answered Louis; "I know you are wrong, and yet I cannot reply to your objections."

"Yes—quite wrong—chapel-master!" added the merchant. "I will venture you do not believe yourself what you say. Swear that you do—in good faith!"

"Ha! ha! ha!" cried Ricco; "you would have me swear to what I have proved! My good Heissenheimer, I will read you the riddle. We Italians are more candid than you. We know well what is wanting in our operas, and have judgment enough to understand that it cannot be otherwise. Where two make a work, the whole cannot be cast in one great mould. If we thus discover disproportion betwixt the music and the text, it disturbs not our enjoyment. But the German will smoothe it all away; he rests not till the faults growing out of the nature of the thing are changed into beauties by some jugglery of the understanding; and after he has in this way deceived himself, he begins to enjoy. If I loved Don Giovanni ever so much, the part of Elvira would not disturb me. I would easily help myself out of the difficulty; I would have Elvira fall senseless on the discovery of her error, and a friend of Anna's supply the sixth voice. What have you against that?"

"In this manner," replied Louis, "you may banish reason from art altogether. I cannot conceive of a work of art, which shall not proceed from the full consciousness of the artist, and contain only beauties designed by himself. Therefore do I detest Rossini's works, void of meaning——"

"Void of meaning? Young man, do not depreciate our master. Think you, he was unconscious of that for which you reproach him, and that he could not have bettered it if he had chosen? But he wished to lead music back to her own natural place; to make her again a science for the ear, and deliver her from your massive philosophical smoke-cells and pedantic fetters. Turn nothing but counterpoint; screw only fugues and canons; write only dissonances, like your Mozart and Beethoven; drive your anarchy ever so far, nature will still be victorious. And then delight yourself in the conceit—that your masters look to the *whole*! Truly, they may have the will, but the vision fails them, and they see no further than a mole on the top of Mont Blanc. Your beloved Don Giovanni, of which you believe that it came forth fully armed from the composer's fancy, like Minerva from the head of Jupiter, is an automaton, whose limbs are fastened together with thongs, and secured with hammer strokes; a thing that has more rents and seams than a clown's jacket; which you can cut up like an eel, without touching its heart;—in short, as I have proved, a thing that can neither live nor stand, if more is expected than that it should be the scaffold on which the musician builds his illumination of tones."

"But," cried Louis, "the splendor of that illumination shall light up the gloom of the most distant future! It shall remain a Sirius, the central sun of stars of the first magnitude, so long as art itself shall exist."

"Ay, and your torchlight, your will-o'-the-wisp, Rossini, shall be blown out by the first breath of time!" said Heissenheimer.

"Friends," replied Ricco, "were it not better that we broke up our conference? Our discourse grows somewhat warm."

"You have chilled me completely, at least, towards yourself," returned the merchant. "But I cannot believe you in earnest with your talk, so I will drink a glass with you. If I did not think you have joked with us, I would have had the wine poisoned for me in which I pledge an enemy of Mozart."

"Have I called myself his enemy?" said the chapel-master. "Who would deny the man genius? I charge him only with a wrong use of it—and of music, which should bring us joy and happiness, not gloom and melancholy. What should I do with wine that did not make me merry like your champagne?"

"So merry," grumbled the merchant, "that, truly, you have made yourself merry with us. But, Louis, why so thoughtful?"

"Pardon me," answered the young man; "I am troubled by what I cannot yet make clear to myself. I would reply to the chapel-master's accusation against the part of Elvira. His opinion is plausible, but he is wrong in reference to the work. I believe I can see a way to lead to a right understanding."

"We cannot reach it to-night," said Ricco, preparing to depart. "It is midnight, and I must go home. Some other time we will speak on the subject; and I will convince you that your conviction is incorrect. Now, fare you well."

"Good night—incorrigible fellow!" cried Heissenheimer; and then put it to the choice of his young friend, whether they should empty another flask, or take a walk in the fresh air. Louis preferred a walk, for he was somewhat excited with the conversation.

CHAPTER III

They walked for some time in the open air. The double row of old lindens that shaded the promenade, rustled in the summer breeze; the moon shone on the tall buildings; all was silent, as if the city were buried in slumber. As our friends passed the dwelling of the chapel-master, Louis stole a look upward at one of the windows, which he fancied might be that of the fair daughter of the heterodox musician. "*She* has a purer taste," said he to himself, and turning to his companion—

"How is it possible that one can be so insensible to the beautiful as this Italian?"

The merchant glanced at the house of Master Ricco, and replied: "The heathenish churl! Yet there is something about him that inclines me to believe he does not express his real opinions. Did you not remark his contradictions? Now he slashed at Mozart, now at the subject of the piece; and, after all, only complained of the part of Elvira. What should he care for the subject, if he be really such an admirer of Rossini, and thinks music merely a science for the ear? His inconsistencies were palpable. Depend upon it, the man has not such wretched taste."

"But why should he speak against his own convictions?"

"Because he is unwilling to confess that his countrymen are surpassed by the Germans in composition. Only one thing staggered me. He permits his daughter to play no music but Rossini's, Mercadante's, Caraffa's, and the like."

"But she sings it unwillingly, surely?" cried Louis, quickly.

"On the contrary; she knows nothing else."

"Impossible!" exclaimed the young man. "How can that lovely face— those eyes—so deceive? How can those features, expressive of a refined soul, be the index of a shallow understanding?"

"Ha, friend! Have Nina's beautiful eyes shot their beams so deep into your heart? That is a precious discovery!" And the little man leaped forwards, rubbing his hands, and chuckling for joy.

Louis colored deeply, and in much embarrassment explained that his acquaintance with the young lady was scarce of two hours standing; but the merchant continued his expressions of delight till they reached Frederick street, and then took his leave with a wish that the young couple might be happy, humming a love tune till he was out of hearing.

As Louis walked towards his lodgings, absorbed in thought, he was startled by the sound of a female voice, singing. In the stillness of night the melody had a magical sweetness. He followed the sound, retracing his steps, and soon came opposite the chapel-master's house. The music came from the windows, which were open, although the chambers were not lighted. Though he lost not a single note, Louis could not determine exactly in which room was the singer. "It is she," he cried to himself; "it is herself:—the beautiful girl!" and leaning against one of the trees, he drank in the melody, never once removing his eyes from the windows.

It was evidently a German song. The voice was clear and powerful, yet soft and touching; the melody had a strange mingling of joy and sorrow, of suffering and repose. The enraptured listener could not distinguish the words, but the music penetrated his very soul. A sigh heaved his breast; he could not tell if delight or melancholy was the emotion excited; but felt, if that were sorrow, he wished never to be happy! The song at last ceased; but another more exquisite, more deeply moving, began. Each verse closed with some words in which seemed to lie a world of feeling. Louis caught the words "*Dahin,*" "*Zu dir;*" and at the close distinctly "*Nur Du!*" It seemed to him like the voice of fate. Tears streamed from his eyes; once again he heard the words "Nur Du" uttered with a melodious pathos he had never heard before; and with strained attention, just as it ceased, caught a glimpse of a white figure moving behind some plants near the window. It passed the next window; he listened for a renewal of the song, but all was silent; and after waiting some time, he took his way homeward.

The earliest beams of next morning's sun aroused our friend from an unquiet slumber. The day was fine, and he had many objects of attention; but the image of the fair songstress alone occupied his mind. He leaned from his window, looking out on a garden opposite, and the scene beyond. A few carriages and foot passengers were in motion, but the bustle of the day had not yet commenced. Only here and there the shutters had been thrown open to admit the sun.

Louis remained some time in deep thought. At length it occurred to him that it was possible the object of his reflections might also be up, and inhaling the morning air. In a few minutes he was dressed and in the street; and a brisk walk soon brought him opposite the dwelling of the chapel-master. The windows were open as the night before, but all was still and motionless. Louis walked for some time under the trees, back and forward, keeping his eyes fixed on the house. At length he discerned a white dress moving behind the plants. In a transport of joy he approached, and stood directly opposite. The white robe was there; the figure rose, turned round, and looked out of the window. It was Signor Ricco himself, in his night-cap and dressing-gown, with a long pipe in his mouth! He leaned out, as if to look at the weather, and must have thought the sky too clear, by the cloud of smoke he sent whirling over his head!

Our young friend shrunk back, but it was too late; there was no one besides him in sight, and the glance of the chapel-master unavoidably fell on him. He was immediately recognized. "Good morning, Signor Louis!" cried the Italian. "So early abroad? or have you been up all night?" Louis bowed in some embarrassment, and answered that the fine morning had tempted him to a walk. "Right!" cried the signor; "I also am taking a peep at the weather, to see if it will do for a drive in the country we have been planning for some time. Suppose you accompany us?" "With the greatest pleasure!" answered the young man promptly. "Come in, then, and breakfast with me," said Ricco; and Louis hastened up the steps.

He found the chapel-master in his music room; the piano stood open; Rossini's Tancredi lay on the desk. Ricco made some remarks on his favorite opera; the eyes of Louis wandered restlessly to the door. "You wonder," said the Italian, lighting his pipe again, "that my daughter does not appear. Ah! she is a sad sluggard! But I shall play her a trick to-day, we will go off without her; I have already sent for the carriage."

These words caused no little chagrin to our young artist; but he was not to endure it long; they were surprised by a musical laugh, and looking up, saw Nina at the door. "Your scheme has fallen through, papa!" cried she. "But really it is true, that listeners hear no good of themselves. Yet I hoped, sir," turning to Louis, "that you would have said something in my defence." She pouted her pretty lips in affected anger, and a little scene of apologies ensued. "All's well that ends well," said Ricco at length; "we will have friend Heissenheimer of the party; now, daughter, let us to breakfast." Nina led the way with a cheerful smile.

Louis had now opportunity to observe the fair girl whose first appearance had captivated him. She wore a white morning dress, with a colored silk handkerchief tied round her white, slender throat. Her dark brown hair fell in ringlets over her cheeks and neck, contrasting with a complexion fresh as the spring rose. Beautiful as she was, he could hardly understand how so much frankness and playfulness of manner could consist with the depth of feeling speaking from her large, dark eyes.

After several efforts to overcome his diffidence, he said to her, "I was made very happy by your song last night, Mademoiselle Nina. I heard you sing after midnight."

"Impossible!" she answered in some surprise; "I did not sing last night."

"Nay—that would have been forbidden," said the father, gravely; "singing late at night is bad for the voice. We are no nightingales; our business is to sleep o' nights."

"You need not deny it," cried the young man. "The music I heard came from yonder apartment, and I saw—pardon me—I saw a lady in white dress pass the open window."

"That could not have been my daughter," repeated Signor Ricco.

"But," persisted Louis, "I could not have been deceived. I heard the sweetest soprano voice, and saw a female figure, which approached the window, and then passed through the chamber."

Nina looked very mischievous, and cried—

"Oh, you are a ghost-seer! I will have nothing to do with you!"

And she began to sing an air in a clear, silvery staccato, making gestures of aversion with her pretty hands. Then the lively girl ran to the window, and exclaimed that the carriage was come; threw on her shawl and bounded down the steps so swiftly, that Louis could hardly keep pace with her. He assisted her into the carriage, and waited for Signor Ricco, who soon made his appearance with a roll of paper.

They stopped at Heissenheimer's house, to take their old friend along. He was just up, and after he came to them, had to parry a great deal of raillery from the arch Nina.

The country was arrayed in all the loveliness of early summer. The fields were green with the young grain, the foliage was in its freshest verdure, the morning air was cool and balmy, the sky cloudless; all things breathed of pleasure and beauty. Little was said by our friends, who each in his own way enjoyed the scenes around, and the motion through the fresh air. It might have been observed, however, that the eyes of Louis rested frequently on the fair Nina, and were withdrawn in some confusion whenever she raised hers to his face.

At length they left the high road and drove through an avenue bordered with cherry trees, past a little village, and into a wood beyond. On an eminence before them, half hid by foliage, was an old hunting-seat, and at the foot of the slope, the water, bordered with trees and bushes. On the other side of the river were situated country-seats.

The carriage stopped here; the friends alighted; and Nina immediately proposed a walk or a sail. The walk was decided upon, as the sun was now high, and the cool shade of the woods particularly inviting. They wandered about for some time, till they came to a knoll shaded by a large, old tree, covered with the softest moss. This served them for a sofa; and then Heissenheimer proposed that Nina should give the nightingales a lesson. She complained of being hoarse, and made twenty capricious excuses, till Signor Ricco produced his roll of paper, and handed a leaf to his daughter.

"What is this, dear father?" asked the maiden. "A composition?" inquired the merchant. "Truly," answered Ricco, "I have attempted to arrange something; it is a cavatina from the 'Gazza Ladra,' to which I have made an accompaniment."

Nina was delighted, and declared it was her favorite piece; Louis looked at her doubtfully. Signor Ricco assigned him the tenor, and the bass to Heissenheimer. Louis hoped to discover by Nina's singing, if she were the songstress of the preceding night. It seemed to him that he was not mistaken; but he could find in her really charming voice not the least of that fervor and feeling which had so enchanted him with the mysterious songstress. His disappointment was so great that he went wrong in his own part, and was only recalled by a sharp look from the chapel-master. Nina seemed roguishly inclined to laugh. At last the piece was finished, and they rallied him severely on his abstraction. Heissenheimer said candidly he thought the solemn wood a place as unsuitable for such a melody, as a church for a waltz or polonaise; and thereupon ensued a renewal of the dispute about Rossini, Mozart, and Mercadante. Nina took a decided part with her father, who at last put an end to the discussion by proposing that they should go where they could obtain some lunch.

CHAPTER IV

The providence of Nina had prepared for them a little surprise—a table spread with refreshments, under a neighboring tree. They talked of other matters besides music, and Louis recovered spirits enough to enter on a lively conversation with the young lady about the climates of Germany and Italy. While the elder guests were deep in their discourse, she proposed a walk down to the water.

The day was delicious; the blue, clear waters reflected the sunshine and the foliage on their bank. An avenue of chestnut and linden trees followed the windings of the river. Nina stood on the bank, smiling as she looked on the lovely scene; Louis was beside her, but a strange conflict agitated his bosom. Her evidently superficial apprehension of art, of that which formed the great object of his life, disappointed him so deeply, that his regard for her seemed nipped in the bud.

After a long silence, he ventured on the question that oppressed his heart. "We are alone;" he said to her in an earnest tone of entreaty; "tell me, was it you who sang last night? I beseech you, answer me truly."

Nina looked at him, and burst into a mischievous laugh. "So," she cried, "you are still haunted by the unknown singer? A strange adventure—in truth; you must have heard a witch! Now I understand why you did not praise my singing just now! And our poor innocent countryman, Rossini, must suffer for it! A young man hears a singer at midnight, and fancies her perfection; next day I sing an air which does not please him, because *I* have not that good fortune! I thank you, sir, for your flattering confession!" and she made him a mocking curtesy.

"But tell me, I conjure you," persisted Louis, "was it not you—"

"Hold!" cried Nina; "not so solemn. I think if I say yes, I can win you for an admirer of Rossini; so I will say, yes! I am a sort of siren, sir, who entices young artists by her song to worship Rossini even against their will."

"Nay, then," answered the young man, "last night's song was not such an one. Now I really believe you were *not* the singer. Heaven knows how I could be mistaken; but I see such must have been the case."

"Then," replied the maiden, "blame not me; I am innocent; I hope sincerely you will soon find out your mysterious singer, who seems to have so captivated you. Be not unkind, meanwhile, to me, because you did not like my song; I have a favor to beg; take me out on the water; yonder is a boat. The shade of the trees on the bank will protect us from the heat."

She spoke with so much gentleness and sweetness that Louis felt his growing coldness melt away. He hastened to push off the boat, took up the oars, and gave Nina his hand to help her in. She leaped in gracefully and seated herself opposite him. The boat soon glided swiftly over the smooth waters: Louis looking straight forward, or at his fair companion's shadow on the water; for a feeling he could not explain, prevented him from looking at herself.

They went on for half an hour without speaking. The boat now glided into a small inlet, shaded by the foliage on high banks. "Let us stop awhile here," said Nina; and Louis took up his oars. The young girl laid aside her straw hat, pushed her ringlets from her fair brow, and looked on the sweet picture with an expression of delight. Behind the wooded shore rose the walls of the ancient looking hunting-castle, embosomed in picturesque woods. The inlet was in deep shadow, which contrasted with the gleam of sunshine on the waves beyond; and the light flashed like jewels in the foliage above. The soft air, the refreshing coolness of the shade, and the fragrance of flowers that filled the wood, completed the effect of this charming scene. The heart of our young artist was full. He looked at Nina; her head was drooped slightly, but as she raised it with a sudden motion, he saw that tears were in her eyes. "You weep?" said he, taking her hand sympathizingly. "No," she answered softly, and with a smile, "but there is so much beauty here!" After a moment she withdrew her hand; but not before a light pressure had responded to the expression of her feelings. So passed some minutes, till recovering her vivacity, she suddenly exclaimed—"Mercy! how late it is growing! We must make haste back, or my father will be uneasy!"

They were shortly at the landing-place again; but found the old people had suffered no uneasiness on their account. Both Ricco and his friend were leaning against the trees, fast asleep. Nina awoke the merchant with a mischievous tickling of his red nose, and he started up from a dream of orchestras and violins. After a walk in the castle garden, they returned to their carriage, and drove back to the city.

The next night saw Louis walking for two hours in front of the chapel-master's house, in hopes of hearing again the mysterious singer. But all remained silent, and he returned disappointed to his lodgings.

As soon as he thought it proper, he paid a visit to Signor Ricco. On the steps he met Nina, going to visit a friend. After replying to his polite inquiry how she had been since the excursion into the country, she had already left him, when she suddenly turned back, saying, "While I think of it, I have found out your wonderful singer; but I cannot approve of your taste!" A flush rushed to the brow of the young artist. "And who is she?" he cried, eagerly. "Oh, sir," answered Nina, "I can keep a secret, I assure you."

"I entreat you!" cried Louis, catching her hand. She drew it away—and with mock gravity replied, "do you think I have so little of the vanity of an artist as to favor so dangerous a rival—one, the mention of whom so agitates you? No, sir, you learn nothing from me; and no one else can put you on the right track!" With this she walked away, leaving Louis embarrassed and disappointed. He had to betake himself to her father, who received him kindly, and invited him soon to repeat his visit, and join them at their family concerts.

Our artist was fain to avail himself of this invitation, and became a frequent visitor. He was conscious of a strong partiality for Nina, which she did not, however, seem to return; at least she treated him with a degree of caprice which he could not help fearing proceeded from levity of mind. Painful was the struggle in his breast; her beauty, frankness, and goodness of heart charmed him, while her utter want of sympathy with all his tastes and pursuits, was a perpetual vexation to him. She seemed to regard music only as a science of sounds, and to be insensible to its life and power; and all his enthusiasm could obtain nothing responsive from her. Louis could not help thinking her, with all her loveliness, a frivolous and soulless being. Notwithstanding, when under the spell of her presence, he could not escape from its fascination. This incessant strife of feeling caused him real suffering.

One evening the conversation chanced to turn again on Don Giovanni, and the chapel-master expressed opinions as strange as before, in the same ironical manner. Nina went even further; she abused the music altogether, which she thought too grave and tragic, and particularly the airs of Anna and Elvira; completing the horror of poor Louis, by declaring she would rather sing anything from Rossini, and that the opera might be made tolerable, if only Rossini would compose all the music anew! That was too much! The artist ventured no reply; but soon after took his leave abruptly — not even hearing, as he rushed from the door, the playful "good night" of the pretty maiden.

On his way home Louis met his old friend, Heissenheimer, who remarked his ill-humor, and drew from him a confession of his trouble. The merchant, enthusiastic as he was in music, gravely remonstrated with his young friend for indulging such large expectations on the score of taste. Louis mournfully insisted, that it was not so much want of taste he complained of, as an absence of true refinement of feeling and mind. The want of an ear was a defect of nature; but Nina had a fine ear, and the highest musical cultivation; hers was a want of *soul*. He who cannot apprehend the beautiful, has no heart for the good. "She is lost to me!" was his final exclamation, uttered in such anguish of spirit, that Heissenheimer knew not how to console him.

They had walked for some time, without giving heed to the direction in which they went, and almost unexpectedly, found themselves nearly opposite the house of Signor Ricco. It was late, and the street was quite still; but low mutterings of thunder at a distance, and flashes of lightning at intervals, foretold an approaching storm.

All at once the softest and sweetest melody rose on the silence of night. Louis started, and grasped his friend's arm; Heissenheimer cried, in surprise, "Who is singing? It cannot be Nina; and it seems to come from that house!" "No, it is not Nina!" answered Louis; "I once thought it was!"

"It comes from the upper story," whispered the merchant: "who can it be?"

"For two months I have longed to know," cried the artist, much affected, "and now I *will* know! *her* alone will I love, whose soul breathes in that music!"

"Hush!" said Heissenheimer; "it comes like an air from heaven!" and leaning against the iron railing, he listened, while Louis drank in the delicious sounds with passionate delight, standing motionless, with folded arms, tears chasing each other down his cheeks.

The full, rich tones were accompanied on the piano; and strangely did the exquisite melody blend, from time to time, with the rolling thunder, that came nearer every moment. But it seemed sweeter from the contrast.

Meanwhile the clouds were gathering thickly over head. Large drops fell, and the wind rushed hoarsely through the trees. Presently a vivid flash clove the darkness, making the whole street light as day, and half blinding our two friends; it was followed by a tremendous crash of thunder, and then the rain came down in torrents.

"Der Teufel!" cried the merchant; "'tis time we were gone! Come, we shall find shelter in the *café royal!*" And seizing Louis by the arm, he dragged him away. Both ran down the promenade to the café, from the windows of which shone a welcome light. "Never mind," said Heissenheimer, as they entered, "such a song was worth a drenching. Let us drink the singer's health."

It is needless to record all that was said between the friends, on this occasion: the result was an appointment to dine together next day, and meanwhile, Heissenheimer pledged himself to do his utmost to unravel the mystery.

CHAPTER V

So deeply had the heart of our artist been impressed by the nocturnal music, that he thought no more of Nina, but only of the mysterious songstress. He waited, with the utmost impatience, for the appointed hour next day. His first question, on meeting the merchant, was "Have you discovered the singer?" Heissenheimer put on an important face, and began to talk meaningly of the folly of being too curious, and the wisdom of Providence in concealing some things from us. From all this Louis divined that his friend had penetrated the secret, but was determined not to impart his knowledge.

Heissenheimer began to quote Faust; his friend reminded him of his pledge to disclose what he should find out. "Well, then," replied the merchant, "you shall guess who she is?"

"I conjure you, keep me no longer in suspense."

"I may not name her; but this much I will say—you have often seen her; now will you guess?"

"I know not," replied Louis; "perhaps the Countess, who lodges over the chapel-master?"

"No."

"Or Nina's friend, Mademoiselle Louise?"

"No."

"Or the Italian dancer, who comes there sometimes—what is her name—Donna Cerconi?"

"No!—you do not go on. See now, how pure is your love for art! you have guessed only those who have beauty of person!"

"Mock me no longer!" cried the young man: "what pleasure is it to you to torment me?"

"Well, then, you shall know; but first, a question—have you never observed a female in the house of old Ricco?"

"Never."

"Strange—and yet you have seen her frequently."

"I can assure you——"

"Hold, sir! no assurances! I see plainly, the young artist so deeply in love with music, has eyes only for a *pretty* damsel! She of whom I speak, is neither handsome nor young. In short, it is no other than the girl who performs the services of maid to Nina."

"Impossible! you are joking!"

"I am in earnest."

"But how could a person in such a station, acquire such perfection in an art which, if she chose to exercise it, would place her above dependence? No—you are in jest!"

"Your incredulity is but natural, considering the ideal you have formed of your singer. But let me tell you how I made my discovery. I went at nine this morning to the Signor's, entered without ringing, and passed quietly through the hall, for my object was to surprise him. I heard nothing in his apartment, or his daughter's; but musical sounds came from a distance. I followed them into a corridor at the end of the hall, and soon found they came from a room above. I went up a narrow flight of stairs, listened, and ascertained that it was really the singer of last night. I held my breath; the voice was suppressed, but it had the same fervor and depth of feeling; I could even distinguish the words that closed the song—'*Nur Du*.'"

"It is the same!" cried Louis, passionately. "I have heard that song—"

"Let me go on.—I could not withstand the impulse of curiosity; I peeped through the key-hole—I confess it—but could see only the bust of a female figure, which, however, I saw could not belong to Nina. I then determined to open the door suddenly, and to pretend I was in search of some one. This I did; the figure turned round quickly, and I recognized Caroline, the maid. She blushed deeply, and seemed much confused; at length she asked—'you wish to see Signor Ricco, sir? He is in his chamber.' I recovered my self-possession at these words, and told her all: how I had heard the music, looked through the key-hole, and finally opened the door to surprise her. I then begged her to sing again, and to inform me how and where she had acquired that exquisite cultivation of her rare musical talents. She refused to sing, but after some hesitation, told me her story. Enough; you know who is your singer: let us go to dinner."

"No!" cried Louis, "I entreat you to tell me what she said of herself; why she has concealed her precious gift—why she submits to dependence, when she might place herself in a higher sphere!"

"My friend," returned the merchant, "I feel it would be a breach of faith to repeat her story merely to gratify curiosity. You scarce remembered her existence—how can you be interested in her?"

"Indeed," protested the young man, "I have often noticed her quiet, modest manners, and interesting countenance. I would do anything to befriend her."

The merchant smiled at this late discovery of her merit, and looked very mischievous. At last he said—"I will then communicate to you all I know—provided you will promise silence—particularly to the chapel-master and his daughter.

"Caroline is the daughter of a poor musician, who lived in a remote village. He was reduced to poverty by the war, and suffered from a long illness brought upon him by the rough usage of the soldiers. In the time of his greatest need, Ricco and his daughter, being on a journey, happened to pass through the village. The chapel-master was detained by indisposition; and to amuse himself, wrote off the parts of an opera he had composed. As he required help in the work, he inquired of the landlord of the mean inn at which they lodged, who bethought himself directly of Caroline's father. But on account of his illness, the poor man would have to do the work at home. Ricco sent Nina, then a girl of fourteen, to his house; she found him in the utmost poverty, with no one but his daughter, who worked to supply his wants. The sick man eagerly undertook the task required; but his over-exertion brought on a nervous fever, of which he died in a few days. During the time, Nina and her father gave the poor old man all the assistance he needed—they have both excellent hearts!—and Ricco promised to take care of his daughter. The day of her father's death, Caroline had gone some miles for a physician; all was over when she returned, but her father had left her a letter, which she showed me with many tears. She accompanied Ricco and his daughter to Berlin, and now occupies a station in his house between maid and house-keeper. Now you know all."

"But the letter?"

"True!—it would have touched you to see the affection it breathed; and the style was that of an educated person. Besides the counsels of an affectionate father, with regard to her future life, he gave her sensible advice about music; alluded to her rare voice, and the cultivation which, to the best of his ability, he had bestowed; with a delicate reference to the shocks to which her refined taste in music might be exposed in her new situation. Art, he said, was a revelation from God; and he entreated her not to display to vulgar eyes the jewel she possessed! Keep it, he said, like a secret treasure; it may yield you happiness when all other sources are withheld, like the hidden fountain to the pilgrim in the desert! And she obeyed his counsels in her prudence. If she has erred, it has been in the sincerity of a pure and loving heart!"

To this relation Louis listened with the deepest emotion. He felt that the desolate orphan could not be happy in the house of the good-natured, but frivolous Italians. He half formed a resolution in his own mind, but said nothing. During dinner little was said, Heissenheimer leading the conversation to indifferent subjects. When the cloth was removed, he said to his young friend—"I see this matter has impressed you as deeply as myself. But whatever may happen, promise me to take no step with regard either to Caroline or her young mistress, without first consulting me." This was readily promised.

The evening came, and the hour for his customary visit to Signor Ricco. Louis, as he went, was far from being at his ease. He knew not, in the first place, how he would be received by Nina, after his abrupt departure the preceding night; nor was he satisfied what course he should himself pursue. All thoughts of becoming the fair girl's lover he had of course abandoned. His passion had grown at first out of the belief that she was what a subsequent acquaintance had proved her not to be. His feelings towards Caroline he could not define. He felt the warmest sympathy for her misfortunes, and a deep admiration of her talents; her gentle manners touched him, and he was conscious, not of love, but of a fraternal interest in her.

He went to the chapel-master's; Nina received him with even more than usual cordiality and cheerfulness, and seemed to have quite forgotten their late misunderstanding. Louis was absent and thoughtful, and even forgot to ask after Ricco, who did not appear, and who, his daughter at length said, had gone to a concert at the ambassador's. How much would he once have given for such an opportunity of tête-à-tête conversation! As there seemed to be some constraint, Nina proposed that he should accompany her in some new airs. They began with Mozart's great duet between Anna and Octavio, from Don Giovanni. She sang with readiness, but without that fire of inspiration, that loving sorrow, which breathe in every note. Then they sang a duet from Belmont and Constance; this also Nina performed with ease, but in as soulless a manner as the first. Louis went on with a species of desperation, and began with a duet from Fidelio; the young lady smiled, as if she were commending her own patience, and sang with such careless vivacity, that her guest's vexation was complete. With a displeasure he could scarcely conceal, he asked, "Had we not better sing a duet from Blangini?"

"Oh, yes!" cried Nina, apparently delighted, "we will have my favorite, 'Fra valli fra boschi!'" And springing up, she sought for it in a pile of music.

Louis struck his head with his hand, and looked fixedly on the keys of the piano; he could have shed tears, but anger restrained him. Nina had found the notes, and stood looking at him for some time. At last she said gently—"No; it is better we should not sing; I see you do it unwillingly. Before you get into such a passion as last night, let us shut the piano, and go up stairs to tea. I have done my best to entertain you to-night, but I see it is in vain; you are dissatisfied with me!"

Her tone showed mortification; it moved our artist deeply, and he would have replied by a confession of his feelings, but was restrained by the thought that he might find Caroline in the tea-room, where she often sat with her work. He only answered, "Yes, it is better; I would rather hear no more after that last duet."

They went up stairs: Caroline was indeed there: he observed her attentively; she seemed conscious of his looks, and anxious to avoid them. She went to prepare the tea; Louis congratulated himself on the superior discernment that enabled him to discover in her plain, and at first sight inexpressive features, the trace of that nobility of soul her singing had revealed. What speaking earnestness dwelt, doubtless, in those downcast eyes! His delight was that of the discoverer of a new land, abounding in unknown treasures. He rejoiced in the thought of offering her his hand, and elevating her to the sphere she was so well fitted to adorn. As she returned with the tea, he could not help fancying, from her apparent avoidance of his glances, that she was aware of his interest in her.

Nina did not complain of his abstraction; but did her part in the conversation with so much grace and sweetness, that the artist involuntarily sighed, regretting that a form so lovely contained no soul. It cost him a severe pang to give her up forever.

Some time had passed in their monosyllabic discourse, when Nina suddenly started up, having forgotten to order lights, and quitted the room. Louis walked to the open window. His attention was an instant after arrested; he heard the voice of his unseen songstress. The sounds came from Ricco's music room.

Softly he opened the door, and passed through the room into another, which adjoined the music room. There, in darkness—for the blinds were closed—he drank in the rich melody. It was the air from Mozart's Magic Flute—

"I feel 'tis gone, 'tis lost for aye,

The bliss of love," etc.

She sang in an under-tone; but this very suppression of her voice revealed so much, that our artist was deeply moved. He could no longer contain his emotion. Gently he opened the door of the room where she sat singing in darkness; and as the song ended, he threw himself at her feet, seized her hand, and pressed it to his burning lips. She sprang from the piano, terrified, snatched her hand away, and hurried out of the room.

Louis stood confused for a moment, then walked up and down the apartment, filled with emotions of delight. Then he seated himself at the piano, and poured forth the feelings of his heart in music. Just at the height of his rapture the hall-door opened, and presently a loud voice cried, "No more of that; you play dissonances! Away with your Mozartish stuff!" It was Ricco. The artist rose, and saluted him with some embarrassment.

"What is the meaning of this Egyptian darkness?" cried the Italian; "and why are you playing here all alone?" He pushed open the doors, and the light shone in from the tea-room, where Nina was seated.

CHAPTER VI

Late as it was, Louis hastened to his friend Heissenheimer, and told him all that had occurred.

"You do injustice to my fair friend Nina," said the merchant; "she has kindness of heart, feeling, and" —

"No more of her!" interrupted the artist: "I have made up my mind what to do, and am determined to offer my hand to Caroline!"

"Well," said his old friend, "then I will say no more. But the how, and when? You had better do it in writing; for you cannot easily find an opportunity of speaking alone with her. I will be the bearer of your letter— your *postillon d'amour*."

Louis agreed with joy, and promised to bring the letter next morning.

After he had returned home, he considered the step he was about to take; and asked himself earnestly, if he believed *a noble apprehension and feeling for a noble art, a sufficient pledge for nobility and purity of soul?* He thought of instances in which the highest taste in art had seemed to be accompanied by a mean and unworthy spirit; but further attention convinced him that in all these cases the taste had been perverted or vitiated, or else the world's judgment had mistaken the character of the individuals.

After some reflection, he wrote a letter containing a formal offer of his hand to Caroline. He confessed his former partiality for Nina, and that his affection had been won by the feeling and soul evinced in her singing. On that security for mind and heart he was willing to rest the happiness of his life!

The letter was given next morning to Heissenheimer, who promised to deliver it. About noon, the impatient artist called again on the merchant, who had left for him the following note:

"Dear Louis:

"Your letter was delivered; but I have no answer for you, for I could only slip it into Caroline's hand, her mistress being present. Ricco and his daughter are gone into the country. They sent to invite you to join them; but you were not at home. Pressing business prevents my seeing you. I send you information, however, as the circumstances may be favorable to you; it is possible you may find Caroline alone at the house. This evening I shall expect to hear from you.

"Heissenheimer."

Our artist lost no time in hastening to the chapel-master's house. He rang, and rang; but no one admitted him. After several trials with the same success, he resolved to wait till evening, when Ricco and Nina might be expected to return. Caroline would then be certainly at home. Who knows, thought he, that she has not some friend, whom she has gone to consult?

He counted the hours impatiently, till it was quite dark; and stood again among the lindens opposite the house. The windows were open, but the curtains down; there was no light, a sure sign that the chapel-master had not returned. All at once he heard the sound of a piano. It must be Caroline, taking the opportunity of the absence of her master and mistress, to indulge herself in her beloved art!

Quickly, but noiselessly, Louis stole up the steps, entered at the door, and passed through the hall. He listened at the door leading into the room; she was singing, with her rich, expressive voice, the same song he had first heard. He could distinguish every word, the closing line being repeated with some variations. The whole song was unspeakably touching, and full of life, love, and hope, such as only a poetic spirit could express. It filled the listener, like magic, with a feeling of delicious sadness; the soft breath of spring, the whisper of love, could alone be compared with it!

Louis breathed quickly. Now is the time or never, thought he, and opened the door. There was only sufficient light in the room to show the outline of a female figure, sitting with drooping head before the piano.

The young man drew nigh, unobserved; and suddenly seizing her hand, "Caroline!" he cried, in a voice trembling with emotion. She started up; he still held her hand, and whispered, "Caroline, canst thou love me?"

The girl trembled, and placed the hand that was at liberty before her eyes. Her lover tried to remove it, and felt her burning tears upon his own. He pressed her to his bosom.

At last, she whispered softly, "Will you love me, questioning not who I am?" Louis kissed the lips that uttered these words, and replied, "Forever and ever!"

Leaning on the arm of the young man, the agitated girl led the way out of the music room, and through two or three apartments, towards Nina's cabinet. As they stood before the door, she whispered again, "Grant me my first petition; close your eyes till the word is given to open them." Louis obeyed, in some surprise; they entered the cabinet; she drew away her hand; they stood a moment still. At last, he heard a strange voice say, "Now, Louis!" and opened his eyes.

The room was lighted up; directly before him stood Heissenheimer; a few paces off, Ricco, supporting the form of a young girl, whose face was hid on his breast. The Italian seemed much moved, but did not utter a word.

Louis stood mute with surprise and embarrassment; at length, recollecting himself, he repeated anxiously the name of "Caroline!" The weeping girl lifted her face from Ricco's bosom, and turned towards him. It was Nina!

"Nina!" exclaimed the young man.

"Nina—Caroline—what you will," answered Heissenheimer; "but the self-same enchantress, whose song has won your heart."

"No! Is it possible? Oh, can I believe it!" cried Louis, looking bewildered around him.

"The same!" said Ricco. And Nina herself confirmed the truth.

No longer doubting, the artist seized her fair hand, and drew her gently to his breast. Long, long, he held her there in silence; amazement—love—unspeakable rapture—deprived him of the power of speech.

At last Ricco, who had been walking up and down the room in great emotion, broke the silence. "Young friend," he cried, "thou hast nobly borne the trial. Art is a divinity—and for the true artist, *no* sacrifice is too great! I vowed—and would have kept my vow—to give my daughter to no one who could not value her mind and heart beyond her outward charms! He who could admire the superficial, frivolous maiden, beautiful as she was, and wish for nothing more—would have been unworthy of her better self. Too often have I heard fair words in praise of art; too rarely does the action correspond; and he alone has right to upbraid his opponents with their want of discernment, who not only has better judgment, but suffers that judgment to guide his conduct. Now, take my girl if you will! I welcome you as my son!" Louis answered by embracing the kind old man.

When their feelings were in some measure calmed, Heissenheimer commenced his explanations.

"You have much to thank me for, young man! Till yesterday I was as much deceived as yourself, and was only let behind the scenes after my discovery. I would have you know, all was truth I told you about my hearing the music, and so forth; except that I surprised, not the maid Caroline, but our sweet friend Nina, while her father was accompanying her in the song you heard a few moments since. There was no escape; both were brought to confession, and having them in my power, I stipulated that you should be kept no longer in suspense, else I know not how many fiery trials awaited you."

"It was my father's will, not mine!" cried Nina; "if you only knew how hard it was for me to play such a part!"

Louis answered by an expressive look; and Ricco said, deprecatingly, "My art—my child—my all, was at stake! We are told to be wise as the serpent."

"But if the issue had not been fortunate?" said the young man.

"Nothing venture—nothing win!" replied the Italian. "We all risked something. Let us rejoice that it has ended so happily."

"Only the poor village musician," said Heissenheimer, "has reason to complain, that I sent him out of the world so sentimentally, without asking his leave! Doubtless he would not be much obliged to me—for to-day is his birth-day, and his daughter Caroline is gone to pay him a visit. But what think you, fair lady, of our friend as a physiognomist? Here he has been finding out that your features were inexpressive—and those of Caroline very interesting!"

"Do not make sport of me!" cried Louis, "you were as much in the dark till yesterday as myself."

"Well!" said the old merchant—"at least I shall claim a kiss for my reward as *postillon d'amour!*"

"Come," interrupted the chapel-master; "let us adjourn to the little back room, where we may find something to eat!" They went, Nina leading the way, leaning on the arm of her lover. The "little back room" was a private cabinet, the window of which opened on a small garden in the rear of the house. Here was an excellent instrument, by which Ricco was accustomed to compose, and his daughter to sing. A large book-case contained, in rich binding, the works of celebrated composers of the old Italian school, down to the latest. There was Palestrina, Lulli, &c., and also Haydn, Mozart, and Beethoven. Portraits of the great masters hung round the walls; the bust of Mozart stood on the book-case.

Louis believed himself in a sanctuary! The fair priestess stood by his side, and smiled upon him. Her usual frank and lively manner was exchanged for something of timidity and reserve; but love beamed in her eyes, and kindly regard was expressed in the looks of all present. Heissenheimer was the first to recover his vivacity; and he brought them back to this world by protesting that he was inordinately hungry and thirsty. He should prefer a flask of good Johannisberger to all the dews of Castaly! And they would not forget to drink the health of all the divinities of love and music; yea, the present company included, besides the poor village musician and his daughter Caroline, who certainly ought to have a share in their good wishes!

FOOTNOTES

[15] The incidents and criticism of this tale are taken from a novelle of Ludwig Rellstab, entitled "*Julius.*"